To Mr. Price

Jersey City to
Escobar's Colombia

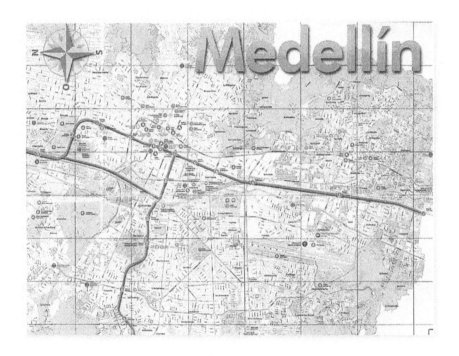

GERARD HORNING

PAGE PUBLISHING, INC.
Conneaut Lake, PA

First originally published by Page Publishing 2021

ISBN 978-1-6624-3433-4 (pbk)
ISBN 978-1-6624-3435-8 (hc)
ISBN 978-1-6624-3434-1 (digital)

Printed in the United States of America

Mom,
My brother, Ricky,
My best childhood friend, Robert,
Roberts uncle, Vincent,
Os,
Monsignor John,
Sister Joan,
Ed and Ben,
Lulu,
To all of the great people in Colombia.

Preface

This book is my memoir. It is based upon my recollection of the facts that occurred during my childhood in New Jersey. For all the people mentioned in this book, I have obtained permission from those who are still alive. For the businesses mentioned here, I have also obtained permission, to the extent practicable, before publication. Because this is a memoir, I have relied upon my own memory in crafting this book; therefore, any misconstrued event is due only to the fault of my memory and not based upon ill motive or malice. Some of the characters' names have been changed to preserve their privacy, and some of the events have been shortened for brevity's sake. Some opinions attributed to some characters are not necessarily those of the characters they are based upon. I have done my best to retell in this book what I actually encountered while growing up, as well as other life experiences.

My best friend Robert (striped shirt) and I on the left

Foreword

My name is Diana Carvajal. I am a teacher in a school in Medellin. I have known Jerry for many years and have witnessed his kindness for my students and others in my area.

For many years, Jerry has donated school supplies and money for our school. Jerry has given toys and other gifts to our students. His generosity did not stop there. For several years, he has dressed as Santa Claus not only for our students but also for many children. When being Santa, he would give many gifts and cookies and cake while standing on the streets, which I thought was crazy. The areas here are not safe. But it did not matter to Jerry. The thing that surprised me was that Jerry was so prepared. He had sheets of music and sung many songs in English and Spanish. He made many children and adults so happy even for just a moment.

That's not all. Many times, he would go to the supermarket and buy many carriages' worth of food and give them out to the poor families. Several times, I witnessed Jerry buying prepared food, and he walked down the street in El Poblado, handing them out to the beggars. Jerry did these things so naturally. During the epidemic, he has sent money to several families in Medellin who are really in need. We call him the gringo laughing, but we all know his good heart. I know of his coming book and some of the things he has done in Colombia. What I can say is that the things he did were in my country's best interest.

My name is Tom, and I have known Gerard for most of this adult life. I know the terrible struggles he had in his life. Being a friend of his late mother, I've seen many of his ups and downs.

7

I've always said to him, "Do you know where you were and where you are now and all the great things you accomplished?"

Gerard would just smile when I said that and say, "Yeah, maybe I know."

He made it by working hard and sticking to his work ethics. It would have been easy for him to quit. I didn't see much of his mother's drinking. Flo didn't do that when she and me and several others were having prayer meetings. But for some reason, I could see that. Gerard did share several stories of the horror and did say that she still did it.

I remember when his father left. When his father left, Gerard had to work two jobs while going to school. I remember seeing all the photos of Gerard with his son, singing and giving out gifts to the children in church in Allentown. I think he did that for twenty years. He would also give turkeys to the church on Thanksgiving.

Gerard informed me of this book, and I know he had a very bad life as a child. The one thing I can say about Gerard besides his good heart is that he can bounce back from anything. And he sure did.

Introduction

Dysfunction was a way of life for us in downtown Jersey City. No matter which way you turned, things never seemed to go right. You were punished for being curious and are called a baboon if you were inventive. In the sixties, the nuns and the lay teachers would immediately let you know who was boss. In their mind, it was either their way or the clothing room. The clothing room was where you could find all the tools for punishments—paddles, straps, cat o' nine tails, shillelaghs. The boys had to drop our pants, and the girls had to lift their uniform skirts to get their behind hit till they fell to the floor.

I remember kneeling on rice or bottle caps in the first grade. I've had someone tell me, "Maybe they are getting you ready for Vietnam." Later, we would turn the clothing room of punishment into the room of seven minutes in heaven. For my brother and me, our home life was worse than school. Our apartment was filled with roaches and mice, and Mom had drinking problems—all these affected my brother and me. My father was absent most of the time. When he did arrive home, he and my mom would have all-out brawls.

Going to Journal Square became an adventure; we had to put any money we had in our shoes. We occupied ourselves with mischievous deeds, and I overcame bullies and survived my brother, who was the downtown tough guy. My brother, Ricky, never had proper adult guidance. None of us really had guidance. Still, some of us survived, and some didn't. Forty people I knew succumbed to alcohol and drug addiction. The example of my best childhood friend, Robert, helped give me direction.

A manager of a major supermarket chain in Colombia said he recognized me. As our conversation went on and I denied what he said, he then called all his associates up to the front of the supermarket, about fifty of them, and said, "This is the man who helped save Colombia."

The second half starts in the early nineties. My first trip to Colombia was during the height of the drug wars. I met a guy named Os (pronounced Oz), who brought me in to seduce beautiful women to get information so he could use the moto girls to kill the dealers and lords. The table in his house was almost fourteen feet long and was filled with photos and information of the most beautiful Latinas in the world, and I got to pick one at a time. I thought I was the luckiest man in the world.

One day, he spoke to me and said, "Never fall in love with these women. They are only for sex and information." One time, the last time, I broke his rule. There were times where we went to Colombian celebrity houses and were visited by them. There was no end to the beautiful women—sometimes three a day in three different hotels. We got the information from them, and we used certain tools. Os was a man on a mission, and he had good reason to do the things he did. Though I thought we were close, it took me almost twenty-three years to find out his reasons.

I felt tears running down the sides of my face. The pain was so unbearable. I dared not move. My hands were pushed hard together. My fingers were pointed straight up, and I had no feeling in them. I was lifting my knees up and down in very small increments. I feared that if I lifted them higher, my actions would be noticed. I never removed my line of sight from the crucifix just above the alphabet.

I was wondering how much pain Jesus experienced. *Did he ever have to kneel on uncooked rice just as I am doing?* The other choice was bottle caps. Then I thought, *Maybe there were no bottle caps when he was alive. When he died, he was much older than I. I am only six years old now. He had a beard.* I had been kneeling for over an hour. I thought, *What did I do to deserve this?*

First Grade

Sister was a very short woman and very old. She was also no-nonsense. She wore all black, and you could hardly see her face. She was what people called a nun, We would never ask what we did to get punished. All we knew was it was frequent with everyone. Sometimes we would sit on our hands; other times, we would sit on the metal lunch boxes with our hands under them. This was either in our desks or on the floor. After a few minutes, our hands would be numb and tingly. If we didn't raise our hand or if we sat with our hands folded or if we asked what she thought was a stupid question, those were some of the punishments. And if we did it twice, then we'd be punished with a trip to the clothing room, where the paddles and belts were.

I asked Jesus, "Does she know we have only been on this earth for just six years?"

> "Sometimes, the only way to heal our
> wounds is to make peace with the demons
> who created them (Dr. Ishiro Serizawa)."

The Start of Grammar School

Guilt is to the spirit what pain is to the body.

—Elder David A. Bednar

The clothing room was a place where we hung our coats and also a storage room. It had one light bulb (a pull light) and a large wall. This was where the tools of punishment were stored—the strap, the cat o' nine tails, assorted rulers. And this was not only in our first-grade classroom but in every class's clothing room—first through eighth grade. The worst fear we all had was being hit with the dreaded shillelagh. This was a walking stick with thorns on it like a rosebush. After all, many of these nuns were from the country of Ireland or had connections there. What a great tool of torture the shillelagh is. It would not only bruise you severely; it could cut you with the thorns. The thinner ones would hit you like a whip; the thicker ones would almost break bones. The fear of those punishment tools would put all of us in great fear! It was pushing us to do the right things, according to the nuns. I had a friend who years later jokingly said to me that maybe they were getting us ready for Vietnam.

There were simpler punishments, such as standing in a corner or being put in the clothing room with the light out and the door closed. One of the biggest no-nos was chewing gum. God have mercy, if you were caught chewing gum, you received a good beating with a ruler on the hands top and your bottom. Then the gum would be put on your nose, and you'd be standing in the corner of the class all day.

All punishments went with a note headed home with you that had to be signed by your parents and then returned. On the first week of school, our parents received a note giving permission for us to be hit by the teachers. It had to be signed by the parents, and all parents signed it.

I was never good at handwriting no matter how many times we did the circles, over and over again in a row. Maybe I lacked confidence or just skills. The nuns were not people who built our confidence. Nothing was good enough for them.

My brother, Ricky (Richard), was just about four years older than I and was much bigger and stronger. I received the honor of walking home with him each day after school. Believe me, it was no honor. It was a very typical brother's torture—only his was worse. My dear brother was a good-looking, tough, nasty guy with a great smile that every girl loved. He was a leader that would do some really dumb things. He would hit me, using me as a punching bag. His middle finger-snapping my ear was always great. My ear was always in pain and my face always red. I received kidney punches as well as Indian burns, where he would put both hands on my wrist area and hold them tight and turn them in different directions. Why they called them Indian burns, I really don't know why. Maybe it's because your arm and wrists turn red.

When we did finally get home, my grandmother was there—Nana, as we called her. I loved Nana very much, but she was older and had issues with alcohol. Her nickname was Ms. Piels. That came from her trips to the liquor store, and she enjoyed a few highball whiskey and ginger ale. Nana loved her soap operas. She never missed them unless she visited Mrs. House's home. She had her spot on the couch with a beer or a highball or maybe even a cup of tea. But one thing she really loved was buttermilk, one of the worst things I've ever tasted. She loved it.

While Mom worked, Nana watched us, but she never really did because her field of view was the TV and her shows. She was blinded by what was going on. I would sleep in a bed in Nana's room, bedroom down the hallway to most of the time. Next to her was my brother; he had the other bed. My mother slept in a pullout couch. Most of the time, I would sleep there next to Mom sometimes. My brother occupied the other bed in Nana's room. The bedroom on the right was my father's bedroom. In my life, I've never seen them together in the same bed. My mother's excuse was that he snored, which he did. But it was not that. I think that the times when I slept in my mother's bed, she did not want him near her and was using me as a shield.

Not only did my grandmother have an alcohol problem, but my mother's problem was worse. She was a very depressed person. She was very lonely, she pushed her opinions on people, and then she drank her highballs and talked to herself all night. After one drink, she would completely change. She'd be crying, angry, and full of self-pity. Then she would wait for my father to come home to have a fight. My mother was a very small woman, 5 feet on 105 pounds, but she had a temper! This was mostly brought on by the alcohol.

Down the hallway, on a wooden stand, was a two-foot Sacred Heart statue (which I still have), and it had been painted several times. In several fits of anger, Mom would pick it up and swing it at my father—or attempt to. And we all would hear the magic word. She always called him a gallivanter. We never knew what it meant. We never looked it up. But we knew it was bad.

I guess that was why I had a security blanket and sucked my thumb. I remember that I would cover my head with the blanket but would also peek out to see what was happening. For so many years, we thought this was the normal way of life.

My father was an auto mechanic for a car dealer in Elizabeth. He would come home late—say, 9:00 to 10:00 p.m.—because he would visit a tavern. I could always smell his breath. Mom would always leave him dinner, a large plate of that day's dinner on top of a pot of hot water on the stove. The only time all of us would eat together was on Sundays, at about 1:00 p.m.

One time during the week, when he saw what my mom left him for dinner, he started yelling, "What the hell is this?"

I was on the couch with my mother and Nana. I did not know where my brother was. My father put his plate on the table, and there were two double-sided razor blades on it, the same ones he used.

Then he accused Mom of doing it. They were put on the outside edge of the plate, so what was the point? Who did it? I didn't know. But my brother was out, and I didn't do it. They were there. I saw them. It was very strange.

The fights always continued till my father left several years later when I was seventeen.

One day, I had an unforgettable experience while sleeping. In the bedroom, my brother was in the other bed, my nana fell asleep next to me. At that time, we had an eight-by-ten black and white picture of Jesus on the dresser. Is was a bit scary to me. It was only his face, and it seemed like his eyes followed me wherever I went. That day, it seemed that, right before I was going to wake up, the picture spoke to me.

Jesus told me to wake up, and I woke up in a very cold sweat. I saw that my nana had a nosebleed. It did not seem like a normal one. Blood was everywhere. I got up with blood on me and ran to get my mother. Nana was taken to the doctor, and he said that she had a cerebral hemorrhage. After a couple of hours and after a few visits to the doctor's, she was fine. Until this day, I still have that picture, and I've even had it blessed by Monsignor John.

It's crazy what things go through your head when someone close to you is ill and you are a kid. I wondered, If Nana does not come back, who will put the newspaper on the floor in front of the TV? Who will put a large dish of cream of wheat with almost a stick of butter in it? Who will make the TV dinners? God, were they bad! She would also make burnt charcoal fish cakes. The best was when she would make a sandwich out of rye bread and raw, right-out-of-the-package chopped meat with a slice of raw onion. Actually, it was not bad, and my brother and I ate it often.

I cannot forget that time when Nana did not answer the door. I was with my best friend, Robert. We just happened to give the door a slight nudge, and it opened. We found my nana on the living room floor, almost completely passed out from drinking. We got her to her feet, the both of us, and then we put her on the couch to sleep it off.

Robert almost never came into the apartment. We met outside, or as soon as he knocked, I came out. The apartment was full of roaches and mice and was not spotless to say the least. There were always excuses, like the fact that my mother worked, my father worked, and so on; but when people are not happy, that is what happens, I guess...

Robert was a great friend of mine. We were the best of friends. He was Polish, and at that time, the Polish jokes were plentiful. He did wear plaid pants and striped shirts and ate Polish food, but he went to a Catholic grammar school as I did. He was two years older than I, and he stuck up for me when Anthony and I got into fights every day at school. Robert was not a tough guy, but he was very smart. He was okay in sports but was never very good, but he loved sports as I did. We would play many board games together, sometimes us only and sometimes with his brother. Risk was a great game for us, as well as checkers and sometimes chess, but our favorite game was APBA baseball game. It was a card game with dice and boards with every team involved, and each year, you could buy an updated game. Soooo great was the game that we had leagues and kept stats on the index cards of every player. You could play with another person or alone. So much fun!

Robert lived in a three-family house. They were on the top floor. He had his mom, dad, and two brothers. He had pet lizards and many games. We were also able to use his basement, where he and his brother set up a race track for Aurora model racing cars. I was sure this was heaven. The track for the cars was huge, and the surroundings had little trees and houses. Wow, it seemed like something built by a professional! The models had small controls, very small steering wheels, and a green mat that looked like grass and felt like sandpaper was put on top of plywood under the tracks. He also had very old baseball bats there and gloves that looked like Babe Ruth used them. But there were also hammers and nails of different sizes and pieces of wood in different shapes. My mind wondered what I could do with these.

I thought, *Hmmm, what I can do with old metal roller skates that were broken and all those nails. What can we build with them?*

Little by little, I was becoming a better athlete. I thought I was very skinny and did not seem very strong. I loved playing ball. Playing with others wasn't the problem. It was always about my confidence, to show what I got. I wasn't as strong as others, but I knew where to be, how the game was played, and always gave the effort. The kids on the block were all different, and many others from different areas (like Peter from around the corner), many of us called one another by our first names, not nicknames or shortened versions of our names.

We played bottle caps: "One, two, three red lights, flies up and out...flies up." You need what we called a high bouncer, a Spalding rubber ball. We used to go to the local candy store and purchase one. Then we removed them from the box and dropped them next to one another to see which one bounced the highest. The price was twenty cents for one. This ball became part of our lives, and we used it for stickball, box ball, and punch ball. Each apartment or house had a basement, which had windows and a windowsill ledge, either slate or concrete. Players would take turns in the field and at bat. We would throw the high bouncer as hard as we could at the ledge two feet away. Sometimes we would almost hit the ledge with our hand with the follow-through, hoping the ball would hit the point area of the ledge. Then the ball would go flying like a line drive or a pop-out (you never knew). There were boundaries off the wall, if there was one, and the base hits.

Many times, people from the apartment would complain of noise. Too bad... When we played after school in the school yard, brothers and priests would complain. Wasn't it better to see us playing instead of doing other things? I always wondered about that. Instead of playing with us or seeing the enjoyment we got out of this, it was always a battle. Remember, this was a city—and downtown, worst of all. So that we could have enjoyment, we used the school yard for box ball and punch ball but needed many to do that.

All the strike boxes were made with chalk on factory brick walls, which were maybe three feet high and two feet wide, and we would pitch from around forty-five feet to maybe sixty, throwing curve balls, fast balls, knuckle balls. But the throwing was fast. The stick ball bat was a broomstick or a shovel handle, or if we'd saved up some money, we would buy a legit stick ball bat, which was nothing more than a thicker broomstick with friction tape on it. The only place where we did not put a chalk strike box was the rear parking lot of the city hall—yes, the city hall.

We used spray paint for hours during the weekends. That was our place. The only problem was that the wall was textured stone, so the ball would not come straight back to you. I pitched to the likes of Robert and many others, even my brother, who would fight with a kid in that parking lot on a regular basis. He was always egged on by Junior, a real instigator, to make them fight. I was the youngest but by far the best ballplayer. I could throw a fastball no one could touch and with a very good curve. Putting a curve on that high bouncer was not easy, but boy, could I do it! Every day I would pitch and practice alone, making up a game and baseball team batters up in my head. Then when I hit, I was very good—not great, but very good.

Then I would practice my St. Louis Cardinals batting order and stances—Lou Brock, Julian Javier, Curt Flood, Orlando Cepeda, Tim Macarver, Bobby Tolan, and many others. I pitched in my mind like Bob Gibson. Along with Lou Brock, they were and still are my all-time favorites. I never seen much of the Cardinals on TV, only when they played the Mets, when their games were set as the game of the week, many times when they played in the World Series in '64, '67, '68, but they were my team (and still are).

My brother Ricky and I

When we played, we had fair and foul areas, and certain hits were singles and doubles and home runs... One thing to remember was that I was three, four, or five years younger than most of the guys I played with and played against. But I was better—I knew it. I wasn't stronger, and I didn't run faster, but I was a much better athlete, as we use to say, much more coordinated than most of them.

One weekend, one of my friends hit a long ball off me that was foul, but he and his brother argued that it was fair. They yelled, "Oh, you are worried because it ruined your record." That was not it, but it did matter to me, of course. They left after that and gave me the business for a while after that. At that time, I was firmly involved in another Catholic school down the block from the Catholic grammar school, and the Little League teams had all the teams with Polish names and the colors black, red, and green. My team had the color blue in the uniform. One was black, one green.

Little League

Showing off is a fool's idea of glory.

—Bruce Lee

How I got on the team? Well, it started when they sent someone down to our school and asked if anyone would like to play in their league. There was only one catch. You had to sign a paper saying you were Polish. Two of us signed up—myself (last name Horning) and a classmate who had an Italian last name, not a Polish name. But they covered it themselves. I had a very nice coach and a very nice team-mate. He caught the ball when I pitched. Many of the players were bad. I mean real bad. They never swung the bat and would just stand there, scared to death. I pitched sidearm, which had a natural curve. I was good... No one hit me. But because of the age rule, I could pitch only a few innings per game. When I hit, I hit the ball hard. I only hit the fence once, but hit many doubles and inside-the-park home runs.

As far as people coming to the games, my mother came a few times. She worked. And then the worst was when my brother and his friends made remarks during the whole game. He got me so mad one time that I hit the ball so hard past the shortstop that his friend said I ripped the cover off the ball. And I did.

I played for several years there and really liked it. They had a glass box in the front of the field. It had a super-high fence around it, and in the box, they would put the stats. That glass box stood for many years even after the league closed for good, and in the box, they had my name with the batting average of 667, the highest ever in that league.

There was only one game I missed. It was a very sad moment in my life. I was very depressed over my mother drinking. She would always hide a bottle of Seagram's Seven, so I would look and find it. Mostly she hid it in the back of a small metal cabinet in the kitchen. Well, I took the bottle and took some and then went outside with it with my Little League uniform on. At that time, they were knocking down the buildings across the street and had one down with only a four-foot platform there right on Henderson Street. I sat there with the bottle and made-believe that I was drunk as many of the families were passing by on their way to the game. I don't remember what happened to the bottle, but I did not bring it back to the apartment.

I never knew which way to turn, between my father not coming home until very late (so he could avoid my mother or my mother's drinking), my nana's drinking, or both of them smoking. My only escape was sports. Even when no one was around, I would go outside and throw what was called a super ball. It was really hard, was smaller than a high bouncer just a bit, but could bounce so high and bounce in different directions. It was fun. I would throw it up to a warehouse's fourth floor over and over again and catch it on the bounce. I was always doing something to avoid going home.

I just hated to see my mother like this. She was such a good person. It made me feel like it was my fault, and I felt insecure inside. Mom would take us all over to the world fairs in New York, to the different zoos, to parks like the Olympic Park in Irvington. Those trips were made with my parents several times, but I think they went to drink pitchers of beer, and it was just another place for my brother to slap me around even more. Inside it was making me tougher and tougher, but on the outside, I only had tears. Many thought that was normal, but my brother had something going on inside of him that started very early in his life.

Given her kind self, Mom always made sure we had gifts and toys, and she worked two jobs to earn money, which was really nothing. She was not a homemaker. The apartment was not the cleanest. The apartment was full of roaches and mice. The washer machine and stove and refrigerator were full of them. We even had a cat to catch the mice, but it was so bad that the mice ate out of the cat's dish. Even during dinnertime, we would use roach spray, but it did not even make a dent. Even so, we used what was called roach bombs, and we would kill thousands of them, which we made into big piles in the middle of the kitchen floor. The kitchen window had a very old removable screen, which was where my mother hung the clothes to dry. It was called an alleyway, but that window was also used by my brother and me to throw the mice out. It was quite a fall from the fourth floor from apartment 401. We used to pull them by the tail from under the refrigerator and throw them right out the window, and when we caught them in a trap, we did the same. Once in a while, the cat would catch baby mice and give them to my mother.

Sometimes it was very hard to find a clean glass to drink from because of Nana was not the best in cleaning and had nothing there to clean with. All I remember is the octagon bars of soap, a cardboard box of Ajax, and Salvo clothes washing soap. The towels were old, and the sink was always full of roaches. The bathroom was about the same; it had only a bathtub, a small sink, and a medicine cabinet, which was loaded with my father's stuff. Nana would wash her clothes with a scrubbing board in the bathtub.

I would take my baths, and more often than not, the bathtub was an escape. I could play with my toys there and enjoy it like a pool. The thing I had was my imagination. And I could escape all the smoking and all the drinking and have a few minutes where I could leave this planet and not worry about getting up for school. I really disliked school. I had a hard time with studying, especially focusing on the lessons, given all the punishments and also my brother's torture. My mother used to keep the bacon fat in the refrigerator—yes, that was how much bacon we used to eat. Well, everything tasted like bacon—even my comb. My brother would leave earlier than me for school, and he would always leave me a gift, like rubbing my comb with bacon fat. No matter how much I cleaned it, the aroma of bacon fat would remain and stick in my hair. So when I got to school, I smelled like I was fresh out of the frying pan.

But even worse was facing another school year and another nun. God help us. She also had all the weapons but had a more sadistic way of dishing out punishments. She would bring you up to the front of the class using your ear to lead the way, pulling you by the ear till you got to the front of the class. She'd stand you up and put your face down on the front of a student's desk with your backside facing the blackboard up in the air. Then she would have you drop your pants; if you're a girl, she'd have you lift your uniform skirt. Brought up to the front once was a nice black kid that we all liked. He dropped his pants, and we saw that we had big holes in his underwear. We sat there in fear—not laughing, of course. We did not move a muscle, gripped with fear that you felt you had to go in your pants. Well, she took a large paddle and a strap and whacked the crap out of him several times till he was crying so bad. When she finally stopped, she then sent him to the clothing room. He pulled his pants up and stopped crying. He was not the only one many of us who got that. Even worse was when the girls got it. The only benefit was that the skirt would not stay up; it would always drop down so many times as they took the beating on the back of the legs.

But no matter how much she beat us, we never stopped being ourselves as kids. At recess, about twenty minutes, maybe ten, we would play games. The boys together, and the girls also together. One day, we played grab ass, which is just tag but tagging one another on the rear—boys only. Well, wow! The nuns saw this, and we were one at a time smacked and told to write how this was wrong, like, twenty-five times. It was wrong, okay, but the nuns never explained what was wrong about it. Remember, we were, like, seven and eight years old.

We always knew how to make money. None of us were lazy in that way. We collected soda bottles. The small ones, we got two cents for those, and the large bottles were for five cents. The empty ones in my house, the Coke and 7 Up bottles were always full of roaches, so I had to rinse them out first. God, even today, seeing a roach anywhere gives me the shakes. We would take them to the Spanish store downstairs, owned by a man named Santos, to get our money. My mother would say many times before that the store had no roaches and mice. Santos was a very small grocery store and had a little of anything, but the only thing we bought there were sweets, cupcakes, and bread pudding, which was only five cents. A couple of men who worked in the store had sons in the Catholic school, and today I could imagine what they made a week. It had to be terrible, and of course, they were Puerto Ricans.

The area really started getting full of Puerto Ricans and some Central Americans. Some were good, but many were terrible. There were fights all the time, drugs, and shaking people down for money. Many just were dirty. The first Puerto Ricans that moved into the apartment were on the third floor, and they never brought their garbage down to put it into the cans. They just threw it out the window into the alleyway. Finally, people complained. For you not to get robbed, you would have to carry a knife, and in school, many gangs from a public school a few blocks away would come down to our school or another Catholic school to start trouble.

Guys would try to pick up the girls in our school, and this started several fights. In particular, there was this guy whose name everyone knew. Physically, he was not very imposing. He wore those leather wristbands that many Puerto Ricans wore. I guess they made your veins stick out in your arms or something like that. The thing was, he had a following and played the game "I'll get you back." So many would not mess with him, and he was the king of the sucker punch. Most of this would occur in our schoolyard over girls or money. He took a big swing at classmate one day, and he was a lot bigger than the thug, but if he fought back, that would be the end of him. What he did was cry and move when the thug swung, and it so happened that the victim (he was my age and was in my class) moved out of the way, it hit his younger brother in the jaw. The punch broke his jaw, and he had a nasty scar just below his right side chin line from the operation.

The only guys that the thug would not mess with were my brother and his guys. My brother had a reputation, and it stood—he was a tough guy and would get you back. The girl the thug would always pursue was a classmate of mine. She was a very friendly, nice person that was a very pretty Puerto Rican girl, and she also had a super pretty sister; both were in my class. Many came to our school not knowing English, so many were older than us. There were many of these in our class because they started late or was left behind because of English language issues.

The worst part of the year was going to get the new school year uniform. The place was just off Newark Avenue, but it wasn't that if we went there, it meant that the new school year was coming. I really hated school, even at eight years old. In my mind, I didn't look forward to more discipline, more rules, and much more beatings. Sister was a real expert at humiliation that seemed to be all of them, but she started early in the school year. She was the one that had you drop your pants (and if you were a girl, lift your uniform skirt) to take the strap or paddle. Then there was always competition with flashcards, with girls on one side of the room and boys on the other side. I was always very good at this game, and it always came down to me and a couple of others. Even then, the nuns had their favorites, and guess what, I was not one of them. So she made the game go faster for the boys and not the girls. We had one second to give the answer, but the girls received more time. When we won, we would really feel great 'cause the odds were stacked against us and, of course, me. Forget about having trust in a teacher, hahahaha!

It would only be another mark against you if they knew something about you or your home—forget it—they would use it against you, putting more pressure on you to get your homework done correctly, as well as your projects. And God forbid if they went to your house. They never went to mine, only to the houses and places they knew they could get something. We were not in good financial shape, to say the least, so my mom would be embarrassed to see them there anyway. There were always the ass-kissers. Mom was not one of them, but with the little money she had, she made things happen. She seemed to always buy something for the school to raffle off—small record player, a tape recorder machine, or a board game. Every year, they would give us raffle tickets to sell in front of the supermarket.

Mom set up a table there, and in her spare time, she sold hundreds and hundreds of books of tickets most of the time for a car raffle. Then they would all go to the card party at the school and smoke and drink, have the pick of the winning ticket. Well, in 1966, my friend Robert's mother won a '66 Buick Special. Wow! I will never forget my mom coming home very late drunk, sitting on the pullout couch, and calling Robert's mother, Ann, and telling her about it. At first, Ann did not believe her and said, "Why are you calling so late?" I heard everything. After Ann hung up, my mom called her back. Not good. Well, anyway, they did win the car and later complained about having to pay for a radio to be installed. The AM radio was an extra back then and had to be paid for. The car was given to Robert's older brother then later passed down to Robert. Ann was a taller woman, a nice person. She was very generous to me but wouldn't think twice about slapping Robert in the blink of an eye. Then the belt came out if he was a minute late.

It was the same for me from my mom and many others from their moms. It was never pretty. We had to be in as soon as it got dark, and I mean the second, like they waited at the door for this to happen. Forget about if you were late for supper. Sitting in the class was not bad enough with the stern punishments, the work lessons, the constant scary looks from the nuns and classmates trying to make you screw up so you could get in trouble. But there was an extra— the terrible smell of the combo from the Hudson River and a factory. Most of the time, we were either sick from the smell or just high from it. At that time, there weren't many rules or regulations, so you could see many suds going out into the river.

There were so many neighbors in the apartment building. Some were close friends to my mom. To some of them, we became errand boys, and we also had to meet their kids and sometimes their extended families. One of mom's closest friends lived two doors down on the left. They were two very nice, generous people who had great hearts. There were four flights of marble staircases, where a fall or a misstep caused a lot of pain and injury. She was a homemaker, and her husband drove oxygen tanks to hospitals. I only knew this because they always spoke about how he would drink a half pint of whiskey as he was driving.

Many times, our errands were to pick him up off the staircase. My friends and I would carry him to the apartment, which was not so easy. We would get his key out, open the door, and set him on a chair or the couch, or she would answer the door and, wow, instant embarrassment. She would be super pissed at him, and that was on a good day. Several times, he would have a cut on his head or was passed out. Their apartment was special, though. It was so neat and clean, and everything was in its proper place. They both also dressed neatly. The best thing about bringing him up or carrying her bags and opening the front doors was that she would see us later and give us money, sometimes a dollar and several other twenty-five cents. Not bad. Another thing was that she could make the best pot roast in the world, and she gave us a taste once in a while.

It was always weird how other people's apartments were always cleaner than ours and much more organized. I could never figure out why. I would think my mom working and helping out at school and my father working and never home had something to do with it, but in my mind, there was no reason. Many kids lived in the apartment, mostly little girls, and a few others, so they were always at my parties. They were always dressed in these white 1960s party dresses, short white socks, and saddle shoes. They were always well-behaved, nice kids. Our thing was pinning the tail on the donkey and so on. Actuary was a fun game. But once in a while, there was a relative of Mom's friend who would come visit. First, I was told she was a godchild and then a niece, but she was six like me or maybe five, and they invited me over every time she visited mom's friend's apartment. We really had nothing to play with in her apartment.

And the questions we asked her was, who was the man who dropped her off? One time, I heard her say that he was her uncle. At another time, she said he was some other relative, but it was always the same guy. She lived out of town, I overheard them saying one day. We always ended up in their bedroom. There were interesting bottles on the dresser and a table with all kinds of bushes on it and a heat lamp, a big silver thing with a red bulb in it. She did have a very beautiful sterling silver large tea set on the coffee table, but that was not something we could play with.

She was not a shy girl even at the age of six, and when we got to the bedroom, she loved to touch. While Mom and her friend sat in the kitchen two rooms away and drank highballs in the afternoon, this little girl began to do super weird things. First, she would pull down her underwear and show me her private parts, which I was so freaked out about. I couldn't move and just giggled and was so red I didn't know what to do. Then she would put her finger in her butt and further up and take it out and smell it. It was that terrible! But it got worse when she pulled my hand with her both hands and tried to put my fingers in her butt. I was terrified. I was so scared and embarrassed. This would happen several times. Every time she visited, I tried not to go there, but we really never questioned anything back then. Several times, she tried to get me to put my hand on her vagina, but I really pulled away. It came to the point where I had to push her away, but she was slick. She would pin me down, and we could never hit or push a girl or else. After a few episodes, I finally sat in the kitchen and watched both my mother and her friend drink their issues away. But I never spoke about those experiences to any adult or even a friend. Later, I wondered as an adult what was happening to her with the man who was always dropping her off and picking her up. Several years later, when mom's close friend died, that girl showed up, and we were introduced again.

Two weeks after Mom's friend died, I saw the girl twice. She was pretty and had orange hair, but we looked at each other strangely, as if she knew. We said hi, and that was the last time I ever saw her. Maybe that was just childlike experimenting on her part; they would use that back then. Or maybe it was not. All things were secrets and nothing was shared.

When you are very young, you only know what you are told or aren't told. We would never get answers to any questions at home or in school. We were told only that we should have known it. It was the sign of the times—ask no questions, and get no answers. We always had to figure out things for ourselves, so it forced us to watch others to see how they did things. Wrong or right, we tried them. This led us to try very daring things.

Ishmael was a Spanish kid a few years older than I, but he was a very nice guy who didn't speak much English. He was super daring. He climbed fences and jumped over parking meters, fire hydrants, and high walls. But the most daring was yet to come. Several years before I was born, there was a ferry boat at the Hudson River in downtown Jersey City, a few blocks from my house. A couple of years after I was born, it burned down along with all the ferries and the boardwalk leading to it and the docks. It was a really great fire. All that was left in that very large area was the pilings. These were large rounded poles set many feet into the bottom of the river. Some were sticking way above the water, some were broken at the water's edge, and some were just under the water. At some piers, for several feet were only the piling standing a couple of feet from one another, leading to a portion of the dock, and then more pilings and then more of the dock. To fall from one of these piling would drop you anywhere to thirty to sixty feet onto other broken pilings or into the river, which would then, with its strong current, bang anything into a very strong bulkhead. At the end of one of these broken docks, the older guys set up a large piece of plywood, where they nailed it onto these pilings so they could hang out, go fishing for eels, and do their drugs.

> Courage is resistance to fear, mastery
> of fear. Not absence of fear.
>
> —Mark Twain

As curious as we were, we had to go there to see the setup. Ishmael was, like I said, a very daring soul. There were several stand-alone pilings before we could get to a solid footing. I was scared just looking down. It would give a normal person a heart attack. Ishmael said to me, "Get on my back." I grabbed him around the neck, hooked my legs around his waist, and step by step, we went one, two, three, four, five, six… I had my eyes closed but could feel his steps. Finally, we stopped and were on firm footing. Wow. I thought it was not so bad, and I laughed. It was crazy. We then made it all the way to the plywood landing spot. And guess what! We see nothing. But the view was cool; it was all open water in front of us. Soon, we went back, and it was just as scary and crazy as the beginning. I counted the steps again, and we—or should I say he—made it. I don't remember seeing Ishmael after that, but it was an experience.

The river always fascinated us. We would go on to have many experiences, many not good. The factory was a large employer on the water then, and there was a real large pipe that was letting some real green stuff into the river, which caused a lot of suds that was so cool it used to turn the water really green. So we would stand there for hours, watching that. The great barges were very large flat ships, as big as an apartment building, and they were always tied together side by side. According to how the current was or what large ship passed by and made waves, the barges would separate about four to eight feet and then slam together. There was a distance of about sixty feet from the top of the barge to the top of the water, so to have fun, we would do a daring thing. We would jump from one barge to another, calculating the distance between them. We would go from dare to double dare to triple dare to get someone to jump. I would make it to four barges, making the jump from one to another with about four feet of separation or even less. There were five of us, as well as John, who really never hung out with us but played some box ball together sometimes. He was not an athlete as we would call him uncoordinated. But daring one another always worked, as it did on me. A couple of guys made it. Then came John. He jumped about a foot a little or maybe more then he fell in between the bulkhead and the first barge. As we looked in horror, his head was crushed like you would see with a hammer hitting a pea. It was a feeling like no other. As we were all screaming and crying, a man walking his dog ran over, saw what happened, and ran to get the police. The whole downtown area was stunned, and a fence was installed with signs.

31

Fences were made to be jumped over and torn down and cut through in our minds, and this one was a mile long and covered many areas. In a few weeks, we would get over, under, and around them. We always think fences keep people out and keep people in well sometimes but not to us. Many times, we would go to what we thought was a point of interest, such as the green street boat club, a dirty place on the water where some of these boats would be docked. I would say these were pleasure boats, but some looked like they were there for a hundred years, nothing big. This was in an inlet on the Hudson River, a super polluted area filled with garbage and who knew what. There were shanties along where the boats were docked. These shanties we were in great fear of. They were filled with very old people that looked like bums and also filled with drug addicts. But on the other side of the boat club, say a block away, was an extremely big inlet for the docking of large ships, with sides that were stone and sand and looked perfect for a nice swim or for just a walk to cool off. We dared one another who was going to break the ice—meaning go into the water first.

One thing we did was to strip down to our underwear bottoms, but we put our sneakers or shoes back on. The reason? Broken glass in the water, pieces of broken steel, and so on. But there were some things that did not bother us, such as the oil slick in the water or the suds from the factory. The one thing that did bother us was swimming around the floating dead animals. If you wanted to visit a petting zoo, this was the place. There were goats, horses, pigs, dogs, donkeys—yes, all dumped into this area or some other area and ended up there. Several times, horses' heads would float by and, many times, a whole horse. It was great to try to get up on a horse and jump off. Remember, they were floating on their sides. When we pushed the issue, tons of fish and hundreds of eels would come out.

We would make a day of it and hang out and chat with each other about nothing, like we always did sometimes about baseball teams or whatever we wanted, a new toy or game, what was on TV, or just our wishes for anything. When we were finally finished and got bored, we left, smelling like a sewer or worse. Thank God there was always a big kid that had a big wrench that would open a fire hydrant, and after letting the rusty water run out, we would drink from it and wash ourselves off. Then if we were lucky, the firehouse across from the Catholic church would have a hose across that had holes in it. Everyone would play and cool off with it, but not all the time. So then we would go somewhere to hang our clothes to dry them off before we went home.

If we went home with those clothes, things would happen. In my case, there was nothing because my mother worked, as did my father, who would not have said anything anyway. But Robert's mother was like a hawk; she noticed everything and would have beat the crap out of him if she found out where we were. We went to an empty lot or warehouses that were being demolished and find a fence to hang our clothes to dry. They never really did. The best case was that they were damp, very damp. By this time, we were starving. I really never went home for lunch. My nana was a terrible cook, and I had to suffer through dinner from her, which was either burnt or undercooked. She did treat my brother and me with raw chopped meat right out of the package; it was made into a patty and put with raw onion on rye bread. Think about it—completely raw meat on bread. Hey, we ate it, and to be honest, it was good. Robert, on the other hand, almost had to be home. His mother did not work, and she played no games. He ate normally. Many times, if I had five cents, I would get a piece of bread pudding in Santos's store and have that. Nana was usually loaded up with Piels Beer, so what she did during the day was drink, sleep, and watch her soaps.

Many of us called each other by our last names or nicknames. I would guess it was making one another feel superior over others, unless you had a simple name like Carl. He was a couple of years older than us—say, two—but he would play baseball with us, so that was okay. We needed the extra players. It's funny how we met. We always traveled in all the streets of downtown Jersey City, knew almost everyone, and had little fear. We were good at getting in and out of trouble. On some Saturdays, we would gather, say, eight to ten of us and head to the Little League field where I played during the week for my baseball team, the blue color team.

On Saturdays, there were no games, and the field was perfect for us to goof around and play in. But there were a couple of problems—one, the gate was locked, and two, the fence was very high. It was a cyclone fence with the barbs facing up at the top of the fence. We always had to climb it. It seemed to be about eight to ten feet high with a metal fence pipe across about halfway up but on the inside. On the outside, you had to try to push your sneakers in the holes of the fence. It was not easy grabbing the fence as you climbed with one hand after another while enduring the pressure from the guys making fun of us for being too slow. We knew we had to get to the other side for another reason. Our gloves, bats, and other things—we threw these over the fence first. The field was on a very busy street, Grand Street, and was across from the school convent, so we had to get in very fast and out very fast.

We had a great time once in. We would have three teams. This was where three bats and the rest played the field. Most of the time, we had the field all day. There was a water drinking fountain there, so we had no worries. But maybe not. There was also a high fence behind the wood homerun fencing around the outfield and also a door with a lock. That fence had barbed wire on top, so we never climbed it. Once in a while, the man who maintained the field would come in from the outfield door and chase us out. We would run like crazy to get out and climb the front fence like superman (remember, to me, it was easier). It had a bar across it, so you could put your sneaker on it as you flew up the fence, except for Carl. He was, like I said, a couple of years older and taller than us, so he tried to get on that center bar and leap over a crazy chance. If he made it, we would all talk about how great that was, so he tried with his short pants on and black socks. But he got caught on the barbs, his groin first, then his whole leg, down to his socks. There was blood everywhere, and we were screaming as he hung there. Poor Carl was screaming so loud and crying I think all the people in New York heard him.

There just happened to be a policeman riding his three-wheeler passing by, thank God, and between him and the field maintenance guy, they pulled him off. An ambulance came very fast and took Carl away. We heard he received over two hundred stiches and had a cast on his leg. It was another sad day that started off so great. It was over. It was the last time we climbed that fence, not because we wouldn't go again, but because they installed barbed wire in the front now. Many months till next summer, we saw Carl's leg, and we heard that he almost died. The leg looked like something out of a horror movie. It was something else we talked about for a while.

It wasn't that we would look for trouble. Sometimes it found us. Well, maybe we started it. John lived in the basement apartment. He was a couple of years younger than I, but one thing for sure was that, together, we were trouble. The giant furniture store closed across the street, and a supermarket opened across the street with a giant parking lot down the block. They had a very different way of using shopping carts. The normal carts could not leave the supermarket, so they had guys called carry-outs who would help the customers. They had these large carts that had shelves on them and two handles and only two wheels, so when they walked with them, they leaned back in order not to let the groceries fall out. They would help the people to their cars and load the groceries into the customers' trunks. What a target they were!

We were always playing army, fighting the Nazis and Japs with our toy guns and fake hand grenades. We realty used our imaginations. John had free roam of the basement of our apartment building, and it had many things an apartment needed for service, including light bulbs and friction tape. What we would do was tape the light bulbs one by one with the friction tape to our belts, and the best thing about the basement was it had great hiding places. Even if you got through the gate and the door, there was a long alleyway and a large wall. We could run anywhere and could not be found. So here came the barrage of hand grenades as a carry-out started to pass. This was across the street, so we had our sidewalk and then the street and then their sidewalk. The street had parking on both sides, and as they passed, the only noises that were heard were those of grenades as we threw up to four light bulbs headed in their direction.

Boom, boom! Bang, bang! It was like an explosion that sounded like that of a shotgun going off. Wow, we really scared the crap out of the carry-outs and the customers, and we were nowhere to be found. We looked through a small basement window for their reaction. They looked around, thought something fell or whatever, and then saw the broken bulbs on the ground. We didn't know if they heard us yell, "Grenades!" But sooner or later, they would. This would go on for a while more, and more light bulbs would be thrown till one day we were seen. They became wise to us. They sent two guys out together. Their plan was to have one guy watch where they came from and then come after to get us. We weren't entirely stupid, but they were older and smarter. Remember, this had been going on and off for months, so we were ahead of the game.

Why did we do this? I don't really know. It was just bad mischief, not good. We did our thing, running out, yelling, "Grenade!" And as soon as we yelled, one guy ran straight at us. My god, we ran faster than the wind, opened the basement door, locked it behind us, and ran into the boiler room to the back alleyway, where there was a window we could escape through. We had a plan, but we were scared shitless. Did he see us? Would he know us? We hid for hours as he pounded at the door on and off. We hoped John's mother would not come home. This worried us for a long time, but we still laughed at the reaction of so many customers and carry-outs being scared to death. Needless to say, that was our last day of the light bulb grenades. There was another reason for it—we were running out of light bulbs.

No matter what we thought, yesterday didn't matter the next day. At this time in our history, we had draft dodgers, guys that burnt their draft cards. There were all types of people that, for whatever reason, didn't want to go to Vietnam. Did we care? Not at all. We used to watch channel 5 on TV, and it would have a roll-down of the men that died in the war. We were warriors even if we didn't really know what was going on. We were battle tested from playing war and watching all the war movies and series on TV. We would kill the Nazis and Japs every day and draw swastikas on walls outside of factories and throw rocks at them and imagine that we were beating the Nazis. Every plastic gun we had, fancy or not, was added to our enjoyment of beating the bad guys.

Caulk was a big thing for us to use; one thing about it was that it could be erased very easy. We had bikes and ideas. I had a very beat-up black Knight with a wheel in the front; it wobbled like crazy. I had that bike 'cause my Schwinn sixteen-inch bike that my mother bought me for Christmas two years ago was stolen from the apartment basement (by whom, I never found out), so I saved up all of three dollars to buy this bad bike. Then the sixteen-inch bikes had what was called a banana seat and could move like the wind and could turn on a dime. There were a few small parks on Washington Street, one across from another that had a few benches and grassy fenced-in areas. Normally, seniors would gather there to talk and gossip, but at this time, those parks were taken over by the draft-dodging hippies—bums with long hair, dirty-looking ripped jeans, jewelry, as we saw them.

They were smoking pot, doing drugs, urinating and defecating all over the place, ruining it for all. So a few of us with bikes put together a plan to really get these bums. Then a light bulb went off in our heads, and we could imagine our bikes as War World II motorcycles and attack them with what light bulbs. The apartment had replenished its stock, and like I said, some things never change. Friction tape was at hand also, so what we did was tie the light bulbs with the friction tape on the side of our belts, making up to six each. There were four of us and four bikes, so there were twenty-four bulbs for us. They were hand grenades, and we meant business. No one was going to draft-dodge the war, and no one was going to look like them and take over everywhere. Just think: we were just kids, and we never were brainwashed by our parents or anyone. We knew in our minds that this was the right thing to do.

So we all had a plan. It was to speed up to the park area, throw a salvo of bulbs at them, and fly away on our bikes. We were on our way from Wayne Street to Washington Street, say, about five or six blocks. We were ready super ready. We raced to the area, stopped our bikes, but didn't get off them about thirty to forty feet away. We threw them one after another. Bang, bang! They exploded like gunshots. These guys ran all over the place, and we flew like the wind down Grand Street, racing as fast as we could go. When we got back to Wayne Street, we were in our glory, laughing and talking about how scared they were. We planned another attack for the next day.

Early in the morning, I would pass by the area to see how many were out there and what sides they were on. The next day, there were only three of us, so we had less bulbs. We went and really hit them with many bombs, and they ran like wild mice like the cowards we thought they were, and again we went home and laughed and had a lot of pleasure in their fear. We planned another attack. Again there were three of us, but this time, they were ready. They saw us coming and tried to box us in. We could hardly get off a bulb. We were very concerned about escaping this time. We barely eluded them. They got so close to grab us by the arm, but we escaped toward the front of the Hudson River, while they chased us on foot. We then separated and went three different ways, only to end up back at Wayne Street. This time, it was our turn to be scared. They got a good look at us, so we decided not to pursue this again.

Many times we would build stuff thanks to Robert's basement supplies—mostly nails and a few hand saws and a hammer. We didn't have any screws or nuts and bolts. What we had were two things—our imagination and watching the *Little Rascals* on TV. They would have box car races. We could see how the kids built them but didn't have the supplies they had, so we made do. We needed three things—a long two-by-four, a wooden milk box, and an old pair of roller skates. We had the skates, the metal kind that had the metal wheels, and had a middle adjustment for size that we could break in half in order to put one end in front of our box car and one end in the back. We scavenged throughout the area and basements for the two-by-four. The milk box was easy; many stores left them out. We would sort of remove them; the best ones we used.

Then we would begin by nailing the box to the two-by-four and nailing the skates to the two-by-four, not really hard. We were at the mercy of what nails we had. Many were too long, so we had to bend them flat when they came through the wood. Then came the milk box. It was great to have the handle hole, so it was a good place to grip. But we needed more, so we searched for two thinner pieces of wood to put on ends for the handles. This took us all day to build. We were so proud of ourselves and also put bottle caps on the milk carton, but lo and behold, our weight was too much for the skates, and they often broke. We felt sad considering all the work we put in.

Across the street was a ShopRite Supermarket, and in the back area, they had a long ramp that went down a long way onto the sidewalk. Then it came to us. We cut the two-by-four to, let's say, two feet or less, and we put the broken roller skates on the far end of the board. Then we rode on that. Wow, we made a skateboard! As Robert and I always said, we invented the skateboard. We had hours of fun going down that ramp over and over again till finally the wheels came off and the separated skate broke. It was so sad. The bearings were all over the place, and now there was nothing we could do.

But we always found some things to do even if it caused us trouble. Slingshots were next on our agenda. Where we bought them from were the backs of comic book ads. In two weeks, we received them in the mail. Mine was large and black with thick bands and an automatic loader, where I could store the peas. Robert's was a metal one; it was a little shorter but still cool. We were in our glory. We saved for these things. It took us forever. I believe they were two dollars each, and we paid by putting cash in the envelope and filling out the order form.

All the changes were taped to a piece of cardboard. Our first plan was to put them to use, shooting at everything. We ran out of peas fast. They were hard, made of plastic, pea-sized, and green, so when we did run out, we bought a bag of hard peas; we bought the kind used for pea soup. Well lo and behold, they worked. But something strange happened. Robert had a pea stuck in his nose—yes, his nostril. Why did he try to put it there? Nuts. But we couldn't get it out, and panic ensued. What to do? This was crazy! We tried every-thing, but it still remained stuck in his nostril. So I said, "Let's go to the pharmacy, the one Robert's family went to." At the drugstore, the pharmacist did almost everything. Even when Robert had a lash stuck in his eye, they got it out. So there we were. Robert had tears coming down, and it made me feel terrible to see my best friend cry-ing, especially since he was three years my senior.

In a matter of seconds, the man came from behind the counter and removed the pea in seconds simply by pushing down and using tweezers to pull it out. The best thing was that these guys would never tell Robert's mother, which was great for us. So what were we to do afterward? At this time, many Puerto Ricans were moving into the area, filling up the hallways with their cooking aroma, which was very strange to us. And their eating habits were very different, includ-ing the food. Some tasted really good.

I would try anything, but Robert, not so much; he seemed to be on a special diet—tough rules by his mom. Later, I would see his health issues at a very young age. We didn't know crap about any-thing like that. We just ate what we liked and even those we didn't like. And we drank soda of all types. But he couldn't when his mom was around. Many years later, after I finally found Robert again through his brother, I got in contact only to find out that he was suffering from diabetes. And what Robert told me, he was at the end of the line. I hadn't seen him in over forty years, and it was so sad to see him with only months left to live.

By talking to one of my friends and his uncle, we found out that the Puerto Ricans loved to eat pigeons, so now we had a reason. For what? To kill pigeons! We would go hunting for them using our slingshots, hitting them from factories' ledges and parking lots. We filled cardboard boxes with them and handed them over to Jose's uncle. He showed us how to cook them. He removed the feathers and cleaned them, and then he made super big pots of soup with them. It was not for my stomach or Robert's, but we thought it was cool for them. I did not eat that.

After a while, we got bored with that, so we would go near the waterfront, where there were railroad tracks and… What else you ask? Rat holes around the tracks! Hmmm…let's see. Robert and I would get flour from our houses and put it on the tracks and wait for the rats to come up for some dinner. It was boring to wait for this. The pigeons were easy, but waiting was not so much fun. Finally, after about an hour, one by one, the rats came up out of their holes. At this time, we were using rocks in our slingshots, and my pellet holder, which was rubber, broke so I simply took a part of the tongue from my shoe and used that. I cut two slits for the thick rubber bands to go through. Now the rats arrived, and we fired very fast at them but were missing over and over again. We hit a couple, but our hits had little effect. They were going back into their holes, and we weren't waiting for the next round, so gone we went!

Going home wasn't the greatest thing. I never really liked my home life. I buried myself in my baseball cards, APBA baseball game, playing with my toy soldiers. But when my brother was home and my mother wasn't, it was really bad. There were also times when even when my mother was home, it didn't matter. In a normal family, a mother would tell her husband about the behavior of one of their children, but talking to my father, as I witnessed, was never easy. Half the time, my father came home late, and then by that time, my mother had a few highballs, and that would mean another fight. Mom took much of the responsibility of handing out the punishment, but I don't really remember my brother being given much.

The first time I really saw my brother act out (he had issues big time) was when Ricky and I were at the kitchen table, having dinner. Mom was a good cook and could really make the food taste great. I guess half a bottle of meat tenderizer would do that trick. The one kitchen window was closed, and Mom was by the sink. I was sitting at the end of the table. Ricky was in the middle front. The table was against the wall. The kitchen was shaped like the letter T. The narrow part was where the window was. I don't remember what we were eating, but the next thing I knew, Ricky said something to Mom. Then he turned with the plate full of food and threw it through the window, smashing the glass. The broken pieces of the plate and food bits were everywhere. It was so bad I thought I was next. I looked at the knives on the table and got up and was really scared. My mom was super angry, but she started to cry as my brother left the apartment. Honestly, I don't think he was thirteen at the time, but I knew from before that he had serious issues and that it would not be the last violent act we would see from him.

I always thought my father was no person to speak to anyone. He was a large man—not fat, but a big man—and he never really said anything articulate. He only had a fifth-grade education and had twenty-one brothers and sisters. On the other hand, he was a World War II hero, as I found out later in life. I never knew what the medals were for. He had a bronze star and several others for blowing up a Nazi bunker with a hand grenade and doing two tours—one in Europe and one in the Pacific. I was later told that he did two tours because he did not want to return home to take care of all those brothers and sisters. I guess fighting the Nazis and the Japs was easier. In those days, fathers really didn't get involved in our sports like many do today. For many years, I blamed him, thinking he was the reason I was not a better ballplayer and made the major leagues. But as we get older and play more, we see our own failings, and maybe look and say, "Maybe I was just not good enough."

It was like Dad was only there to help pay the bills. He worked as an auto mechanic or something like that. I knew where he worked and went there a few times. He was popular with the guys there but not at home. I could say he really wasn't a good father at all. But I was told by my cousins when he died (I think it was the second time I saw my cousins on his side) that he spent all his time with them and that they loved him very much. I could have cried. I never knew the man. I never had more than a one-minute conversation with him, and that was about sports teams. I won tickets for a giant game one time, and I wanted him to go that time they played at Shea. It was super cold, but we went, sat there, and never said much. I never saw him and my mother in the same bed. I had never seen any romance between them at all. Nothing. Never. They were just two people that didn't like each other, and they only stayed together because, in those days, it was the thing to do. I don't think I had ever seen a couple that were married and happy together back then. Either they were drunk or fighting or both. And the supervision was either wielding a belt or throwing shoes or several different objects (ashtrays, glasses, etc.). Maybe it was just the apartment we lived in?

It wasn't always going home that was the most difficult thing and depressing. It was the journey around the city, especially dealing with some Puerto Ricans. We called the bad ones spics. I never knew what that meant. And the Blacks we called colored kids. We really didn't use the *N* word; it never came up. There was one colored kid in particular, a big kid a year or two older than us, that happened to be around more than normal. He was living in the projects on Grand Street, Jersey City. He used to come down to our area because he attended a public school. This was a really bad kid; he would rob you and threaten you in a second. We always had a certain fear of black kids. Only if they were from another school. Other kids that attended Catholic schools were our friends, but others, no. He saw us as an easy target, but the reality was that we had nothing on us—no money, no new clothes, no new sneakers or shoes. It looked like we were in the same boat, but no, he figured out that we may have toys at home. So he would take a very sharp object, such as a stick or a piece of broken glass, and hold it over us.

He always used my best friend Robert as a potential victim if I did not go up to my apartment and get him a toy. He would have Robert cornered, and Robert was so scared half the time, crying. I had to do it. I would get him toy soldiers and a few lesser toys to appease him from harming Robert. I guess you would call him a real shakedown artist or, more appropriately, a real piece of crap. This would go on several more times until we avoided him by being in other areas or taking off when we saw him. In other words, we would hide and duck into alleyways or hallways. Then he didn't come around for a long time. We met again in very different circumstances where the field was balanced.

On occasions, we would be able to save some money by gathering soda bottles and opening doors for people and carrying groceries up the stairs for people and asking my mother or father for change. It was difficult to save anything 'cause we liked soda and all kinds of cupcakes and sweets, but in my mind, I wanted this thing and thought it was the greatest thing when I saw a first baseman mitt. Wow, I thought. It was so different, so special, but I never played first base. It only had that use, but I wanted it. There were only two places that would have it; two were the so-called sporting goods stores. One would be the Levy's sporting goods store and the other was the Simonetti and Sullivan on Jackson Avenue, which was not a good area if you were white kids. The sporting goods stores back then were nothing more than Army and Navy stores with a few more things, such as uniforms and bats and gloves and high school uniforms for the three sports—baseball, football, and basketball.

They had the object I wanted, but first, we went to Levy's. They really didn't have it. We were very shy about the owners; plus, it was a long trip for us on the bus. We were living downtown and had to get on a strange bus and go to a place we had never gone to. So we sat on the bus, worried about the area we were going to, knowing it was an all-colored area. Fear was mounting. Robert seemed to always sit on the window seat to see where we were going and to be ready to pull the cord in order to get off. As people got on and off the bus, there were only colored people, but it was good for us that they were adults, not kids our age or close to our age. Then it was time. The bus seemed to take forever, at least an hour, maybe more. Then it was our stop. Robert pulled the cord, and the driver stopped. I felt as if we were being stared at over and over again, so I flew off the bus and saw the signs for the two stores. It was a blessing that they were within a few other stores of each other, so after leaving Levy's, I was hoping Simonetti and Sullivan had what I wanted. All my dollar bills, along with change, were in our sneakers. We kept them there 'cause when the colored kids tried to rob us, they always outnumbered us and made us turn our pockets inside out.

So there we were in a better store, and there were so many gloves on display. And there it was—the giant first baseman's glove. *God*, I thought, *I hope I have enough money for this.* All the fear, the stress! It had a tag on it, a small white one, with a string. Robert was looking at the other gloves, at how great they were. He already had a good glove, a normal fielder's glove. I wanted something different. I turned the tag and saw the price. Oh god, it was super expensive! It was almost seventeen dollars. Then the sneakers came off. Most of the time, we paid two or three dollars for sneakers, and we wore them till they had holes in the bottom of them. We would put matchbooks in the sneakers to help seal the bottom, but now I took off my sneaker to double- and triple-check the amount of money I had. I had two fives, a few bills, and some change that I needed for the bus and more change in the other sneaker.

I was praying, *Please, God. Please, God!* The bills were smashed and wet from the sweat from my feet. We counted, and it came to fifteen dollars and change. But Robert was able to give me a dollar in change. His sneakers also came off there. I was shaking and worried about whether I would have enough. Just a bit short maybe? No, just enough? Yes, it was enough money. Yes, I was so happy it was big, but it was also very stiff and had to be broken in. The guys who worked in the store (I assumed they were the owners) just liked everything about Robert and me. They knew how we saved and how we hid our money and even asked us if we had bus fare. We nodded and then said that we at least thought so? He gave us fifty cents each back, double of what the bus fare cost. The man gave me good advice. "No bag," he said. "Put the glove under your shirt, half inside your pants, and don't remove it till you get back home." I took his advice, and we made it back traveling a little more scared than coming because we had the glove—the great glove. We had many good reasons to be worried about being robbed by the colored kids and had several experiences to prove it.

Back at the apartment, I also always had a problem. I seemed to feel insecure. If it wasn't the colored kids, it was the Puerto Ricans or my brother. Other than school, it was home life in general. I came home for some lunch. I knew that if Mom had the day off, she would make me a sandwich or something to eat around twelve noon. When I arrived at the front door, so did a repairman. I didn't know the reason he was there, and I didn't care. He said who he was, and we entered. He could have been a mass murderer. Didn't matter. We never looked for identification. We took people's word for it—strange but true. He had a uniform and tools, so he entered. Mom was in the kitchen, and it looked like she was doing some last-minute cleaning. The washing machine needed to be repaired, Mom said, so I sat at the kitchen table, watching, and of course, eating. It was left-over of something, but the ketchup or mustard killed any bad taste, and the soft white bread helped also.

The repairman then put his tools down, took the cover off the dials, and said with a loud voice, "Oh god! I can't touch this!" I saw why. There were thousands of roaches coming out. It was terrible! I felt low, real low, so the guy pushed the cover back on, said sorry, and left very quickly. What I saw made me feel so bad and even more insecure. Mom broke down crying, and it was so bad that she went to the floor on her knees, saying over and over again, "What am I going to do? What am I going to do?" I had tears coming down. I could not find the words or any word on what to say. I just felt like I was low, very low. What I remembered in the next few days was washing the clothes in the sink and bathtub with a scrubbing board, which was a wooden board about twelve inches wide and maybe eighteen inches long and had a metal part toward the top with waves in it. My nana used it several times, but now it was used regularly.

After that, there were even more heated fights between Mom and Dad. They were always centered about money, but that was only part of it. There were deeper issues. Now Mom said over and over again that the machine was broken and that they needed a new one since the guy would not fix it. Nothing was ever discussed. It was just yelling, and most of it was done by Mom. She had many issues and all her pain, and these came out by yelling and drinking. She would then cry. Most of the time, my father gave in. A day after the battles, I would feel nervous and tried to push this from my mind by playing with my toys and ignoring all this. My brother had it better. He just wasn't home. Where he was, no one knew, but that was better for me.

Mom was still waiting for the kitchen window to be fixed with new glass from my brother's plate throwing. I do remember Mom saying a few times to Dad the issues my brother had, but it fell on deaf ears. Dad was not a talker. He had a low education and spoke only about sports or John Wayne movies, and even then only a few words at that. I would be waiting all my life for him to say something to me that meant something, but later on, he did give me advice. Thank God I didn't do it, and I made the right decision not to do it. It was one that started my journey to be someone. They did buy a new washing machine. I saw it come in a big box and put in place, and the roach-infested one was gone. It was so cool to get a new thing. We looked at it as if it was gold. It was so cool; it was like we felt better about ourselves. It was a weird feeling to have, but it was there. So things were calm for a while—a very short while.

Robert's brother was several years older than I. He seemed to be a good guy and had his set of friends. Once in a while, they would play touch football either on the corner of Henderson Street or Lincoln Park. I would go along with them and Robert to Lincoln Park, what we called West Side Park because it was off West Side Avenue. It was not even a challenge. Even at my super young age, I was a much better athlete than any of them. I was always better than Robert and now really embarrassed his brother and his friends. I threw a football much better at one point. They said they may even ask me to play quarterback for them in pickup games. I was at least seven years younger than any of them, but from all that time alone, throwing balls against the walls and up toward the fourth and fifth floor of the Singer building across the street, I build up a super strength in my right arm. Playing flies up and out caused me to have very good lateral movement. The one big negative was that I was skinny and my overall all strength was limited. But I never quit. I pushed myself to be better always and had dreams of playing organized sports at a higher level. It was so difficult. It was not like today; there are so many leagues so many teams.

Sports was always a high for me; it was my drug, my escape. Green Bay Packers was always my football team. I loved Bart Starr; he was my hero. Though the Pack was not a flashy team, it was steady and followed a routine. I would lie in bed and name all the players over and over again. It was a great way to annoy my brother, who was in the other bed in the same room. He would get super upset and even call Mom to intervene. I had protection, and it was a way of getting back at my brother from the tortures he brought upon me. When my brother did play football with me and my friends on the street, his mission was not to win the game; it was to kill me. He would go after me and me alone. He would hit me whenever he could. If I was not his man, then he would switch. I would beat him all the time. It wasn't easy to avoid his flying elbows toward my head. Remember, this was a two-hand touch. No one would stand up to him. No one. He was too tough, too crazy, and too angry.

The game stopped, and the reason was that I was running up the left side of Wayne Street with the football big gainer. Then there came my brother, not with two hands out, but with a swinging right elbow aimed right at my chest. I saw it coming at the last second. I made a move, and my brother, who was swinging his elbow, hit the side mirror of a car. Wow! Thank God it wasn't me. He knocked the mirror right off the car, broke it completely off. Then the game stopped as he had hurt his elbow. I dared not laugh. I held it in and scored the winning touchdown, and my friends and I went on our way very quickly and left my brother to attend his issue. I never understood the sibling rivalry thing through the experiences with my brother. All I felt was that he wanted to severely hurt me, and I never felt comfortable being with him alone.

One thing I did notice was that many people who knew him didn't bother me. I found that very interesting.

There was a very interesting game we played on the block, and till this day, I've never heard of it. It had one of the strangest titles ever. No, it wasn't one, two, three, red light or tag or even jelly belly. It was not hide-and-seek—close to that. Let's say it's a bit more violent. It's called hot beans and butter! Do not ask me where the name came from or how that title makes sense, but it came from somewhere, and that is what we used to call it. There was one girl and her friend and about five boys. To get the girls to play this game, we always said it was not so bad, that it wouldn't hurt, and a few more little lies. The game consists of a home base—in our case, a streetlight pole. If your hand was on it, you were home safe; if not, you were a big target. The other main piece in this game was a belt, one you wore around your waist. First, we did the shoe choose game in part to see who first got to hide the belt. Let's say we all had our foot in, and it started with "My mother punched your mother in the nose. What color was the blood?" The person then would use their finger to do this rhyme, stop at a person's foot, and then they would choose a color. So they said red!

Whomever the shoe touched was last. Red spells red. Then that person got to hide the belt. They would hide it somewhere on our block. Of course, the person would let us know when to go and look for it. We had our backs turned and our hands covering our eyes. Then the hot and cold part would start. Anyone that was near the hiding place of the belt was told warm or hot or boiling hot. Anyone that was near the hiding place of the belt was told by the one who was hiding the belt to give the clues if you were warm and you were somewhat close, and boiling hot meant you were next to the belt. If you saw it, they would get close to you and say, "Ahh, I found it. OMG!" Then it became a mad dash to the home base. Why? The belt was swinging and lashing and hitting anyone that was close. The boys were much faster than the girls, and they were an easy target. I can remember one game where I found the belt, which I did many times, but this time, I had Sandy in my sights. She was a pretty girl and had a backside to die for. She was wearing tight white shorts. I think I hit her behind several times before she got to the home base. The funny thing about it was that she just laughed.

I'm afraid to lose you and you're not even mine.

—Author unknown

Hmm... that was very interesting. She didn't go to my Catholic school, like most of us. They went to another Catholic school, so we only knew them from living on our block—Wayne Street between Grove Street and Henderson Street. They were cool girls, really. We also played spin the bottle with them, and I always wanted to have the bottle stop at this girl. I thought she was pretty. It was one of those things. I liked her a lot, more than she liked me. The kisses weren't that great, if they even were kisses. The board games we played were checkers and go to the head of the class, but one day, she brought out a weird game called Ouija board. If someone didn't tell us how to say it, we would never have known how. We setup a card table; it was a small table that was used for four people to sit around to play cards; we set it up in the hallway on the first floor by the front door entrance. We sat around the table, three girls and me. The thing about this game was that it was banned by the Catholic Church, or so we were told. But that made it more interesting and more exciting.

There we were, ready to put our fingers on this weird sort of oval object with a see-through glass toward the front of it. The board had letters and a few words like yes and no. She knew how to play this game 'cause her mother used it. Of course, everyone was trying to get an edge and know the future. With our fingers on it, two fingers each, we started. I remember a few stupid questions like "Who likes me?" and "Who among us likes a certain person?" It was weird. This thing was moving around the board by itself. I knew I wasn't pushing it, so I figured the girls were. If I had hair on my arms, it would have stood up! The object moved faster and faster no matter what question we asked, like "Am I going to get honors in school?" and so on. So she, with her smart mouth, said, "Is Gerard going to marry Cindy?" I was so embarrassed, but I loved the question. I figured Cindy would push it toward the word no, but she took her fingers off at that moment. Then it moved around the board and finally moved to no. Cindy pumped her arm and fist, and said, "Yes!" Boy, was I hurt! but I was also very scared that this thing moved by itself. No kidding. We became scared, and it went very quickly back into the box and further into back of the closet.

There was something else that was scary! Many of our families could not afford a private phone line, so party lines were popular. In other words, if you shared a phone line, you could pick up your phone and hear the conversation going on from, say, a neighbor. The party line was shared by just one other family, so once you heard the click of the phone handle being picked up, you knew that someone was there, unless you could be slick and hold the buttons on the top of the phone just enough not to click. It just goes to show you that her family phone was our party line connection. A party line phone in the sixties was a phone line that was less expensive because it was shared by another family on your block (same area), living in another house. So I asked a big favor of her to call Cindy and give me the time for their conversation so I could listen. Well, she was going to ask Cindy if she liked me. I couldn't wait. I waited for the time. Then I listened. I held the buttons just right and heard them talking. My god, was I nervous! It was so stupid and dumb, but it was a chance. I then heard the answer after she popped the question to Cindy.

"Do you like Gerard?"

Cindy said, "Well, what do you mean?"

"Do you want to be Gerard's girlfriend?"

Then came the answer I didn't want to hear.

"Naaah, not really."

At least I knew, so my crush was over. Dead. A few years later, maybe four, I saw Cindy again. She had lost weight, had a sort of bad acne, but was still pretty. She had a Puerto Rican boyfriend, so I moved on.

Jackie was the big sister of Cindy. She was a couple of years older than Cindy, and she also went to other Catholic school. The big thing for some of the girls then was to look like Cher of *Sonny and Cher Show*. So what many girls would do was first iron their hair and lose weight and wear dirty bell bottom jeans, a bandana around their forehead, and around their hair. Her mother would then speak for the whole block to hear, she had a really loud voice. I didn't like the look Jackie had. It was too different, and she was super pretty to begin with. But at that time, things were changing. Younger people started to be a big argumentative with their parents. The times when you would never talk back were starting to fade. Many parents did push back harder, but it didn't matter. The kids would just walk away. That wasn't a good thing. Her mother's husband was a big man and very quiet, one of those guys that would politely say hello and good night. I guess he became tone deaf from the loud voice from his wife.

He would go out after work every day and clean the sidewalk, not only in front of his own home, but the neighbors' also. Many did clean their sidewalks and tried to keep things in their area in order. The people on the block were from many different places around Europe, Poland, Italy, Ireland, Ukraine. But they worked hard and were super clean.

Jackie's father was out doing his thing, cleaning the sidewalk and using a long-handled square shovel at the end; it looked very heavy. I was in front of the apartment and hitting a high bouncer against the wall. It must have been fall. I had a long-sleeved shirt on, and her father had a light jacket. There was a very old lady. I knew her by seeing her. I think she rented a place down the block. She had a heavy long coat on with her hat and was about halfway down the block, walking toward me. She had a medium-sized pocketbook that was hanging by the handle from her left arm. I noticed a tall young black guy coming around the corner where Santos's food store was. It was the Spanish store that had mostly food but a few home goods. This began the sign of the times. As the black guy appeared, he brushed by me and walked very fast down the block. Real fast! I was watching him closely. As he got closer to the old lady, he really started to move, and then it happened. He pushed the lady down, grabbed her pocketbook, and took off. I was frozen. I just said, "Hey! Hey!" I was very loud, but to no avail. Did I really think that it would stop him? But one thing did.

The old lady lay on the sidewalk, yelling, "Help!" It was the first words I ever heard her say. The black guy ran down the block, racing faster and faster. All I saw was Jackie's father cleaning the street gutter (the side of the street) with that large shovel. He had his head down and seemed not to be paying attention at all.

The black guy was coming close to him, a few feet away. And then it happened. *Bang! Smack!* Then again another *smack*! He nearly took the black guy's head off with the shovel. Down he went and the pocketbook also. The guy was stunned and almost down for the count. I was elated. I ran down to try to help, but at that point, the guy got up and ran away—this time, without the pocketbook. We helped the old lady up, and I was so stunned at how that happened. A few minutes later, the cops came in, and a police car took a report, asked the lady if she was okay, and that was it. I never saw that guy again. Maybe he learned a lesson—a good one.

The worse time of the year came, and it was time to return to school. I heard we were going to get another nun, another bully, famous for her two-handed slap. I couldn't be more depressed at this point. I really disliked school, and this was only the fourth grade. There was no fun, nothing new. It was the same classmates, many I haven't seen for several weeks. But that summer, Mom decided to start taking my brother and me, and of course, Nana to a place called the Highlands in New Jersey. It was down the Jersey Shore, but it was the start of the summer to me. I never knew how Mom got the money to do this, but later, I figured it out. The place we stayed at was called a bungalow. It was a small beaten-up, very old house. There were, like, ten of them in a row and a very big main house at the end of them. They were off a highway and behind a Catholic church. What was the best of all was just below. It was the coolest thing—the twin light towers. In reality, it was not far from Jersey City, but it seemed like we traveled forever to get there, though it took less time to get to the Poconos.

The Poconos was a whole different thing; it was a boarding house with a lake behind it, and just between the lake and the boarding house was a gigantic cesspool. This was where all the waste went to, and if the wind was blowing the right way, it was a bad day for breathing. We traveled to the Poconos, which was in Greeley, Pennsylvania. We went many times before the switch to the Highlands. In the boarding house, we had breakfast no one would forget. The bell rang at, like, seven in the morning, and you got about thirty minutes before you had to be downstairs for breakfast. We stayed in one room with two beds—one for my brother and me and one for Mom. The shower and bathroom was down the hall and difficult to get in 'cause it was shared by all that stayed on that floor.

Breakfast was special. As the three of us sat at assigned tables, the platters came out. OMG! There were stacks of bacon, stacks of pancakes, big platters of scrambled eggs, ham, potatoes, and bread. And there were big pitchers of orange juice and milk—it was crazy! There was so much food. The tables were full very long. There were maybe twenty or more people at each table. And those people could eat! There was so much sweet syrup as ever for the pancakes. But I didn't eat that much. Especially in the morning, I always seemed to have a weak stomach, and orange juice gave me heartburn and stomach pain, so I ate very little. I loved bacon, but I always felt indifferent about it and the aroma 'cause it reminded me of the past and present when my brother would put bacon fat in my comb and I would smell like bacon in school, which was not so great.

My brother did eat more than I, and maybe that was the reason he was so much bigger and stronger than me. He was also a few years older and a head taller. There was much to do there. There was a nice lake and trails to travel on and more trouble to get into. I would wear pants called clam diggers. They were three quarters long, just past the knee, and had a rope as a belt and was, of course, white. During the day, there were watermelon-eating and pie-eating contests, which were cool. And there was also a corn-on-the-cobb cookout. And many games were played with us at night. Across the road, there was a tavern. Of course, they always found a place to get smashed. Once in a while, my father would come down and keep everyone awake with his snoring. My uncle and aunt and my first cousin, who was a year older than my brother, also came for a few days. We took walks through the trails. There was a work glove nailed to a tree where one would leave money. None of us ever did. There was a cool stream leading to the lake. Just past the woods was a store, like a camping store, but it sold many wood carvings of animals and had leather wallets and handmade things. Hide and seek was a popular game there in the woods, and believe me, I always felt like I was the odd person out. After a long day, it was dinnertime and more platters of food. There were incredible platters of turkey, ham, roast beef, mashed potatoes, vegetables, and desserts (pies, cakes, and more). I ate then after a long day of goofing around. The food was very good.

And I then got to see her. She was a server and worked in the kitchen, even though I was only a kid, but she happened to have the look I loved. I really was attracted to her, and she had a beautiful face, dirty blond hair, and a super beautiful tan. She was way older than me, maybe seventeen or eighteen, but wow, was she pretty! I would think of her for a long time because she was so perfect to me. Then, of course, my brother, my mom, my aunt and uncle, and a few of their friends would go to the lake to swim and smoke and drink. They would keep the beer in a cold stream that went into the lake. I would be in the lake or fishing off a rock, but my brother and a couple of other boys. They got an idea, and I was in on it 'cause they had to take me with them. A row boat and a couple of canoes were always around, and the rowboat was large, about twelve feet. His plan was to take their beer and put it on the other side of the lake. So he rowed the boat to the area of the spring that was draining into the lake, took all their beer, and rowed away. We all were giggling about it and were headed toward the other side, and we then put it in a swamp area and went back to the beach side, where the adults were. Soon the shit was going to hit the fan. They went over to get more beer, and none was to be found. It was gone. Very soon, the four-letter words came out. "Where the hell is it?" "Who took it?" Then they figured it out. You would think it was gold. They made my brother go and get it. They were cursing for over an hour. Bad stuff, I guess. They became too drunk to pass out punishments or they'd just forgotten maybe.

Another day went by, and another breakfast, which was large as every other day. But now came a real issue, a bad one. My brother was always the leader no matter where, and he seemed to be the king of bad ideas. This one was no different. There was plenty of green apple trees around, and of course, what else would one think of then? A green apple fight! Only these apples were as hard as a rock and easy to throw. They were a little smaller than a baseball but were very easy to hurl at anything or anyone. The sides were chosen, and each collected tons of apples on each side. One side was on one side of the cesspool, and the other was on the opposite side. There were big kids and smaller ones like me. Soon we began firing! I would and a few would throw them like one would a hand grenade, looping them into the air. Believe me, even that way, they would hurt if it hit your head. But my brother always played to do damage and was throwing with all his might. As he was, a little kid smaller than me was walking in front. Now there had to be eight on each side throwing apples, but my brother was firing them full speed as hard as he could. And then it happened! He hit the little kid in the face. The kid went down screaming, uncontrollably crying, like I had never heard before. Many ran, but I guess the kids that knew him went to get help. We panicked. My brother took off, and I was upset and crying. The worst had happened. He hit the kid in the eye with the hard green apple. It was terrible! There were no words to describe it. For hours, my brother was no place to be found. He was hiding in the woods, as I recall. He did come out much later, but the worst was yet to come.

The next day, the boy's mother took him to our room and showed what happened. He not only had a bandage on his eye but also a big black patch like a pirate. I would not forget the lady yelling at my mother that she was going to bring a lawsuit on us over and over again. We were stunned. We didn't really know what that meant, to be honest, but we could see Mom crying. We packed up. We were leaving very soon. Nana loved the place, but she was going back home with us. We never knew what happened to the boy, and we never heard from a lawyer, but again, I saw my brother at his worst, always wanting to hurt someone.

The Highlands was a cool place because it was different than downtown. Where we stayed was close to the bay and the marina, so there were things to do other than get into trouble or have trouble brought upon us. My brother was there, so I knew problems would come with him being there. Where we stayed was nothing special at all. You can say the apartment was as good—well, maybe not. Down from the bungalows was a major highway that we had to cross to go down a very steep hill, where there was a well with fresh water running out of it, flowing to the top. You could fill a jar or whatever and take it with you. My nana thought it was like a fountain of youth, and she and my mom drank from it frequently. Farther down, it led to a main street. There was a bar called the Wagon Wheel and a few stores that sold beach stuff and comic books, which were good for us. Down farther was the bay area. It had a sandy beach and a roped-off area about twenty feet out into the water. If you walked the other way, there was a very small movie theater that happened to be showing two very scary movies: *The Pit and the Pendulum* and *The Werewolf of London*. That was great!

Now we went to the marina, where all the big fishing boats were docked. Such a great place. We could see the boats leaving and arriving, and we even would go fishing off the dock area. Even a longer walk was the bridge over the inlet of the bay, and below it was a small beach area called the mud hole. The current in the bay and the inlet was terrible very. It was very strong, and if you went too far out, unless you were an excellent swimmer, you would drift most likely to your end. This place was new, so exploring was going to be a super thing for us. It was soon after that when my brother made friends and even had his friends from home visit for a couple of weeks. It was a bit strange. He got bored quickly and got homesick fast. I found that crazy! He lived a few blocks from us across from city hall, and he was bored and lonely here?

Behind the bungalows was an open field, and most of the time was filled with yellow jackets. They scared the crap out of you, and their sting was no joke. As we all went to the bay and fished and had some fun, he wanted no part of it and wished to go home. He was there for only a couple of days, and he wanted out. As he stayed behind, he did something good. He had a pile—and I mean a pile—a giant super big pile of dead wasps. It was maybe two feet high. It was bizarre how he did this using only a fly swatter. But who cared? And the next day, my father came up and drove back home to Jersey City.

Next up was our neighbor. Her two kids were a perfect match, right? Maybe my brother had many fistfights, and they were so brutal. Blood would flow. Back home, there were many troublemakers, a guy a year or two older than my bother. This was a guy that would never fight but always loved to instigate one, and who best to fight one another than two hotheads? My brother and one of his friends would fight. He would put a piece of wood on Ricky's shoulder, and the other would knock it off. Then off they went, full punches, grabbing, headlocks. This was always in the parking lot behind the city hall. Most of the time, even though his friend was bigger, my brother would win one time. Ricky had him down with his legs wrapped around his head, only to see him bite a large scab off my brother's leg. It was bad, really bad. It then was broken up by all who was there, but I just watched and was glad it was not me.

One of the best things we did was go night fishing down at the marina to catch eels. It was so cool because they gave you a fight, pulling them in. Between the party boats that were docked, we fished. We would use anything as bait, and we were pulling them in one after another. My brother and his friend even more. Suddenly, my brother's pole bent like I hadn't ever seen before. One end was touching the middle of the pole. Wow, a big fight was coming, and this time, it was what was on his fishing line. Everyone stopped and watched. There were several of us there. After a several minutes of fighting, it was an eel but not a normal one. It was a giant, a super big eel! We all watched as my brother landed it. It had to be almost five feet long and four inches thick, a real monster. It should have been in the newspaper or something, we said. We were so proud, so we put it in a big bucket with the hook still buried inside of it. We took turns carrying it to the bungalow to show it off. We thought so.

As we walked along a few streets and up the very steep hill going up to cross the four-lane highway, he was talking my brother into laying it on the highway to see the cars run over it. I didn't say much, but I was hoping that Ricky would not listen to him. It looked like jealousy to me, and I wanted Mom to see this monster, but that was not going to happen. As we finally crossed the highway, the deal was made. His friend talked him into how cool it would be to see. We always raced across the highway, and this time, nothing changed. So as we waited on the other side, they were putting the eel on the highway. After this, there would only be a story to tell, and that was what his friend wanted. As car after car ran over it, no real enjoyment came out of it.

We got back and told our story of how my brother caught a big eel, and it didn't get Mom's attention. She was drinking and was more concerned about their own storytelling then ours. It was more of the same—always drinking. More of a bad feeling more of seeing people doing that, especially my mom made me depressed. I always thought, What does make someone happy. Is this normal, and if so, why? I became more insecure about my feelings, not knowing how to act or feel. The best thing was having something to eat, maybe a sandwich, and going to bed. After a few days, we wanted to go to the fishing pier in Long Branch. Mom's friend drove, so she and Mom took us to the pier. It was so cool. It was a long pier that went into the ocean. We could catch anything. The time was set. They said we would be picked up at 7:00 p.m. After only catching dogfish, it was the experience in Long Branch pier that was great. It was maybe eight miles, but to walk it at night—and a cool night at that—was not so good.

Truth is everybody is going to hurt you.
You just gotta find the ones worth suffering for.

—Bob Marley

Well, it happened. They were drinking and forgot about us, at least the time. We waited till eight. Still they didn't show up, so we began to walk back along the high stone wall along the highway. I guess we walked about three miles before we saw them coming. They blew right by us. OMG! Terrible! They didn't even see us! We decided to keep walking. They never seemed to turn around to come back. It was only a two-lane highway, one coming and one going, but my brother, who had big courage or something, started to put his thumb out and hitchhike. Within a minute, a man picked us up! He was drinking also. We could smell him. I knew the scent. I could pick it out anywhere. But he was a good guy and took us right to the front of the bungalow. We hardly said thanks, but he understood. About an hour after that, Mom's friend and Mom got back. They said they were so worried. Maybe yes, but if they were, why were they so late? Just another thing to block out and blame on the drinking.

After many trips to the mud hole, a name the adults used, it was really a narrowing part of the bay that ran under the bridge—the bridge, which was about fifty feet above the water. My brother and his friend and a few other kids would walk to the bridge and climb down a few feet and jump into the mud hole. It took guts and it was a big risk 'cause the current there was strong. But Ricky wasn't scared of anything I had ever seen. He could be dared to do anything. It was a super sunny day, and we went to the mud hole, only us. My heart was pounding through my chest. I knew what was coming. They were going to force me to jump. I was at that time a poor swimmer. The only person who helped me learn was Mom. And I was not as strong as they thought. First, one kid jumped, then another. Then they set up a line so they could catch me when I got to the water. My brother and his friend helped me over the guardrail. My brother jumped, and then his friend jumped with me. I held my nose, and my eyes were tightly closed. And then I hit the water. I was hurt but not so bad. I was just stunned, and they helped me to the beach area. I could hardly catch my breath. I was shaking so badly, but I did it. I wasn't proud, but I was glad I did it. I never did it again.

I enjoyed going to the twin towers and walking up the hill with Mom and her friend, playing ghost. It was a game where we named a movie star or a famous person going through the alphabet, as well as states and capitals. If you missed, you got a letter until a person lost, ending up with the tin ghost. One time, as we walked, Mom saw a house for sale right near the twin towers. It was beautiful. It was stone, and you could see the bridge and the inlet. It also had two stone round ponds in the backyard. She was so excited she went to the local realty company, and we checked on the availability. It had black-painted casement windows. What a great thing to be able to move there. Mom was given the price. It was 13,500 dollars. With Mom and Dad working, it would be no problem. My father was a veteran, and even better, it was not far from Elizabeth, New Jersey, where my father worked. The next step was Mom telling Dad about it. Well then, she did. He wanted nothing to do with it. His excuse was that it was too far a drive to work. Well, to me, not really. He just wasn't interested. His interests lay elsewhere, and the dream Mom had for us was painful for years to come. We paid the price for that. We visited once I remember, but our dream became their future. Mom always used that experience for what could have been, and maybe she was correct.

There was a bar on the main street in the highlands. It had a big wooden steering wheel from an old boat above the door. Mary and her husband were the owners. They were nice people from what I knew. They were nice to me anyway. It had a long bar and a big yard and had a bottle cooler with some tables against the wall. The cooler was filled with sodas and beers to take out (meaning, purchase to take out of the store) and also had a super chocolate drink I loved in a bottle. Boy, was that good! I loved it. It had so much chocolate on the bottom of the bottle. You had to shake it well to mix it. It tasted like heaven and was really cold. Mom would go into this bar during the day with me and leave me at the table, and she would sit at the bar and talk with Mary and, of course, drink. I was left to drink Yoohoos till I almost drowned. I was so bored and so unhappy. The only thing there was a television playing baseball games. The Dodgers and the Reds were playing, so I watched that from the table. Then I asked Mom for some money to go to the 5&10 store to look at the comic books and some small toys and balls, just to waste time till she left.

For the few times we went to the Highlands, my brother didn't come. He stayed home, which was weird 'cause my father worked all day and Nana was with us most of the time. I knew Mom left money with him and left a lot of food for him. Again thinking about it, I felt safer with him not here, and I wondered what kind of trouble he would get in with nobody around. I guess that didn't matter either. He was the tough guy of the area, and so he would survive. I felt alone and scared and worried about Mom. Maybe it was because I'd seen her feel that way. I was shy around many people and wished to just play with my toy soldiers. Many times I would get comic books and never read them. I just looked at the drawings and imagined things, maybe just to tune things out about Mom and Dad's fights, my brother's bullying of me, Nana's drinking, and what was going to happen next.

I missed my friend Robert, but he had his friends also. He was two years my senior, so there was a difference. The biggest fear was school the next year. I would be entering the fourth grade, and I was starting to dislike school more and more each day. My next teacher was another nun, a bigger woman known for something special—the two-handed face slap. We would get info from kids who had her, and there were always rumors. At such a young age, we were worrying so much. But when you didn't like school, this was what was spoken about. When we arrived back in Jersey City, the first thing was school uniforms. There was a store around Second Street that sold them, and that was where we went. There were ties, shirts, jackets, pants, green ties, and green jackets with the emblem of the school on them. Then there were also the notebooks, the book bag. Many had an attaché case, a vinyl-covered wooden rectangular shape with two snap locks on it. Very cool but expensive. So a book bag was good for me and, of course, a lunch box and a thermos. Many had designs of a television character—for girls, maybe Barbie, and for boys, an army theme. There were also Peanuts, Batman, and Snow White. We had to be careful because the nuns were always watching, so if you got one that was different, they may tell you it was no good. Strange but true.

Always, the first couple of weeks were okay in class, but then the punishments started. Previously, in my first to third grades, I had been on the honor list. I knew all my timetables and was good at the flash cards, addition, and subtraction. Mom worked with me on those things. Fourth grade was harder. English was a tough class. My handwriting was bad. This could have been a lack of confidence or just sloppiness. This was a number one priority for the nuns, along with drawing small circles. I did it over and over again till I could not hold a pencil. Now things were really getting difficult for me, and I was getting worried. Then it came, the sister thought I was joking and I was doing it on purpose. She called me up in front of the class. Of course, it was to humiliate me, like she did to many others. But really it was also to teach me a lesson. Would getting slapped several times help me with my handwriting? Of course not. But maybe, in her twisted mind, it would teach me a lesson.

It began first with the ruler on my hands, back and front. I guess that would improve my writing, but maybe not. So she slapped me with both hands twice till I had tears running down my face. Then I was told to sit down and write more circles. Of course, I couldn't. My hands were hurting as my face was. God help you if you really started weeping You would stand in the clothing room. Going home that day, I was popular. The girls would always feel sorry for you, but they had to also watch out. They could be next.

We always had fear and wondered how we could escape these things. School was no safe haven, and the streets weren't either. The parks, such as the West Side Park, were good places to play baseball and football, but that trip was on the red bus, the Montgomery bus. Many of us went, so it was a little safe. The library on Jersey Avenue was a good place. It was a big place. There were so many rooms and some cool projectors, but it was downstairs where we wanted to go. Why? Because we couldn't. It had a scissors metal gate locked and a sign that said, "No one under the age of eighteen is allowed." It had playboy books and other magazines that had naked women in them, we were told. Why else would it be locked with a sign like that? And besides, my friend Dennis made it down there and saw many X-rated books. We were so curious. But we were watched, like hawks. The older woman working behind the large desk kept a keen eye on us, so our efforts were rejected.

Now we could have been there to do book reports or study or even do homework but nope. It was always escape something to distract us from the real world. Robert never came with us to try those things. His mom could get info from him very easily, so there were some things he didn't do. School was an issue as always, but now it was getting more and more of a problem. I was so bothered by it. The only reason to go was to see some friends. One was not Anthony, whom I was fighting every day as soon as we went to recess. This was like a fifteen-minute break when we went outside to run around like crazy, like kids did. The word was out. Anthony would tell someone to meet me after school, so then the stress started. After that, I couldn't focus on class and got into more trouble by not paying attention to the nuns or class. That meant more whacks with the rulers and more slaps before class ended. I was always distracted by thinking why only certain people rang the bell to end recess or played jump rope with the nuns more and more. They were the goodie girls or the goodie boys, who acted more like the girls.

Most of us never got a chance or a thought. We were marked as bad actors or baboons, as we were called. Then class did finally end, so in front of the church, Anthony and I fought. It seemed always to be a draw, and a few times, my anger heated up as the fight went on—ripped jackets or shirts and ties pulled. But then Robert was always there to break it up, or a few times, the brothers from the church came a few times. Why so many fights? I never knew. I had nothing against him, but a couple of years later, he was transferred to a public school, which was not a good thing.

After many years, believe it or not, we met again as adults when a guy from my baseball team brought him in to play for us. It was my team. I could not believe it. It was Tony. We never spoke much about what happened when we were kids, but it was good to see him. The next year, I was hoping to see him again, but to no avail. The person that brought him to us to play informed me the bad news. He died of bad circumstances. I said to Bobby, who knew him and had brought Anthony to me, again that he was just one of many. I thought later that maybe if the nuns had given him a chance. things could have been different. What was his problem really? Why did he want to fight all the time? Why was he the way he was? The same could be said of my brother. The nuns reacted to things, but the only solution was to punish or push us. Where was the love? It was about control. Maybe the area affected them as much as us.

Going home from school each day was sometimes a challenge. There were some more fights, either being in them or seeing them. They changed the times for the dismissal of our school and the public school because of the issues. There was a boys' club on Grand Street called the Whittier House. We called it the Woody House. Mr. B was the head guy. Mr. B was an older man but ran this club like a no-nonsense guy. Black kids, Spanish kids, and white kids joined there to play pool, ping pong, and basketball and also learn to box (as in gloves and punching). According to the age and years, the membership cards were in different colors. Many of the kids were from public schools; only a couple of us were from Catholic schools.

Next to that was a candy store, and wow, it was packed after school. Many of the students went there. What you could get for ten cents! I loved the red-hot dollars, two for a penny. Seeing all the different girls wasn't bad either. We would cut down to Henderson Street and turn right and get almost home. There was so much going on. There were so many houses now being demolished for the Gregory projects. All the homes from across Wayne Street were going to be gone. When the houses were being demolished, a supermarket would be built and a big parking lot with it. The houses were the place to investigate. Wow, spindles from the staircase were great for guns. There were so many things to be curious about. Then there were the old sheds in the back of the houses. My brother and his friends made one of them into a clubhouse and even put a lock on the door! We got around that by screwing off the hasp. We were far smarter than they thought. Inside was an old couch and chairs and other things—naked centerfolds of women!

Wow, we were in our glory sex education first-hand. No one ever told us about any of this, not in school and never at home. We looked and pointed and saw the big chests and the hairy private parts and the very pretty faces. This was even better than the Christopher Lee vampire movies, which had the Englishwoman with half their chest showing. Never forgot those. We felt like big guys and soon got out of there. But there were traps. We were told this included boards with nails through them. They were hidden in the dirt all over. My brother and his friends made them in order to get the guys who were going to eventually tear down their clubhouse. How bad was that! But my brother was busy. He was an excellent dancer and a party type of person, and all the girls loved him, especially the Puerto Rican girls, who always asked me about him. Where was he? Dancing on the Zacherley Show. He was a guy that dressed like a ghoul and had a dance party show, I believe, in Newark, New Jersey, which was a few minutes away by train. He was popular and had his gang and was also popular in the boys' club. No one ever bothered him. I had never seen him lose a fight, and in the girls' opinion, he was good-looking.

He ironed his hair with a hot iron and rolled up his T-shirt's sleeves to his shoulders. I didn't admire him. I knew he had something wrong with him beyond those silly things. I also knew one thing. I was a far better athlete, so that kept me somewhat satisfied. The brothers from church liked him, and the nuns liked him or were maybe scared of him. But they didn't know him as I did. They didn't see so many things. When the streets were piled high with snow and the sidewalks were also full, he would chase me, and when he caught me from behind, he pushed my face into the snow until I couldn't breathe. My arms were spread. Thank God.

Mr. K, a hero with the shovel (the one who hit the black guy who was stealing the old woman's purse), pulled my brother off me and told him, "Are you crazy? You were killing him! Look, he can't catch his breath! What is wrong with you?" he yelled at my brother.

Ricky never flinched. He walked away. I got up as Mr. K helped me up. I looked at him. I couldn't talk, couldn't even say, "Thank you. You saved my life!" I said nothing. I guess maybe I was worried my bother would get me in another way or hurt Mr. K. I really thought I was going to die. When we were both home that night, I never spoke to Mom about it, and my father didn't come home from work or the bar till late, I guess hoping that he could avoid any fights, hoping Mom was asleep or was too drunk to argue. Mom was awake, and so was Nana. They were watching TV, and we went to bed. One bed was next to the other. I would recite the entire Green Bay Packer roster. I did this many times through the years when he was sleeping in the bed next to me. I knew them by heart. I loved them, and they've always been my team even today. I would start always with Bart Starr and then Travis Williams, Ray Nitschke, and Willie Wood. This killed him, annoyed him to no end. He screamed again and again for Mom. Too bad. I had my chance to get him, even though I knew his revenge toward me would be far worse.

Halloween was a different time, a real time of fun and more abuse. The big guys, including my brother, of course, filled socks with flour. This would make another weapon. It hurt when you got hit with it. It would be swung with purpose, like a mace spiked ball, and it marked you with flour stains all over. Eggs were so popular and not used for eating. They were thrown at everyone and everything—buses, storefronts, signs, and of course, one another. The costumes we were wearing were 5&10 store plastic Frankenstein or Wolfman or Dracula, all popular movie characters. These were the masks with the thin rubber band around your head, and you could hardly breathe. Or you make up your own mask with face paint—as a hobo (whom we called bums) or as a pirate. None of them helped from the punishment of the floured socks or the eggs.

It was a crazy day and night. We went from house to house, begging for candy. For those who did not answer the door, they were abused and marked by my brother and his friends. The Jewish people and some others in the apartment did not practice Halloween, so they answered the door and yelled at us at my brother and his gang. That was a big mistake. Dog shit was popular, and the eggs came into big use. Just ask Mr. T. He lived on the third floor, a floor below us, and was a nasty guy. He was always angry, always yelling at us for anything. Hey, we were kids. Yeah, right. He paid for it this time. My brother got a big pile of dog shit, and they put it in a paper bag and placed it outside his door. But that was not enough. He set it on fire. Wow, I couldn't believe my eyes. The smoke, the terrible smell!

Mr. T opened the door and began to stomp the bag over and over to put out the fire, but he got a foot full of dog shit. Not only that; he was pummeled with at least six eggs before everyone ran down the stairs, tripping and falling over one another, laughing so loudly. They could hear us for blocks. If only the nuns could see us now. Maybe they would have a reason to beat us and punish us, but they never knew. It was so funny in a weird way. We never thought of them when we left class for that day, even if I was punished or beaten. Anything we did was a great escape from them. We never picked out people 'cause of their religion or faith or creed. We just never cared about that stuff. We had enough fear from the Puerto Ricans and blacks. The ones we were friends with were cool but one guy I had an issue with.

Mr. B at the woody house took a liking to me. For what reason, I don't know. He wanted to train me to box, and so he did upstairs, where there was a basketball hoop and also boxing equipment. So he showed me how to put on the boxing gloves and throw punches. So cool. I loved boxing since my brother practiced on me all the time. And from throwing a ball all day against the walls and pitching so much stickball, I had a very strong right hand. Donnie was a friend of mine and played ball with me for Little League, a good guy. He was a year or two older than me but was taller and bigger. He put on the gloves, and I had my set on. Then we went at it. First, he just pushed me and rubbed me on the top of the head. I still was so skinny, but my temper got to me. I let Donnie have it. I hit him with a couple of big right hands to his face. Most of the time, when I threw punches, I had my eyes closed, but I hit pay dirt. I busted up his face. There was blood running down from his nose.

Everyone yelled and screamed and started calling me Little Ricky. Wow! What respect! I was being compared to my crazy brother. They all knew him and how tough he was. Now I was being compared to him? I hated myself for that. I liked Donnie. He helped me so much with pitching. He was my catcher and helped me. I didn't know what to say to him. His other friend was Gary. He was a good guy also. We used to sneak off to the Yankee stadium together and sit in the left field for seventy-five cents. I even told Donnie to hit me to make up for what I did, but being the good guy that he was, he said, "You beat me fair and square." I looked at the ground, and we went on.

> I've come to realize that the only people
> I need in my life are the ones who need
> me in theirs even when I have nothing.

> —Cheryl Ruebel

Soon I would practice more and more and cause more trouble. Robert and I were playing around on Wayne Street, and I told him what happened. He was amused and laughed, so I said, "Let me show you what I did." Now he was by far my best friend, and I so respected him, so we were kidding around and boxing. Then it happened. I let my right hand go and bang right in his nose. Another bloody nose! God almighty, I almost started crying as he had tears coming down his cheeks. He went home to get attention for that. I did not know at the time that he suffered from diabetes. It was many years before I found out.

The next day, I saw his mother, and I was scared. I usually said hello or waved, but I crossed the street. I was embarrassed, ashamed. I knew she knew what had happened. She knew Robert and watched him like a hawk. Later that night, she called my mother and was not mad at me for what happened to Robert. It was that I crossed the street on her. Mom didn't have to say anything. I told Robert's mother I was sorry. She said okay, and it passed.

Robert's uncle was a savior. I never really knew his name. I think it was Vincent, and he was Robert's mother's brother. He was a single guy and lived on Van Vorst Street, and he told us he was a welder. I often saw him in Robert's house. Robert lived in the last house on the block on Wayne and Henderson Streets, on a third-floor apartment. His uncle would often sit in the chair, watching the television show *Wild Wild West* and eat an onion—yes, an onion. He would eat it like you would eat an apple. I believed he lived with his sister in a brownstone on Van Vorst. Though a short man, he had a big heart and loved Robert very much. He took us to so many places.

Bowling was his sport, and he would take Robert and me bowling all the time. He was good, and so was Robert. They had their own balls. I always came along. Mom would give me a dollar or a little more, but he never took my money. He always paid. I was not that good at bowling. To me, it was not a contact sport, and I was not that interested. But I liked to be in their company and going to different places was special to me. Many times, he would take us golfing in the back of Lincoln Park off West Side Avenue. I really liked that, and it was like a par three course. I was good at it, really good, and I would win many times. I could really hit the ball well and straight. I think playing baseball helped me with that. We went several times, but the last time we went was the saddest, a very difficult day in my life.

The best place he took us to was the Palisades Amusement Park. Wow, it was so great. There were so many rides, so many things to do, and of course, he paid. On the way in, they would give us a paper pack with all kinds of goodies in it and even Tang, which no one liked. I always gave my bag to Robert's uncle, and he picked through it and gave me back what he didn't want, which was fine. The greatest thing there were the freak shows and the deformed animals—the cow with six legs and goat with two heads. The human freaks were also cool. We were amazed by them. There were animals in jars, and the best one was Jolly Jerry, the fat boy. He was the same guy we saw in a carnival in Washington Park in Jersey City. He was in a large steel chair, and he must have been four hundred pounds or bigger. As we walked in, to the right was an amphitheater, and guess what. That day, the Supremes were singing, and I knew their songs!

But it was the rides and the freak shows that mattered to us. The best was the dog with human skin. They couldn't have made it up. All it was, was a shaved dog. What people would do to have a show! We figured that out pretty fast. They had a parachute ride that went around and around. We went on that first. When we got off, I had my head in the garbage can, throwing up. I hated any ride that went in circles like the round-up ride and so many rides there. It was always a good time as long as I wasn't getting sick. It was a beautiful ride there. There were so many trees and nice, clean roads. I never knew how to act with Robert's uncle—what to say, how to thank him. He did so much for Robert. I remember he collected bottle caps with certain inserts with baseball players in them, Mets and Yankees. We stuck them on a paper that matched their names, and when the card was full, we took it to Coca-Cola, and they gave us prizes. We both did it. I hated the Mets and the Yankees, but I wanted the gifts. I think it was a Yoohoo thing. I noticed one thing. Robert started to drink club soda from the bottle, which was odd. We always drank soda, and Robert would drink weird sodas, such as pineapple soda and Fresca (not for me) and Tab soda (a sort of diet soda). I wondered why, but he never would say why.

One of the cool things Robert's uncle would do was collect cigar bands but certain ones 'cause if you had enough, you would get prizes. I think one was Admiration cigars and also packages of certain cigarettes, but it was the cigar bands that would bring in the big prizes. Robert's father worked for the railroad. I only saw him several times. He slept during the day and worked at night, so it seemed I'd only seen him when he was headed home. He would collect many cigar bands along the railroad tracks. When he'd had enough, he would send them in to a company. This time, it was a special prize, a five-inch color TV! I would never forget. They put this TV. Now remember, no one had color television. They were just starting to become popular, and no one could buy one. It was way too expensive, so thinking back. It was funny to have everyone sitting in their chairs or couch, like ten or more feet away, watching a five-inch television, but people did it. At that time, the 5&10 store was to us like how a dollar store and supercenters are today. They had these plastic screen covers that, as they said, would make your black and white television into a color TV by taping it on your current television. It was blue at the top, red in the middle, and green on the bottom, and that was what it was—a rip-off! There were so many so-called bargains.

Fourth grade was always the same with the goofy stuff we had to do. There were school plays, and again the sister slapped clothing room punishments, standing in the corner, and a new one. There was an the influx of new students (Puerto Ricans and Central Americans), we had a great age difference. They were like three or four years older than us, and some had facial hair. The girls were, let's say, bigger everywhere. But the funny thing was that none of them spoke English. Guess what. That's why they were in the fourth grade. The nuns had no patience with that. They were intelligent, but the nuns would talk loud with them. They thought that, by yelling, they would understand them better. The new students would urinate on the floor through their uniforms. Wow, that was so bad. Then the upper-class students, like my brother, would come in with the mop and red sawdust to clean it up. Yes, these nuns were so compassionate. What a joke that was.

They had old uniforms sitting around for these students to change into. These were placed in the office outside the principal's office. Sister, the one who loved to beat us with her shillelagh, was a tall bitter old lady with a hard face. She knew how to smile only when our parents brought her gifts or donated things to the school, like my mother did many times. The upper-class kids, seventh and eighth graders, got to be patrol boys. These were like crossing guards. They had ranks also—normal a white silver badge or a lieutenant or a high-ranking captain, which was the rank of my brother. He had all the badges and was Mister Popular. If only they had seen through that and seen the real things he did, but they got out of him what they wanted. The nuns or the lay teachers never cared what went on at home or on the streets. They were just interested in getting where they wanted to go, and only God knew where that was.

The next step was the school plays. The *Mary Poppins* movie was still popular, and the school took us on a trip to see it. I guess it was okay. They decided to make the boys dress up like the chimney cleaners. My poor mom had to get black dress pants then sew red stripes down each leg and have a corn broom. Not good. Mom was a good cook, not a good housekeeper and not a seamstress. She pinned the strips—yes, *pinned* the strips—on the pants legs. I bothered her to get me a black corn broom, and she did. We did find one.

Nice! There was also a red cross tie and a white shirt. And of course, we learned a song from the movie "Chim Chim Cher-ee." And we messed it up by saying *chimney* instead of *cher-ee*. To normal people, it was an honest nervous mistake but not to the sister.

But the main event was coming. The older classes had special plays, more serious ones. We were still the cute kids. They had to get really dressed up, and many Puerto Rican girls were in those classes. So pretty they were to see, so beautiful. We waited outside in the hallway from our normal classroom. Our classes were separated by the auditorium, a really large hall with an upper area and an area with a few hundred seats downstairs. It was used for the mass until the normal church building was finished being built. We also had gym there and recess when the weather was bad. On the other side were the sixth, seventh, and eighth grade classes.

As we stood in the hallway, the auditorium upper doors were pushed open in a severely violent way, like a person was bursting through it. It was half a flight of stairs up, so it was very clear to see the area, like ten feet away. One of the nuns had a beautiful Puerto Rican girl by the hair and was pulling her like you would not believe, so violently. The girl was screaming, crying. You see, she had these big curls in her hair, and the nuns were going to take care of that. The nun had scissors in her hand, not just scissors but large metal shears. They were very popular then, and she started to cut the girl's hair off right in front of us. The girl grabbed her own hair, trying to stop the nun. The nun cut the curls out, pulling and pulling right on the staircase. The screaming! The crying! She may have been heard for blocks. It was terrifying! We almost started to cry. Then it stopped, and she pushed the girl down the stairs toward the principal's office.

Well, you see, girls were told curls were never allowed, and Spanish moms loved to curl their daughters' hair. I was sure the girl told her mom no, but it was for the play, and the nuns had to make an example of her. They sure did. And guess what. The play must go on, and it did. Did we screw up? Yes, but the parents and friends loved it. We made it funny and cute, but not to the nuns, with their hard faces and mean streaks. I don't know if I'd ever seen that girl again. Too bad.

We had a classmate who was a really nice kid. He was a Puerto Rican kid and was a good person. You could really tell he was a respectful guy, and the older kids would always want to talk to him. We knew why. He had the most beautiful sister I had ever seen in my life, and she fit that name—long dark hair, big brown eyes, and the most perfect body. She put Natalie Wood to shame. She was a sweet person and many from the public school came by to just take a look. When we got lucky enough to deliver something to the other side, the upper grades, we always took a look. She was an angel, a real one. But a few friends had another thing in mind. His father worked in Santos's market below where I lived, so we knew what hours he worked, and his mother worked as a seamstress somewhere. We also knew when she would be home, so we had the all the times set. We also played sometimes in his house on Mercer Street, but the best thing we knew was that when his sister came home.

We would always talk about his sister to him, and he used to rub his head, saying, "All everyone want to do is talk to me about my sister. The older kids, you guys, and everyone."

We would ask more probing questions, like "Have you seen her naked? What does she look like?"

He would tell us, "Yes, and she is beautiful. Her body is perfect. Even though she is my sister, I have to say that I have peeked into the keyhole when she was taking a shower."

Oh boy, what an opening for us. Day after day, we went to his house, waiting for her to take a shower. You see, the old house still had skeleton keys with a big keyhole, so you could get an eyeful. It was planned well, and she got into the shower. We all started to take a look one by one as she took off her clothes. The whispering was so loud I think she suspected something, but no, I saw her. Oh my god! I had never seen that in my life. She was skinnier than I thought and beautiful. As she stepped into the shower, I saw everything. I still have that image to this day! I will never forget the good guy. He was a good person seriously, but my vision was still of his sister.

There were many places we would sneak off to, and one place was the movies. The beautiful Loew's in Journal Square, the newer State Theater around the corner from it, and the Stanley across the street from the Loew's. The Loew's always seemed to have the better movies, as in the James Bond, Dracula, and karate movies. The State had more serious movies, like *The Train* and *Von Ryan's Express*. The Stanley was known for the close-circuit boxing fights. When a big movie came to town, the lines were long. Robert and I would take the path train there or, as my nana would say, the tubes the path. It was two blocks away, and there was one train to Journal Square. Robert was the expert on what train to take and what side of the platform to wait by. Remember, he was a couple of years older than I. The movies would cost seventy-five cents and sometimes ninety-nine cents. It would take a lot of saving for this, and if we had more money, we would get a hot dog or a slice of pizza when the movies were finished.

Outside on the side of the Loew's, there were eight-by-ten photos of some scenes that were so cool to see. We would look at them and say "Hey! I remember that one!" and so on. But no matter where we went, there was always something that would ruin our day or put fear into us. As we came out for the path train, there was a long alleyway, a type of area that had many stores and bars. When you came out of it, the Loew's Theater was right across the street. But just as we would start to get ready to cross the street, there would be four to five black kids, some our age, some older. Many times, there would more than us. They would hang out there. It seemed they were waiting for anyone to take advantage of, and we were always targets. I hated it. This was a common situation. If it wasn't the bully we knew, it was them. No matter where you went, it was always this crap. They were always trying to rob us, and we maybe had less than them.

It started with "Hey, you got any money?" It was not a question. Many adults passing by would do nothing. We would always hope someone would say something to stop this. This wasn't the first time, so we were a little slick. They would say, "All I find, I keep." This was repeated to us over and over again, but by this time and from past experiences, we would keep a dime and a couple of pennies in our pockets. Our response was always "We got nothing." Then they would turn our pockets inside out and find the change and see it fall to the ground. Robert was full of fear, and they sensed it. Sometimes pushing went on, but then some adults walking by would yell, "Stop that!" For a minute, it would stop, but usually, when they saw that we had nothing, they stopped. But we outsmarted them. We kept our money in our sneakers. As beat up as our sneakers were, who would look there? We fooled them, but the abuse would go on and on. Then there was a day that I fought back, and I sure did with a lot of fury.

Though my brother had big-time issues and I feared him as many did, sometimes I wished he was there at those times. He was only a year older than Robert, but my brother being tough was in a different universe. I had never seen him fear anyone, and I was sure those guys would have paid a big price. The thing was that he would have not done it for us. He would have done it 'cause he liked it, meaning beat the crap out of those kids. Bending over to make believe you dropped something in front of the movie theater was a trick, and I was sure the ticket person didn't like that. But money was money, and so on. We didn't go to watch many karate movies 'cause when the movie was over, the black kids that was there, thinking they knew karate, would see us and decide to try their kicks on us. So we either waited till they left and sat there or left early to avoid them. I said Robert had much fear. I started to boil inside. Be careful of the person that has tears coming down his face and has anger in his heart.

Another summer was coming to an end, and that meant another year of school. The fifth grade was looming, and the uniform thing and supplies and book reports were due. The books I had to read were not read yet. I had a week to make a book report; it was going to be due. I had great fear of the unknown and a lot of anxiety. No one ever asked how I was doing and if my work was complete. Mom's issues were still there, and she seemed never to leave drinking and smoking and crying and talking to herself. It left me feeling insecure and nervous.

I just reminded her over and over again what she was doing: "Mom! You're talking to yourself again" or "Your ashes are falling on the rug." I tried to avoid bringing any friends up to the apartment because of that and the apartment being a mess. That also hurt. I just played ball or with my toys and tried to block that out. Everything was always last minute, and the fights between Mom and Dad went on bigger and louder. I really had never seen an older couple who was happy together or hugging or kissing. They all looked very unhappy together and spoke at each other by barking orders. Many times, we would go to my aunt's house. It was a small house, but they owned it, and it was in the Jersey City Heights, a block away from the hobby shop Robert and I loved. My father and mother and I would go. Sometimes my brother would go too, but as he got older, he seemed to do what he wished. There was a really big backyard and plenty of space, so my cousin would go and their parents and also my aunt Wanda and uncle Billy, my mother's brother.

Uncle Billy was a war hero. He never said much. He was captured by the Japanese in World War II and came back home weighing sixty-five pounds. My nana, his mom, had several letters from Eleanor Roosevelt, saying they were doing all they could to locate him. He never spoke of this, but everyone knew, except his wife and their son. Many years later, at my mom's funeral, I told them of this and what he went through. They were in shock! I thought they knew this, but they didn't.

At my aunt's house, we were the beer deliverers, and we were happy to do it. We had the can opener (church key), and it was something to do. It looked like we pleased them. More arguments would come out of this gathering, more people drunk. When we left, Dad said nothing. Mom said nothing. With their blind stares, it was like they were daydreaming all the time. They were so unhappy. With all of this, I felt like I was the sponge absorbing all the dislike they had for each other. When they got back to the apartment, my father went right for the back room. I guess to avoid fights, but my mother would not let him get away so easily. After a few more drinks, she sat on the end of the couch. She was getting more steam to start or finish the fight. Then it began. He would end up closing the door and holding it. She would then start crying and then go back to the couch to drink some more and cry herself to sleep. It becomes normal. It was the same thing over and over again. I had those feelings of insecurity and fear and of being lonely. It was good to me that both of them were there.

I can't remember ever asking, "Why do you fight so much and drink so much and smoke so much?"

It seemed one day just went into another. When I was a kid, I didn't spend much time in my mind. Who belonged together or who didn't never crossed my mind. But I could feel the stress. I always liked my uncle and my aunt, but I could see they didn't like each other either. Uncle seemed kind of quiet, and my aunt was louder and expressed her feelings easily and directly. But they were always good to me. So I liked visiting there. Back home, we would play football in the supermarket parking lot. We played two-hand touch mostly among ourselves, but once in a while, we would get a game against some of the kids from other Catholic schools. Many of them lived on a street only a couple of blocks from Wayne Street. They were all Polish, and we called them the morons.

They were more organized than us and had good plays. We could tell they played together a lot. But we had a Puerto Rican kid named Doodlebug that's what we called him because he had great moves and was super quick, as we would say (weave Jim). That's when you put a great fake on someone and go around them. I never knew where the saying came from, but it was cool just saying it. We all practiced the move. It was a quick move of your hips one way and then moving them quick fake to the right or left to get around them. All the games were close, and we lost some and won some. But we, for the most part, got along.

Many years later, I dated one of the girls. She was very bright and fun to be with. I asked her what she thought of me when we were small.

She replied, "Well, I thought you were quiet and nervous."

Interesting, I thought.

She asked me the same about her, and I said, "Remember when the firehouse used to put out the hose with holes in it and all of us used to go there? I would see you run to the hose that lay on the street." She had on white shorts and had a great backside. When they were wet, all of us would stare. She just laughed.

Now I knew summer was over, and now it was time for the fifth grade!

If you didn't think for yourself, you didn't get much help. It was not as if you would go to your parents for advice or answers. They were always busy working or drinking or doing other things or not around. How could I go to my mom for answers when she had so many problems? My father was never around. Then when he came home, it was fights and sleep. There was no hugging, no respect. Television shows like *Father Knows Best* and *Leave It to Beaver* looked like they were from another planet. Those families, those homes were nothing like mine. It was easier watching *Lost in Space* or the *Outer Limits* or even the *Twilight Zone*. I never saw in those shows black kids robbing us or Puerto Ricans fighting with us or nuns beating us or parents beating us. Did the Beaver ever get wacked around for coming home five minutes late? My home was not as organized as those showed in the television shows. In my mind, it was all fake, or those people were very wealthy. It was so confusing, but it was normal for us. You learned for yourself, or you were left behind or abused. It was all normal for us to make fun of others, to hit one another, all in a normal day. What we called bums living out of the garbage cans was never explained. It was just normal. That's why they were called bums. What was right or wrong was taught with punishments and never really explained. Maybe you knew what you did wrong or maybe not? Why didn't Bud or Beaver ever get hit?

The upcoming year of my life would impact my life forever. The fifth grade was coming, and I was more insecure than ever and was not ready to deal with this year. But I was never going to forget it. We found out we had a male teacher this time. This was the only time we had a male teacher, so it was different for us. By this time, my brother was in the eighth grade, his final year. He was still a nightmare for me, but it was all the same for him. We were never told what was expected from us for the future, college, trade school; no one sat down with us and explained any of that to us. Mom was trying to do it all, working, doing so many things for school, buying small things, such as radios, to be raffled off so that the school could make money. She had such a good heart. I guess it was her best way of making up for the things she felt inside that were missing in her life. Even though we had very little money, she found a way to give. Her kindness was a way to give to us comfort. She was not the hugging type or the type to say "I love you." I know she felt it, but it just didn't come out. Only her kindness showed. She had so many demon's things. We found out about those things in our adult life.

My brother's life would surely turn when he graduated from eighth grade into high school. He was do different then. He covered up so many things with his tough-guy, violent ways, but he never did it at school. I'd never seen him get into trouble. That was amazing. He did that only outside of school. He had his ways and his violent actions at home and with me, and still he was so popular with the girls and was the most popular boy in school. Many people would call me Little Ricky, which I found annoying, but it also felt like I was someone, which was very weird to me. We would still never see much of the older grades because they were still on the other side of the school—sixth through eighth, that is.

We had about thirty students in our fifth-grade class. Many new students that came in year by year were mostly Spanish kids and were very smart, very good in math. And there were also very pretty girls. On our first day, our new teacher went over the rules, many of which were written down. It was the first time for that!

I remember thinking, *Hey, maybe this could be a guy that could give me advice and guide me.* It really popped into my head.

In the morning, I had a cup of tea with a lot of milk in it and a very large multivitamin for breakfast. I would get chest pains from heartburn. I could never eat breakfast 'cause of a weak stomach, so I suffered through all that. Mom always made me take at least the tea and vitamin. All the sugar I put into the tea didn't help. We really didn't have cereal in the apartment. The roaches or mice got to it before we could, so if we got a box, it never lasted much more than a day before we finished it. The sugar-frosted flakes had so much sugar in it, and we ate it like a box of candy. This year, the subjects were much harder. The math was tough, as were many of the other subjects. I knew I could get by maybe second honors, but home life was getting worse than normal.

The Real School Bully

As we got older, we noticed more and got worried more and were embarrassed more. Nana was drunker more and more. Mom was working more and more. Nana had to cook more often. It was terrible, burnt food all the time. My brother and I would use a bottle of ketchup for every meal, but Mom had an idea—frozen TV dinners. You just had to pop them into the oven, and they would be cooked half an hour. That, and chicken pot pies. We lived off them for a while, from meatloaf to spaghetti. No one was there to help me with homework. If I dared ask my brother, he would tear up my books, and then what! I was embarrassed to ask anyone else. I did it all by myself, and to be honest, my handwriting was bad, real bad. I had to take my time, and the stuff wasn't as neat as many other kids, though I really tried. We would hand in our work to this teacher, and he would go over it. I would have all red all over my pages, and the teacher would rip my work, saying it was really bad. There would be circles all over the papers, and then he would flip my notebook at me and a few other students and say, "Are you kidding me?" It was the fifties. He wrote on my homework, and I thought it was correct, but I guess not.

Mom got home late, and I had to have her sign my book. I told her I didn't know. She yelled a few times, but it was still no help. Back in class, there were things I could not understand, so I put my hand up. The teacher would not give me attention. He'd seen my hand up but would not call on me. I was the only one to have my hand up, so I put my other arm up to hold my hand up. Still no attention. Nothing. Finally, I spoke out to the teacher that I didn't understand some things.

Well, I finally got my answer: "Mr. Horning, you are to write one hundred times, 'I must not talk in class.' It is to be signed by your parents."

I said, "But, sir, I only wanted to ask a question."

He said, "Two hundred times."

I almost had tears coming down. How was I going to get this done? He piled us up with so much homework, and it took me forever to get that done. When I got home, I cooked the TV dinner and started thinking how I was going to do it? Each page had twenty-five lines. I would go straight down, writing *I, I, I, I*. Then *I must*, then *not*, then *talk*, then *in*, and *class*. It was an issue, and my lines were slanted, like they were going downhill from left to right, front and back of the pages. But now I was learning. This so-called man, this teacher, was not a good person. He was the same as the nuns but even worse.

The next day, it was signed, and my homework was completed and handed in. As I approached his desk, he stared at me, and it was right into my face. So I began to smile. It was not because I was happy. It was because I was nervous, but again, it started.

"Why are you laughing?" he said.

I responded, "I am not laughing!"

He yelled and said, "Go back to your seat!"

He still had my books, and then he started class. I had no books so after about ten minutes, I raised my hand and waited and waited.

He finally asked me, "What do you want?"

"You have my books," I said.

Many started to laugh out loud in class. And guess what. I was told get out go to the principal's office. I was upset. Why? Why? Why was he doing this to me? When I went, the principal met me downstairs. Then she asked him what happened. He said that I was acting out in class. I said, "No, that's not true." I told her what happened, but all I got out of this was a finger pointed into my face and my cheeks squeezed together with her right hand. And then I was told it would be worse next time.

Thank God a field trip was coming up. Most of my classmates asked me, "Are you going? Are you going to be in school?"

I didn't think anyone else noticed that I was absent more than usual. We were headed to Valley Forge, Pennsylvania, the place where George Washington was. Most of us could not care less. It was a free day from school and mostly my teacher.

Mom would make fifty or more chicken legs—the whole leg! She was a great cook, and they were always great along with noodle salad. While on the bus, she would hand out all the food, and the kids loved it. Mom was always kind-hearted like that. We always knew we would get a test on this trip and hated that we had to think for this. When we finally got there, everyone ran for the bathrooms. A few of my classmates, my teacher, and I hung out together and had discussions about our favorite Marvel characters: Iron man, Hulk, Spiderman, and so on. My teacher brought his wife and hung out with Sister Joan and a few others. Sister Joan was a super nice person and was also the school guidance counselor. Many years later, Sister Joan left the convent and become a psychologist and did special things for my family when my brother died.

The tour started. There was nothing special, only a few old cannons, a lot of open fields, and a few cabins but nothing cool. As the tour went on, the man who was the tour guide told us a lot of people died and blood was spilled on this field. We didn't see blood and graves, which would have been cool, but there was nothing we could see. It was so very boring to us. My teacher was watching all of us always as if we were doing something wrong, but he seemed to be on his best behavior. Maybe it was because his wife was there, as well as Sister Joan. Most of the time, we were free, but if we laughed or joked, the dirty looks came. So again we had to watch out as we knew he played the "I will get back at you" game. God, I hated that man. He reminded me of my brother with even more authority, the real bully type. Where was the man that would just talk with you as a person or woman that would not hit you or belittle you? A caring person that would sincerely help you with your life? There weren't any! Did they ever want you to really know the subject or just want to get through the pages? Did they know I didn't comprehend what I was reading? The speed was so fast.

As we returned to school from the school trip, we all went home. What a long ride. It had to be three hours. Mom walked in with that blind stare like she was daydreaming all the time, always thinking what she said wrong inside, always correcting herself. Then she was talking to herself. It was so weird to hear a conversation like that. Who was she talking to? She was so lonely and wondering about the future. I think inside she knew things were going badly—me with school and the things my brother would do. Maybe if she ignored it, things would change.

I would miss more and more classes. As the morning came, it took a lot to even get to school. When all things went right, there would be more tea and the big multivitamin and more of getting dressed. Most of the time, my shirts were not cleaned or pressed, and there were stains on my tie. I always wondered where I could hide. The weather was getting colder, and it was near Christmas, and more vacation was coming. But it was a stranger day even more than normal with my teacher as we stood and said the pledge of allegiance and a prayer.

He said, "I need a boy to guess a number that I am going to put on the blackboard and hide behind the chalk eraser." No one knew what was going on, so he said with the bland voice he had, "I am putting number one through five. The first one to pick the correct number wins."

Win what? we thought.

He scribbled a number as he stood in front of the board so none could see. Then he covered it over with the eraser. The first guy he picked was a good guy, my buddy.

He said, "Number five!"

The next was Raymond. He shouted, "NUMBER ONE!"

Whoa, not yet! The teacher looked around and then looked at me, and well, guess what, he said, "Mr. Horning."

I looked at him in amazement. *Me? This can't be good.* I said, "Number three!"

I had never seen him look so depressed. He said with a low solemn voice, "You're right. I will tell you after class what you are to do. You have to see Sister."

I thought, *Yuck! What is this, a special smack, a new way of punishment, or what?*

What my teacher said to me was he didn't expect me to win; it was only guess a number. Even then, he put me down and tried to make me feel bad. What did that mean? Why would he say that? Now even when I did something right and good, he still had to humiliate me. Now what was next?

When I went to see the sister, she started to explain to me what I was to do—the great deed, the good person, the charitable thing.

I stood there thinking, *What is this? Where is she sending me, and why?*

Then finally came the explanation. Looking straight into my eyes, she told me I was to be Santa Claus. Yes, Santa, with the red suit, beard, glasses. The whole deal!

But I am just a kid! What is she talking about? I'm supposed to see Santa, not be him!

I didn't really pick the right number. I didn't get lucky. I was going to be giving gifts, not getting them. And I was way too skinny. I was thinking all of that and more but never said it. I couldn't survive the beating I would get. Now it was time to listen to her plan. Now came the military speech, which was over the top: I had to do it this way and do it that way. I am telling you! The plan came together. I was to be at the convent at 1:30 p.m. dressed with the costume on. How was I going to do that? Where would I get dressed? I started to move my lips.

"Sister," I said, "I have to walk eight blocks with the Santa costume on?"

"You can't get a ride?" she responded.

I said, "No, Mom works. She doesn't drive. Only my father, and he's working too."

Well, my dad didn't work on Saturdays, the day it was planned, but I could not ask him for that. Who knew when I would see him? He always came home later than normal.

She said, "Okay, you can get dressed here, so be a half hour early. Be here at 1:00 p.m."

Sister informed me that her nieces and nephews were coming and that she wanted me to take photos and give gifts to them. I was planning this in my mind. Now I was wishing I hadn't picked the right number.

The week came and went very fast, and it was a few weeks before Christmas and two weeks before our Christmas school vacation. A lot was going on at home, school plays, the stupid stuff. We were also singing Christmas songs on stage in the auditorium. We were going over the songs over and over with Sister. My teacher, the person I hated, I knew he could not sing a note. But the Santa date came very soon, and there I was, walking to the convent, very scared and worried that I would make a mistake. Mom knew, and so did my brother, who just laughed and said, "What a joke." I was lucky he didn't hit me. I was always leery of that. The convent was on Grand Street next to the rectory and church. It was a longer walk than normal because of the stress. Doing anything for the nuns was dangerous because if there was a mistake, they never forgot about it.

Then I knew she would get back with the info to my teacher, and then in his mind, he could use that to punish me. And believe me, he would. I was at the door of the convent, and it was just before 1:00 p.m. Sister was waiting. Her nieces and nephews were already there.

She whispered to me and told me, "Here, get dressed here." It was in front of the convent, like a waiting room or a sun room. So I got dressed. There was had no mirror, so putting on the beard and hat was extremely difficult. Sister came out to see how I was doing. She was putting on her happy face. I guess she didn't want to show her relatives who she really was—a slapping, beating child abuser. Now I got a peek inside. The woman who worked in the convent was cooking and opened the oven. The aroma was incredible! All those pork chops cooking in the broiler must have been twenty!

I was thinking, *I can't wait to eat them!*

Anyway, I was now inside, all dressed, saying, "Ho! Ho! Ho!" And then I sat in a big chair set up in the living area. There were four kids, none above five years old. There were the gifts all wrapped up. Over and over again, I gave them to the kids. The flashbulbs went off over and over again. And I was sweating more and more. Then the songs came. It was already an hour, and the aroma of the food was making me more and more hungry. I haven't eaten all day, nothing at all.

Sister then yelled out, "Santa has to leave now!"

Thank God, I said to myself. So I went back to where I came in.

Sister whispered, "Leave the costume here. I will put it quickly in a bag so they won't see it."

I was thinking, *What dumb kids. They don't know?*

Then I was back in my street clothes, sweating; it was so hot in there. Now I was thinking that I could not wait to eat all those pork chops, all the great food. I was sitting there, waiting for the sister to invite me. Then she came and opened the door, and she had a plate with her.

She looked at me and said, "This is for you."

I looked at the plate with amazement. *What is this?* I was saying to myself. *What am I going to do with this? Yuck!* I kept repeating to myself. She handed it to me and walked back inside. It was one Twinkie! One Twinkie! One Twinkie! I hated them! I never ate them! And this was my reward, my gift, from the sisters. They had all that food, and they never invited me in! They didn't even offer me a glass of water or milk. Nothing! Sometimes when you are a kid, you don't think of how adults really are. You think that, much of the time, they are right in the things they do. This is the problem. They always fool us into thinking that what they're doing is okay. They fool you.

Many years later, in my adult life, I would be Santa Claus at Christmastime for Sacred Heart Church in Allentown, Pennsylvania, for the poorer Spanish kids and families. I would buy the kids many gifts each, make a lot of food for them, and we would sing many songs in Spanish and English. I would do this for over sixteen years there and for a couple of years in Medellin, Colombia. It was about doing things the right way, not the way or examples that were given to us by the nuns. Never forget where you come from.

Things go in and out of your head when you are ten. No one was on the street. Many people were home. It was Saturday, and it was cold. I was so hungry and was just wondering what I was going to eat when I got home. Who was there? My brother or my nana. Was he going to start a fight or hit me, or was I going to find Nana on the floor, again intoxicated?

I thought at that time, *What will I get for Christmas?*

Mom was always generous, her way of showing how much she loved us. She always seemed to leave the prices on the gifts she gave, as if she wanted us to know how much she spent. Maybe that was a way of making up the love. She felt she wanted to give but couldn't. Hugging and kissing were not big in my family. Drinking and fighting were big. It was as if no one bothered to talk. They would immediately punish us or yell at us. It was not that Mom didn't try, but it was her past and the mistake of marrying a man who didn't love her. All I did was react to things—to my brother, my mother, my father, and all those teachers in school. They all had their ways. It was way too much to think about.

I always wondered, *What did I do wrong? What's next?*

Playing sports helped me find friends, and talking about sports and playing sports helped. Being home was the last thing I wanted next to being at school. When I found an adult who spoke about sports, that was big! Wow, he knew the past players and the games. Even when Mr. Smith was sitting, talking with us, he was about seventy or more, he would talk with us. But when a very pretty Polish girl walked by (she lived down the block and would wear short skirts and had great legs), Mr. Smith would say, "Look at her. Wouldn't you like to bang that?" We would just giggle, but we did notice how pretty she was.

Now it was wintertime, and I had as many days off as I did in school. The word *hate* was not enough to describe how I felt about my teacher and the school in general. If it was a different experience, if at least someone cared, maybe I would feel different, but it was always "What is next?" I wasn't back to school for a week and received my summer book report back; it had so many red circle corrections. I felt sick. There was no reason why things were wrong; they were just wrong. When he handed it back, I just shook my head. He changed my seat to near the front, the middle second desk from the front. I liked my old seat 'cause it was close to the wall. I could lean into the wall with my shoulder. I always felt sick after lunch. Mom would make many different sandwiches for my lunch, and let me tell you, they were made in a manner not made for human consumption. Spiced ham with a lot of mustard—it was always slimy, and some of the white bread was old, sometimes stale. And then there was the roast beef from the Sunday before that was so hard and had a lot of gristle and a lot of mustard. It would slide right out of the bread. I was so hungry I would pick it apart and eat it anyway. But the worse was the tuna fish sandwich.

Remember, there was no tuna in water, only tuna in oil, and Mom didn't really drain the oil from the can. She mixed the tuna with oil and mayonnaise and put all this between two slices of white bread, place it in a paper bag. In my book bag, the oil and all seeped through the bread and then the paper bag. Then the book bag would smell. I always looked at how neat and well made all the other kids' sandwiches were, and then mine was wrapped sometimes in old aluminum foil. I had to eat most of it. I was hungry. In class, I felt like I had a heart attack and a stomach virus. It was a combo along with my teacher, and that was like getting hit with two atom bombs. I looked at my book report, and I shook my head.

Bang! Bang!

He was watching me all the way, and now it came. What did you do?

"What did you do?" he said to me. I looked surprised right at him. He raised his voice. "Shut up! Sit down!" he yelled.

I am like "For what?" And I was sitting! What did I do?
Then the punishment came down. "Mr. Horning!"
"Yes," I said.
"You write 'I must behave in class' two hundred times."
I said back to him in a normal voice, "What did I do?"
He raised his voice. "Three hundred times."
I looked down and almost started to cry. He saw that and said,
"Five hundred times, and I want your parents to sign it!"

I was very upset. How could I ever do that? It was impossible!
Just more hatred entered my mind. I never pictured him dead. I
never wished him dead. There was only a lot of hate. At home, it was
the same thing again. Page after page, Mom helped me with it. It
was not easy. It made her handwriting look like mine. Handwriting
wasn't my best thing. Again, it took hours to complete five pages,
front and back. The next day, I handed it to him signed and all, and
I looked at him without a smile or with fear but a blind stare of hate.
He looked at me smugly, but inside I knew he would really hurt me.
He always had the advantage.

There were about two weeks left for school, and I had a bad
feeling. I missed almost half the year of classes, and my schoolwork
wasn't the best. It was not normal for me. I would get by just when
I needed to, but I had no incentive to do anything. I just wanted to
escape. The whole thing was a joke. I hated my teacher. He was a
mean-spirited man, with no understanding of any of us, especially
me. He would humiliate me any chance he had. He was married
and had a newborn baby. I guess that was another example of how
marriage was. I wanted to tell him many times that he was garbage. I
had it going around and around in my mind all the time. At the end
of class that day, he handed out a few very thick white envelopes to
about five of my classmates and me.

One of my classmates who was a good guy asked me, "What is
it?"

I said, "I think chance books for my mother." But inside, I
thought it was bad.

At home, I opened it up before my mom got home from work. It was summer school papers, and if I didn't attend, I would be left back. Terrible! It was almost six weeks of more school in the summer. Well, Mom finally came home and read it. She didn't say much but went out and bought me clothes for the summer school classes. I felt so stupid and felt rage and humiliation all at the same time. All those years before that, I was on the honor roll, either first or second honors. Now this happened. Didn't anyone see this? What happened? Didn't they understand? Didn't they see what this small man was doing? I guess not. They were all on the same team. We were on the wrong one. we were the bad ones. But in the end, it was my fault for missing so many days. I knew it was wrong that my mom let me do that, but she was at fault, too, for drinking and failing to set the alarm clock. But most of all, why didn't she see how bad this guy was? Now she felt guilty and bought me more clothes and some toys. Summer school was very easy. We had a teacher we had never seen before. There were only seven of us in the class and two from another school, which was fine. One kid was starting in my school, and he needed to catch up.

The best thing was lunch. I would go to a German deli across the school and get a ham sandwich and a small potato salad. They made the best! I couldn't stop eating it. I sat by myself on the fire escape behind the rectory, enjoying it. I had white jeans my mother bought me. I loved them. They were so different from my normal pants. The weeks flew by so fast, and the teacher let us go home early all the time. It was only the humiliation I felt from being seen going to summer school. They thought I was dumb. But they really didn't know why. I never said much about it. The real reason was that it would make my mom look bad. And the kids forgot anyway. We played ball when I went out.

Pablo was a classmate, a Puerto Rican kid. He and I would hang out sometimes. He lived around the corner on Mercer Street. He would jump over parking meters and fire hydrants. Very cool! But not easy. It took a lot of time for me to learn. These kids were ahead of me in strength and height for now. As the years passed, I moved way ahead of them. Many of the deliveries to Santos's food store came in wooden boxes. As the year passed, some came in metal milk boxes. Our brains started working. We figured if we turned the box upside down, it could be a grill. There was a really big garbage dump at the end of Jersey Avenue and Grand Street. We thought it was a good place to have a barbecue, so I took some chopped meat from my house. He would bring the box. We only had rye bread in the house, so I brought that. In the middle of the garbage dump, using some of the fire that was burning all the garbage, we started to barbecue. We turned the red-painted milk crate upside down. The bottom was also painted red, but I was smart! I brought a piece of aluminum foil. So then we made the burgers. Sitting around with all the tons and tons of garbage around us, the smell was really terrible, but we cooked and ate. Looking around, there was garbage for as far as we could see. There were mountains and mountains of more garbage and more trucks coming in all the time to dump. Soon we finally left, but it wouldn't be the last time I would be there. The next time, it would not be so much fun. Every time we passed Pablo, we would end up hanging out more and more with a bully, a real bad guy. It was like he was always recruiting for his gang. His gang were Puerto Ricans and many not good ones.

Several years later, after I just graduated from high school, I visited my grammar school. I was, of course, much bigger and much stronger and athletic. I don't know why I wanted to visit at that time. Maybe I wanted to show them who I was now. There were no security people at all, so I just walked in. I saw all the little kids in their uniforms similar to ours and classes that weren't crowded. Ours had been so crowded. I roamed around. I didn't know the teachers or nuns, so I went across the auditorium to the other side, where the sixth to eighth grades were, same as my time. I peeked into the classes, and there he was, teaching one of the sixth-grade classes, still there. I could not believe my eyes. I opened the door to his class, which was unlocked. He saw me, and his eyes opened so wide underneath his silver-rimmed glasses. I thought he knew it was me. I looked at him, and he looked so scared, so worried. As I approached him, the entire class was staring at me.

Who is this? they thought.

He backed up on the other side of the desk. What a coward. What if I was there to hurt the kids or do something worse? He stood on the other side of the desk. I stared right into his face.

"Do you know who I am?" I said.

"I do."

"Who am I?"

No answer.

I repeated, "Who am I?"

"You are Mr. Horning," he said.

"Good, and I know who you are, and I remember."

I saw the fright in his face, and I knew he was scared. The students said nothing. None of them moved an inch.

Then I said, "Good to see you." I turned and walked out of his class.

What a punk he was. What a loser. I smiled as I walked out into the hallway to another class and another so-called teacher I wanted to see.

The next teacher wasn't there, but he was now teaching in another school. Interesting. I went to see the sister next, to see if he was there. She informed me he was gone, though she didn't tell me what school he had moved to. It was interesting that she would not give me that info. Maybe she knew something, or maybe she was covering for him. I had this sister in the eighth grade. We spoke for a few minutes, nothing interesting, just catching up. Then my teacher opened his class door. It was just down the hall. He looked around and then went back inside and closed his door.

Most of the nuns didn't even look like nuns. All were wearing street clothes or habits far back off their heads, if they even wore them. Many of them had left the convent by then, and more were leaving. Several in high school left, some accused of sleeping with some students. So be it. I left the school, where I remembered things I hated and had endured cruel and indecent punishments. But now

I was headed to the sixth grade and a female teacher, a beautiful woman, everyone's dream.

With the sixth grade coming for me, my brother was starting high school, Saint Michaels. He didn't know much about high school, but he was going to find out. He started to play the clarinet and really got into music. He had a new friend coming over, Ricardo, a fat guy whom my brother said used to eat fish heads and rice. I never knew if that was true or if it was a joke. Ricky then hung out in a hippie store on Henderson Street, a place that sold bongs and other drug paraphernalia used for pot and other stuff. It had posters used with black lights to make them glow in certain ways. There were posters of Jimmy Hendricks that glowed in the dark. There was a guy who gave karate lessons, which my brother took advantage of. I thought this place was the beginning of the end for my brother, and he used this for his escape. I knew of the black guy who owned the place and couldn't figure out if he was a good guy or a bad one. He was friendly and spoke to all of us.

I was too busy trying to figure myself out, and I wanted to play sports and was learning about girls and grown women. My teacher was one of them, and all the boys were interested. She was our new teacher, and she wore above-knee dresses and skirts, and all were form-fitting. She had perfect legs, red lipstick, big brown eyes, a beautiful smile, and thick lips. Even when they tried to speak with her, the boys started to stutter. Just by her mannerisms, you wouldn't want to upset her. She was so sweet. We were so curious about her.

That year, new Spanish girls started in our class. They were sisters, and both were super pretty. One was a year older than the other, and older was a bit prettier. The moment I saw the younger sister, I liked her. I was back on the ball and made midterm honors, but math was getting really hard. Mom was going to more card parties and fundraisers at school. She came home smelling more and more like liquor and cigarettes. She then would sit on the couch and burn more holes in the arm and the end of the table. Then the crying started again like clockwork, then talking to herself. When I said something, she told me to shut the hell up. Now I wondered where my brother was. I would see him come home with his new school jacket and tie, but I really didn't see him much.

I often thought, *Why be home and see what he'd been seeing for years longer than me?*

Maybe he went to the hippie store. Then along came Charley Black! The end of the school year was coming. I was super relieved I made the honor list and proved to myself that my old teacher was the asshole I thought he was.

Charley Black was something. He would wear an army jacket, ripped jeans, and boots. I didn't think he was a draft dodger or a hippie. He was a couple of years older than my brother, or so we thought. The cool thing about him was his superhot girlfriend. She had shoulder-length curly hair and a pretty face like an angel, and her smile could stop the war. She had a very nice body. She wore tight-fitting bell bottoms. She was friendly. She said hello all the time and smiled so sweetly. The other thing was that she hung all over Charley all the time and wore his jacket a lot.

Many of us wished we were Charley. She had a girlfriend named Can Opener. What kind of name was that? She was tall but not pretty but had a big chest, and she had a very gorky way about her. She had a severe overbite and smoked a lot, and they all smelled like pot. We would see them hanging out in the Gregory Apartments parking lot, where Charley's car was parked. It wasn't really a special car, but it was okay. He seemed to be always there. We never saw him work. His area was one of ours, but we used that area to play ball, sometimes football and other baseball.

One day, we saw Charley sitting in his car, and it seemed to be in the same spot all the time. But this time, he was sitting in the passenger side with his head back and the window open. His arm was holding the outside of the door. His facial expression was really strange, and he seemed to be moaning. We were parked two cars away, but on his side and between another. Then he took his outside arm and brought it inside the car. We snuck around the back of the parked cars to get closer. We stood up to try to get a better view. We got within a car, and he still hadn't noticed us. Suddenly, a head popped up, and it was Can Opener. She took a quick look toward our direction but then spit out a whole mouthful of Charley right out the window. We were shocked it wasn't his girlfriend, that it was Can Opener. We all burst out laughing and started to move away. She was so pissed off and cursed us out. Charley just laughed. What a cool guy. As we went back to that area, we never saw Charley again or his friends. Later, I asked my brother if he knew of him. He told me yes and asked why. Interesting.

Though we found Charley interesting, we really only wanted to see him to take a look at his girlfriend. We sort of knew he wasn't a good guy, but being bored most of the time, we looked for interesting people and things to do. The supermarket parking lot was where most of our sports activities took place. Today we were distracted. There were still a few stores left on Henderson Street, and at the back of the stores, there was fencing. As we went by the fence, we noticed in one of the fence posts that there was a rolled-up magazine in it. Well, you know, we assumed it was a nudie magazine. We tried to pull it out, but it only tore, so now we were really thinking of how we could get it out of the post. Robert figured a saw, and he was the only one that would have one in his basement. We went there on a mission. He had wood saws and hammers and so many tools, but how could we cut this and get to the magazine? We did find a hacksaw and a coping saw, but the blades were terrible. We had to try cutting this metal, but it was not easy. We took turns, and the saws were hardly making a dent in it.

Finally, we went to this store on Grove Street. It had everything in it, but the only thing my mom ever bought there was a window shade and clothes lines. They had it! Hacksaw blades! We had enough money to buy two. We weren't sure which end was the correct one to put in, so we tried both ways, even used a file that Robert had. It took hours, and we all took turns. Our arms were so tired. Finally, we were at the point where we could hit the post with a hammer to try to bend it back and forth. We hit it. We pulled on it with all our might! Finally, it bent. We were inches away from pulling it off. Then the cops came. Someone had called the cops. We knew who it was. It was that old lady, Mrs. G, a terrible old woman who complained all the time about us making noise. She was a bitter old bag who sat in her window on Wayne Street right across the parking lot.

So the cops were asking us, "What are we doing?"

The Wicked Witch

We stood there, and finally, Robert said, "We have one of our magazines stuck in this pipe, and we are trying to get it out." By this time, the post was cut, so we had a twelve-inch piece of pipe lying there.

They said, "Keep out of trouble." Then they left.

You see, Mrs. G's son was on the police force. They always came when she called. But now we didn't care. We only wanted to get the magazine out. So we pushed it from the cut part. Not good. We took it down to Robert's basement, put it in a vise, and used the hacksaws to try to cut it so we could sort of peel the metal back. We were able to cut one inch down the top of the pipe, cutting the magazine in the meantime, but now we were desperate. Finally, we pushed the bottom with a hammer handle, and it worked. We were now able to pull it out. It was badly damaged, but we were right! It was a nudie magazine. Now we saw what we wanted to see, and the women were perfect. All the girls were so beautiful. We still didn't know how real sex happened. We knew kissing and holding hands, but what else? We knew what happened in our pants when we saw a girl we really liked, but no more. After all of us looked at the magazine several times, we hid it in the basement. I never saw that one again in my life.

From time to time, many of our friends and guys we played with went away. They moved or just moved on from us. We didn't really know. We just looked forward to meeting other people or playing on our own. Robert was in the eighth grade now, and he started to have more friends his own age from school, so that left me to find others to hang out with. I always found people. I didn't care what they looked like or where they lived, like Gary and Donnie, who were Yankee fans and only a year older than I. Many times, we used to sneak to afternoon Yankee games and sit in left field for seventy-five cents. No one was at the games, and many times, the Yankees lost. Good. I loved the Cardinals and hated the New York teams.

There were times when we would see brothers of guys we knew doing drugs and sitting on steps, passed out, looking so helpless. My friend Carl had a brother who was one of them. Carl was such a good guy, and his mother was a sweetheart. But what can a person do? How can you stop a person from getting caught up in that world? Look at what happened to Anthony. As I said, when I saw him again later in life and played ball with him a few months later, he died. He was thrown out of the Catholic school after the sixth grade. I knew he and I fought so many times in the previous years, but to be thrown out and sent to public school, my god! What a punishment. That school was bad and had so many kids that were in gangs. Did the nuns just give up on him? Was he that bad? What was the real problem? No one knew. Only he was gone and died way too young. Where was the help that he needed? There was also plenty of bums around. One was Charley, whom we used to talk to. There was also a very old man that would sift through the garbage cans, eat out of them, and take things from them. We used to ask him and ask why he was doing that. He wouldn't say much, and if you pushed him for an answer, you would get "Don't bother me."

Gloria, the janitor, was a nice lady but not very educated. She was abused by her late husband, as many of us witnessed. Now another man she lived with abused her more. She just put up with it. I guess he helped her with bills. She even took in an old guy named Leo, a very cool guy who had a bed and TV outside her basement apartment. He also had nothing and had nowhere to go. He was a super good guy and watched sports all the time, especially college football. I used to sit and watch it with him on his cot, but it was very difficult to sit there for long. He smelled like urine and old clothes. It always seemed as if you didn't have a person to take you in; you lived as a bum or like Leo. Nothing was explained—why they had to live like that, why people did drugs, why people got thrown out of school, why people died. No answers. Nothing. We were like robots: "Do as you were told!" "Do this, do that." "Don't ask questions." If you acted out of line, pow! You were hit. Maybe if you were lucky, you would only be yelled at. We reacted to those things by doing mischievous things.

Once in a while, we found an adult who spoke to us almost like a father figure, which many of us never had. We only had fathers that worked and came home only to eat and sleep. They hated their life situations. We had to figure everything out. Mom tried over and over again. She took us to places, volunteered in school, but she had her ghosts as well, and they only made me feel more and more insecure. So the example we had was a father who didn't talk to us. He never kissed my mother. The two of them were always fighting. My brother had big issues, and no one seems to see this. My grandmother was intoxicated more often than not, and neighbors were always fighting and drunk. The nuns and priests in school would sooner hit us or punish us than listen to us.

Now you know why I just disappeared into sports and had to argue about things even if I was wrong. It's because I felt so insecure. Many said I should be a lawyer. What was the escape? Where could we turn to? Got it—girls! We were getting old, and the girls looked prettier, so it was time to notice them.

The seventh grade... Well, let me get started. By this time, my brother was really going crazy. He seemed to have his own gang and was giving Mom such a difficult time. Mom usually reacted by yelling or throwing anything near her at us, but now my brother was uncontrollable. He just walked out. He had ordered some really strange things from the comic books, and I was the target of what was coming. Meanwhile, Mom had a very big box with her sewing stuff in it, and that included, of course, many wooden spools of thread. To this day, I still had the mark of one of them, a spot that never went away at the bottom of my thumb. In what was called my father's room, there was the dresser with Mom's hair brushes, nail polish stuff (including a nail polish remover), and the box with the spools in it. Maybe there were twenty or thirty of them with needles still in them, pushed through the tread.

I was in the room, looking for a few toys or baseball cards I might have lost. Then my brother entered, and I stood in the corner of the room very close to the room radiator toward a window. He started to fire not with a gun but with the spools. I was screaming as he fired one after another, throwing them with all his might at me. I had my face and my head covered the best I could. They were bouncing off me, my arms my head and my hands. Some still had needles in them, and they hit me in my back and legs. I was screaming, crying. I could not move as my brother laughed. He finally stopped only because there was nothing left, but as he was throwing them at me, he apparently bumped into the dresser and tipped over the nail polish remover, which had a loose cap. Mom did not tighten caps on anything, and it spilled all over the dresser, practically bubbling up the finish, ruining the top of the dresser. At this moment, I was beaten up from the spools hitting me. I had marks but were not as bad as what was coming.

He left finally, again laughing. That night, he said he'd had enough of Saint Michaels and was going to leave. He hated it, and his grades showed it. All the people liked him, the church brothers thought him as the greatest altar boy, and all the girls loved him. He was the great patrol boy. Where were those people now? What I knew all along was coming to a head. My father, who was never around much and didn't want to deal with anything anyway, only had fifth-grade education and was one of twenty-one siblings. He never spoke to us about anything, never mind knowing what my brother was all about or even me. But the violence that was going on before was picking up now for all to see. What was I to do? Many in the area feared my brother as the rumors got around. He put up with nothing and would soon hit you before you had a chance to talk. It was so strange.

Me, I took this almost as a badge of honor, like he was the great protector for me. It was so twisted, but living in the area, I was in it. The more popular he was, the safer I was. At different points in time, his friends called me Little Ricky. I didn't like it, but I felt very cool. It was as if I was someone, a person of importance. But for my brother, his life was turning, and it didn't stop turning and not for the best.

Now the girls that were in the seventh grade were for the most part well developed, and Latinas had beautiful eyes, long black hair, and olive skin. They were so distracting. There was also a special one. Everyone in my class thought that we were perfect together. She had long dark hair and pretty eyes and was pretty. Also, she was well developed, might I say, since fourth-grade people thought that. She was nice and always there, and also there were many people who thought I should be with her. She liked a few guys from sixteen schools, not a good thing, but those guys were always hanging around our schoolyard to try to get our girls.

The other Carol was also pretty and friendly. She had blond hair and blue eyes but was never a match for me. And there was also the very pretty sisters Reina and Isabel. With all that said, the younger one was the one I really liked, but for now, we had to worry about our biggest problem. Our biggest problem was our seventh-grade teacher, a rather overweight man with a large head, big ears, big lips. He sort of looked like the actor Charles Laughton. He was closing in on middle age too. He also thought he could really sing, and it was funny. He could not hit the high notes, so he sort of pinched his throat. Every time he tried, we all made fun of him. He would teach with super vigor, too fast for me and for many. Several times, we would raise our hands to ask him if he could repeat what he said, and he would. He would do it once, maybe twice, and then the violence would follow—and fast.

The Brute

If he had the pointer in his hand, it would be swung, the pointer first. It was about three to four feet long, made of a hard wood, and had a rubber tip. Being swung by a grown man with the intention of afflicting pain, it was no joke. He was right-handed, so as he walked down the aisle, which was narrow, even his backswing would hit another. He moved rather quickly for an old man, and he would have a kind of weird look on his face as he hit us over and over again on our left arms and shoulders. He would even catch us on the side of our faces. The smash hits on our shoulders, nearly blinding the person behind him with the back swing. We just ducked, and when he stopped, we would see many red faces, some with their heads half toward the top of the desk and some just staring with an angry face.

There was a tall Puerto Rican kid who just looked like he wanted to do big-time harm to the teacher, and the teacher noticed this, so he told him to leave the class and wait in the hall. Within ten minutes, our lessons stopped, and he left the class and went to the hall to talk with the student. When he was in the hall, we went on our way, talking, guessing about what was going to happen to him. But it was not only him. We all were hit. However, he got the brunt of it. Then Victor returned. We could see he had tears coming down his face, tears from frustration. He sat down in his desk but not so easily. He sort of jumped into his desk and immediately put his head down on the top of his desk.

The teacher yelled, "Mister! Pick your head up!" But the student's head still remained down. The teacher yelled again, "Mister, pick up your head up!"

We all felt terrible for him. He was humiliated, and he didn't want us to see his tears. But the teacher insisted, so he had to raise his head. Thank God! His face was red with a look of anger. The lesson went on after that. But as always, more over-the-top things were to come.

This was the time we were figuring things out about girls—what we liked and what we didn't. The first thing was watching them go up the stairs in school. We always waited at the bottom of the landings and waited till they went up the stairs. You ask why? Let me tell you. We could see their underwear, and it was special! They had great legs, and we saw the panties too. It actually became a game. We would call out the color of their panties. Then what started for many of the girls was to hold their uniform skirts close to them when they moved up the stairs, but not all did! Some of the girls would let it flow and laughed along with us. Maybe those girls were ahead of their time and enjoyed the attention. But there was a problem. A few of us liked certain girls, and knowing that other boys were doing that, we ended up telling those we considered our girlfriends what was going on, so they made sure to hold their uniform skirts close to them.

It always seemed that the more restrictions we received from the nuns, the more we wanted to push to the limit. Anyone who chewed gum would have to clean the stairs and scrape up any gum that was under the desks and under the handrails on the staircases. Remember, all of this was done after school, so no one wanted to do that. The school had a lunch program, and they had a cafeteria with food. It was the same place that had bingo twice a week, which Mom attended. The best thing about the cafeteria was that there were no more sandwiches from Mom. The worst thing was the menu. Grilled cheese was okay, but they put tomatoes on it. Not good. Hotdogs were okay, and so were the hamburgers, but this was the kicker. They had big bowls of mustard and ketchup, and this became a big problem. They also put out salt shakers and sugar, so you could imagine what happened. Kids would dump them into the large ketchup bowl and mix it in, so if you put those things on your hotdog or hamburger, it was like eating a mouthful of salt or sugar. Not good! We avoided that.

At that time, there was no such thing as healthy food, no labels with ingredients, so you never knew how old the food was or what was in it. We ate by taste or the look of the food and even the smell. Only a few things had expiration dates. It was back to class. The bell would ring, and that was it. The stupid beatings continued each day, it seemed; my teacher would find a reason to do something. Several times, he would use his fat fingers to hit us in the head, use his index finger to jab us in the back of the head or the side of the head, sometimes the chest. I mean, it was not an easy jab. It was like he was throwing a punch. Then there was the day of Yellow. On this day, he hated how the entire class was answering the questions, so he decided to put the colors on the board one at a time, very largely written in red. Then he made us repeat it and spell it all out loud and together: "Rrrr eee ddd." It was like we were second graders. Then he went to blue: "Bbb lll uuu eee." Then he went with yellow: "Yyyy eeee llll llll ooo wwww."

Then something happened. I broke out laughing. I couldn't hold back anymore. He stopped and looked at me. The stare didn't stop me from covering my face, and I continued laughing. Everyone was looking at me, and they were sort of laughing too. But now the fat man turned, and with his face fully super red, he grabbed the pointer, the three- to four-foot rounded wooden stick with a rubber tip. With his jacket flying open, he moved like lighting with the pointer in hand and raced toward me. I sat about four seats back to the left of the center aisle. Then he arrived, and I knew what was coming, so I covered up over. He hit me over and over again with full swings! It seemed that, with all his might, he could have taken off my ear or nose, but I was covering up with my jacket to help stop the pain. My left arm was taking the brunt of the hits. Then I fell to the floor, and he continued hitting me! He hit me again and again, trying to cause more pain. By now, I was in the fetal position. Then he started on my legs. After a quick look at his face, I could see how this so-called man was enjoying this. He had such a satisfied look on his face.

Then something happened. The rubber tip flew off, and the point cracked and broke. But he had another move. He was really angry. He ran back up and grabbed the yardstick, a heavy thirty-six-inch-long ruler with metal edges. It was a little more than a quarter-inch thick.

He yelled, "Get up! Get up! Get up!"

I was trying to make it to my feet, and the whole class was looking. I would never forget the girl I loved looking at me with such pity; she was almost crying for me. As I stood up, he told me, "Put your arms out straight." Then he swung and swung at my forearms and my hands. Finally, he got what he wanted; he saw tears. He swung and hit my wrists and the back of my hands, which really hurt. I knew then that there would be a time in my life that I would get back at this guy. I knew there would be a day.

My nana once or many more times always had clean underwear on in case she got hit by a car and had to go to the hospital. It was a common phrase all around. Many a day and night, we would play two-hand touch football on Railroad Avenue. I was always the youngest, of course. The games would go on till dark, and we would only have the streetlights to be able to see. After that, we would hang out on Grove Street in front of a store or another. There was a policeman, a tall tough-looking cop.

Then the cops used their nightsticks often to poke us or to keep us moving. The words they used were "No loitering!" This would go on all the time, and he knew many of us by name. One day, he approached me and asked me if I liked basketball. I was shocked! He spoke to me in a normal voice. I was in the seventh grade and loved the attention from a real policeman. I told him yes! I loved the game, but I was only a so-so player. He then told me he helped coach a team called Team Post from the CYO, and they traveled to many places. He then went on to tell me that they traveled by bus and that all the players traveled that way. He would also bring his son, who was very young, maybe eight years old. The first place he told me we would go was Connecticut.

So cool! I thought.

So now I would have to tell my mother what was going on. She knew of the policeman, so she was good with it. Now he informed me what I had to bring: shorts, shirt, white socks, and sneakers, of course. And a duffel bag. Well, we had a cat at home, and it would spray on anything that was on the floor. The duffel bag—I had the old canvas one—was loaded with cat piss, so that was out of the question. The only thing I had was a brown paper shopping bag. It was embarrassing, but I had to put that behind me; it was very normal in my life. So the first game was on a Saturday. The policeman, with his son, picked me up on the corner of Wayne Street and Grove. We then drove to the bus. It was in the Greenville area of Jersey City. As we entered the bus, I saw that there were fourteen guys, all black, and one white kid around my age. All these guys were big and very strong, especially to a skinny kid like me. They seemed very friendly to me, and that was cool.

The drive took a couple of hours. I didn't really say a word for the whole ride. We arrived at the gym. It was nice. There were chain nets, I remember, and also a big court, so we went to change in the locker room and came out to warm up. I felt so out of place. My sneakers were two dollars, and I would slide on the court and really couldn't stop quickly, another thing in my life. The game started, and these guys were good, quick leapers, and fast. I knew I could not fit in with that. They were too big. It was a blowout, and our team was winning. With two minutes left in the game, he put me and the other white kid in the game. I ran to the right hand corner. I was not covered but was frozen out. The other white kid got one shot off and missed, but I was open every time but never received a pass.

After the game, they showered. I didn't. I never worked up a sweat. I put my stuff in the paper shopping bag and met the policeman outside with his son. He bought me a slice of pizza and a soda. I was starving again. During the bus ride, I just sat there and thought if I was going to do this again. I didn't really want to, so I hoped he would not ask me, but he did. I just sort of said, "Well…" He got the hint, but at least he knew my name was Gerard. He was a very good guy. Everyone thought was a bad guy and a bully, but he was a nice man. Now I felt good when I saw him.

There was news coming. My brother was leaving Saint Michaels and was now going to a public school. This was an older public school. Mom had more pressure on her. She couldn't get him to stay in Saint Michaels. He fought her in every way. Now it was a public high school, not good. From what I heard, they were building a new public school on Montgomery Street, so who knew what the future would bring? But I knew at least I had a feeling what was coming. Now at this time, my brother was very happy. The reason was that he just got a BB gun in the mail and even thought it was cool. I knew that at some point I was going to be the target. It was not the only one he bought. Another also came. This one had an air cartridge and could load several pellets in it. The other one had to be pumped up and could fire one shot at a time, but both were handguns.

When the both of us were the only ones at home, he would fire the pump-action one at me. It was crazy. Again, like the sewing spools, I covered my face and head, and it hit me on the side and back, and this was far worse than the spools. The pain was terrible. I made it to the front door and got out of the house, tears coming down my face. This was not the only time this happened. Several more times and many times, I would run out with no shoes or sneakers and only in my socks, which always had holes in them. I used to pull them forward and stuff the front of the sock around the top of my toes and then shove my foot into the sneakers so it would stay that way. I would tell Mom about me being a target. I guess she would yell at him, but now she had more pressing problems with Ricky, and she was getting very worried. I never knew if she had conversations with him about what he was doing or what problems he was having. I knew my father didn't. He would never say more than two words to us. But I do remember her telling my father to do something, and he just walked away into the room and closed the door, never knowing what was going on and never wanting to know.

This never happened on television shows, but I always thought that was fantasy stuff on TV, even the trouble The Beaver from *Leave It to Beaver* TV show would get into.

We would laugh only because we were so street smart and would never do those dumb things. Mom was so kind and had a good heart, but she seemed to never be able to have meaningful talks with us about what life should be and why we were in the situation we were in. The things we heard in the fights between her and my father were how we figured things out. If they fought about money, we knew money was important. If they fought over anything, that was how we communicated. We experienced the places she took us to, so many very nice places, but we also experienced Mom and Dad sitting next to each other at Olympic Park in Irvington, New Jersey, and not saying a word to each other. We could only see them drink, so what did that teach us?

My brother was three years older than I. He picked up more and understood more and was affected more than me over the years. But it felt better when we were together. It was so weird, the feelings. You never really hear of people leaving each other back then. They only did that in the movies. I guess as my brother got older, but still a young teenager, that it finally affected him. Whom could he have talked to? He was far more popular than me and had more friends, and the teachers always liked him. The brothers liked him. Some of the nuns also liked him. But where were they now?

We were not all thumb suckers with security blankets. We took a lot of pain and grief, and there was plenty of it. My brother had a good friend named Tony. He was a very good-looking kid. He would even bring him into our apartment, not so easy when it was a mess most of the time, but my brother did. Mom even knew Tony, and he would even say hi to me, which was unusual, because many acted like I wasn't there when they came over. I used to hear stories about my brother and his friends going down to the harbor side terminal. This was a warehouse with some stores in it and was right on the Hudson River. The roof was overhanging the water. This was a metal corrugated roof around the buildings. In the water were several broken pilings, some hidden into the water. This was because many years before the ferry launch area was there, a fire had burned everything, and the ferry service ended. But not the danger that was in the water. The water was so nasty with sludge and suds from the factory that to see beyond a foot into the water would be a miracle.

It was a normal day. I remember coming home and seeing my brother crying. I had never seen him cry. Never. Then Mom came home, and I found out that my brother and his friends had been jumping off the roof and into the river. Then the worst happened. Tony hit a piling head first. He was killed instantly. They had to race to a phone to call the police. It was terrible, so sad. I could see how it affected not only my brother but also so many people in our area. Tony was popular and a good guy. What followed was something strange. A couple of weeks went by, and there were stories about several kids dying the same way. Nothing was done about it.

His Death Is Only
the Beginning

Then I came home one day, and as I entered our apartment, not only was my brother sitting there, but there were also two men in suits. They acted surprised to see me. One was standing, and the other was sitting in my father's chair. My brother was sitting on the couch, so I didn't say a word, but they asked me who I was and told me why they were there. They were asking my brother some questions.

I was thinking, *This is wild. What is going on?*

Then they explained. Now think. We were both underage, and neither of our parents were home. They asked me if I knew Tony. I answered yes.

"Do you know that he died?"

I said, "Yes!"

"And do you know how he died?"

I paused and said, "I think he drowned."

The detective said, "Yes, something like that."

I said to my brother, "Where's Mom?"

He said, "She's working and cannot leave or she will lose her job."

The detectives had spoken to her already, and she said that it was okay to talk to Ricky about Tony. I missed many of the questions they asked Ricky.

I felt weird, like, *Cool, look at these guys here, talking to us!*

But soon they went away and left their business card. That was it. Ricky would not say what they asked just to bust me. Mom told me they thought there was foul play involved, like someone had killed him or pushed him or something. In the end, time passed, and Tony was for the most part forgotten. We never find out what really happened, only what people said, that he jumped and hit the piling.

Through it all, there was much tragedy around us, but we found some interesting things to do. My teacher would ask many of us to stay after school to clean the blackboard and clap the erasers that were full of chalk and wipe off the desks. Many times he would ask for volunteers, such as me, and some classmates as well—sometimes some of us and sometimes all of us. But we always had a plan. We would go get the buckets with super speed and open the windows. Then we'd clap the erasers, sometimes against one another, like if you were clapping your hands together, or we would hit them on the outside of the window sill, which would leave chalk marks. But we would pour water over the sills to sort of clear that up. The blackboards were wiped and washed with water.

We sped through this. Why, you ask? It's because we had plans, and it was to play Seven Minutes in Heaven. The game was the reason we stayed. We had to have a lookout. That was Raymond. We used Raymond because he liked to hang out with the girls but really didn't like them. He stood outside the classroom door. Raymond was good in getting info from the girls to see whom they liked. The stage was set. As always, one couple would go in the clothing room. It was where we hung our book bags and our jackets and had all the weapons the teachers used to beat us with and also had some class supplies. The clothing room was about seven feet deep and maybe four feet wide—perfect for us. As the couple entered, we would close the door and count down to seven minutes. How the name came about, I don't know. But it's perfect.

When in that room with each other, you would start to kiss and maybe get tongue if you were lucky. The key was you didn't go in there with just anyone but with a person that liked you. Then you hoped to get a feel—maybe touching the girl's butt or maybe, if you were really lucky, her chest. You were always nervous, taking a lot of deep breaths. Seven minutes could be a long time. Kissing was the main thing, and when the two came out of the clothing room, they would have smiles! Then it was my turn with the girl I liked. She was a taller girl with long dark hair, dark eyes, and a big chest. She had a very pretty face. As I said, people always thought we would be together forever, so it was easy to go into the clothing room with her. We kissed, and when I went for a feel of her back side, she sort of pushed my hand away gently. But she let me feel her chest, which was large and hard. I guess she had a hard-material bra?

This would go on for many weeks, and it was always enjoyable. At one time, my teacher came back and almost caught us, but we always got out of it. We were cleaning the clothing room! Two Spanish kids instead of us started to stay after school to clean. He picked those two? We started to figure out why, and our thoughts weren't good. Maybe he was playing favorites but had his private reasons as to why he wanted those two. None of it made sense. Why would he have taken so much interest in them? Our teacher would often ask us who was the best-looking men in Hollywood, and when we said John Wayne, he would contradict us and say, "No, Rock Hudson is." Our opinion didn't count, but it would go on. He would work that into our class conversations. None of that mattered to us. The next day, the conversation changed.

Some of the time, we were no angels or saints. We always had a plan to find out more about the girls in school, if it was not Raymond telling us about the girls. It was about what they wore, and I am not talking about their uniforms. As the girls walked up the stairs, we would let them go up, let's say, a flight and then look up their skirts. Wow! Some of them had better legs than we thought, but the best was their underwear, the panties. Seeing them was special, and when we did, we called out the colors. This was started by a few kids who were the ones who introduced me into that type of behavior.

Then one thing t happened. One boy had a sister in our class, and she was super pretty. That was when things changed. He informed his sister about it. I guess he didn't think she would inform the other girls, but she did! From the next day on, they would hold their uniform shirts close to their legs with both hands as they went up the stairs. As I said before, all girls did this except Mary. She was a pretty girl and, let's say, overly developed. She seemed to enjoy the attention and didn't bother to follow the other girls holding their skirts close. A new rule came in. The girls that used to wear saddle shoes now would wear penny loafers. They could not wear shiny patent leather shoes because they were shiny, and the reflection would allow a person to look up their skirt. This was what was on the nuns' minds.

A couple of kids and a few others would put pieces of broken mirrors on their shoes and stand close to the girls to see up their skirts. Even I thought this was unbelievable! But they did it, and many of the girls became aware of this. Then the slaps started coming. The girls really didn't go tell the nuns, but they found out and would start inspecting the shoes! This was something else for them to do, and they would try to control us in any way they could. What the nuns would do was get the class back and then question the class and try to get each person to turn on one another to tell who was doing those things. Many of us knew but would not tell. The nuns or lay teachers would say, "Are you your brother's keeper?" That fell on deaf ears. No one cared about the guilt trips they tried to lay on us because we knew they were liars also and would give the one who admitted it and then the class corporal punishment for what they did. To them, it would be a teaching moment. To us, it was just more crap. The only thing that would come out of this was that the guys in the class would say they did it though the nuns knew they didn't. It was quite noble of them. Then after they said that they did it, many of us said that we did it. Then the nuns would punish the whole class. We would sit after class with our hands folded, and the nuns would let a couple of us go a little at a time. All the girls would be released first 'cause, in reality, they didn't do anything wrong.

Then something really funny happened. A tall black kid who sat in the back, in the right hand corner, stood up and said, "Okay, I've had enough of this." Then he yelled, "Whoever did this, admit it!" No one would, but we all laughed. The sister yelled at him to sit down and to keep his mouth shut. We sat there longer and longer till she let us go. The only reason was that she had something to do. Then one day, a Spanish kid continued to use the broken mirror on the shoe and got caught. I remember his parents or his mother came to school to talk with the principal, but he was back in class, and all was forgotten till the next punishment.

I had such a crush on the younger sister. She was so friendly and had beautiful olive skin and pretty eyes and a great smile! Everyone always had me with another girl, like she was it for me. It's not about what you're told. It's what you want. I remember it was Sunday, and the sisters were at a house on Grove Street, very close to Jersey Avenue. A classmate that liked her was going over there also. We walked over, and to our surprise, there was a real idiot and his idiot older brother.

One liked to talk a lot, and we always thought he was a little different. His brother was a jerk. He would look for anything to make fun of us. That day, I had a light-brown suit on, but I didn't like the pants. They were straight, and bellbottoms were in fashion. I had a pair that were close in color but not quite the same, but I wore them anyway. To the older brother, that was an opening to make fun of me. As we stood on bottom of the steps and the sidewalk, I ignored him. He was such a jerk, and hitting him was a waste of time. I was more interested in the younger sister, and so was my classmate. I could not forget what she was wearing. She and her sister had on identical suits. They were sort of dark gold, but the suits had short pants (culottes). They looked beautiful!

My classmate walked up the steps and had a look on his face full of lust, like he was eating his favorite food. Seeing that look, I felt disgusted. Things were getting worse. Not even listening to one of the idiots run his mouth was this bad. He went into the hallway with her. She happened to be having her arms stretched up over her head as she fixed her hair, and she even had a bobby pin in her mouth. He went up and kissed her on the lips. I guess it was nothing different from them being in the clothing room at school when we used to play Seven Minutes in Heaven. Seeing it was so different, so painful. My heart was so broken. Her older sister didn't want anything to do with that or the situation. She went into the apartment. I was so hurt. I did not even hear anything the two idiots said. They were two dumbasses, anyway. I didn't know that the younger sister knew my feelings. We all were just dumb kids anyway.

A couple of days later, I received a letter. It was handed to me by Raymond. He was the go-between and hung out with the girls. When you were having a life like we had, for someone to think of writing you a letter was a big deal. I opened it and started to read it. It started like this: "Hi, Gerard. I am writing you to tell you that it was not the other guy I wanted to kiss me. It was you that I wanted to kiss me. Written and signed with love and kisses." My hands started to shake. I felt so different, so happy that someone would say those things to me. For it to be her, it was special.

I kept the letter under the carpet in the apartment for quite a while. Once in a while, I would read it, but one day, I looked, and it was gone. I guess Mom got it, or my brother did. I never asked about it. I just remembered it and never forgot it. She lived near a public high school and ended up going there. But nothing ever happened more than that letter. I went looking for her a couple of times when I was in high school, but I heard she married and moved away.

Raymond, who was, as I said, the go-between the girls and us used to give us sex advice. Who knew where he got it from? We had a good idea, but most of the time, when we spoke about him, it was to ourselves. He wasn't a bad guy at all. It was just that he was not the type of guy you would hang out with. He would rather hang out with the girls, but it was not because he wanted them. The advice this time was to masturbate in the shower or bathtub with a lot of soap. We would just look at him like a weirdo. Why would a guy tell that to other guys? Not good, that stuff, that was very private.

We spoke of girls and about how much we hated the nuns and teachers and homework and television but not that stuff. The one thing we learned was that when someone told you something like that, it would stick in your mind. Not good! Sports was a good topic for us. I loved it so much. A few of us saved for an official-sized hard-rubber football. We had those balloon types, but they were terrible, so fat in the middle and no threads. Real garbage. To us, they were cheap to buy but hard to throw. Now we went to two guys in a big department store, and we all chipped in and got one. It was a real official-sized hard-rubber street ball. It was so cool! We all could throw it, but when you caught it, it sort of hurt your hands. Our spot was the supermarket parking lot. We would play two-hand touch all the time. Two big lights in the middle of the lot went off. We knew then that we had to go home.

A couple of days later, it was Saturday, about 5:00 p.m. There were about eight of us playing in the parking lot with the new football that we had all saved for. It had cost us a lot. Then a bunch of black guys showed up. This was strange 'cause we had never seen so many together. There were about eight of them and were around our age. Two of them walked toward us. I had the football in my hands, and many things were going through my mind.

What did these black guys want? Already many of us had so many bad experiences with those guys. They were the reason why we had to put money in our shoes when we went to the movies and anywhere where these guys were. Now what did they want? The kid approached us and said to me and Robert, "Do you want to play us in two-hand touch?" We looked at each other and said okay. Now the game was on. We told them the ground rules, what was out of bounds, touchdowns, etc. Then we went over the rules. They agreed, but they seemed to walk away too easily, too normal. Something had to be up, right? We spoke and said yes, that we would trust them. I always had a big arm and would be the quarterback. I could not only throw the ball far but really high. At twelve years old, I could throw it almost fifty yards. Then we lined up. They were in a huddle. Okay, maybe they had a plan—could be a spot pass or whatever.

Soon we would find out their move. I was back behind our guys, ready to run down to touch the ball carrier. I ran up to the line of scrimmage and threw it, and I mean I threw it far and high. They ran back and caught it. Then it happened! What we thought they would not do! They took the ball and started to run the other way with it, out of the parking lot, and toward Railroad Avenue. We went halfway but could not catch them. They laughed at us. They stole our new ball that we had all saved for. Now we only hoped they would be hit by a bus or run over by a train. After that, we didn't speak for a while about it. I guess we were so upset that we showed so much trust in them and were again disappointed. And it wouldn't be the last time.

The Garbage Dump

Then there was a second trip to the garbage dump, down off Jersey Avenue and Grand Street. This time, we weren't camping. It was just something to do. Robert, John, and I headed there just to wander around and find cool stuff. This trip was not going to be pleasant. As we walked through the mountains of junk and garbage, which was super high and smoldering, we never cared about how bad this might be to our health. We never cared or thought about those things. We went about our journey. Then we encountered two black guys around our age, maybe a little older, and we all knew what was coming. If we had any dollar bills, they would be in our sneakers to hide them. Change pennies or nickel would be in our pockets, maybe a few cents. Then the black kids saw us, and they made a detour toward us—to harass us and rob us. We knew this was coming.

Robert and John, at that time, were a lot bigger than me, but they didn't have what I had. I had great fear of my brother but not much from anyone else. I knew this before they came.

"Hey!" they said. "What are you doing here."

I stayed quiet, and so did Robert and John, which to me was a mistake. They should have said, "Hey, what are you doing here?" But they didn't. So now they had the advantage. They walked toward John and Robert and immediately got into their faces and said to them, "What money you got?" They raised their voices loudly then started to go through their pockets while pushing them. No one had money. Now it was getting worse.

I stood there and thought to myself, *Why doesn't John do anything? He is so tall, and Robert is not far behind.*

But then it got worse. They had tears coming.

Ugh! Terrible! I thought.

I stood several feet away while one of the black kids picked up a nasty four-foot hose and started to hit them with it over and over as Robert and John cried. The mounds and mounds of garbage were surrounding us. Some were burning and some smoldering. I couldn't watch anymore. I was almost crying. Then I did something. I ran as fast and as I hard as I could as if I was giving a football block. I hit the kid hitting John and pushed him right into a superhot area that was burning. He went shoulder first into it and rolled on his back. Then I picked up a can of food, a small can, and threw it at the other black kid. All of us ran as fast as we could out of there through the small areas. There were like roads to us or maybe like highways to get out, and finally, we did escape onto Grand Street. We didn't stop there. We walked fast and then ran again until we were back on Wayne Street several blocks away from the dump.

Never again did we return to the dump, not even with Pablo to have a cookout. When all was calm, Robert and John never spoke of what I did. For a moment, I felt like a hero—only to myself, I guess. They were embarrassed to have a smaller guy like me save their asses. I never said anything about it. I just knew then what kind of guys they were. But they were still friends. The one thing it did do was that it made me feel bad. They were so scared and didn't fight back. I knew then and in the future how I would beat them in sports. I would be better than they were.

Sunday was here, and it was another depressing day. It was time to get up early and serve mass. Yes, I was an altar boy! I never really liked it. It meant more things to think about and more responsibility, and I always felt stressed over that. But I seemed to get it done. I lit the candles and put on my garments, making sure I had the right size and that they were clean. We had lockers and had a TV in the locker room, and many times, my friend Carlos would serve with me. Carlos was quiet. We were friends in class, though not so much outside of school. Maybe it was because he lived up just off of Newark Avenue. I remember backing Carlos for class president. Everyone seemed to be more prepared than I. Their clothes were neater. Their lockers were more organized. I put that on my list as things I didn't care about. Sometimes I wondered why.

But I knew why. I didn't want to realize it was too depressing. When I would get ready for mass on Sundays, Mom would still be sleeping, and my father would be leaving. I really didn't know where. He would come back with great cut fresh rye bread in that white waxed bag, and my brother and I would eat all of it before Monday arrived. Mom was passed out, I would guess, from working all week and from drinking the night before. Over and over again, it would ring around in my head—her talking to herself like she was auguring with everyone. She would say what she really felt. The people she was talking to were not named, but I heard everything. That always stayed in my head no matter what I did. Every place she went, she drank, and she wanted to argue with any adult. All it did was make us feel smaller and more insecure. The pain that Mom had was real, but she didn't realize how it affected us, her kids. My father more and more would leave early and come home late except on Sunday, when we had to be home for afternoon dinner. Before that was Notre Dame football highlights and *Sons of Hercules* movies.

When Nana was around and not living with us and living with my aunt in the Jersey Heights, she would go to mass to see me serve. It was Sunday morning, the day after Saturday, so there could be cool things to see. As I walked, this day was different. I was seeing all the different styles of cars back then. They looked so different, a very noticeable thing. They were missing radio antennas.

I thought, *What happened?*

It was over and over again, more and more cars, then my father's car had the antenna broken off; then many people figured out why it was happening. It was because of gang fights, and it was mostly the Puerto Ricans who did it. Now it cost people money, and that was a big problem. People bought a sort of spring type of antenna, which you could bend like a sling shot, which we did. The gangs and the fighting were happening more and more. When I arrived at the church, we went into the locker room. Most of the time, Carlos and I would serve together. One brother was a very good guy and always prepared us. But he was leaving for good, and his replacement was another brother who was not a good guy—another reason for not wanting to be there. He was a real disciplinarian and was also a guy who kept certain altar boys coming in at different hours. But we said nothing. Brother would hit you with no problem, so you wanted to get in and get out fast. I really hated Sundays 'cause of that and 'cause I knew school was the next day, and I had those feelings of fear and hoping the alarm would not go off.

When it did and we arrived at school, things were so different. The black kids who were our friends and whom we hung out with would not talk to the white kids at all. We knew what happened. MLK was killed, but we didn't really care. None of that mattered to us. We were kids. The same as Kennedy being killed—we really didn't care. Even if you spoke directly to the black kids, they looked the other way. So weird, we thought. The only thing you would think would be that their parents told them that it was our fault! It's possible that our classmates overheard bad things. These were our friends, and it really hurt. Again, no one explained a thing to us, only to do what they told us and to not really think for ourselves. In other words, this is the way these things are, and we should just deal with it.

Mom took us all over. We had vacations everywhere. The way she saved the money was a question I often thought about. She would buy insurance policies and use them to sell later and get the money from it. She also hid money under the carpet, which Robert and I found one day by seeing a bill sticking out. We pulled up the carpet and saw many dollars underneath. Mom made no money working in the stores on Newark Avenue. After that, she worked for Great Eastern, taking two buses and walking down Carbon Place to work there. Mom had a great heart, as I said, and she tried to do all she could for us. But we saw her through the eyes of kids. Now my brother was really starting to push her to the limits, where she would never recover.

Ricky was threatening to leave high school. Then he finally quit. He left Saint Michaels, transferred to a public school, and now after that, he wanted no more of school. I guess when you are involved in your own misery as Mom was, she didn't see things. And she also gave in a lot. She was always in between trying to work, keep the apartment, and take care of us. Nana was way too old now to know what was going on, and she seemed to be getting senile. There was a battle between Mom and my aunt about whom was she going to live with. Then my father didn't want to know anything. He just kept away and was not involved. He came home late at night. Between Mom drinking and fighting with my father when he came home, she was overwhelmed—drinking and talking to herself every night. It wearing on us, especially me. I felt so much stress inside. I remember crying and hoping she would stop. When I did say something, she again told me to shut the hell up. Mom would also go to attend bingo at school and card parties and Chinese auctions, especially when they had liquor. Several times, she came home only to throw up in a bucket she put by the bed.

I would always ask her "Are you all right, Mom?" and repeat it many times.

She would tell me yes then go to bed. "There is school tomorrow," she'd say and then forget to set the alarm.

Then I would miss school, which I liked anyway. I never knew where my brother was, maybe sleeping in the other room or somewhere? Was he sleeping over at a friend's house? Who knew? And I didn't care. I would avoid him as much as I could. We were very different. He hated everything I liked—sports, games, etc. It was difficult to know him. He had his friends, and I had mine, but the mystery was why two of my friends left us to go to hang out with him. Both were older than me and didn't like sports like I did. They seemed to be nice guys. One was a good guy, and he was funny. His mother didn't speak English and had chickens in their backyard. I remember his mother yelling at him all the time. He lived a couple of blocks away around Morgan Street, but like us, he was poor.

I remember another time when he was wearing penny loafers, and it was pouring rain out. It was him, Robert. and I, and the water was shooting down the curb toward the sewer. He removed his shoe, which like ours had a big hole in the bottom, and put it on the street side of the curb, and it was like a river was running downhill. It took all of our speed to get it before it went down into the sewer. It was so funny! But we didn't care. It was funny. I guess to us it was. Another kid was also around. He played army with us several times. We would always kill the Nazis and the Japs. And we also talked about war movies.

Then one day, both guys changed and went to hang out with my brother's gang, a sure trip to the dark side. They grew their hair long and wore peace signs and headbands and old ripped-up military shirts and seemed to join the hippie era. None of that was good to me. I never liked those things and was not attracted to that at all. But I could figure out why they left. I only thought they hated sports and wanted to get into the drug culture or something like that. All I knew was that I didn't want to do their thing.

It was two days after Christmas 1968, a week before my brother's sixteenth birthday, and he went off to New York City to buy a Fender amplifier for his Gibson SG guitar. Now he was in some sort of band. For that time, the amplifier was super expensive—195 dollars plus tax. In New York, the tax was 2 percent then. I would never have guessed he got the money from Mom as a Christmas and birthday gift combo. But how she saved it. I was not sure. Mom could really save. She, as I said, bought and sold insurance policies for money and ate American cheese sandwiches for lunch for herself every day. She was doing her best to do something for Ricky so he would have direction. There was something missing, though, a father figure, someone who would tell us what was bust, what was the future, and what was the journey.

Mom did her best but never had any advice, and my father, I don't remember him ever completing a sentence for us. As each day went by, he and Mom hated each other, and Mom criticized my father all the time. He would fall asleep in the chair and snore and rub his feet together. She needed money! I don't remember ever asking my father for money, but he would give me a dollar if I cut his ear hair. Then I lost that job when with a pair of scissors I was using cut his ear! My mistake. I was watching TV as I was doing it. Man, did he get upset.

I remember watching the Celtics when they were in the playoffs and when they played the Knicks and became a Celtic fan and then a Packer fan. I loved John Havlicek and Bart Starr to this day. The only thing my father and I had in common was sports, but even at that, it was hard to get into a conversation with him. I've never heard him or seen him talk with Ricky ever. Many times, it was gifts from Mom that showed us love, never words. When you're small, you don't see how hard things are, I guess. You don't see all the little things—the cooking, the working. You feel bad from what you see—the fighting, the drinking, the talking to themselves. You can't figure out some things, the pain is the only thing you see. At that age, we didn't know how to react. We only felt insecure and found places where to hide when there were fights, a place to bury ourselves in our toys, escaping into an imaginary time till the fights stop.

My brother was not around when there was fighting, but I am sure he'd seen his share. But what was his escape music? A band? Or maybe his escapes were not good enough again and again. Where was the help? Where was the person he could talk to? Who would ask him if everything is okay? As I said, not in school, not in church, not our neighbors. They would just gossip. No matter how poor you were and how clean or dirty your home was, it was important to let people see your family as good, having no problems. The neighbors only spoke to you when you bothered them, like if there's noise from playing ball or seeing a ball going in their area or if you hurt their kid while playing ball. Otherwise, they assumed and didn't care about you. But I thought they knew. Why? Because so many were in the same boat and had all the same issues. When you start to get older, you see things a little more clearly, as I did with my brother. His time was coming with his destructive behavior and the wrong people he hung out with.

Now you would think my brother attending a public high school was bad. The worst was yet to come. He was sixteen and now wanted to quit school. Remember, my father was not a talker and didn't have a positive thought that I could remember. He was not an example after all. Again, he only went up the fifth grade and had twenty-one brothers and sisters. I had only seen a few of them once or twice in my life. Though Father did get a bronze star in World War II for blowing up a Nazi bunker, he never said anything of worth, never advice, never information on how to live your life. Nothing! The only thing we knew was that I had never seen my parents sleep in the same bed. I had never seen any affection between them. Nothing. There was only fighting and distance between them. My mother was drowning in her own problems by drinking or smoking.

But they did set one thing as an example. They worked and worked hard. There was never a speech on education or that we had to go to college. Nothing. Maybe it's because they didn't go. It was not important to them who tried to speak to my brother to try to inform him on what was important and what wasn't. No one. Maybe my mother did. She was once in nursing school but had to leave it. I don't know why; it was not explained. We only needed to know certain things, and that was it. Mom many times helped with our homework, but she was so distracted working and, as she said, trying to make ends meet. For a long time, I never knew what that meant. I always thought it had something to do with food.

Why the ends of meat? I thought. I guess I didn't care or didn't want to think it through.

The time came, and my brother was looking for a job and wanted a car. Thinking of what his prospects were, I would say not good. I was now in seventh grade and headed to eighth, and my only thought was staying far away from my brother. He had long hair, and it was so funny that he would try to iron it with a regular iron all because his hair was a little curly. He finally found a job. It was in the harbor side terminal, right on the Hudson River. It was the last stop by the path train before New York. There were a few warehouses inside, and the one where my brother found a job was in a small factor for cigar box wrapping. There he would steam the plastic on the cigar boxes. In reality, it was a job that would go nowhere; it maybe paid a dollar an hour. I can remember him walking there to work and walking home always with a smirk on his face, almost like "I know I am not going anywhere, but I cannot let anyone see what I am feeling." Think about it. At his age, he had no advice. He felt pressure but had no direction. Then one day, I was asked, "What is your brother doing? Why did he quit?" Most of my friends were all older than me, and we played sports together. It was not that anyone cared, but they would ask, and I said, "I don't know."

Many of the guys I played sports with had some family structure, and their parents would not have let that happened. Most of the guys I played with, except for a few, survived and went on to college or trade school, but many didn't. Many fell to drug and alcohol abuse. What was the future for me or my brother? We didn't know. I always wanted to be an archaeologist and found out that if you couldn't spell it, you couldn't be it. I recall Anthony asking me if he could be one also. I was worried that it competition, so I told him I was not sure. We wanted jobs we thought were cool—astronaut, president, cowboy, James Bond. But they were so out of reach. Maybe garbage man was good enough. I think the nuns and lay teachers told us to become astronauts and other things to have us see what we could become and brighten our horizons. It was just something to say. They never really knew our home lives and our situation as my brother had. After all, he was so popular in grammar school and a great crossing guard and altar boy. Once you graduated, for the most part, you were history except for maybe one nun.

Summer was near, and my last year of grammar school was approaching. The depression was setting in. I thought good things, such as "It's my last year!" Then what? High school was coming. Where was I going? To Saint Peters Prep, Hudson Catholic, Marist? I was not really smart enough to get into those even if my test scores were high enough. Then the money to attend—that would be an issue. Maybe Ferris? I didn't know. I didn't think about it, and my parents didn't either. I knew of a sister, and she had no patience, just what I needed. When she got nervous, she stuttered. We had all seen her because my old teacher and her used to talk in the hallway. They had connecting doors between classes. We knew and heard from people what she was like. In other words, she was a typical nun. Smack or beat first and then ask questions later.

Again, we had to get permission notes from one of our parents in order for them to hit us. Of course, all parents who sent in the affirmative on that didn't want their child singled out so they went along with the group of parents. Only God knew if they said no! What would they have done? Maybe flunk the kid? The yes check mark was always marked. She had tiny envelopes for us to put a quarter in for the collection for the 9:00 a.m. Sunday mass. More things to worry about!

Beyond that, I wanted to enjoy the last few days off before school started. Mom was always last minute with buying things for school, so I had to buy them from the school to cover what I needed. My friends and I would still play baseball in the parking lot and get as many of us together as we could to make it seem like a full team. And we would make sure that the baseball we had was covered in friction tape in order to save it. Otherwise, it would get chewed up on the concrete or the blacktop we played on. Think about how fast a baseball came at you on a flat no-grass service, and one time, it did. Billy was hitting, and I was in the shortstop area. When he hit a rocket toward me, I was right in front of it, coming superfast. Then it hit a stone, and the misdirection caused it to short hop me and hit me right in the balls! I mean my balls! Between my legs! Oh my god, did I go down! Tears were coming down superfast. There was such a pain in my stomach. I couldn't move for an eternity. Finally, I came to my feet, but still I was in pain. I didn't go home right away.

When Mom got home, I explained everything, and then one of my balls started to swell up. The next day, we went to the doctors. The fix-all doctor with the black bag, his office was on Grand Street. We entered his office. Mom was with me. The next two moves were so embarrassing. I had to drop my pants and underwear and get up on the table in front of my mother. Ugh! Then if that wasn't embarrassing enough, he squeezed my balls, especially the one that hurt. So I let him know right away. The next thing was a prescription for a pink liquid medicine, which seemed to help. Who knew what it was? The next week, I was ready to play again with the guys.

Now another thing happened that would change opinions and the way we felt about one another's lives forever. A few of us got our gloves and bats and were looking for a classmate. This classmate had a cousin from Central America, Louis, who was only about nine years old. But he was another body, so what the heck! We went to the classmate's house, but no one was there. Then we looked around the block but couldn't find him. We asked around, but no one knew. Finally, we thought to look into the basement below the apartment his family lived in. There were shutters. It was ground level, so the four or five of us started to pull the shutters open, and we pulled them wide open. The windows behind the shutters were wide open. These were almost full-sized windows, not the small basement type. Then we saw it—the most shocking thing all of us had ever seen in our lives for sure!

Louis was face front into a mattress, leaning onto a column, and my classmate was having anal sex with Louis! Others and his brothers were waiting their turn to rape Louis. Louis had tears coming down his face but was not openly crying.

All these things kept spinning around in my head even though we made fun of them. I started to think about the fight I was involved in and getting hit in the back of the head with a baseball bat. The sex thing they did with their own cousin, a male a boy, was something I could not forget. He was eliminated from our circle. We looked at him as a homo, a faggot, a rapist. Even at our age, we knew that was not normal, and his cousin didn't even know a word of English. It was his first week in America! That was his welcome. It was not that we were angels, but this was over the top.

Robert was not around much anymore. He was deep into high school, and he started to have his own older friends, but once in a while, we would see each other to go bowling, which I hated, but his good uncle took us and always paid for it, which I never forgot. What a good man he was, and such a generous person. The one thing I noticed with Robert that was he was drinking beer! I would see him with a quart bottle of beer even walking by the apartment building. I would be hitting the high bouncer off the wall, and he would pass by and just say hello. I hated that. I was losing my best friend not only to age and new friends but also to liquor, the thing I hated the most. When I saw that, I saw Mom and all her drinking and all the troubles that it brought. I'd seen many things in black and white. What was right was right, and what was wrong was wrong. It was because of what I felt—insecure, of course.

Why did my brother quit school? Why should I keep going to school? Why, why, and why did different rules apply to me? Could have I said to anyone what happened to Louis? No, of course. Who would listen? I did tell someone about it, a guy I played ball with on the street. He was few years older, and he did not think much of it. He told me it was called old hat. What that meant I never knew. Many pieces of the puzzle were what we heard from classmates and friends and overhearing what my mom said. Then we would listen and think about what sounded good or stupid. Most of the time, it was stupid. And that would come from mostly girls, whom we became more and more curious about. They were a big distraction from our terrible lives. But as time went on, something big was coming—that was high school. But bigger news was coming—a big change. And it was a big change for my brother.

All those things were coming to an end—the weeks at the Poconos and the Highlands. Those days were in the mirror, very far behind. We were surviving the stupid Mets winning the World Series and the terrible Jets winning the Super Bowl. Both we thought were fixed, as did many. I never liked any New York teams. Now many kids jumped on the bandwagon of those teams, something else to argue about and debate with one another. They were things to think about, such as school. And my brother finally quit school and now was working in a cigar wrapping place in the harbor side terminal right on the Hudson River. It was a dumb job that a monkey would do, but what can you do when you quit high school? He always complained about his knee hurting and his eyesight. He started to wear glasses, and he had asthma. All of that never stopped him from being popular. He still had his idiot friends and always the girls. But now where was he going? I always had great fear of him. I liked the respect I got from being Little Ricky, which was what many called me. I knew it was a good and a bad thing. Maybe it was his fear of things that drove him out of high school, or maybe it was the frustration of having no one he could talk to, no direction.

God knows I knew because I felt so many of those things. I knew Mom loved me and us, but we were never the touchy-feely type of people. Only when we got hit or yelled—that was our attention. Maybe we acted out of order to get attention. Maybe that was it! It was not because we liked getting hit with so many different objects. That was not a joke. Now my brother was working forty hours a week. My friends and I never really spoke about all the abuse. We just knew it was understood—normal, if you will. Now I was in eight grade and was getting through the torture from my teacher—the hitting, the belittling from a very unfairly man. We could only wait to get through the eighth grade to leave this place. Sister was no joke, a really nervous nelly, and had very little patience, also a big hitter. She was thin. She thought she could sing. Most of them thought they were the singing nuns. To this day, I don't even want to look at them. To me, they were just a bunch of frustrated women, angry and bitter. They were like the gunfighters who said, "Shoot first! Ask questions later." They hit first and then asked questions later.

Here we were learning math, a new math, and God knows that if it wasn't the timetables. It was not good for me. Also diagramming sentences was a mess. I just didn't get it. My lines were sloppy. The inside of my desk was not in proper order. My book covers were made from supermarket paper bags, which I could never get to stay on. My pencil bag was full of all kinds of crap. Sometimes I looked at the schoolwork and figured how in the world I would ever figure it out. Maybe ask the sister? Not a chance. She was not a teacher who would know how to explain it to you in easy terms. It was her way, and that was already shown. Explaining it again in her way never worked, and she was so nervous in an angry way. She made us more nervous. I shook my head like I got it, but I never did. I had to have help, but I never really got any. No one would help you.

In the class, they had their ways, almost like they wanted you to fail. It was like a competition sometimes. When we had tests, the ones who knew had the answers would wrap their arms around their papers like they were holding a baby so no one could see their paper. I always found that strange. Who cared if someone looked? I never did. There were always cheating and mischief going on and crib notes. Many times, we would be kept after class, holding our hands tight in a prayer position with the point of our fingers pointing up, and we would sit perfectly still. She let us go one by one. Of course, her pets, such as some girls, get to go right away. But us? Not till very last thirty in the class, and one by one, she let us go.

She asked over and over again, "Who did it?"

We knew it was Hector, but we would all say, "It was I!"

We were almost like what Spartacus men said in the movie, but the tall black kid went too far.

He stood up and said, "How stupid this is? Why are we all punished 'cause of one person?"

Sister's reaction was incredible. She was talking without words coming out. The tall black kid sat in the back because he was very tall, but that didn't matter. This was the second instance with him. Sister raced to the back and began swinging her hand toward his face. She had to swing up 'cause of his height. But then he grabbed her arms. Wow! We all turned toward them to watch this.

As he grabbed her arms to stop her from hitting him he shouted loudly, "My mother doesn't hit me, and you sure aren't!"

I think we all had our mouths wide open. It was great!

But then she grabbed him by the arm and said, "Get into the hallway now. Get out!" she screamed. "You wait for me here."

OMG! As we finally left one by one, the poor guy, our hero for a day, was waiting in the hallway with tears coming down his face. We all snuck a peek to see the hero for a day!

There was a girl in my class, a very friendly person with great humor, whose mother used to own a store downtown. She worked in her mother's place, cleaning and organizing. This was done late at night and even before she went to school. She was a really special worker. Another special thing about her was that she played the guitar. The worst thing was that the nuns found out at about the same time they found out I could sing. What that meant was that the nuns were going to put both of us in a position to work together, have us do an act during mass. Here's how it went down.

After class, the sister would give us certain songs to learn to sing and play for the 9:00 a.m. Sunday mass. Besides that, I had to be a lector, meaning I had to read one or two of the readings and do the announcements. It was maybe a big responsibility, and believe me, I was super scared! All those people were looking at me and listening to all my words. Doing both was crazy. She and I practiced almost every day the several songs for Sunday, and the reading I had to do by myself. Sister was calmer with us after school, not the nervous nut she usually was, and as most nuns, she was like a cowboy in the movies: shoot first, ask questions later. This was not the only thing I had to do. The next project was her teaching me how to play the guitar. OMG! I was like a mental patient trying to do three and four things!

Why did she pick me? I often wondered.

It was the same thing as being picked by my teacher to be Santa Claus. The next step was singing at mass and reading the scripture and the announcements in church. I was to read a couple of things from the paper that was given to me before mass and then jump back with her to sing the opening hymn. This was a lot for me, an average student who had to work hard to be above average. This week, things started easy. The announcements went easy. We started the song. As I looked up, I saw the other nuns standing next to her; they all were there, staring at us like "Don't make a mistake!" The back of the church was packed! All the classes had to attend the 9:00 a.m. mass. They even gave us small special envelopes wherein we had to put a quarter, and believe me, you had to! They checked the envelopes on Monday, and your name had to be on it. God help you if you didn't put that in the Sunday collection.

"Here we go." And she started.

There was always a warm-up first, but then I noticed something. She was wearing her school uniform. No one wore that when they weren't in school. She had to wear her uniform 'cause she didn't have nice clothes to wear to church. It was sad. None of us were rich, and many of us were poor. But she had such a sense of humor, and like most of us, including me, she used it to cover up her insecurities, sources of embarrassment, etc. The best thing back then was that we made fun of one another, and that sort of eased the pain. Many of us began to take turns doing the reading.

John could really read well, but there were mistakes. I said, "The propaganda of the faith." Big mistake! I was misreading it. I should have said, "The propagation of the faith." On Monday, I was corrected and not in a mild manner. I was yelled at, with finger in the face, of course. But the one thing I did well was sing, and they loved it. I was a fixture with her and only read once in a while. Another thing that has happened recently in life and for many previous years is that I have sung solo in mass and sang in many different places even in South America. I also used Santa Claus to give gifts to the poor kids in church for over twenty years. I sang with my son, who played the violin, at mass for almost ten years. I still sing today. At the time, the bigger question was, Where was the credit due to—the teacher, the sister, or myself? Was that something I wanted to do? Was that something I felt in my heart? Maybe all of them.

There was always a question for it: Was I forced to do all those things? Of course! The nuns worked with fear, saying, "You do it or else." We did it so much that it influenced my life, and I am sure many others have similar experiences. They used to look at many of the girls and say, "Maybe this one could be a future nun, or maybe that one." There were two top candidates, I would guess, but I don't think they ever became nuns. Believe me, there were no priests in our class for sure.

It was just another day, or so I thought. I walked home and turned the corner, going to make a left toward home. Then I saw it! My jaw dropped, and then depression and anger all at the same time kicked in. It was my clothing room girl who I thought was always mine! I didn't know why? I just always thought that. She was walking toward me, but she was not alone. She was arm in arm with Rolando! OMG! I could not believe it! I so mad and angry and, of course, jealous. I did what most guys would have done. I confronted them and said, "She is my girl! What are you doing?" I was holding my book bag in my right hand, which was always heavy. I had a real bad tweed jacket on over my sports jacket. I had very little room to maneuver, but again, I didn't know what to expect. I was just overreacting. Then Rolando swung his right arm and hit me right in the face! Boy, did everyone go nuts. I pulled his arm away, but he hit me pretty good. We were pushing and pulling, but she, who had never said much, was yelling "OMG!" over and over again. But nothing happened further, and I had some tears coming down as I walked home.

That six-block walk became a journey. I was so depressed. I guess I realized things weren't the way I wanted them to be or I imagined them to be. Rejection was something I was used to. Even though it bothered me, I moved on. I didn't pay much attention to her after that. Those seven minutes in the clothing room were in the past. After graduation, I never really saw her again except that one day after I was out of high school. I saw her going in with two guys. I think on Route 44. She was with someone. I was walking in another direction and realized who she was, but I avoided her. I don't know why. Who knows? Maybe I still felt rejection or depression.

I returned home, where I could be distracted by something—my APBA baseball game or afternoon television. My brother wasn't around much. He was working, I guess, or hanging out with his stupid friends. But some things real bad were coming, and I could feel it. Big changes were also coming.

Donna was a pretty girl, taller than most of the girls in the class. I think she was smart. The Reyes sisters were very cool girls. They were very open about themselves and were fun to be around. She was living with her dad and her sisters across our church. This year, as with most girls, they were really noticed by us guys. She sat at her desk to my right, two seats behind me, on the window side. I remember looking back, and she would always have her legs tightly closed as if she was very cold or something. She sat like a respectful girl, not so much for many of the other girls in the class.

One day, we were in the middle of a subject, and in the afternoon, most of us just watched the big round clock in front of the classroom, high up on the wall, just counting the minutes to get the heck out. I had to remember what day it was because I had guitar and singing practice with AD. Ugh! Soon some action occurred. Donna started crying and got up and ran from the class. What happened? I turned quickly and saw blood coming down from her legs and dripping on the floor. Wow! What was that? Some of us knew and some of us didn't. As she ran for the door, the sister quickly followed. She then left the class alone. A big mistake! Everyone was like "What happened?" Some were laughing. Then one of the boys yelled out, "She got her period, you idiots!" Laughter was still going on but not so much. The sister returned and had two boys clean up the floor quickly. A mop was needed. Then we returned to normalcy. Or so I thought.

One kid was sitting to my left, one seat in front of me. He was a funny guy with great humor and would ask some really dumb questions that broke up the class. This time, he came up with the best. Sister explained that Donna had a nose bleed. Now nearly the whole class had seen the blood coming down her legs, but as always, the sister decided to not tell the class something she would have to explain!

As the sister was explaining, one of the Puerto Rican boys interrupted and said, "Hey, Sister, how was it a nose bleed? If blood was coming from between her legs, how did her nose get there?"

Everyone laughed, and the sister went nuts! First, she bit over her lips, as she did when she was ready to explode. Then she went off, grabbed the kid by the ear, and threw him out of the class. Boy, was he red! His revenge was coming soon. He would play "I will get you back." Many of the Puerto Ricans had big pride, and getting humiliated in front of others, especially girls, was not a macho thing. It hurt his pride.

The class ended, and the sister canceled our practice because of what happened. So we all just went home. The next day, more was to come, the same as the day before. We would get yelled at, called stupid, but the most used word was *baboon*. I guess we learned a lot about animals by being called an ape, a jackass, and a baboon, which they loved using. The class started, and the sister was doing some heavy writing on the blackboard.

The Puerto Rican boy got ready. He might have thought of this all night, or maybe it just came into his head. We had these like nine-inch tubes of paste in our desk. They were so useless, but they were required as the sister had her back to us. He took out the paste and started like he was masturbating with it, with the top off. I could not believe my eyes! Then he squeezed the tube hard with both hands, and all of the paste shot out all over the back of the sister! It was like he had just ejaculated, and it went all over her back. It was so crazy! I burst out laughing! I couldn't hold it in. Then she turned and took three fast steps to me. Squeezing her overbite top to bottom, she hit me in my neck and shoulder area with her forearm! It must have been twenty times. I heard something crack, not to me! It was her arm. She was in pain and then asked another teacher to take over the class. It was easy 'cause the doors were connected. I was in great fear. I was scared to death! The next day, she had nothing more than an Ace bandage on. Too bad. She deserved more! Remember the saying "What goes around comes around"? Well, this is why you should never wish for anything on anyone, not even a nut like this sister.

We were playing football in the parking lot on that Saturday, and there were many of us. There was the throw-off, and now this was in the all-black top parking lot, where we played most of the time. I returned the ball, and as I made a cut, so did Sammy. I tripped over his legs and went down hard, arm first! It was a bad fall. I went down hard and right on my left arm. I had no feeling in my arm. It felt terrible, so then I went home and called Mom at work. The next thing I knew, we were at Saint Francis Hospital. They took x-rays, and back then, things took even longer than today. They said it was not broken. They wrapped it with—guess what—an Ace bandage, and home I went. I had no sleep that night. It was a Sunday, so there was no mass that day. I went to school on Monday and was still in a lot of pain. Then something happened. The hospital called Mom and told her they had to wait for the x-rays to dry. My arm was fractured. The x-rays had to dry. That was what they said. Then we headed off to Saint Francis Hospital. They put a cast on my arm.

At school, you would think many would sign it, but maybe I was not as popular as most. Elle was one of the few that did. Elle was a Puerto Rican girl who always seemed to have her skirt higher than other girls. She was very aggressive. She might or might not have been active with the boys. On Fridays, they would take us to a big room that was next to the cafeteria to watch movies on a bad sixteen-millimeter projector with terrible sound. We were lined up to enter the room, and Elle was in front of me. On the other line were two boys right to my left. The next thing I felt was Elle smacking the crap out of me. I mean whack, whack! Then I put my arms up and held hers. Of course, the two boys were laughing. They put their hands up her skirt and grabbed her ass. Then they bumped me into her. Though they were to my left, we were all shoulder to shoulder, so it was perfect for them to do their act. But boy, was she pissed! Like a lot of Spanish girls in our class, she also had a good body. I noticed everything but never touched her like that. It was not that I didn't want to. We did play seven minutes in heaven with a few girls, but it was not like I was forcing things. Believe me, those girls knew more about sex than us.

Working? Yes! I started working, and I remember going down to public school number three to get my working papers. I think I was thirteen then. You know, when the doctor made you cough as he grabbed your balls and looked down your throat with the tongue depressor? It's always embarrassing. It was the same stuff we went through in school every year, but this was different! I was on a mission to get my working papers, and I got them! I felt good about that, very good. Even though I had a paper in Little League baseball, my name and batting average were still first in the glass case. I did it!

Now to get the job in school. The sister was looking for a few kids to help clean the school and wash the bingo buckets. After school was when I started. I was busy practicing for the songs at mass and now working. There were, as always, bad things. There was the janitor. He was a big man and, of course, older but would not show us anything and made everything harder for us. Watching him work was scary. He would mop the floors in the auditorium and then use the same water to wipe the tables down. Then it was my job to stack the chairs and tables with him. The mop was heavy to me, and the work was not easy. I did it.

Then came the worst job—the bingo buckets. These were red small buckets that were put on the tables for the people playing bingo to throw their garbage into, including empty cigarette packs, gum, napkins, and some foul stuff. There were plenty of buckets. First, it was cool. I would dump the contents into the garbage can, then run them through the big commercial dishwasher. It was not bad. I could do four buckets at a time. I stood there and waited for them to go through. Easy, right?

But then the next time I went to use the dishwasher, I could not believe it—there were two padlocks on the doors, so I couldn't use it! I couldn't believe it! Who would do this? Yeah, I knew. It was the bitter old janitor. Now I had to do them by hand in the sinks. It was terrible. They were so nasty, and also this would take me over an hour longer. That meant I would leave at about 6:00 p.m., and once I left, there was no way of getting back in. I had to make sure I put everything in the proper place, and the lights were off. This job went on for a while. Each Friday, I would get paid. I think I would work maybe fifteen hours a week. The sister would give me a tan envelope with cash in it—a whole eight dollars and forty cents. I could remember opening a Christmas club with it, but I never kept up with it and had just twenty-seven dollars in it around Christmastime.

Bigger news was coming, and it was news to me for sure. My brother, who had quit school and was working in the harbor side terminal, wrapping plastic on cigar boxes, was going to join the Navy. Mom was not happy. We used to watch Channel Five news, and they would show the names who were killed each day. They would roll down the names. My father, I never knew what he thought. I never knew what he thought about anything. He never spoke with us and wasn't around a lot. When he was around, he and Mom would just be fighting. I didn't know what I thought, only that he would be away—and away from me. I didn't even know why or when my brother chose the Navy. So around April 1970, he was already in, and he was writing many letters to Mom. This was the Vietnam era, a bad time. I think the logic behind this was that if he joined, he could pick what branch he would be in, and he went in on the buddy plan, which never worked. They always separated buddies. My brother was tough guy, but he had issues—a bad knee, bad eyesight, and the big one, asthma! But I guess that didn't matter to the Navy. He was just another body. To Ricky, it was another escape. He was leaving the area, and maybe it was for the best, or at least he thought so.

My brother was now in the Navy, and my mother was always writing letters to him, wanting to visit him. One of his first stops was Maryland, where he was taking classes. My aunt and Mom were making plans to visit him, but Ricky would write back: "Please don't visit. They won't let you see me. It would be a waste of time." Mom always wanted me to write to him, but I never knew what to say. My handwriting was terrible, and I had always had fear of him. What was I going to say? Anything? He hated sports. I never listened to his music, and many of my friends left me to go hang out with him. Mom made me write to him, though. I had to write a letter, and I did. In one of his letters to Mom, he said that my handwriting was terrible, and he would say "How is the brat?" or something worse— never good compliments. He was always asking for money and worried about his eight-track player he'd bought through the mail in was one of those "Buy 8 eight-track tapes, and get the player for free." It was only that you had to buy, like, fifty more to really get it for free. He wanted Mom to send the player and some tapes to him.

March 2019 was the first time I read his letters to Mom. All together there were maybe thirty. They were all saved by Mom all those years! From his first one in the early 1970s to the last one in March 1971, I will talk about my feelings and read them later, but it was not good. I will include a few of them in this book so you can get a bit of an understanding of where he was at that time and his mindset. Being three years older than me, he had seen a lot more of what went on at home and outside and the friends he was hanging with. I knew he loved Mom. One thing I didn't see in the letters was him saying anything about Dad. He was our father but was never there. You just don't see how bad relationships affect the kids. What we see, what we hear, and what we have to lie about to our friends so we won't be embarrassed—we bury ourselves in distractions.

Even when they take us to a nice place, a lake or an amusement park, or take us on a vacation, I could see they just didn't want to be there together. Even when Mom took us to so many places, it made me wonder what it was for. Was it her escape from her misery and feelings of loneliness? I could always feel what she felt—wanting to help people, to do so many things for the church and school. But even then, when she would, she had to drink. I could see how all of it affected my brother. As kids, we never spoke about it. All we would see was our nana and mom drunk, especially when they were alone. Okay, many people drink, but as I have said, it is the things that come out of their mouths that bring fear.

Now my brother was on a big adventure and one that had real rules and consequences. As June was approaching and we were taking our tests to see what high schools we were going to attend, I knew I was in trouble. First of all, I never did good on these tests, and we had to put down the top three high schools we wanted to attend. I knew I was not smart enough to make a high score on the test to enter the very good high schools, but I put them down anyway.

All along, my brother would write in a letter: "I guess Gerard is going to Ferris?"

Ferris was a public school a few blocks away and was a new school, but Mom saw my brother drop out of St. Michaels and Ferris and didn't want me to go there. After a while, my score came back. It was not good. My grades were good but not my scores. Now I didn't know where to go. Mom would never be able to afford the top two schools anyway, so where was I going to go? I and a few others were called to the guidance counselor's office, and guess what, the nicest nun was there—Sister Paula! She was a really even-tempered person who was super tall and a really good athlete, especially in basketball. She was the best I'd ever seen in jumping Double Dutch rope, where there were two ropes and two girls on each end, moving their arms inward in a circular motion over and over again. The sister would jump in the middle. She moved fast. She had a nice way about her, and it made me think that maybe one out of a hundred nuns were okay.

Now came the word! Did we know why we were called to her office? Nope! It was to me more stress. What did I do now?

She handed us envelopes, saying, "Well all the paperwork is in the envelope."

What! What paperwork? What did I do? All of this was running crazily in my head. Then it came right out of Sister Joan's mouth: "All of you are to attend St. Mary's High School, and in the envelope are the enrollment papers and so on. Give them to your parents and have them fill them out."

Wow, I thought. *Where is St. Mary's? I've never heard of it.*

Then the other kids knew some info.

"Third Street!" one said.

"What?" I said.

"I think Cole Street?" another said.

"Ahhh," I said. But I still didn't know. All I knew was that it was somewhere close to Newark Avenue.

As the next couple of days passed, I asked Robert if he wanted to go for a walk. Robert was already in his second year of high school. St. Anthony's was sort to be a Polish school to us, and many from OIC went there. Even though Robert went to my school, it was not big deal. The next thing was for Mom to send the papers in and pay the tuition, which wasn't easy. I think it was around four hundred per year, but for us, it was a lot of money. I knew Mom was happy, and that was a really good thing.

It was a short summer. My brother was in the Navy, Mom was even more nervous, and my father was never around as usual. Things were very lonely. Most of my friends were on their way to different schools, and all the kids I was friends with in grammar school were gone for good. I remember Mom taking me to the highlands for a week. We stayed in a house near the bridge where the mud hole was. The bridge going to Sandy Hook was the one where my brother used to jump off and also the bridge where he had pushed me off into the bay. All that was on my mind was fear of the unknown again. There was no one to assure me and talk to about it. All I knew was the high school, and I was on my way. As usual, I had to think for myself, and sometimes that wasn't the best thing! Because I always thought I made so many bad judgments in the past.

When we got back to the apartment, my brother's letters kept on coming. In one, he asked, "Did you buy the house in the Highlands? Are we going to move?"

The house in the Highlands was beautiful and was up by the twin towers. There were two stone ponds in the yard. Yes, that one! The view that was looking over the inlet was so beautiful, and the price, of course, was thirteen thousand, which would be pocket change today. My father, a veteran, could have gotten a low-interest loan called a VA loan. I remember my mother practically begging him about it. She, I guess, knew what was coming and had seen how my brother was acting. What a dream! The house was a true dream. Then all the cards fell off the table when my father complained and said no because it was too far to drive to work. As I said, he worked in Elizabeth, not far at all. As I said, he just wanted excuses to get out of any responsibility. After that, Mom cried and drank more.

Disappointment! I don't think my brother knew unless Mom told him in a letter, but I didn't see anything he said that would tell me that he knew. So now this part of life went on. We were always looking to talk about something except the terrible apartment and a place where my brother would never bring a girlfriend to or would be too embarrassed to bring friends. I can remember Mom receiving a letter from my brother on my birthday, May 11, but I never read it. I don't know why. Maybe I was just not interested, or Mom didn't offer it to me to read. Again, later, I wondered how often Mom would read the letters. I was now playing a lot of sports with many friends on the street, stickball and two-hand touch, and was still playing in league, which I found more and more boring. I had so many distractions going through my mind.

I would let many friends know I was going to St. Mary's, but no one really cared. All the others went or were in Ferris. I never said anything to them, but I wanted to play football and baseball in school. I found out they didn't have a football team but had a baseball team, only one baseball team, not like a junior varsity team. I didn't know what that meant anyway. I knew nothing about those freshmen teams and varsity teams anyway. That was something I saw on a television show a lettered sweater may be on leave it to Beaver, or father knows best television shows. To me, those shows were the same as science fiction—not true; those people weren't real. Who would explain anything I was in for? No one. The time to attend a new student opening was getting close and to see what classes I was going to be in and who my new teachers were.

The bedroom where my father slept now had a pullout chair so my brother could sleep there when he came home from the navy. My father's bed was moved over to make room, and an area carpet was put on the center of the floor. It was on the street side, Grove Street. The two windows in that room were on the fire escape side, third fire escape up. My grammar school days were behind me. It was more difficult to find friends. Everyone I went to the grammar school with was going to different schools all over the place, and now we all were strangers to one another. My brother was in the Navy, and Mom was more and more nervous every passing day. Dad was gone more than usual, and many times, I would play ball with myself. I would throw the ball over and over against the walls outside until I saw some friends and played stickball with them. That was only on the weekends because they were older and worked regularly and went to classes for their careers.

One day, I was in the bedroom, overlooking Grove Street, and there was Lana. She came to my school in the fifth grade and didn't know a word of English. Many started to come then from Latin America. She had beautiful olive skin and was sort of pretty. She had big beautiful eyes and long dark hair. I believe she came from

Nicaragua, the same place as two other classmates. Maybe they were related. She moved into an apartment with her cousin's family on Wayne Street across Grove Street, about a block away where we lived. Also, a couple of times, we were in the same place at the same time in Gregory apartments, where a classmate also lived. His father traveled, so he and his brother were living there. I'd never seen his father, but we used to watch some football games in his apartment. One day, Rosa was there.

I thought, *But why is he there?*

I think he was trying to get her to go with him. I liked Lana but never spoke to her that much, but I always stared at her, noticing that she was getting better-looking all the time. I never knew what she did with him, but one day, later in time, I happened to be looking out of the right side window of the bedroom and saw Lana.

Wow! She was hot! She had white tight pants, a halter top. I mean she was really nice. It was about 6:30 p.m., and I raced around to get a toy pair of binoculars I'd had for years. By the time I got back to the window, she was still there but with a blonde Spanish kid. I had seen him before but was not sure what school he was from. Across the street also was Patrick's barbershop, and it had a small closed-in area in front of the main door, about five feet deep and five feet wide. Vestibules, they were called. Now I had an empty feeling in my chest again. The two of them stepped into the vestibule area. The barbershop was closed for the day, of course, and they started to make out! He was really making the moves, feeling her up all over the place. I was so jealous with that same feeling I had so many times before. I was so bored, and so I did what anyone one would do. I went and found a whistle and stood by the window and blew it as loud as I could. I then peeked to see! They stopped and walked away fast. Lana did look up like she knew it was me. A few days passed, and I saw Lana.

"Hello," I said.

She looked at me like she was looking through me. After that day, I would never see her again, and life moved on.

Many letters were coming from my brother. He was in some sort of training. Now he found out he was color blind besides having asthma and a bad knee. One letter was dated May 11, my birthday, and it was not good. Imagine being in the Navy and being told that maybe at best you could only be a dishwasher or a cook. Now looking back, where was the advice he needed? If only he'd been advised, "You could learn to be a boiler mechanic and get your proper seals, low and high pressure, so when you leave the Navy, you can have a great job!" But no, he had no advice from the Navy and certainly none from home. He was being set up for failure, just like back at home. You can see he was just another number to them, just like he was in grammar school and in high school before he quit.

When you think there is hope and maybe a future for yourself, you just need a break. Good luck. Maybe you can meet the right person who can help turn your life around. But there was no one there for us. The so-called father in our lives was too busy working and hanging out in bars to escape his lousy life. The one time in my life my father gave me advice, it was the wrong advice. He said I should keep a job that was going nowhere and not take a chance and go to engineering school. Thank God I decided to go there anyway. School helped change my life for the better, with special thanks to a couple of guys named Ed and Ben, who were nerdy smart. Through their example, I found direction. As my journey continued and the things I did in my life, these built confidence in me.

I can say this over and over again, I really didn't know my brother. I knew the things he was going through, but I was still a kid and knew only my fears—and one was him. Playing sports was an escape from my loneliness. We all had friends, but we would really not speak about our issues 'cause all of us were in the same boat. When we did run into kids that had great toys, board games, and footballs, there was always the question "How did he get that great stuff?" All of our learning for the most part was learned on the street, what we thought was good and not so good, whom we thought told the truth and who bragged about what they had.

While my brother was away, I ran into some of my brother's friends. They called me Little Ricky. Sometimes it felt cool and sometimes not. When I saw they were around, I also saw they were with red eyes all the time and that their speech was a little slower than normal. Drugs, I assumed. I was right. Many times I would watch where they were going, and I would see some very strange handoffs—not like handing a football off from a quarterback to a running back but one guy walking one way, another walking toward him, and a left hand meeting a right hand. It was like they never knew each other. But then they passed again, and this time, it wasn't drugs; it looked like one guy was getting money. I was never interested in drugs and had long decided to never do drugs in my life. Events in the near future would cement that attitude. With all the smoking of cigarettes around me, which I really hated, God knows how much secondhand smoke all of us had been breathing in since we were born. You would wonder how anyone survived that. I've included here several of my brother's letters so you can really feel what he was communicating by seeing his own words.

164

May 11, 1970

Hi Mom,

Today I received really bad news. I had that eye exam over in the other camp + they classified me as color blind so when I broke my glasses + went for another pair I asked for another test + it still came out the same. The bad news is that I can't go into any A school like aviation or electronics. The guy told me today the only thing I probably could get into is dish washing. So it's truly really a waste of 4 years. You bet it is. I should of stayed out of all the services with my bad knee, asthma, heart ect. These would of even kept me out of the army. I don't know why I did this because at night + when we work out lately my knee hurts like hell + if I tell them anything I'll probably get a general discharge for lieing on my inlistment papers. Well forget about all this how is everything at home is nancy still feeling bad. I hope I get a letter from you today the mail call is every day at six o'clock. I miss you guys alot. I wish you the best of health

Love Pinky

P.S. Send me a ~~50¢ a 60¢~~ 16 ¢/00 stamp
+ some 10¢ ones in a envelope

Now when you are so unhappy, what do you turn to? That was the next question for my brother. Me, I was entering high school. It was my freshman year in a new school. But in a way, it was still the same nuns but different names. I had the same problems with math, and the work they were giving me looked more like someone in NASA should be figuring it out. The classes were very difficult for me. Many kids were from other schools all over Jersey City, as far as Central Avenue and Dwight Street and in between. There were a few from downtown but not my area, like Third Street and around. I did notice some cute girls, such as Cathy and Maryann and a few others. Again, I felt alone.

But there was something coming. It was baseball signups! I'd always wanted to be on a team like I was in Little League. I knew it would be difficult. I was skinny but could run and knew the game. I also knew another thing. No one could catch a ball like I could. It would be hitting. That is the problem. Soon, there would be a meeting. I guess the coach just wanted to see how many kids he had. He already knew the kids he had coming back, so he was seeing the newer kids. It was in the gym, a very small gym. It had a curtain in the middle that would be closed for gym class. The girls were on one side, and the guys on the other. So there we were. There were not so many kids, maybe six or seven. I saw one kid I knew—Richie! He played at the same Little League I did. He played with the green team. And there was also his brother, Ray, who was a senior. I also remember him! Ray was there to introduce his younger brother.

The coach was a big man named Rocky Pope. He seemed to always have a cigar in his mouth. He spoke with a gravelly voice but never really yelled; he just spoke loudly. We met, and he informed us of tryouts and where and what time there were going to be. So there I was. I didn't know anyone. Really, I didn't have a ride to go anywhere, and I had to find the place to practice. Many were at Lincoln Park, so I made it there. I took the Montgomery bus and walked through the park to where practice tryouts were. Wow, the kids were so much bigger than me; they looked stronger too. It began, and my glove was even big for me. Now we squared off, throwing to each other. Each person had a partner. I had a guy named Bob, who had a nickname. I called him by his nickname like everyone else did. I didn't know how he got the name and never asked. What I noticed was his bigger brother Ray. Guess what, they were Cardinals' fans. Wow! It was this great having someone to talk to about the Cardinals. This was 1970, and they were two years removed from the World Series. It was great. It was like heaven talking with two people who really knew the Cardinals.

Back to throwing. Man, these guys could throw hard! Much harder than I was used to! There was no freshman team, no junior varsity, only the varsity team. I knew I had to prove myself to everyone. I watched and learned. My baseball knowledge was really good. I knew the game! We always did run down tag plays back on Wayne Street. I would always win. I could assume and estimate things well—when to stop and when to fake in rundown plays. We started lining up. He had what he thought were his regulars in the infield, and I lined up to get into a rundown between first and second bases. I was in the middle. I knew what and where they would throw, so I played sucker and waited for them to make the first throw. When they did, it was my game. I was so quick, and I forced them into so many bad throws. Rocky would make them do it over and over again. They would catch many others, but not me. A couple would see that I knew the game. I was hoping the coach did.

Many practices passed, and my problem was hitting. My fielding in the outfield was great, but hitting, not so much. They threw so hard. I would foul off a few but not many in play. I was worried about making the team, but I thought Rocky was a fair man who might have seen positives in me. I always hustled and never dropped a ball and even warmed up the pitchers. I caught some in Little League, but that was a joke. These guys threw hard, and the practice mitt sucked loose and was old. My left hand would kill me after. Also, I didn't wear a cup, so it was double danger! No matter how things hurt, I never showed it. I never missed a practice and was there on time. Sometimes some nice guys on the team who were seniors and had cars would give me a ride home. Some players' fathers also did. I was lucky.

The time was right. There was no list on who made the team, but Rocky had only so many uniforms. They were blue pinstripe. As he was giving them out, he had two shirts left but no pants. So he gave me a shirt but told me I would have to get the pants to be on the team. I asked Mom for some money, went to Kuchar's Sporting Goods, who just happened to be the basketball coach, and tried to find a pair of baseball pants to fit and baseball socks. I found the pants, the only pair. They were small for me, but anyway, I bought them. I had an old pair of baseball spikes. I was ready. The pants were tight and high, so I really had to pull up my socks to make them acceptable, but when I showed up for the first game while wearing them, the comments came from some but not all.

Pony was a junior and was super nice to me and was always my throwing partner. I didn't play much at all, but I learned a lot and practiced hard. It was so nice to be on a team. Really, no parents ever really showed up for our games, maybe one or two, not like today. Rocky was a good man and a good coach, but at the end of the year, he would leave to coach at Hudson Catholic, a big loss for me.

I used to think, *Why? Why did Vince Lombardi leave my Packers?*

I could never figure that out. The team just won the Super Bowl, and he was so popular. Everyone knew his name in my area. You didn't get to read a lot about him in my area and not much about him on TV. I never had answers. All I knew was that it made me sad. None of my friends cared. They weren't Packer fans, so again, I had to figure it out myself like everything in my life. Even worse was that I now had to deal with death and the death of the man I just worshiped. Before he died, he had left for the Redskins. Why? But now he was dead. The news on TV said it was cancer. Cancer was another thing that was not explained to us. People then didn't know cigarettes were causing cancer. If they did, I didn't know. Most things were kept secret and quiet; it was almost as if it was better for you if you didn't know. Even if you asked a question, you got an answer but wouldn't be sure if it was true or not. They just gave you an answer to shut you up.

The sister was asked the question, "Where did God come from?"

She answered well. "Something so good came together and formed God."

"What?"

We sat there and listened to this stuff only because they couldn't say they didn't know! Never would they admit to anything.

"Are you smoking?"

"Oh no!" Even though they had a cigarette between their fingers.

"Are you drinking?"

"Oh no!" Even with the whiskey bottle on the table next to them and the glass half full.

This would leave you with another feeling called mistrust! I knew they were lying, but these were teachers, parents, and friends. It would make you think, *Should I act that way or not?* We were always given great examples, weren't we? Besides the feeling of fear, insecurity, now we have also added mistrust.

Now a big thing was coming. My brother was coming home on a leave. When he arrived home, there was not much excitement. Mom was working but came home early. My father, I really don't remember if he was there or not. Ricky was home for a couple of weeks. Mom made special food and, as usual, overdid it. There was so much food and gifts for my brother. But he was home only for a short time. He went out with his friends. A thing he should have learned is that those people weren't really friends. To me, they were what we call users to me. He always seemed to be their leader. He was always in the front. Since he came home, he was making trips to New York City with his friends and to a store on Newark Avenue. I didn't really get the full experience of what they were doing till they came over to the house. It was bad, really bad. Nana was staying with my aunt for a while, and I was the only one home during the day. Mom worked, same as my father.

The Beginning of the End

When my brother came into the apartment with a few of his friends, I knew it wasn't going to be good. The bedroom on the right side was where the fire escape was. They would head to his room. He was joined by his friends. Two of the guys were also my friends at one time, but not now. They only hung out with my brother. That was their loss. I always felt they weren't any good at sports. That was why they entered the so-called drug scene. The new pullout chair in the room was super heavy. When my brother and his cohorts were in the room, they would push the chair against the door. It was mostly because the lock on the door was so painted over that it never worked.

I did notice that they had several paper bags, small ones, and these were loaded with stuff. At the time, I couldn't tell what the ingredients were. At this time, this store had small models for fifteen cents, mostly World War II airplanes. They were cool and easy to build, but you also had to buy a tube of glue. This was modeling glue in a four-inch tube. The other thing was that it had a very strong odor, a very strong chemical odor. Many people were going into this store, buying only the glue. They then made a rule that the only way you could buy a tube of glue was to buy a model.

People were thinking, *What is the glue used for besides models?*

I sat in the living room, watching TV. My brother and his crew were all in the bedroom, and I would smell things from there. First, there was a very strong scent of the glue, and second, there was an odor of something that was burning but not food! It was a foul smell. It was crazy. I couldn't quite understand it. I also wasn't stupid. I'd seen people smoking pot before and remembered how it smelled, so I knew it wasn't good. They opened all the windows in the room, but the breeze pushed the odor under the door. They were ready to leave. I could hear the chair being moved from in front of the door. When I went in there, I smelled everything—the glue and my mother's hair spray (which they used to cover up the smell)—and I saw some things in between the cushion of the chair. It was a pipe and not a normal one. Later, I figured out it was called a hash pipe. That was the odor I smelled. Yuck! I could see how they squeezed the glue into a bag that was left behind.

The one thing I really remember was my brother saying to me, "Don't tell Mom!" He had that look of "I will kill you." This was not a one-time thing, and the return of his friends to that room was almost routine.

Many of my grammar school classmates had issues at home just as I did. We were all good at covering them up. Mom was friends with a few moms and often went to card parties and play bingo with one woman who liked to drink. I didn't really know her kid well, but it seemed we were always being set up together by them. Mom would tell me stories of what was going on in their house, and it wasn't pretty. I always wondered if they knew what was going on in our apartment. Mom would say how the kids hid from the battles they had. My safe space was between the beds and playing with my baseball cards. One time, Mom picked up the Sacred Heart statue in our hallway (it was on a small table), and she tried to hit my father with it. The punches she was throwing at my father didn't work. When you thought you were the only one, it wasn't true. Many of my classmates from grammar school had those issues as well. One girl's brother missed a year of school and then came back, and he was far from normal after an operation. It wasn't explained to me what happened as normal. We had to figure out what happened to him. I wondered often if the teachers and nuns have an idea? If they did, they never said anything to me. What I do know is that many of my brother's friends died years later from overdose.

You would think my brother would use the time home to be more constructive, but that would never happen. He would only talk about his next potential leave in a few months. Mom was so nervous about everything, but if she only knew what Ricky was doing, it would kill her. A couple of days passed, and his friends were back in the house and doing the same thing. This time, a heavy odor from the hash was coming from the room, and it was all over the house.

Terrible! I thought. I couldn't stand it anymore. I went to the room and pushed the door with all my might and moved the pullout chair. It was super heavy. Then I saw everything clear as day. Now I was thinking that I had to tell Mom. My brother then came out of the room and told me, "Stay the fuck away or else!" That was the first warning from him, and I knew he meant business. He might do something serious to me. My brother never bluffed. I think that was one reason he had so much respect on the streets. If he said he would get you, he sure would. I knew he was going over New York. He had a girlfriend he was talking to and had some photos of them together in the Washington Square park area. I had never met her or seen her with him. I didn't know what school she went to, but when he was home, he used to pull the phone cord into the closet to talk with her.

I never asked questions because I knew what was coming from him. But drugs were something else. I knew it was bad just as alcohol was. Seeing Mom and many other relatives taught me that. Even though I had never really seen junkies, being in high school started to show me a lot. Many girls in our freshman year were popping pills and smoking pot, and many were very high in class. The draft dodgers who were hanging in the park were always smoking pot. Robert always set a good example. He was two years old than me, and I had never seen him do that stuff. Many of the guys I played ball with on the street never did those things, so I never felt pressure to do it, not that I would anyway.

One day, when Robert was into his own thing, hanging out with some older guys his age, I was playing OUT against the apartment wall as we had done in the past so many times. And here came Robert around the corner with a quart bottle of beer in his hand, drinking. I said hi and not much more as he went by. It seemed to be a regular thing for him. I seemed to connect everyone who drank alcohol to my mother. The feeling I had seeing her when she would drink was branded in my mind. That was how I felt, and when I saw a friend also drinking, I seemed to lose my connection with them.

Another day passed. I was home, and my brother was ironing his clothes. I walked to the back room. He started to come at me like a crazy person. I started to push the bedroom door shut and got it to close. Then he started to kick it over and over again. Finally, he got in. He brought with him the superhot iron, the one he was using to iron his clothes this time. He pushed me into the wall and put the iron within an inch of my chest. I couldn't move. If I did, my arms would get burned or my hands. As he held the hot iron near my chest, he said over and over, "Do NOT TELL MOM! Do not tell Mom!" I was scared and crying. The fear he put into me had lasting effects, and I would end up making a big mistake because of it.

Carlos was a sort of quiet guy. He always sat next to me in class. He was a nice guy. Four of us used to play Avengers in school. He was Captain America. I was Iron Man. Jose was the Hulk, which he hated, but he was a little chubby, so he had to be the Hulk. Sometimes we had Louis there, and he would be the Sub-Mariner. We had some comics of them on TV. There was a cartoon of them that was really good for that time. We would run around the schoolyard, doing the voices, chasing one another, making crashing noises, and falling down like we were hit with a ray gun—all until the newest brown-noser shook the big bell. On the first bell, we would have to freeze. Seriously, we didn't move a muscle. We froze in the body position we were in at the first moment of the bell ringing. Then the second bell would ring, and we would then move to form a line back into the school for class. Many played jump rope with the nuns, of course, and kick ball sometimes. Then when we returned, and it was time again to tolerate the nuns. It was so funny when we took quizzes or tests. Carlos would cover up his paper with his arms to block anyone from looking to see his answers; he was very smart.

I liked Carlos, though we really never hung out after school. Sometimes he would play baseball in an annex across from the prep. He always wanted to be Brooks Robinson, the third baseman of the

Orioles, who was a super fielder. I was a center fielder, but other than that, we spent most of our time being friends in school.

I remember he was to go off to a Catholic school. He made that school but ended up in a public school. It's possible the Catholic school was too expensive, as it would have been for most of us. But the last time I saw Carlos was when St. Mary's, whom I played for, played his school. We saw each other and hardly looked again. I don't know why. Maybe we felt we were on opposing teams, and it was not proper or whatever. But it was a sad moment.

Paola was a very pretty Spanish girl in our class, and it seemed every boy was interested in her. She seemed to like hanging out with some nice girls and was a really nice girl. To be honest, I really didn't know her well or hung with her at all. What I had always seen was her very cute smile. When we graduated, she went on to a public high school, and I never really saw her much after that. But what I was to find out was that she became connected to bad people who led her in the wrong direction, into drugs. It soon took away not only her pretty looks but also her soul and then her life. She died from drugs very early in her life. The man she was with didn't help her be a better person; he helped her fail.

When you do not see a person in such a long time and hear what happened to them, you can only picture them as when you knew them. The picture in my mind, that of the pretty girl in her school uniform hanging out with two other Spanish girls (forming maybe the three prettiest group of girls in the school)—it was another difficult loss. I used to think to myself why she didn't go with me. Maybe I was not as cute as the *papi chulo* guys, but my intentions were better. Or maybe it was a way to say that even with all my issues, I was better than them for her. Either way, she was gone.

My brother now was headed to another area to attend a school in the Navy. He took a bus there and got lost, but now he was out of the house again, and I had his secret in my head all the time—the stupid things he was doing, the drugs, and the bad boys he was hanging out with. I saw them on the streets, and now it was official. My nickname was Little Ricky. It seemed as though I was being protected by them, another way of boosting my ego, like I were someone else. I always wondered why my father didn't drive Ricky to where he was going. Why did he have to take a bus and then a taxi and still get lost? It was in Maryland again, a few hour's drive by car, but I guess my father was too busy. I could imagine being in a car with my father for hours and the two of them not saying a word to each other. As I remember, I don't think my father said five complete sentences to me in my childhood other than some things about sports teams. When my brother was there, taking a class, he was talking about coming home for a weekend.

For whatever reason, he told my mother it was to see her. It was not the truth. It was to hang out with his so-called friends and do drugs. Every time he came back home for a weekend until he was shipped overseas, he would remind me about not telling Mom. Now if I told Mom, what would have happened? I would never know that answer. But each time, I couldn't figure out what I should do. It was like something you just wished you had the right answer for. I only felt that pressure when he was around because I was involved in my own issues—new school, new friends, and now getting older and still having nothing. Living in this terrible place dictated who my friends were. As my friendships in freshman class evolved, I realized that most of my new friends and I were in the same boat.

UNITED STATES NAVY

July 28, 70

178

Hi Mom,

I finally made it to this place Sunday with a lot of unneeded effort. When I arrived at the airport in Baltamore I had to take a cab to the bus terminal & then wait two & a half hours for the bus. then when I got on the bus I missed my stop & ended up somewhere in Deleware then I had to take another bus back to Perryville when I got there I had to take another cab to Bainbridge. this place is in the middle of nowhere. the barrax I'm staying in now has four guys to a room which isn't

UNITED STATES NAVY

②

179

had at all but all we do everyday is go on working details & in this heat you really suffer. You see, my school is supposed to start on the third but no one here ever started school on time. The biggest goof so far is that when you get off at four you can go anywhere you want as long as you are back by 730 the next morning for work. Wow big deal there is nothing but hickesville for about 75 square miles.

I may be home this weekend if I don't get duty, but knowing my luck I'll be here for the next year without beating the duty.

③

180

Oh I have some more good news. When I checked in for school I was talking with my buddy a chef + he said that when we compleat school we have a 50 50 chance of going to nom.

Another reason I want to get home this weekend is to get some clothes you don't have to wear this crumy uniform after working hours. Well I'll be going now beat bord once a day for me.

Love Ricky

My brother was now off to Spain, and his journey was coming to a full circle. It looked like he didn't know what he had gotten into and was into something he was not prepared for. He never received the proper direction on what type of career he should have taken. After he found out he was color blind and could not take electronics, what he did at home was what he did in the Navy—looking to get out. Today I understand his issues. For many years, I thought he was just a failed leader who had many followers follow him to a dead end. He was popular back home, but for whatever reason? Birds of a feather flock together; they sure do. Given all the things that many see as destructive behavior, now I could see how really scared he was; he wanted to escape.

Think about it again. He had seen himself as a failure back home, so he quit high school and got a low-income job that was going nowhere. Now he was seeing an opening. "Hey, I will join the Navy, learn electronics, and finally move on with my life!" At eighteen years of age, how do you keep getting up from the ashes? You can with advice and help, but for him, where was that coming from? Not our father, not the Catholic schools we attended, not our friends. They were for the most part in the same boat. And even if they did move on to college, such as my best friend Robert, many became self-destructive, anyway. Eventually, they end up killing themselves with alcohol or drugs. Now as I look back, what was the answer for my brother? Many could not get past the frustration of how we grew up, where we came from, and what our family lives were like. We all covered up all the embarrassments in our lives to hide our insecurities. I can remember recreating the altar from the church on our dresser and making-believe that we were priests saying mass. Then we had the scars from the beatings and humiliation from the nuns from being altar boys. After the mass, we would go inside the sacristy. We would kneel and ask for the priest's blessings, and after being blessed, we would get hit in the head hard or smacked. Why would we make our dresser like an altar in our room and make it as though we were saying mass? What were we really looking for? My brother was overseas. My father and mother brought a surprise; it was a small color TV for our room.

I thought, *What a great thing!*

My brother would be so surprised. That was the reason Robert and I hooked up the big antenna on the roof and lowered the cable to the bedroom window. We strapped the antenna around a big pipe on the top of the roof, not a small feat for a couple of young people with only a pair of bad pliers and a wood-handle screw driver. Reaching our bedroom window to grab the cable was no joke, but we did it. As we adjusted the antenna, we yelled from the roof to the window. Too funny! In the alleyway area, the echo was loud, and everyone knew what we were up to. I could not believe it. Robert was older, and I had only seen him once in a blue moon. But the TV was special. A few weeks passed. I was coming home from school when I noticed that the screen in the alleyway window near the building hallway was pushed out and that the front door to our apartment was ajar. I went into the bedroom. The TV was missing! I called Mom, who was working then in the Great Eastern, about an hour away or more by bus and walking. She called the police, and they came over and filled out a report.

Two days after, we received a call from the police to come to the station on Newark Avenue. We did assume that they had the TV. We had to describe it, and then they gave it to us. You could see it had a big scrape on its side. The officer told us that they saw a couple of guys with it. Then they dropped it when the cops saw them. Dropped it? Would it work again? They were very strange. I remember that one detective showed us a polaroid photo of what looked like two gay men.

He said to my mother and me, "Just think. It could have been worse. You could have sons like that."

I never knew what that meant or what the photo was really all about, but we got the TV back, and that was great. One of the policemen gave us a ride back home with the TV. I carried it up, and that was not easy. It was super heavy. But guess what. It did work! When my father got home late as usual, he looked at it and didn't say much, only to say some four-letter words about the guys who stole it. I think, to this day, it was a couple of my brother's friends who stole it for drug money. They knew the apartment and knew that my brother wasn't around. Seeing the antenna didn't help. It was back, and now I could watch the weekly football highlights and hope they showed a play or two from a Packer game.

U. S. Naval Station
ROTA, SPAIN
FPO
NEW YORK, NEW YORK 09540

★ Air
Mail

184

Oct 16, 70

Hi Mom,

I had written you a letter earlier today but decided not to mail it because that was back in Spain. Now I'm some-where in the middle of the Mediterean floating around on the San Diego. That isn't my ship but I'll probably be on it for a few weeks till it gets me to mine. I'm having a hard time writing this letter there isn't even enough room to sit up in bed & my neck is getting stiffer by the moment. No work has been done by me yet, but I've heard you really bust your chops.

Speaking of busting chops

GERARD HORNING

U.S. Naval Station
ROTA, SPAIN
FPO
NEW YORK, NEW YORK 09540

★ Air
Mail

②

185

what a time I had getting
to spain the fog was too
thick in Jersey so they bussed
us out to Kennedy airport. The
flight didn't leave till about
9 that morning & I didn't get
a wink of sleep. When I
arrived there it was about ten at
night the flight was a long
seven hours so a few guys I
& myself took off for the
club & had a few drinks.
The only two things that
was good were the bars &
the girls but the weird plants
& trees are quite beautiful

168

U. S. Naval Station
ROTA, SPAIN
FPO
NEW YORK, NEW YORK 09540

③

186

★ Air
Mail

From the way people talk around here I doubt if even my ship ⊗ will be in the states for the next seven months & if there work to be done on Christmas day you work. It look so beautiful when you set up topside & see the blue blue water all around, but it all turns black when you dont know why your heart all you do is I hate it. Soon I hope I'm out of it one way or another. I've found out all you have to do is tell them

169

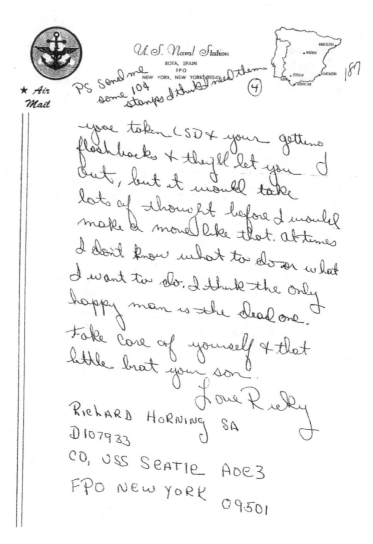

★ Air
Mail

U. S. Naval Station
ROTA, SPAIN
FPO
NEW YORK, NEW YORK 09540

PS send me some 104 stamps I think I need them

④

you taken LSD & your getting flashbacks & they'll let you out, but it would take lots of thought before I would make a move like that. At times I don't know what to do or what I want to do. I think the only happy man is the dead one.

Take care of yourself & that little brat your son.

Love Ricky

RichARD HoRNING SA
D107933
CO, USS SEATIE AOE3
FPO NEW YORK 09501

I think back to all the things I survived when living downtown, all the things we'd done. I think, *Why we did those things?*

There was the great fear we had of the nuns and the teachers and our parents, the lack of communication, the one-sided conversations, the beatings we received, and of course, the belittling. It was like we never noticed these things or felt that they affected us. They did, but we thought it was just another day in our normal lives. I could see that my brother's friends were pieces of shit. In a way, they were cool, but why are we attracted to such people? What makes us follow them? To have a better way of life? Don't they make you worse?

To me, we were all set up to fail from the beginning—where we lived, who our parents were, who were our role models, and whom we hung out with. Still some of us made it out, but it was not without scars. As for myself, I never did drugs, I never drank liquor, I never had an addiction. I loved sports. That was my escape, but I did not walk away without scars. My personality may have been affected. It showed in the way I acted with people in general and the issues I had with commitments in relationships. Seeing the bad relationship of my parents and just about everyone I knew, I always felt that I never had enough to survive in a relationship—either money or things. I thought things were more important than feelings of love. It took me a long time to notice this in myself, the feelings I thought I had and didn't have. I could not separate what was love and what was need.

I wonder how it all affected my brother. I have only ever seen violence from him. When he became a teenager, it was hard to distinguish what was normal sibling fighting and what was genuine desire to hurt. Looking back, I now feel so sorry for him, knowing what he'd seen and noticed for much longer than I did. I am lucky. I really think so! I made it in a sense. Many of my friends went over to hang out with my brother, and some of them were doomed and even died very young. They had bad lives, such as being addicted to drugs and alcohol. Mom again did her best. She was limited but had a good heart. But she was filled with guilt and was in a very bad relationship with my father. She worked so hard long hours and then came home, made dinner, did her best, but also was weakened by alcohol. She helped at school as vice president of the library and bought many things to be raffled off in school, even with the little money she had.

I learned from her how important it is to have a good heart and to be generous. I learned from her the work ethic of showing up early and leaving late. I learned how lonely she was, how much pain she really had from so many things that turned bad in her life. From my brother's letters, I could see how much she really loved my brother even though I had never seen what she wrote to him, and I also found out how much my brother loved her. I was too young to know any of this. It was a silent love. Our family never hugged, never kissed one another on the cheek, never really communicated—only barked orders. But through my brother's letters, I could see so many things. It always seems as if "I knew now what I didn't know then." I was just too young, too stupid, and too scared with my own insecurities to notice.

The things Mom did were amazing. The vacations and the day trips, I never knew how she managed to finance them, only that she got some money from the insurance company she saved with. To us, everything was normal. This was the way things were. Mom died on July 8, 2014, at the age of ninety-one. She had Dementia for a couple of years before her death. I took care of her as she had taken care of me as a kid. It was not easy, and many times, I lost my patience. But to see a person like her, who was such a survivor and had lived her life for me and my brother, was so painful that many times I cried alone.

On January 26, 1971, Mom received a letter from my brother. It had a lot of good news in it. He was heading home for a leave again!

January 26, 71

192

Hi Mom,

What's happening? Sorry I haven't written in awhile, but we have been busting chops lately.

Thanks for the money, but I still think it was too much. You know you have to save your money for the new house your going to buy.

Hey guess what ?? I graduated high school. Yes I received my

result from the ged Test now what
I have to do is go through a line
of bullshit before I get the deploma
First I have to fill out a form
~~which~~ the ~~ship~~ is out of at the
present. then ~~they~~ send it ~~to~~ USAFI.
upon receiving it USAFI sends the state
proof that I passed then USAFI sends me
a letter telling me they let the
state know, then I have to write
the state, send for luck
name of the school, then + only
then I get my deploma. Wow!

Mom, did you get a w2
form from the place I yourse
too work at? If not please

Call them or drop ~~them~~ them a line saying I need it. I don't remember the address but it in the phone book

Gary? to LTD

—Exchange place

I'm sending you my w2 forms from the navy. I don't know if you want to get involved with my tax ~~return~~'s, soooo if you have all my w2 forms see if you can get the jerk accross the street to do it + I will give you the five dollars. Don't worry if you can't I don't think I'll get anything back

———

anyway.

Due they have changed my leave
time to the 18 of march I had no
choice. I may try + make it home
a weekend after the first I don't know
Well thats about all for now
Be good + take care, I hope
everyone is well

Love Peace Hoppyness

Ricky

195

I did the typical dumb stuff. We all did while growing up in my area. It was never the real bad stuff, in my opinion. We threw rocks to break windows of vacated factories and houses. We threw snowballs at buses, and when we hit the windows where people were sitting, it was a super bonus. We looked up girls' skirts, called one another retards, but never made fun of disabled kids. Now remember, none of this was explained to us, why they were that way. It was just something we had to figure out for ourselves. I cannot remember a good marriage to give an example for us in the future. My father never spoke to us, and when I was eighteen and I had just graduated from high school, he left for good. My mother was crushed, not because of love, but because of need—his part of the rent and so on. It was bad. I was going to school and working. Now it was more pressure. I remember going to his work and asking him if he was ever coming back. I never got an answer. He never did return. As you can think, we had to move to a cold water flat, an apartment where the stove had to heat the apartment. Here we were going backward again.

Many years after that, I became successful from hard work and school. Mom's help was always there. I then got in touch with my father through Salvation Army. Remember, there were no internet or cell phones back then. They had a way of contacting people. So they found him, and they never told me. But they did send a letter to him. Then we spoke on the phone. When I visited him at Hockey Motors in Newark, he still had nothing and was living in a terrible apartment in Irvington above a bar. It had one room and was super dirty. After almost twenty-five years after he left us, he still had nothing. He never really wanted any responsibility, so now he got what he wanted. I brought him up to Pennsylvania, but first, I explained this to my mother that he was not staying, just visiting. When he first walked in, it was like everything was the same. Nothing had changed. He had nothing to say, nothing of importance, just like it had been when I was a kid.

Now I saw this as an adult, not as I did when I was a kid. And now I could see why. He visited a few more times till one day I received a call from St. Michaels Hospital, telling me he was there. I

177

went to visit him. When I got back to work, I received another call from St. Michaels, telling me he had passed. I then left, and he was still in the hospital bed. I kissed his forehead. It was the only time in my life I can remember being that close to him. I shed several tears. The date was August 9, 2001. He was eighty-three years old. He had many health issues that were brought upon by himself. I had him buried in the Veteran's Cemetery. There was only room for one more in the plot in Holy Cross, North Arlington, and that was saved for Mom. Dad had received the bronze star for blowing up a Nazi bunker during WW2, which I didn't know about; he never spoke about it. I still have the medal today. I know it's his because it has his full name on it. It was one of many. Mom made me wear it in grammar school when we had patriotic school plays, but again, I never knew what it was, as usual.

My brother finally came home on leave, and this time, there was a very strange feeling about it. He had a very scary smile on his face, as if he was up to something. As always, I stayed away. I told him about making the baseball team and a few other things, but he seemed not interested in anything. Mom was so pleased to have him home she cooked roast beef with mashed potatoes, and all seemed great to her. A few days passed. I was still in school and struggling through all the classes and math especially, wondering how I would pass that class. One day, I came home and saw no Ricky. Then another day the same and then another day; it was the same.

I asked Mom what happened. She thought he was visiting his friend Ricardo, but I knew he wasn't friends with him anymore; they hadn't been for a very long time. This was very strange. I asked a few of my friends if they had seen him. "Nope!" was their answer. I saw a couple of his friends. "Nope!" was also their response. *Hmm,* I thought, but I went on with school. The end of the first year was coming fast and then on to my second year. I could see Mom was super worried, and she spoke to my father to look for him. Did he? I didn't know. Now Robert and I started to look around. It had been a few weeks; my brother was still missing. I thought maybe he was with his girlfriend. I never met her; I had only seen a photo of her.

He used to talk her on the phone. He also spoke of her in a letter he had written to Mom.

One day I was sitting on the couch, and there was a knock on the door. When I opened it, I saw two military police officers standing there. The only thing I knew about the military was what I saw from watching war movies and the TV show *Combat*. They came in, looked around, and asked me where my brother was.

I said, "I don't know. We're all looking for him."

They asked me, "Where are your parents?"

I said, "They're working." And I told them where Mom worked.

They left a letter. It was sent from the Navy, saying he was overdue and AWOL, absent from his post. This was serious now. After that, Mom's drinking got worse! We were all stunned but never thought the worst. Each day, when I came home from school, I expected my brother to be there, but there were no phone calls, nothing from his friends. Then believe it or not, my father asked around. I never told anyone he was involved with drugs. I was stupid and scared. He put such fear in me. I just couldn't say anything. Maybe if I had been pressured or even asked, I would have, but no one was curious about it. By the end of the school year, while sitting in class, I was called out to the principal's office. She was waiting in the hallway with Mr. Sam.

I was thinking, *What happened now?*

> We never seen eye to eye, we never got along, and
> we were very different in all, but I still miss you
> and love you, Ricky, my brother...
>
> Sincerely,
> Gerard

I heard it when my brother was alive till after his death, and it still rings in my ears as if it was said yesterday as it was told to me by Mom, "You don't have a heart! Ricky had a good heart, not you!" I never responded to Mom. I just took it sometimes, thinking it was true, but other times knowing the pain she felt from my brother being gone.

We went to the office, and I was thinking that I got left back or something, but that would have been better news than what they told me. I was told that they had found my brother and he was dead. I didn't know what to think. I didn't know what to say to Sister Ann. Mr. Sam gave me a ride home; he was a super nice guy. I had him for general studies; he was a short Indian guy. He drove me to my front door then said to me how sorry he was. The short drive home to Wayne Street seemed like a lifetime, but when he stopped, he also said, "Your mother needs you now." I had tears in my eyes. I opened the door to his car, said goodbye, and made the long walk up the four flights of stairs to the apartment. I had the one key I needed to open the door with the new lock we had installed after the TV was stolen. I was the first one home, the only one there. I saw a wire hanger on the couch. I picked it up and started to bend it back and forth and call my brother's name out. Then I looked toward our bedroom.

Soon after that, Mom and Dad came home. Mom was a wreck, worse than ever. She had to go and identify my brother's body, her son's body. She was told he was found in back of a truck in the fetal position, having died from an overdose of drugs. Mom told me she had thrown up in the morgue and needed to take medicine to stop. All was a mess now. She had to organize everything. She started calling everyone with the terrible news. Soon the wake was being organized but with controversy. Would Ricky have a flag covering his coffin? The Navy said no because he had been AWOL when he died, but an angel appeared—Sister Joan.

She showed up to help, and she did. She argued with the Navy, and lo and behold, she got the flag. It was quick! My brother had been popular, and many came to the wake. The coffin was closed because, as Mom explained, they had to break his bones to straighten him out. He was all black from rigor mortis. That was why his coffin was closed during the wake. Maybe it was better because of the emotions. Even some came from my grammar school, nice girls like Nilsa and Maria. But many of his friends who knew what really happened stood in the back of the parlor. This lasted for a couple of days. I remember Debbie and Danny coming. I didn't know how to act or what to say to anyone. Most just said that they were sorry and shook my hand. Two close friends of Mom were both very upset. They said to me, "Your mother really needs you now." I didn't know what they meant. Needed me, how?

During the funeral mass, as we walked by the coffin down toward the altar in the church, I was next to my father. Then he almost collapsed, but he caught himself before he fell. Mom had food at the house with some friends and relatives. During that, I didn't want to stay there, so Robert's uncle took Robert and me golfing in Lincoln Park, par three course. Not one word was spoken during that day. Nothing at all. I would wear my brother's dog tags for a long time after that.

To this day, I never knew how I really felt about him. I never really knew him. We grew up together, yes. We lived in the same room, but in the end, who was he really? I learned many things by reading his letters to Mom, how much he loved her, and how his digs at me were from jealousy and just being my older brother. As I write this, I have tears in my eyes. He was so popular, very good-looking, but also so misguided. What had to be done for things to be different for him? I became a different person after that. Some things stayed the same, though. I never drank alone. I never ever smoked or did any drugs. I never did and never would.

Finally, I received the correct info from a friend on how the last days of my brother went down. In one of my brother's letters to my mom. he wrote about being a failure in the Navy and that the only way to get out was to overdose on LSD. It's fatal drug, but overdosing doesn't mean you're going to end up dead, just enough to put you in the hospital. When he returned home on leave, he started by hiding in all his friends' homes. As he went from house to house, many told him to leave because he was doing the wrong thing. I guess he figured doing some heroin would get him into the hospital. It didn't. A man walking his dog on Washington Street found him in the back of a straight job truck. The heroin killed him, my brother, who was always looked for a way out but found one.

Today I often wonder how life would have been if Ricky had survived, how my life would have changed. I knew how much Mom loved him. He was her life. She always told me he was a loving person, unlike me. Mom often compared me to him—but me in a negative light compared to him. I knew how she felt, so I let it go. I couldn't say anything back to her. I didn't want to hear more. She had to deal with crap her whole life. In the future, I helped stop her from smoking and drinking excessively, but in 1995, she stopped everything. She lived to 2014, so it took a while, but I got something right.

Tom, a good friend of my mom, one day said to me, "Do you remember the terrible life you had? What you went through? And now look at all the great things you've accomplished in your life!"

I looked at Tom and said, "Maybe I did, I surely survived that part of my life."

My life could have been different. I knew how much Mom loved Ricky; he was her life. She always told me he was a loving person unlike me. She often compared me to him—but me in a negative light. I knew how she hurt, so I let it go. I couldn't say anything back to her. I didn't want to hurt her any more than she was already hurt. She had to deal with all the crap her whole life. In future years, I helped stop her from smoking and drinking. She stopped everything in 1995 and lived till 2014. It took a while, but I got something right. Tom, a good friend of my mother, one day said to me, "Do you remember the terrible life you had? What you went through? And now look at the great things you've accomplished in your life."

I looked at Tom and said, "Maybe I do remember!"

Team Post Basketball

They were all looking at me the skinny kid. They seemed very friendly to me, and that was cool. It was a couple of hours' drive. I didn't really say a word the whole ride. We arrived at the gym. It was nice. I remember there were chain nets and a big court. We went to change in the locker room and came out to warm up. I felt so out of place. My sneakers were two dollars, and I would slide on the court and really couldn't stop quickly—another thing in my life. The game started. These guys were good, quick leapers and fast. I knew I could not fit in with that. They were too big. It was a blowout, and our team was winning. With two minutes left in the game, coach put me and the other white kid in the game. I ran to the right hand corner. I was not covered but was frozen out. The other white kid got one shot off but missed. I was open every time but never received a pass. After the game, they showered. I didn't. I never worked up a sweat. I put my stuff in the paper shopping bag and met the policeman outside with his son. He bought me a slice of pizza and a soda. I was starving. Again, in the bus ride, I just sat there and thought if I was going to do this again. I didn't really want to, so I hoped he would not ask me, but he did. I just sort of said, "Well..." He got the hint, but at least, he knew my name was Gerard. He was a very good guy. Everyone thought he was a bad guy and a bully, but he was a nice man. Now I felt good when I saw him.

Nana once—or many more times—said to always have clean underwear on in case you get hit by a car and had to go to the hospital. It was a common phrase all around. Many days and nights, we would play two-hand touch football on Railroad Avenue. I was always the youngest, of course. The games would go on till dark, and we would only have the streetlights to be able to see. After that, we would hang out on Grove Street in front of a store or another. There was a policeman, a tall guy, a tough-looking cop.

The cops used their nightsticks often to poke you or to keep you moving. The words they used were "No loitering!" This would go on all the time, and he knew many of us by name. One day, he approached me and asked me if I liked basketball. I was shocked! He spoke to me in a normal voice. I was in the seventh grade and loved the attention from a real policeman.

I told him, "Yes! I love the game, but I am only a so-so player."

He then told that me he helped coach a team called Team Post from the CYO and that they traveled to many places. He then went on to tell me that they traveled by bus and that all the players traveled that way. He brought his son, who was very young, maybe eight years old. The first place he told me we would go was Connecticut.

So cool! I thought.

So now I would have to tell my mother what was going on. She knew of the policeman, so she was good with it. Now he informed me what I had to bring shorts, shirt, white socks, and sneakers, of course. And a duffel bag. Well, we had a cat at home, and it would spray on anything that was on the floor. The duffel bag—I had the old canvas one—was loaded with cat piss, so that was out of the question. The only thing I had was a brown paper shopping bag. It was embarrassing, but I had to put that behind me; it was very normal in my life. So the first game was on a Saturday. The policeman, with his son, picked me up on the corner of Wayne Street and Grove. We then drove to the bus. It was in the Greenville area of Jersey City. As we entered the bus, I saw that there were fourteen guys, all black, and one white kid around my age. All these guys were big and very strong.

During a conversation with a clergyman, I said to the priest, "Father, you know I am not a saint."

He looked up at me and said, "I never accused you of being one!"

On to Colombia

What man is a man who does not
make the world a better.

—Kingdom of Heaven

After my brother died at the age of eighteen and my father left, my life turned in many directions, but the one direction I never expected was that I'd end up in Colombia. Yes! The one in South America.

The girl I knew was super pretty. She had brown hair with lines of blond in it. We were together for a while, but I never felt secure with her. Things seemed to be good, but she always wanted to go back to Medellin and wanted me to visit with her. This went on for a while. I had heard many bad things about the place—the drugs, the killings. And this was primetime, the very early 1990s. She would often tell me about the issues there and about her father but never about her mom. Even when I asked, it was the same story—well, you know. I figured they were divorced. I wasn't a super smart guy, like a math or chemistry genius, but I was smart enough and was very street smart. What that means is that you know when to run, when to hide, when to fight, when to talk, and when to keep your mouth closed, which I always had a problem with but learned as the years went by.

As Yuliana and I discussed our or my new adventure, she said she may not be returning to the USA.

Wow, I thought.

Then she explained to me that she was on a six-month visa and was already overstaying. When you do, that it's a big no-no, and she may be penalized and may not be able to return to the USA. When something like that comes up in a conversation, I always look to see if she's sorry or cares or something, like, "Hey, does she really care about me?" But she was a bit cold as a person but knew when to be intimate with me. I guess it was to make sure I was interested in her. Most of the time, she never went overboard but did all the right things. She advised me to get a passport so I could come visit her.

With her beautiful body and face, I thought I would have gone to Mars to be with her again. When you only look at one thing in a person and the other person knows about it, then they can sort of manipulate you through it. They can bring you around on a string, and you follow along just to get that one think you want. Then after that, you're done.

But she stayed interested long enough for me to get a passport. Now she was leaving. It was sad going to Newark airport and saying adios, and then when she was going through the final gate, she turned and looked at me. Well, she did that, and my ego went up a bit. When I finally went home, I felt alone. I would wait till I get a letter or something to communicate with each other on the Web. At that moment, I knew I would be traveling soon, very soon. I knew I was a bit older than her, and I felt I had to act a certain way, but she never minded that. And she reminded me that age never mattered, only the person. Again, she always knew what to say. So I was ready and wanting to leave to see her. We spoke through the internet. It was all that lovey stuff: "I miss you" and so on.

So after months, I was leaving to travel. It was a real pain traveling to Newark and then to Florida and then to Panama and then to Medellin to a scary airport in the city just under a group of large mountains or in between them. It wasn't long before I went through customs and saw her. This time, she was with a very short man who was a bit older and also another man. It was super strange, my Spanish. As a woman whom I would meet later said, it was fatal, the way I spoke. Yes, she meant my Spanish was bad, and it still is.

I walked up to Yuliana, and as I went to kiss her on her lips, she tilted her head and kissed me on my cheek. It was proper to do that when family members were present. There were so many more things I was about to learn, and some were not very good.

As we were driving out of the airport, Yuli and I were in the back seat, and her father and the other guy were side by side in the front. They were driving like crazy guys to a place called Envigado, a *barrio* in southeast Medellin. I had no idea what was going on, only to be in my best behavior around Mr. Ossa's daughter. Finally, we arrived, and an old woman welcomed us into their home. I was very polite in my bad Spanish, but since Yuli and Mr. Ossa could speak English, I was in the clear.

As strange as things were, I felt very scared. I was thinking to myself, *Why did this guy come with her father for the ride? Is he just a friend or what? And why do I care or even think of that?* To me, the guy looked weird. He had strange eyes, like that of a nut/crazy person, totally opposite of Mr. Ossa's eyes. His eyes looked like he was always thinking and thinking ahead. I was not even listening to the constant rapidly speaking friend. When they spoke fast, forget about it, I couldn't understand a thing. But if I had a hint of what subject they were talking about, then I could separate the words and understand a bit. Colombians spoke so differently from the Puerto Ricans back home. It seemed more proper, and there were no English words mixed in. Right away, they offered me a cerveza (beer), a very popular word, and also another drink called aguardiente. It was terrible. It tasted like cheap mouthwash, but I guess they used it for a cheap way of getting drunk.

Os then explained to me where we were and how long they had lived in Envigado. This was their home. As the conversation went on, I never heard them mention his wife, nor did I ever hear Yuli speak about herself. Now I was ready to hear where was she or if they were divorced or if she died. Who knew? Yuli was sitting next to me on the couch. What I noticed first was that the rooms were super small in the house and the toilet, which I had yet to use, had no toilet seat! Yes, no toilet seat! So when you took a crap, you had to squat over the toilet. Believe me, it was not good. I said something to Yuli, and she told me that they were buying one tomorrow.

Thank God, I thought.

Now we all sat down to eat. The table was small but okay, and we had a knife and a spoon but no fork. Then came the old lady. They called her *abuela* (grandmother), but she was not related to them. So why? I didn't know, didn't care. I was just very hungry. So then came the food—a lot of rice, a lot of beans, and many fried bananas. They looked really tasty. Then there were also some meat and chicken. The table was full of what looked like carrots and cabbage cut up, and there were also very green tomatoes—not good. So we ate, and the conversation began with my talents.

"My daughter tells me you are a good mechanic, that you can fix anything, and that you are very athletic."

I said, "I am, and I try to keep in good shape."

Then the next question was strange. "Do you know guys?"

What? I thought. *Do I know guys? What, like a friend?* I thought, *What kind of a question is that?*

I replied, "Well, I know them but really don't use them. I don't care who uses them—none of my business."

Then he got up from the dinner table and brought two guys in—a handgun and an automatic weapon. He asked me, "Do you know these?"

I said, "Yes, I have seen them on TV."

Soon after that, we went to a house in the back, about fifty feet from the one in the front.

This is getting very creepy, I thought.

As we walked, Os said to me, "You are tall and have blue eyes and are a gringo." I guess I replied to that. Then he said, "You would be very popular here in Medellin."

I say, "Why?"

"Well, the men here cheat and lie and have many women each."

Then Yuli caught up with us. He rattled something very fast to him. I had no idea what he said, only now I felt that it was stranger than ever. As we entered the house, the one in the back. It only had a couple of rooms, but this was different. It had steel doors with cages.

I was thinking, *Now what's going to happen to me?*

I was now waiting to hear the words from every horror movie just before you're killed: "Just relax." But no, he moved with intent and was business as usual. Then he said something more curious.

He looked at me and said, "The women here would love you—tall blue eyes, good shape, gringo."

I thought that was really bad on his part, saying that with his daughter right with us. Maybe he was drunk or what. I tried to stop guessing. Then he took his keys out and opened the one big door. It was all steel, and behind it were—wow!—so many weapons. I couldn't count the many cases of guns, automatic handguns, what looked like hand grenades, knives, vests, all kinds of special stuff.

I said, "Are you going to start a war?"

He turned and looked at me and said, "On only the evildoers."

"Where are they?" I said. I didn't really know what to say. I was only going to be in Colombia for two weeks, but now I was wishing I was going home the next day.

"My daughter said you brought gifts. Let's go back to the house and see them," Os said.

"Sounds like a plan," I responded.

I had bought him a watch, a few shirts, and a lot of chocolate bars. He really liked the stuff, and now the subject was changed for the moment. But I realized that he never asked me about my feelings for Yuli, maybe another day.

Day by day, it seemed Os was trying to teach me things—mapping the area and weapons, which I had nothing against. But really, for what were they? To kill people?

He told me, "Colombia has gone to being so bad. People can't live normally. They have to be in fear of him."

I assumed he was talking about Escobar, the big-time drug trafficker, but *him* was a word he seemed to use for all of them—all the drug dealers. Yuliana didn't seem to be around so much. She would sort of slip out, especially when her father was showing me things, and our relationship was almost like a business now. I was wondering why I traveled all this way, and of course, it was to spend time with her, not so much her father. Os was intensive with me. Each minute he was teaching me more Spanish and more how to get around the city and later all the barrios in Medellin. There were so many little towns. He would show me maps of San Javier, Campo Valdez, Aranjuez, Santo Domingo, Itagui, Belen, and Bello. These were all small barrios, which meant neighborhoods in English.

When I had been in Envigado for four days, we traveled to Sabaneta for a couple of hours. Os introduced me to a couple of guys in their early thirties. They looked rough. From what I could pick out in their conversation, they spoke of guns mostly and the government. It was so difficult for me 'cause they spoke so fast. I could only pick out some words, so I did my best to eavesdrop. When I asked Os what was going on, he would say that they were his business partners and that they had several things to talk about. The next thing was Yuli teaching me about the Colombian peso. It was not as confusing as I thought, only that the US dollar was worth a lot more than their pesos.

We went to a small area in Medellin. The city itself reminded me a little of New York City. It was super busy. We walked a couple of blocks and passed by a couple of kids openly pissing on the street, which was not great to look at, but I had seen the same in Jersey City. We walked through an alleyway to a stone-front building. It looked nasty and real bad. I just followed and didn't have time to ask questions. Yuli told me we had to hurry before everything closed.

I asked, "It's early. Why would they be closing?"

"Well," she said, "it's almost siesta time."

I remember hearing that about Mexico, but here? From 2:00 p.m. to about 4:00 p.m., everyone rested, she said. I couldn't stop laughing.

"How lazy is that!" I said.

She said, "Someday, it will stop 'cause all the people have to work long days. The banks close. Everything does."

Now we had reached the place. It was a dump in the middle of an alley. She asked for the money, and he took it, the guy behind the counter. He reached into his pocket and his drawer and pulled out a pile of bills. I mean a lot of pesos. He counted it, gave it to Yuli to count, and then we left. The car that had dropped us off was gone, so she wanted me to go on a bus to learn about it. Now it was like school. Everything was a learning experience. Many of the buses were colorful and open, as in no windows at all. Now we had to get on the right one, and there were lines for all of them. We went on this one line, and soon we were off. What was a twenty-minute ride in a car now took an hour on this bus.

She pointed things out on our way back to her house—stores, restaurants. And she explained how the streets worked. She even told me about the several churches we passed. We finally got off, and as we did, I noticed that everyone on the bus was staring at me like I was the missing link or something. I was one of the few people who was wearing sunglasses, but I was a gringo. There seemed to be no other gringo, only me. When we got off the bus, we had about three blocks to walk to her house, and I knew more lessons were coming. When we walked into the house, it was more lessons about money and what could be bought for how much.

By this time, I had been in Medellin for six days, and my head was going to explode from all the stuff being force-fed to me. And like a dummy, I wasn't asking the right questions for what again and again. Then Yuli took me to the back house, and now I wondered what was up now. When we got in, she turned off many of the lights, and then she removed her clothes.

Finally, I thought.

She put two blankets on the floor, locked the door, and things got a lot better... We were close again for a short time, but it seemed like a reward and to keep me interested rather than genuine lovemaking. I was being used, and I hadn't figured that out as of yet. But for what? That night, while in bed, I was thinking of every horror movie I had ever seen and wondered how this one would end.

But me trying to outthink Os and knowing his plan or why he was showing me all these things was not going to happen. In the seventh night there, I spoke to Yuliana at length.

"What is going on? Why is he showing me all this stuff and his house full of weapons?"

191

She did not answer. All she said was "He is trying to be friendly."
Nah, I thought. *That's not it.*

I had almost a week left here, so I figured I would confront him with the same question the next day. What I did notice was that he was always on the phone and in communication with people all over Colombia. There were also had a couple of guys coming to the house. What I noticed was that they would leave with a couple of weapons. It looked like he wanted me to notice it, like he was finding out if he could trust me. We always had breakfast together. The conversation was simple, but we ate eggs, cheese, and *arepas*, a round small bread shaped like a disk.

Again Yuliana left for the day. When I asked her where she was going, all she said was work.

"Work?" I said. "Where? What?"

By the time I got the second word out, she was gone. So it was the same routine again. This time, Os took me to meet some people, and he sure did it. There were several girls on motos (a small motorcycle), and the girls were dressed to ride—high boots, tight jeans, black helmets, and black jackets—all very tight. All of their bodies were perfect, and they also were very pretty. He introduced me to all of them. I shook their hands. Not one removed her gloves to shake my hand, and all of them never even cracked a smile. After that, we went to another house. I decided to keep my questions on who they were to me till later, but by then, I knew this was very serious and that I was being led to a path that I was getting very scared of.

Then I found the guts to say, "Hey, Os, who were those girls, and what's going on?"

He replied, "They are friends who deliver messages for me."

Now I was going to figure it out for myself, and my imagination was running wild. I sort of knew Colombia was Wild West City from some of the stories I had heard and that coming here was no joke. Something that I noticed was that no one called Escobar by his name. They had to use a word to substitute for his proper name—El! Wow, everyone was scared of using his name, and rightfully so. From what I was told, he had paid spies all over, and if you spoke his name, you would be accused of spying on him. Then the bad news came—you wouldn't live another day.

That day, I went to play basketball in a small court in Envigado. It was nice to get out and do something else. Then a car pulled up. The court was only down a block, but it was Yuliana who popped out of the car.

She came right over to me. "Let's go!" Then in the car, she told me, "Ne never wander off like that again."

I said, "How did you know where I was?"

She said, "Don't worry."

Then an argument came. I was worried. She replied that she was sorry for yelling.

Then she told me, "You're being watched."

I almost pissed in my pants. I said, "By who? For what?"

She told me, "You will find out very soon."

We were back at her house, and there was more food on the table. Her father came in and said he was sorry for scaring me that way.

Then he told me, "Soon all things will be explained. But first, I had to see if I can trust you and see if you are the right man."

I thought, *The right man for what?*

But in my mind, I knew this was all a plan—a big plan—and that I was being set up for it. Trained maybe?

Os said, "I have many things to tell you. For one thing, you can deliver many messages for me."

I just looked and was thinking, *Now I have to get back home and work.*

Each passing day, more came out his plans for me, and it seemed it always involved women and many women. He was very careful not to tell me everything at one time. He chose his words very carefully. At this time, I was starting to feel very comfortable with him and less with his daughter, Yuliana, whom I thought was my girlfriend. But I felt less and less that in this trip, I was going to get the whole story and plan. And as I thought, he said that in the next trip, I would know more.

The next day, I was leaving. My two weeks were coming to an end, so that night, Yuliana spent the whole night with me and was more passionate than normal. I didn't eat the next morning. There was no time to do so. I was off to the airport. It was a short drive in a dump of an airport and a nice sendoff by Yuli. I received a nice kiss as I was dropped off and an "I'll see you soon."

As I flew home, I wondered, *What the hell have I gotten myself into?*

As soon as I got home, it seemed my phone always rang, and it was always Os asking me how I was and how I liked Medellin and when I was coming back. Only in the next week did Yuliana call me. For me to call them, it would take a calling card and hoping someone answered, but again, I knew the time was coming for what I had been trained for. Os kept delaying the conversation, telling me we would get to that soon.

He said, "Talking to Yuliana and a few of my amigos, you are going to be perfect for our plan."

I told him straight out, "I will not at all deal or take drugs."

He laughed and said, "Don't worry. You will not do any of that. We will discuss the plan when you come again."

During our conversation, I was hearing a beeping sound on his phone. I thought he was recording me, but that wasn't it. He had some sort of scrambling device on his phone so it would not be traced. Yuli had told me about that briefly before, but I never paid much attention. She didn't really explain things clearly; it was always half a story. So I made plans to travel once again, and this time, it was only for a week.

I thought for the next few weeks, *What in the name of God is the plan? What does he want from me?*

During the time I was home, I would call Yuliana's house. She answered maybe twice a week, and the conversation was very low key. If I spoke about her father, she would become quiet, and if I asked about anything about her mom and what happened to her, I would get no answer. The same went with anything to do with any of her father's friends. She became very quiet. I sort of knew she was going to do that, but I was bothered by it. I am not a person that likes mysteries. I did not bring up any of those things again. I told her the date I was arriving there, and she took all the info and said they would meet me at the airport. I never really traveled much, just around my country, so it was an adventure for me. But inside, I felt it was not safe for me or anyone.

Then I was on my way. The time had come. As I was riding to Newark airport (next stop was in Miami), everything was going very smoothly. When I arrived in Miami and headed to my next flight, I was approached by a guy as I was boarding. He looked Spanish, most likely Colombian. As we were walking, he started a conversation.

"How are you?"

I looked at him and said, "I am fine, and you?" I was just curious. "Who are you?"

Believe it or not, he sat next to me. Now things were getting really strange. I was a little angry. I guessed it was to cover up my nerves. Finally, we took off, and our conversation started.

"You can relax. I hope I didn't bother you."

I replied, "Naaah, don't worry. I'm cool."

Then the big news came out. He told me he was a friend of Hector.

I said, "Who the hell is Hector? I don't know anyone named Hector."

He laughed and said, "Hector Ossa."

Now it was my time to laugh. "Okay," I said. "I didn't know his first name."

He apologized and moved on, saying, "Hector sent me to walk with you and watch over you."

I laughed and said, "Who is watching *you?*"

Now it was his turn to laugh, but it was okay. We spoke about simple things, and he asked me how I felt about Yuliana. I told him that I really cared for her. He nodded his head as if to say okay. Nothing reassuring was said by him, but during the time that our conversation went on, I never got his name.

I said, "What's your name?"

He smiled and said, "You can call me Comigo."

I said, "That's not a name, but if that's what you like, okay, Comigo."

The plane finally landed in the Medellin airport, and now he told me to stick close to him and follow him. Customs was a breeze. I don't even remember if they stamped my passport. We picked up my bags, and off we went. Two guys met us, and we all got into a car. I always thought that if I was going to get killed, they could do it anywhere and anytime. So I just did my best to relax.

My only question was "Where is Yuliana?"

Comigo told me, "You know her. She has a mind of her own. Maybe she is working."

I smiled and said, "Yep, I know."

When we arrived at Os's house, there were a few more guys there and no sign of Yuli. I was disappointed as usual. It seemed I knew how to deal with rejection and projecting, which I was good at, thinking things were over before they were. There were six guys in and around the house and one guy in the back house.

Things passed in my mind: *Why didn't I tell anyone back home about all this?*

It was very difficult for me to keep things to myself when things were not going well in my life. I usually shared it with friends, but not this time. It was too strange, and they wouldn't be interested in my business anyway. All those things ran through my brain.

Afterward, the others disappeared. Now there were only three of us in the house—Os, Comigo, and myself. I popped off right away.

"What the hell is the plan, and what is this guy's real name?"

They both laughed and then Os said to me, "His name is Juan Jose."

"Oh, wow," I said. "He does have a real name."

We shook hands.

I said, "What do you want with me?"

Os went to a table behind him, took a very large envelope, and started to put eight-by-ten photos on the table. He attached to them the person's profiles. There had to be eight to ten women in all those photos.

Os looked at me and said, "Pick one."

I said, "For what?"

He looked into my face and said, "For a girlfriend."

I was in shock. Then I said, "What about your daughter?"

He told me, "We have much to talk about, so let's start now."

I raised my voice, "Explain everything!" Now I didn't care that these were tough hombres or were people that were mixed up in something not so good.

Juan Jose just looked at me and said, "You are going to be the luckiest gringo in the world."

I felt so disappointed. Now I was starting to see how I was being set up. Yuliana had been very, very involved.

Os looked at me and said in a very comforting voice, "Don't worry about my daughter. She really cares about you, but she understands what we are about to do is far more important than any relationship." Os began to explain. "Now the game is to begin," he said. "Look at these photos and the women's info next to them and tell me which one you would like to meet."

I thought, What is this?

Then Os said, "After you look them over and pick one, we can get into what the next step is."

So when I was alone that night, I picked one. It was like picking a woman in a beauty contest. All of them were super beautiful, more beautiful than anyone could imagine. The one I picked was incredible. She was about five feet three and had mixed light brown and blond hair. In the photo, she was wearing a halter top and hip-hugging jeans and a face like that of an angel. She was so beautiful, and her name was Diana. The next morning, I put all the rest of the pictures in a pile and left her info and photo separate.

When Os saw it, he told me, "Interesting choice."

I said, "What is the plan? I must know everything."

Os went on to explain to me, "You are a gringo."

"Okay, I know that."

Then he said, "You are tall, have blue eyes, and you are very different. Here, that's what many of the girls are interested in. They can get the stupid good-looking boys here, but all they do is leave them with babies and terrible places to live and no future."

I said, "Okay then, how do we meet? And what is it that you really want?"

Then it finally came out—the whole plan. Os explained, "All the girls in those photos are somehow and in some way connected to big-time drug dealers. They are friends of small-time guys who in turn are connected to big-time lords. So now you can start to see the plan. These girls will talk either by their actions or by trying to get you involved. If they don't, in time, we have our ways of them to lead us to the lords' front doors. It may take weeks or months, but eventually, we will find out."

I look at Os and said, "Why are you doing this? Isn't the government going to look for these guys?"

He told me, "We have a job to do, and once in a while, we get help from the government and lawyers and doctors."

I didn't pay attention to much of that. I thought about meeting Diana, so I asked, "When do I meet her and how?"

He said, "A meeting is being set up now by Yuliana."

I said, "What! Yuliana?"

"Yes," he said. "She is a friend of a friend and so on of Diana."

"So on my next trip, I am to meet her?"

"No!" Os said. "It's going to be before you leave."

Wow, I thought.

It's my land what would I be if I
didn't try to make it better.

—*Kingdom of Heaven*

Os felt that, since this was his country, he wanted to do something about what was going on. Bombs were going off every day. The other day, there were fourteen dead. A bomb in Medellin was set off by El, and more were set in Bogota, the capital, almost every day. Fear was all over the place. I admitted I felt the ground shake many times from the bombs going off. In almost every street corner was a military man with an automatic weapon and a big ugly dog.

I remembered the first setup meeting between Diana and me. She was so beautiful and super pretty and had a body that was incredible. I bought her flowers, and she posed with them for several photos. The way we hit it off was interesting. I could tell she was really interested in me, but our barrier was the language. My Spanish was so-so, and her English was only a few words, but there was a big plus. She had a girlfriend who spoke good English, and that was cool. So when we went out, it was the three of us. But when sitting there with them, I would think of what Os and Juan Jose told me and the real reason I was with her. I knew it would take time to do the things they wanted. The plan was spinning around in my head, and every time I looked at this beautiful woman, I wondered how long this would take. But nothing was my decision; it was up to them. Os was very anxious to see how his plan would work, but he knew inside that no matter, it would work. He had so many connections but always wanted to be sure. When the plan was explained to me and we put it into action, I was amazed how sure he was, anxious or not.

I sat in the chair that night—no Yuliana, only me, Os, Juan Jose, and a couple of other nobodies.

Os then said to me, "I see you like pretty women."

"Of course," I said. "Who doesn't?"

Then he told me what happened. He explained how his loved ones were killed by bombs that were set up by Escobar and his followers. Though he did not say it, I knew it was his wife who was killed, and this was why he had this plan. This plan was not going to end in any simple way. This was something he was going to do for a long time. When I was sitting there, I was trying to put this together and figure out my part. Yes, of course, it was the girls. I would get the relationships and the sex and what else ran through my head, and before I could think of the rest, Os said he wanted the info of where and who were involved, as well as the addresses of the drug dealers.

And not just them; he wanted the higher-ups too, the so-called lords. So after a certain period of time with these women, it would be my job to get all the info.

I said to Os, "Then if they don't say or won't say?"

He said, "There are ways to get them to talk. When we are near that part, then you will know."

I was pretty scared at this point. He always had a stare as if he had x-ray vision. It was looking right through me. But now everything was becoming reality. I was with Diana, and I felt in my next trip back that we would be sleeping together. How could I tell? She was giving me a list of things she wanted when I returned to Medellin. When I got back home, no one knew that I was down in Colombia. I showed photos of Diana to a few people, but they really cared. They saw she was very pretty and young. And they didn't want to hear anything else, but in many ways, that was so good for me. I didn't have to talk about it, though. I wanted to. I feared that if I did, I would get into some big problems with Os, who maybe had ears all over. Remember, many were just jealous when they saw you with a beautiful woman or say she was looking for money or things. They always had to rationalize things to make themselves feel better.

When I showed some dumbasses photos of the girls I was with, they would respond, "I don't need to see your girls." Others would say, "I get it." I got a good laugh out of that, and that helped me keep my mouth shut also.

I went about my business, and Diana and I spoke almost every day on the phone. I would be spending much in calling cards. The best thing was that Os would pay me for the cards, and he would call me also every day to get dates of when I was returning. The problem was vacation time. I only had a few weeks left. But Os left nothing to chance. He wanted me to start to travel on Friday nights and return on Sundays, especially when I had a three-day weekend. For me, it was so stressful. With so many things to do, I was starting to get stressed. At night, in bed, so many things were going around in my head.

Should I be doing this? What is the reward? Only sex. What if I were to fall in love? What if I want to quit? What would happen then? But my selfishness always won over the pretty girls. The ego.

Things started going off in my head no matter where I was. It was like I was being watched. Maybe I was just not used to this. And another thought was what the end game was. My life was always in turmoil. There was always something stupid going on, and it seemed stress would always be there for me. But this was something different. It was not only me. I calmed myself by repeating in my head how lucky I was to be with such a beautiful woman. It seemed to boost my ego and calm my nerves.

Now Diana and I were in a serious relationship. It was so crazy, though. We had sex three times a day, morning and twice at night. It was so cool. She would either stay with me at a hotel or visit me in the morning. She told me her family was always looking into her business, and it was becoming more and more difficult for her to stay overnight with me. When she brought me to her family, she had two sisters, her mom, and her niece there, waiting for me. It was cool. I enjoyed her family, but there was one thing. Her oldest sister was always giving Diana hard looks. I would say they were dirty looks. I caught that a few times. It was almost as if she knew something about Diana, and it wasn't a good thing. There was always something about Colombians. If they didn't want you to know something, they would talk very fast and use expressions I could not figure out. So they had me in that bind. And that evening, that was aplenty.

Soon Diana showed me her room. It was nothing special. There was a very small twin bed, one small dresser, and a wood box where she kept her keepsakes. When you see what little they have, you start to feel bad and want to help. I would buy them food and some daily necessities. In my mind, I was thinking that Os would be so happy knowing I was building confidence with Diana and a lot of trust for what he wanted. We needed to have all that from her.

Sometimes her friend would tag along, which was fine. She spoke good English, and she helped me translate what I was trying to say to Diana. We would go to local restaurants or go around to

Parque Lleras, a small area in Medellin where there were a lot of restaurants all over the place. It was also known as a place where the prepagos were. There were two translations for that word—women who used you for money and things, or as some say, prostitutes. It was a populated area where there was much loud music all around, but in the places to eat, the food was real good. It was a nice place to hang out and have a few drinks also.

But I could see the women looking at me almost like the way vampires would look at a person for dinner. But for me, they looked at me for money and things. And let me tell you, the girls were beautiful, like Barbies. They didn't care if you were with other women or not. They checked you out and wondered if the girls you were with were competition. I was told the music there did not stop until 4:00 a.m. It was not a place for me, I thought, but when I thought it was going to be a quiet night, the girls decided to go to a club in an area called Las Palmas, another barrio in Medellin. This was a club, and in a couple of minutes, I was there. As we entered, I thought that this wasn't a place for me. The first thing that entered my head was that I was the first gringo ever to be in this club. As we sat, a bottle of vodka was put in the middle of the table, and then we had to pay for the setups, so here it came, the one thing that would give me heartburn—orange juice.

So the glasses came, and the vodka was just poured over and over into the glass. I had, and at one point, it was straight vodka, so as the night went on, so did I. I got up and danced and took both girls up, and we began to dance to all types of music. The more I drank, the more I moved around, dancing with several girls on the floor. The band played different types of songs. It seemed then that the girls were getting more and more nervous about me. I could see it, so finally, we sat down and stayed calm. But the place was packed. The bottle of vodka was almost empty, but I still felt good. We left the place and went to a restaurant next to it with a super view of the valley. With all the lights on in the valley, it was a beautiful sight, almost like Christmas lights all over for miles away, and looking down toward it was even more breathtaking.

Even at the time we were there, the place had a good amount of people in it, and the food was superb. It seemed that all we did was drink, eat, and made love—not a bad life. But it always didn't work that way. The hours the people had to work in Colombia were long, and the pay was small, so there was always the pain of reality for them. But for a minute and a day, it was an escape. I felt good that I could help them with that. Diana's friend said something to me that caught me by surprise. She said they had a friend from the West Coast of the USA who would visit. He had a girl here whom he was in love with, and he visited her often.

I thought, *Wow, cool!*

They also said he was a gringo but spoke good Spanish. They thought he was in Medellin now. Then my brain started working, and I thought that I didn't need another person asking questions I may not be able to answer if he were to stumble across something.

So I said, "Good, maybe we can meet."

But something worse happened. A couple of days later, I believe it was on a Wednesday, a guy walked into the disco club we were just in and opened fire with an automatic weapon, killing fourteen people.

I just thought, *What was I doing? It could have been me that was killed.* So many negative things born from fear ran through my head. Yes, my brain-dead self.

It wasn't a couple of days later when my phone rang. The voice said, "Hi, I am Howard. How are you? Are you Jerry?"

I said, "Yes. Howard? How are you?"

Howard was Diana's friend from the USA West Coast, the guy who had a girlfriend in Medellin. So now the conversation started.

"How did you meet Diana?" he asked.

"Through a friend," I said.

So as the conversation went on, I found out he had his own business. He was a tax man accountant who had his own firm and had several people working for him, he told me. We spoke about how hot Diana was, and we also spoke about her friend and other people Diana knew in Medellin, basically all the people she knew and how he hung out with them many times and how he lived in Medellin for over a year and learned to speak Spanish fluently. I just listened most of the time, and the conversation switched to his Colombian girlfriend.

Hearing his words, I could tell he was super in love with this girl but was having a hard time with her. He didn't feel that she loved him. He would buy her stuff and take care of her family, but still she was sort of cold toward him. After more and more of hearing that over and over again, I realized he was like a stalker. He was always checking up on her. If she didn't come to the phone, he would ask her mother or sister where she was.

What a nut, I thought. But then I thought, *Play it cool. Humor him. He could be useful—a smart guy who's with a girl who doesn't love him and a relationship that's going nowhere.*

I finally asked him, "Did you ask her if she loves you?" He said he did. "Then what?" I said.

"She said she doesn't know yet."

I said, "Hey, Howard, find a new girl." He was convinced she was cheating. I said, "Why be with her?"

And the old words came out. "Because I love her!"

"Not good," I said. Howard agreed. I told him I was going to be there soon and hoped we could get together. He agreed and gave me his phone number. Then we hung up. Now I knew someone who really knew Diana's friends and possibly many other people, which was very good for me. Now I could speed up the process, all the things Os wanted.

On my next trip, I met Howard. He was a small guy, not particularly good-looking, a bit out of shape. First thing that popped into my head was that his girlfriend was with another guy. I always turned the conversation around, trying to find out about Diana's friends and what she was doing. He told me more he didn't like some of her friends, but he liked her main friend, the one that hung out with us. She told me privately that Howard was a fool. He was a bit of a nice guy but a *bobo* for staying with that girl. I just nodded my head. Then Howard called her Alice.

I said, "So that is your name, Alice?"

She said she always went by a nickname. "But that is the name my mother gave me."

I said, "Really? From *Alice in Wonderland*?"

She laughed and said, "Yeah, that's it."

But I found out so much more from Howard. I found out that when I went back to the hotel, Diana never went home. She went out to party with different friends. He went on to tell me that she would smoke pot and drink wind with a couple of friends. There was a guy I didn't know who would pick her up.

Howard went on to say, "Yeah, he is bisexual, and they would hang out."

I said, "Really? She could have fooled me."

The plot thickened. Howard had a motor mouth. He said it was harmless; it wasn't like she was cheating. I said nothing. I just listened, hoping he would talk more. Then he went into her body.

"Yeah, she also goes for hot towel treatments to get rid of the fat she has on her stomach."

I said, "What is that?"

He explained how it was done.

"Wow," I said. "Many should get it done."

He told me, "Don't tell her. I like her as a friend. She really is a good person."

I said, "Don't worry, but thanks for telling me. That was super nice of you. And I won't tell her."

Os would often tell me not to fall in love with these girls. "Think of this as a novella [soap opera]. These girls are not worth your life. They are only looking for things and money and sometimes visas. You are with them for a purpose, so enjoy the sex with them and get the info and think of yourself."

I often thought about what he said, but it was not easy. Diana was sweet and beautiful and would be easy to be in love with, and it was so hard to make a relationship as a business without her knowing. But again, maybe Os was right. She was doing the same and after getting set up for this by Yuliana, his daughter, I could see his point. But now I knew after months of being with her and building a relationship that the time was coming close.

Howard was still calling me and wanting to hang out, and many times, Alice would join us. So what did the three of us talk about without Diana there? Her! Diana was always good gossip for me. I would follow up with silly questions, but when I spoke about Diana's life when I was not around, Alice became really quiet. Alice was smart, and she was a step ahead of me, but she had no clue what I was really after. She thought I was very much in love with Diana and was a bit jealous. How did I know those things? Howard was the best at giving up info. He told me what the girls really thought of me.

The negative about hearing from Howard was his never-ending sobbing about his girlfriend over and over again as he told me about her and how much he loved her. He would ask if I thought she loved him. I would respond, "I don't know her. She seems very private and secretive, and that's not what you like. Maybe she does not love you and feels like you are buying her affection because of all the things you buy for her and the money you give her. You are making her dependent on you, and that's not love!"

He would only then become quiet, but I'd told him the truth. I had to be careful. I did not want to ruin our relationship because he was a great fountain of information. I would give him tips on what he should do.

I said, "Leave her alone for a few days, and see what happens. Let her call you first."

I knew inside he couldn't do that. It would kill him. After all, he put so much into the relationship. It was coming down to Valentine's Day in Colombia. It was September there, so I sent flowers to where Diana worked. It was a perfect opening to get to know her boss. Francisco was a super nice guy, and our conversations were long, much about his family and Diana. He would always tell me how smart she was and that he was so happy to have her working in his office. Knowing him was a big plus for me. He was just another to put on the list of people who knew Diana. It would be important in the weeks and months to come.

So now I would speak with Francisco almost each week, and it was so easy. Every time I called to speak to Diana, he would get on the phone just to talk with me and tell me all about her and his family. He would tell me her sister was here today or her mother, but he would become a little quiet sometimes with me if I called around lunchtime, especially on Fridays. He would only say she went out with a friend for lunch. Now an alarm went off, so my next move was to see if I was right. I would have to go to where she worked and wait across the street and see who dropped her back. Francisco would drop hints to me and say she would be back in an hour, which I knew already, but I knew what he was trying to tell me.

So I left for her workplace, and I had to be slick, so there was no way she could see me. Across the street from her workplace was a store front store, and I was thinking of waiting inside the doorway. But then she often stopped in there to get gum. Another thing her boss would say to me a few times in the past. So now I was worried that I would miss her. I walked back down the block on a side street, and there she was, getting off a moto. I almost walked right into her. Wow, I was sweating, and I had seen the guy she was with.

She kissed him on the cheek and said, "Hasta manana [see you tomorrow]."

And tomorrow was Saturday, another party day for them. Now I knew she didn't want her boss to see her, so he dropped her off over a block away. And then she went to the store to buy gum, so putting two and two together, they weren't eating but smoking pot. This was what Howard told me. She was doing this all the time with him, the bisexual guy with the moto. But this guy was not the guy Os wanted. I thought he was way to low level, but he was the trail leading Os to the bigger fish.

I informed Os of what happened that day. He advised me not to go too far yet but that the time was close. Then he joked with me, telling me, "Hey, you guys look like the top of a wedding cake when get married to her." I just shook my head and laughed.

I would ask him time to time, "Is it your intention to hurt Diana?"

He would only say, "It depends on the information."

I could not forget at any time who were these guys I was dealing with, and I would think more of my life and less of anyone else's. There were times I thought long and hard about Diana. What was going to become of her? When I was with her, I felt happy, and I even thought of a future with her. But then again, I had to get my head back to reality. I had to fear what would happen to me if I screwed up and what would happen to Diana if I didn't.

So the plan was going into place. Howard was a part of it, a surprise part and a good surprise. He was a smart guy who was also a blabbermouth. He had a girlfriend who was keeping him guessing. It was the perfect situation to keep him talking, and the more he spoke, the more information came out. Now I was learning where all of them hung out and where Diana was meeting the bisexual guy. Even photos were showed to me by Howard, so then I could give this information back to Os. I would respond to Howard by saying, "Wow, I love that photo. Could you give me a copy?" And smiling and proud, Howard would oblige.

One day, Howard gave me some super info. It was about the clinic Diana was going to. She had stomach issues, apparently, which I did remember. But this time, she was going to a clinic (which were really hospitals), so again I said to Howard that I didn't know and I asked him to show me where. Of course, he did so. I would never forget how curious he was about why I was taking photos of the streets and the clinic itself. I had to be careful 'cause I never wanted to have him catch on. Then I heard something from Howard that I didn't expect. Diana was having stomach problems from nerves, and she went and smoked pot to relieve the pain. Then he added that she thought I was putting pressure on her in the relationship. Before I said anything, I thought that if she thought me being around was pressure, she was really going to be sick when the shit hit the fan. But I thought the pressure she was feeling was the sneaking around, and I was right. Howard told me she was worried I was such a straight and conservative guy, that I would be angry if I ever found out what she did at night, and she also told Howard to please not tell me anything.

Now I went back to Os with some of the info he wanted. He was super happy with it, especially the hospital.

I thought, *Wow! Why that?*

Then he said, "The puzzle is starting to come together."

I was clueless at that time and thought long about it that night. But step by step, it was coming together, and Diana was giving the information and still didn't know a thing. Now that I was given the info by Howard about Diana saying she was being nervous, I could approach her in a much different way. But I had to be careful. She knew Howard and I were speaking, so if I screwed up, she would know he said something to me. I was real careful about my words.

I said, "I know you spend a lot of time with me when I am here, but if you would like to spend more time with your friends, I could go back to the hotel early and enjoy the pool." She smiled and kissed me and said I was such a good guy. Then I said, "I just don't want to pressure you at all." Again, another kiss.

I knew Diana was smart. I bit my lip many times, and I had to think carefully. This had been going on for months, and I was not complaining. She was beautiful, and the sex was very good. Her company was good also, but I thought one night that this was not much about the other people but more about Diana. Then I was spinning my wheels and overthinking this.

The next day was interesting. Diana spoke about her stomach to me. I was scared to death that she was pregnant, but that was not the case. She told me she had a very nervous stomach and that she had been to the doctor's several times for that.

Then I asked her, "Did the doctor help you? Is he any good?"

She said, "Yes, medicine helped."

I responded, "Great. What does he do with you?" I mean, this is where you go for woman's issues also, right?

She looked at me and laughed. "You are so cute, but yes, there are many doctors there."

I stopped asking questions. I was going so far, and I thought again, *Don't push it. Don't push it!*

But I knew this was some more info for Os. That night, Os said that the time was coming, the right time. Hearing the way he said that, I knew and felt that someone's life was coming to an end.

The next conversation with Os was a big one. He started to tell me what was going to happen and that he was sure that Diana was going to get the info he wanted, but first, he went over to the table and handed me a photo of a girl.

He then said, "Hey, look, she has fake tits and big. You will like that one."

I just looked at him and said, "What is this?"

Then he said, "She works for the government." As I was just going to ask which government, he cut me off and said, "The Colombian government."

"What is her name?" I asked.

"Andrea," he said. He showed me a few other photos of her. She had skinny legs, a pretty face, and super large breasts. Then he explained, "She goes around to real bad barrio in Medellin and checks the young and old women's breast milk."

I just laughed and said, "For what?"

"Drugs," he said. "They get money from the government for certain things, and if they check positive for drugs, they take the things away."

I said, "What about their kids? Do they take them away?"

"I don't know," he replied. But then he went back to Diana. "Tomorrow is the big day, and we have it all planned out. This is what has happened and what is going to happen, so pay attention." Afterward, he told me what was going to happen. I nearly got sick. But then he handed me a folder full of papers and then explained to me what was in it. I could not believe all that had been done and that this was his plan. I thought this is not a great plan, but then he went into detail of what was done and how it was going to work, it was my turn to really listen. So I knew my job, and then I knew what I was going to say.

I said, "Let me ask her nicely."

But he said, "No, we cannot afford for her to tell anyone."

So we had all of this planned, and the girls were already paid to do their jobs. They only had to know who and where we had to have this confirmed.

I said, "What? What girls?"

"You will soon find out, my friend," he replied.

I could only think of the times Diana and I had together, and though I kept my real feelings to myself, I still had strong feelings for her. After all, we had something, but as I went back and forth, I remembered I shouldn't ever get serious with these women. It was one thing to put that into your mind and another thing to follow the unwritten rule. I had to think and remember what to say. And I had to get to bed. I had a long day ahead of me tomorrow.

I met Diana on Wednesday at 6:00 p.m. We went out to eat after she finished work. She said she had a few things to do, so she had to make it an early night. but I had a sense it might be the last night we had together, so we walked to a park near San Jose church and sat. She asked me several times what was in the folder with me. I had such a tight grip on it that my hand was numb. I was a bit worried, even scared, but a few feet from us was Juan Jose and his buddies just sitting there, watching us. I knew that it was part of the plan.

As I sat next to this beautiful woman, I said, "A guy I work for wants information from you."

She just looked at me with a shocked look on her face. "What info?" she said.

"I am going to explain. You know, your friend you hang out with, the bisexual guy you go out and smoke pot with after you leave me?"

She tried to say, "What? Are you jealous?"

It's an old game women always play, I thought.

I said, "I am not that. We know he is dealing drugs, but we don't care about him. We want to know where he is getting them from—the name and location."

She became very upset and said, "I don't know anything, and I don't want to say anything." She started to cry, but I thought she was really going to cry in a few minutes. Then I handed her the papers. It was a nice stack of papers. She looked through them in total shock.

"What is this?" she screamed over and over again.

I said, "Read them."

"I did! This is a lie!"

"Well, you signed them."

She was shaking her head back and forth, side to side. "No way, this is not me."

"Look," I said, "if you do not give me the info, these papers will go to your family, friends, relatives, and your workplace. And no matter where you go, they will follow."

Her tears started to flow, and I mean really flow. "How could you do this to me?"

I then said, "I am sorry, but you know your Colombian brothers. That's the only thing that came to my mind that I could say. She started to get up. Then I told her, "Look at that car." I pointed. She looked, and Juan Jose gave her a little wave. He had a big smile on his face. I told her, "These guy do not play games, so it is best to get and give the info that they want." I informed her she would be watched. "So please do it."

The next two nights were bad. Finally, she went out with the bisexual guy, a real close friend of hers. I really didn't know what she did with him, but she finally came back with the info all written down. I asked her if she was sure. She didn't look at me but told me yes. I said it would take a couple of days to find out if she was lying. A few days passed, and then everything came down. I was told what had happened. They got the bisexual guy, and parts of him were put all over Colombia. And the big-time drug dealer was shot in the head and killed. What Os did was get several women on motos with pistols and paid them fifty dollars each. Women were the best killers, he told me. Now I was worried and scared. But what was on the papers? Os had connections all over Colombia, and he knew lawyers and politicians, so he paid a lawyer, I believe, two hundred dollars to go to a clinic, the one that Diana was using. And he paid a hospital administrator to forge her papers that said Diana was HIV positive, with Diana's forged signature on them.

A few days later, Diana was, let's say, shipped to Panama alive, and she started a new job there. Several years later, I tried to get in touch with her and was disconnected. I couldn't blame her. But I had a connection in Panama. Her name was Maria, who kept an eye on her for me.

I had several conversations with Os about the welfare of Diana, and he said she would find her way and build a new good life.

"You didn't fall for her, did you?"

I told him the truth. "No, I did not."

So the topic moved on to Andrea—the milkmaid, as Os called her. He explained to me ad nauseam on what to expect and what I was to look for. He informed me I was going to be in a place that hadn't seen a gringo like me. I laughed but was scared.

"What is the name of the barrio?"

He said, "San Javier." He followed up by saying, "They rob the paint off cars in that area, and guess what. You are meeting her tonight. A friend of Juan Jose will bring you guys together."

After seeing several photos of Andrea, I thought that she was pretty, very pretty, but not super beautiful. So I left in the early evening to go to Parque Lleras, one of my least favorite places. The evening came, and I took a taxi there. Of course, I was early very early and walked around for a while. *Annoying* was not the word I thought but *crazy*. Several prepagos approached me; they were all super beautiful and all totally plastic. They had obviously had implants, lipo, butt injections. They had perfect bodies, but that was the norm there. I went to the restaurant Andrea and I were to meet, and sitting there were four girl friends, I assumed.

So I started a conversation with them, and they laughed as they knew how bad my Spanish was. I was still thirty minutes early, so all four girls and I chatted. The four had above-average looks. A couple of them were sort of cute but had good bodies. As they were ready to leave, one gave me her info, her phone number, and email. She told me her name was Louisa. I told her how nice it was to meet her while the other three looked on with smiles on their faces. So I took her info and put it in my back pocket.

As they walked away, there came Andrea walking very fast with a purpose toward me.

She said, "You are early."

"Yes, I am always early, and so are you," I said, "about ten minutes."

Both of us smiled. We sat and ordered food and had a good time. She was telling me about her job and how important it was to check the breast milk for drugs. It was so difficult to hear her story because I already knew it. So I had to stay quiet and not say a word. I could tell she was bright and would pick up on anything.

I joked, "How do you check their milk? Do you squeeze their breasts and put it in a bottle?"

She laughed. "No, not really. We use a pump and test it right there, but I do not tell them what I find 'cause that could cause a problem."

I said, "Violence?"

She replied, "Yes, very much so."

I was looking toward her chest when she was telling me, and she noticed. "Yes, they are new, only a year old."

I was embarrassed, but I laughed and said, "They look beautiful."

And just I was thinking that this was a super nice girl, she said, "Wait till you see them naturally."

Then I said, "Well, I hope soon."

Her face was nice, but she had some acne marks on her cheeks. She had a small butt and skinny legs, like I'd seen in the photos. But she was definitely great to go to bed with. We would go out to eat many times, and in that time, she was scared she would lose her job because of possible government cuts to programs. I felt so bad for her. She was a nice girl. I bought her a nice watch. She really loved it, and that night, we went back to the hotel and had sex. It was okay, but she hated it from behind. Maybe it's because she was insecure about her skinny butt. I didn't care about her thoughts. I just enjoyed the moment. I found many Colombianas worried about something on their body.

We actually started to be friends. Andrea was bright and very nice to talk to. The sex was okay but not great. It was what it was, I thought after a while. But I had some things to do, and it was to go with her on her work trips. I didn't have to ask. She invited me, but first, we had to go to her apartment. She told me she lived with a guy.

I said, "What?"

"Don't worry. He is gay."

I almost said, "Another one!" But I caught myself.

So the next place we would go to was Aranquez, another barrio in Medellin, another poor, bad place. As we went on the elevator to go to her apartment, she was telling me that her parents were in Bogota. They lived there.

"So you pay for this apartment?"

"No, they do. The guy I live with is my best friend. He works and is hardly home."

"Great," I replied.

Then she opened the apartment, and the place smelled bad and was a mess. I just ignored it, and I used the bathroom. I could see she was not a maid for sure, and the guy was a pig. I found the mess a big turnoff, but she told me the next day that I was going with her to check several women.

I thought, *Finally, now I can see where this leads me to.*

I never really liked Andrea. She was annoying to me. She acted as if she was so smart and knew everything, but I dealt with it. I knew there was a bigger plan than to worry about her. She was also difficult to sleep with. She was very demanding on how she liked certain things with sex. In the end, I did what I wanted with her anyway. I didn't want to treat her like a whore or anything like that, but it was tempting to do so. She constantly worried about the little bit of acne on her face. She would spend hours in the mirror just getting her makeup just right. Man, did I hate that!

I was thinking, *Can we get on to the next woman already?*

But I would now be accompanying her to do her work. She dressed and acted like a doctor, but she was far from that. I played along. The place we were headed to was San Javier, just as I was told. I knew already that this was a bad place, but again, I had to go along with Andrea. She told me every place was okay, not too bad. We took a car there. It was only like a twenty-minute ride, but with the traffic in Medellin, it took more than that. As we drove through, I could see this was a really bad area—very poor. Then we stopped. Of course, I paid the driver. We went to what I would call an alleyway with really decrepit houses on each side. Kids were all over the place, and there were many babies. We arrived to what Andrea would call an apartment. As we entered, I was looked at like someone from Mars. Not too many had seen a gringo in this area, but I was playing it cool and quiet. I only nodded when Andrea said anything to me and said yes or no.

The first apartment was terrible, maybe the worst place I had ever seen. My stomach jumped into my throat. I was starting to feel sick. The smell of shit and urine was overwhelming, and there were kids with black dirty diapers, many with no clothes. Many of the kids would shit and piss in the alleyways along the street and run around with nothing on their bottoms, only a dirty shirt on top. Then Andrea would talk to the so-called mother and ask her if she had taken any drugs or smoked anything. She had a complete list of questions. Then to get their things from the government, Andrea would use a pump and a cup to test their breast milk. I left the room when that was taking place. I was already nauseous.

She was about to go to the next woman when little kids came in with babies. By my estimate, these kids were about eleven or twelve, all girls, of course. They were carrying babies. I thought they were sisters or cousins. Then I saw something that completely shocked me. Andrea went toward those little kids to test them. I then spoke aloud.

"What is going on here?" I asked Andrea.

She replied, "Those are their babies."

I asked, "How old are those girls?"

I was told something that made my nausea come all the way up. "Yes, the babies are theirs, and they are eleven."

I left and ran out the door and to the street. I actually sat on the curb and had some of the nausea come to reality, throwing up right there. I was sick and angry. I sat there for about an hour and then made myself go back into the alleyway. I saw Andrea. She looked at me and saw the shape I was in.

Before she could say another word, I said, "Who did it to them?"

She said, "I check them, but the government does not know about them and doesn't care anyway. And the question you wanted an answer to... They were raped many times by their cousins. You see, Gerard, they all sleep in the same bed—old, young, babies. It doesn't matter. Think about it. They only have two rooms, and all those people live there."

I could see now how Andrea was a sort of cold person and lived the way she did. Seeing those things every day would make a person block out everything and make you like a zombie. I thought back to what Juan Jose and Os told me about that barrio. Now I knew why he wanted to know where the drugs were coming from. In other words, who was the seller and who was the producer. This time around. I really wanted to do this. And how would I explain this to Andrea and what do I hold over her head? This was going to be real difficult.

Louisa was an interesting woman. I met her while walking through Parque Lleras, a place in the Poblado area that had many outside restaurants and many prepagos. Despite all that, it did have several good places to eat in my journeys. There I met a woman named Louisa. She was better-looking than the average Colombian woman, had a nice personality, and was very friendly. This was completely out of the blue. I could say she was not on Os's list. We hit it off so much that we had lunch together. She told me she was meeting a few of her amigas there for lunch, but they were late, so we sat and ate. Louisa told me she worked in the area for a construction company and had a son and lived with her mother. Of course, she supported them both. It was a relief from Andrea, who was really a pretty-faced big-tits bitch, but Andrea was my work, as Os would have said it. But Louisa and I hit it off, and we planned to see each other again. So we kissed each other on the cheek, and that was it for that day. I had plans to meet up with Andrea that night.

That night, Andrea came to the hotel, and we did what we usually did. We had sex with her. It was almost as if it really was work. She was not really sexy, but as I said, her face was nice. She had large breast implants but a flat ass and thin legs, so her body was weird-looking. Most of all, she, for some reason, hated to have sex from behind, which I really liked. But I could not push things. I didn't want to get her real angry, so I did what she liked. I could not lose her. She really liked flowers, so I gave her flowers almost every week. But the one thing she was into was watches. She told me how the big-face watches were the ones she loved. But I had to remember what I was going to hold over her head to get her to do what Os needed. The information he wanted was about the dealers who were supplying the woman in San Javier with the drugs. I always played it close, and I really wanted to get rid of Andrea as fast as I could and move on to the next job. As I said, patience is not my strong point. So now Andrea told me she had a few more trips to San Javier to complete that area, so this Thursday, we would go again. I found it amusing that she asked me how I felt after seeing what I did 'cause this woman seemed never to care about anything in my life or person. I smiled and said I was happy and that those things surprised me and that, to be honest, it made me sick, as she'd seen. Andrea maybe became immune to all this, and maybe that was what made her so cold as a person. Again, I could not worry about her psychological makeup. I had to focus all the time.

The next day, I received a call from Louisa. I didn't even think. I gave her my info, but it was cool. She wanted to meet again, so we made plans to go to eat the next day. But there was a problem meeting with Andrea, so I had to plan this carefully and watch for two people, Andrea and Os, whom I know would find out. But I was lucky, and I mean real lucky. Andrea got sick maybe from food poising the next day and could not go to work, so we had to delay our meeting, which was great for me. Now I would have little stress and meet with Louisa.

We met for dinner that night and went to a restaurant that had great steaks, and we both ate too much. She had wine, but I could tell that she was not a drinker. Soon after dinner, we took a taxi to Parque Llaras and started to talk about being together on only the second meeting, but in reality, I just wanted sex. I asked her almost right away if she wanted to go to a hotel and make love. Almost immediately, she said yes. Wow, did I think I was the stud! My ego went through the ceiling. There was a hotel right near us, and we walked over to it. As we entered the so-called front desk, there was a tree stump. Seriously, there were maybe two together. It was varnished with a clear stain, and two guys and a girl stood behind it. I asked for a room for the night and gave the guy my credit card and my driver's license. After running my card, he said it didn't work. I had a bad feeling about this place anyway. I thought to myself that this was a shady place, so what was going on?

Then he said to me, "We are sold out anyway."

I said, "What? Is it my card or what?"

Then the guy got wise with me and told me, "Keep it down, stupid guy." Now this lobby was right in the middle of their restaurant and bar.

I said, "You want to repeat what you said?"

And he made a big mistake. He repeated it with two stupid guys added. That was it. I lost it and hit him with a hard right hand to his forehead super hard. I thought I killed him. He hit the wall behind him super hard, and I felt no pain.

I told all of them, "Go fuck yourselves." Then we walked out.

Louisa was in shock, and so were the people all around us. As we left, we both jumped into a taxi and took off to another hotel. The next hotel was only a few blocks away, so we went there. It was amusing that my credit card worked fine there, so we got a room for the night, but it really wasn't for the whole night 'cause she had to go home to her son and work the next day.

As soon as we entered the room, she was ready. She took off all her clothes. She had a nice body and was in good shape, no fat at all. She pulled my pants down, and wow, this girl was in heat! She did everything super hard. When she got on top, she was like a jack-hammer. Everything was with great passion, not really with heartfelt feelings but great. She also told me she loved it in the culo and that, next time, she wanted it there. I said I had to take photos of what we were doing, and I did. She didn't notice. She was so into the sex. To be honest, she bruised me right on the bone above my penis. I could have handled her better. I was so surprised by her super aggressiveness. Then she jumped into the shower and came out and said she had to go. I was almost speechless. We kissed. She opened the door and then asked me for money for the taxi. I gave it to her and told her to call me. She nodded and kissed me and then left. I still think I didn't blink that night.

Many of my meetings with Andrea were important for getting a little information. I knew again that the time was coming to get the info Os wanted, and I knew Juan Jose was keeping an eye on me. Everything that was done was a delicate matter, so any interference by anyone would scare the victims, and they would not give any info. It seemed all these people trusted women way more than the hombres. You never know what is going to happen in life, and I was really worried about me and how this one would turn out. Now I had been in this area a while back, and I was worried about being spotted. Or maybe I was just being paranoid. So many things were going through my head again and again, so I often turned to Louisa to make me forget. We would frequent the local hotels, and my stomach muscles were more sore than ever. She was the human pogo stick. I guessed if it was on film, it would be the closest thing to a porn film you could get—no respect, just plain old hard sex. And the harder, the more she loved it. In a way, I was lucky Andrea was not so into sex as Louisa. When Andrea and I were having sex, it was like a vacation, and that was what she liked—very calm, normal sex.

The next day, I had a visitor. Juan Jose met me in an outside restaurant with two of his guys standing on the corner. I always looked for those guys first just to see how they played the game. I was always joking with them in a good way. I never wanted to get on the wrong side of them. God knew what would happen if they took something the wrong way. I would hear over and over again that any teenager would kill anyone for you if you paid them fifty dollars. The hit men charged four hundred. That was one thing I would hear for years, and I guessed the price never changed. Juan wanted to know how things were. He always had a twisted, dirty mind.

"How does she fuck?" he asked as usual.

This time, I was honest, and I told him, "She sucks at sex."

Then to my surprise, he said, "What about the other one?"

By then, I knew I could never fool these guys at all. I said, "Oh, you seen her?"

"Yes, we see it all, my friend."

Then I said, "She is crazy in bed. Super! Does everything and is like a jackhammer." I explained to him what that was. Juan Jose was a pervert and loved to hear these things.

With a smile on his face, he told me, "Be careful with these women, my friend. They steal your heart and then your money."

I then laughed and said, "You're right. You are always right."

He said, "Soon we need the info. We have many other jobs and many in other areas of Colombia."

My eyes became really big, and I said, "Where?"

I got the usual answer: "We will tell you soon, my friend, and where we will send you to has many hotter women and hotter places." He laughed again. He put some money on the table and left. Gone in a second.

That night, I met with Andrea and asked her, "When are we going back? I wish to help those people there."

She thought that was very nice. "But with what?"

"Maybe ice cream?"

"No," she said. "We can bring then candy."

So we went to the local supermarket and bought a lot of candy to give out the next day. I thought this was a good idea. They would trust us more. When she had to get the information, it would be easier to obtain. The next day came, and again I felt uneasy. I really couldn't handle seeing these kids with babies, so I completely closed my mind. As we walked into the alley, I saw a few hombres I hadn't seen before. They were real lowlifes. I right away concluded that they were the dealers, but again, these were the small-time guys. But now they'd seen me, and that was a bad thing not only for the plan but also for my life. Andrea told me that no matter what, I shouldn't speak. I should keep my sunglasses on and say nothing. If someone said a word, I should just nod my head, so I did.

One woman said a few things to me. I had seen before, but I just nodded and looked away. The hombres were gone. They turned the corner and took off. I put a picture in my head of them so I wouldn't forget them. Then like it was automatic, the women and the girls started to take their breasts out of their blouses to give the milk for a test, but Andrea interrupted them in such a polite way. She was so good with them. She informed them that this was a different visit. Then she opened the big bags we had and started to give out the candies. I also helped with it. It was like the walls opened. So many came in. The candy was gone in seconds. For such poor, needy people, they were so thankful. I had tears in my eyes, and again, I had to leave. I often thought of when I was small. We were poor, but we were nothing like this. My heart was breaking. I felt I could never do enough. But then again, I had to get this done. I had to talk with Andrea and get the info from them so the real business could take place. The next time we would go for the breast milk test was the end of next week. Maybe that would be a good time, I hope.

The week went fast, and us being together at the hotel was really getting strained. The sex was very straight and normal and almost routine and not much fun. I might as well had a blow-up doll. At least some conversation came from the final week, which she didn't know. Andrea opened up a little about how she was almost married to a German guy and that it ended the last minute. I just listened because I thought Germans were cold people with no feelings, and though Andrea and a German guy would be a perfect couple, she was one of the few Colombian woman that was not sensual. She said he got cold feet and left. I felt kind of bad for her. She had a kind way about her, especially with the poor moms and the kids, but she was not into sex that much. Only for duty. I was wondering where Louisa was at this time. I didn't think of who or what she was. I just thought of the passionate sex with her, how into it she was, and how she turned me on.

As my mind swung in different directions, I knew I would have to explain things to Andrea. After the first experience, I thought, *Would she be surprised? Would she believe me? Or would she just laugh?*

I wanted to go back home soon. I had so many things to do and my real job also. I happened to call Louisa and got her where she worked. Louisa told me many things and all as I thought, but I must not forget these women would tell you enough for you to trust them but would never tell you everything. She agreed to meet but sounded cold. Everything she said was quick and not even a hola. The day passed. Then I had to sit and talk with Andrea on what the plan was and who I was. It was tough because I didn't know who I was. We went out to a very bland dinner. She liked no spice at all on her food and always worried about her complexion. I always followed suit. I just wanted this to end and as soon as possible. Now Andrea started to tell me about her family. She was really for Bogota, which was the capital, and she had moved to Medellin because of work. I listened but with only one ear. I really didn't care at this point, but I was glad she was talking because I felt that it gave me an opening to tell her what I had to say.

I started with "I have to tell you something," which was a good opening line. Then I said, "I work for some bad boys that need and want info from you, and there are things that you are going to have to get." Andrea just stared at me. I said, "No games. And what I am going to tell you is God's honest truth. These guys want to know about the hombres that are dealing drugs to the kids and the women in San Javier, where you go to test the breast milk. They want all the info."

Andrea was smart and didn't ask any more questions. She sort of knew what she had to do and knew in her mind whom I was

223

connected to. But she said, "Only if I get a big-faced watch and one that costs more than five hundred dollars, and then I want money to travel back to Bogota and get my contract renewed for work."

Wow, I thought, *a lot to get done in a short period.* The contract she was talking about was a work contract. See, in Colombia, they worked on three-year contracts, so it was easy to get rid of workers and hire others for less money and for a minimum wage. It was like two hundred dollars a month, and it was possible that she made four hundred a month. So now I had to explain this to Os and hope they wouldn't go after her and threaten her. I knew these guys were dead serious, but I had to tell them what she wanted.

The next day came, so first, I saw Juan Jose and told him. Then he and Os together, I told them of her demands. They said, "No problem. Tell her she will go back to Bogota and get her new contract. And she also will get her watch and traveling money." I thought I knew they had connections, but now I know they were connected with the government there. It took only one phone call, and everything was covered. Os told me she would be very well taken care of. "Now, Señor Gerard, get the info."

I went back and told Andrea everything was covered. Now she wanted to wait a week to see. I butted in and said, "These are not guys to push."

Soon, that evening, a guy showed up at her apartment with flowers. It was a fake delivery service. As he went up to her apartment, she received a super beautiful big-faced watch and a renewed contract with her job. Also, there was some traveling money, and the guy left her another message: "If you screw this up or lie or play games, many more people will suffer." This was a warning that her family would be hurt.

Then next day, she showed up at the hotel, looking like she hadn't slept in months.

I looked at her and said, "You came here to sleep?" I laughed a little.

Her head was down, and she told me, "I can do my best, but I don't know if they will tell me."

I said, "You are going to have to be yourself. They love you, those people. They depend on you, and look, do better than your best, and all will be okay."

She looked into my face and said, "Who are you, and why are you doing this?"

I told her, "It's all for the betterment of your country."

As she entered, I removed her clothes, and for the last time, we had sex. And believe it or not, it was better than normal. After she showered, she asked me if I was coming.

I said, "Not this time. It is all on you." I knew this was not going to be easy for her. Every time she felt pressure, she would get loud, and she did. I said, "I will be here. I need names, areas, and photos if possible—and also how many big guys and little guys there are."

She said she would need a few days. I informed Os of what she said, and he didn't say much. I guessed he knew.

I said one last thing to her, "He has people all over, so be careful and tell the truth."

Two days went by, even a third, and Andrea returned. I could not believe what she had—names, maps, areas, and even a couple of addresses. She knew a few of the women there who were sleeping with these guys, and using some of her money, she paid off the women and warned them that she would turn them in to the government and they would lose their benefits. She had everything. I knew what a bitch Andrea could be, and she really turned it on. I told her I would get her money back.

I soon met with Os. I had never seen him so happy. He gave me the money plus more to give to Andrea.

He said, "Make sure she stays here another week."

I said, "Okay, I will."

Moves were being made. Again, the girls on the motos were at it again. Altogether there were four girls. Six drug dealers were dead. The girls would wait to ride up to and next to the drug dealers, the big-time guys and the little guys, and that would be the end of them. These girls were quick and smart and were dressed to kill. Many would drive up to outside restaurants and shoot these guys always right in the heads. Os would pay them fifty dollars a head, and that was what they did—right in the heads. When I saw Os, he would have a smile on his face, but his eyes had a blank stare.

He then told me, "Tell the girl she can leave now. And remember, let her know the risk of telling anyone."

Soon, I saw Andrea. We kissed, and she left. I would never see her again. But I didn't care. I was headed home for a while. The next one came into my life.

I really started to respect the Colombians. The more I got to know them, the more I liked them. They were very hard-working, but the hombres, they were another story. They seemed to be serial impregnators. There were so many young girls around with babies and not only from one guy but from a couple of different men. In my travels, there were two women with five kids each from five different guys, so then you had ten kids and ten so-called fathers. So troubling. The guys would skip out on support, and if the woman filed papers to get child support, the guys wouldn't work. But many of the women were *lolitas*, meaning "promiscuous," as I found out. Hey, I was using them also, but at least they received things in return. But if you thought for a second that these women were dumb, think again. They weren't.

I finally made my way back home. I landed in Newark, New Jersey, and had over an hour's drive to my house. As I was driving, I received a call. I saw the exchange, so I answered it.

It was a guy on the other end, and the first thing he said was "Do you know Louisa Lopez?"

I said, "Yeah, and who is this?"

Then he said, "How do you know her?"

I said, "Who is this?"

And he told me his name was John.

I said, "How did you get my number?" It went on so fast. There were many questions with no structure, rapid fire. Then I stopped. "What is this about?"

He repeated, "How do you know her?"

Then I said, "Who are you to her?"

He then told me he was her fiancé.

I asked, "How did you get my number?"

He then seemed to calm down a bit. Now we could have a conversation. He then told me he had tapped her phone and her laptop and knew whom she was talking to.

I just said, "Wow! What is the issue?"

"Well," he said, "I called several different people and they just laughed at me and hung up when I asked questions." Then he informed me that he worked for the government here in the United States.

I said, "Okay, so what is the problem?"

"Again, how do you know her?"

"Well, the truth is, I do some things in Colombia. I met her, and we have sex many times." Before I could complete my thought, he asked me for proof. I said, "You have my info and our conversations? What does that tell you?"

He became quiet. Again he asked me for proof, so I felt bad for the guy. I could see he was in love with her, but he never knew her or was just in denial. I always kept things to show what I did with all the women, so Louisa wasn't any different, even though she was not involved with bad things—well, not drug dealers anyway. I told him the truth and also told her she went with other guys and also on trips to Panama, all over. Then I gave in, which was taboo. I sent him photos of us having sex. It was not smart. He then forwarded them to her, and then all hell broke loose. I was called every name in the book by Louisa. It was crazy, not the thing I wanted to get involved in. It was a killer.

This guy was far too trusting of those women. I received a couple of phone calls from him later, and he would cry on the phone and tell me how in love he was with her.

I told him, "You're nuts to even think of her. She's nothing more than a puta (whore), and you still love her? Wow!"

This would go on for quite a while until finally, he sent me pictures of a new girl he was dating in Colombia. Man, this guy went to the well too often. She was super cute, the new one, and she had black hair in the photos, but I knew her face. I couldn't remember where. Maybe it was in a photo on Os's table. I was straining my mind to remember. Seeing the photos he showed me, I could see he was not a good-looking guy, but he bragged about being able to sleep with women there by giving them gifts. Time would go by, and I would see how he made out with the new girl. I would still see Louisa when I returned to Colombia, but she was not the same, so I cooled it and went on for what Os wanted me there for.

He reminded me, "No distractions, and stop with these new putas you found."

I listened, and we were ready to go to the table and see who the new one was. Such a choice. I picked a beautiful girl, but she was from Cartagena and had teeth braces. But she was so pretty, and her name was Maria. All of a sudden, I was thinking of the song from *West Side Story*. I started singing it in my head. Os just looked at me with a look he often had for me, the same as the nuns had: "Hey, be serious!" I didn't remember to see if she was John's new girlfriend, but who cared at this point?

Maria was fine, and I couldn't wait. But how was Cartagena?

I asked Os, and he said, "You will find out. Besides being hot, it's crowded and has a lot of foreigners. It's a big tourist trap. Do your homework, and I will tell you more about Maria and the Italians who go there tomorrow."

My trip to Cartagena was cool but not the weather. It was super hot for me. The thing I liked was really the historic giant wall around the city and the many beautiful old churches. I was to meet Maria close to a hotel in town. I had a picture of her in my mind. She was easy to remember because she was so beautiful and had braces on her teeth. I was told the meeting was set up by Yuli, who knew a friend of Maria. I didn't know if Maria spoke any English because my Spanish was so bad and I wanted to impress her right away. I made it so I was in front of the hotel a bit early; let's say thirty minutes. I was always early all the time, and usually the Colombian women were an hour late, so that was always an issue—the stress of waiting.

But this time, I was in shock. There she was, getting out of the taxi across the street. Wow, she was special. Her hair was super long, and her body was toned. Seeing her face, I could see she was very young. She hadn't seen me yet. I was off to the side, but as she crossed the street, I moved in front of the hotel, where she could see me. She looked at me and stared.

Then I walked toward her. "Hola!" I said. "Encantada." (Nice to meet you.) I continued, "I am Jerry or Gerard—whatever you prefer."

She looked right into my eyes and said, "Muy bien, I am Maria."

I was stunned. She was super sweet, and I almost lost my train of thought. What was I going to say next? So young and beautiful was all that was on my mind in that moment. But she had no problem entering the hotel and asking what room we were in.

I told her, "404."

She said, "Okay, I have to get to the front desk." She went over and gave them her ID card, and they registered her. We were on our way upstairs, and I finally kissed her on the cheek. Then she made me laugh. She said, "About time. I was waiting for that." She told me she loved my eyes. "So blue," she said. Her English was not that good but passable for me. I had a king-sized bed in the room and a view of the ocean.

So beautiful, I thought.

She then spoke about her friend who told her of me.

I said, "Are you pleased?"

She laughed and said, "So far!" She called me Gerard, which I liked.

I thought, *Cool, she remembered.*

I asked her if she was hungry, and she said, "Sure." So we went to eat. We had fun, laughed, joked. I asked her if she was staying with me in the hotel, and she said, "Not tonight." She had school and work tomorrow. "But I will stay on the weekend." She told me she wanted me to meet her friends tomorrow.

Wow, I thought, *so soon.*

She was so sweet and nice, but in reality, I had work to do. I was here to find out the info, to have as much sex with Maria as I could, and to meet her friends to get all the information I needed.

The next day couldn't come fast enough. I wanted to be with her so badly. I had to meet her in a restaurant. She said her friends worked there, and I did dinnertime. This was a big place in an area that was a distance from the great wall. As I walked in, I saw Maria in a white top and a very sexy red skirt just flowing, and then were several other women but older. It was hard to say, but maybe they were in the thirty-five to forty-five age group. Really, they were a group of very attractive women. This place had a few stages around for preforming, and they also had the same clothes on as Maria did. There was a long staircase with a red carpet in the center, and between them were the stages and a balcony around the top. I was early. Only they were there. Maria called me over and introduced me to all of them—maybe eight or more. They were very, very sexy women, and there was only one young one besides Maria.

I looked at Maria and said, "You work here? Seriously, what do you do?"

She said, "I perform."

I said, "Perform what?"

She laughed, "We sing and dance and maybe take some clothes off. I need the money to pay for school and my grandmother."

Boy, did I feel bad! But did I really? I knew what some women did for things and money here, so why think differently? Now I knew why she had no problem coming right to my room. Now they had to practice, and I was here to watch. They all bounced down the stairs and sang and acted sexy with all their moves. Then they went off to the different stages, three to each stage, and danced and removed some of their clothes little by little. Some of their lingerie was shown. It was very sexy, and Maria was by far the most beautiful girl there. She came over after the practice and hugged me and kissed me. Then we left, heading back to the hotel.

This was the start. I knew where this was going, but for now, I kept my mouth shut. The next morning, I met Maria at the hotel, and then she came to my bed. She jumped into the shower, told me to wait. She then came out in nothing but a towel.

She is so beautiful, I thought.

She came across as innocent, especially with the braces on her teeth, and I also had to remember she was super young. She just started university and just turned nineteen. Soon she jumped into bed and was instantly passionate. It sure wasn't her first time.

I thought, *Maybe not the first time today.*

But she did everything without me asking or even wanting. I was almost stunned. She really enjoyed everything. My ego would not permit me to think that it was because of me. I would have to be a fool to believe that after knowing her for only a couple of days, but Maria really enjoyed it. And by the way, so did I. She would not let me finish. She told me to wait, so this went on for almost two hours. I was even sore, but I had to keep up.

Then I thought, *Is this how it's going to be every time? I have to get into better shape.*

And even with braces, she was still great with her mouth. Then I finally finished with her permission. I was spent, and she was never more beautiful. I lay there and just stared at her. She was so tan and perfect. Her hair after all of that was long and straight, and her face was like that of an angel. I always put into my mind a wall to block from falling in love with anyone. As difficult as it was, Maria was going to be tough not to fall in love with, and I used the age gap to help block it from my thoughts.

As the days passed, my stomach muscles were pretty sore, but I never complained. I knew the next step would come soon. I had a feeling Juan Jose was around. I could almost smell him. He would always want to check out the girls and make perverted remarks. He would get off on that. But he knew his job and wanted to make sure I was doing what I had to. Each day, I met Maria's coworkers and got to know them a little more each time. Some were so hot and sexy and seemed to put it out there. Let's say they were super flirty to be polite.

As I started to leave, I thought, "If she is going on that big boat with them, they will each take a turn fucking her, along with her friends. And if she refuses, she will be food for the fish. We know they are bad guys, but we need our excuse to end them. I don't care about the girls. All I care about is what you can get for me. So if you want your girlfriend to come back with a normal-sized pussy, do something about it."

I was thinking out loud and said, "What can I hold over her head to get the info?"

Juan Jose looked at me as he walked out and said, "Her job and her university. Remember, she is an okay girl but not a super nice one. Now get the info."

I was thinking how I could get the information and keep Maria safe. I really didn't want her to go on that boat with those lowlives, but it was all about the money with them. If they were going to make money with those animals, I couldn't match it. Now there was another issue. Os knew I could deep-sea dive, and I had done it several times. The call I just received from him brought that up. You see, he never wanted to bring any of the guys to justice. It was all about killing them.

But for many reasons, he wanted proof of their wrongdoings, and that was my justification for his actions. So now I had to think up a plan. Many things ran through my head. Maybe I could pay off Maria to get the info, and maybe I could use her grandmother as a tool to get the info. Almost all the time, Os had me thinking up the plan to get the info, and if I even asked him for help, he would tell me, "What do I need you for?" Talking to him was a waste of time.

That morning, Maria and I met again, and it was sex first. It was almost like she was taking all my energy and thought patterns after hours with her in bed. My head was spinning to be nineteen again, but I also enjoyed sex as much as she did. I didn't want it to end. Then again, I knew it was going to sooner or later, and I wanted it later. I figured I could get another few days out of this until the boat ride. But sometimes I could not keep things in, so I told myself I would tell her the next day or the day after that. That night, I met with Juan Jose. I told him my plan or what I thought was my plan.

He said, "Tell her you would have her grandmother killed."

I looked down toward the ground and said, "I thought of that and a couple of other things."

He said, "If she does not do it, we will kill her grandmother."

I knew that was coming next. He looked at me and said, "You're not in love with this girl, are you?"

I said, "No, but she is a nice kid." I started to smile. "She is so good in bed. Anyone could love her."

He turned to me and said, "Tell her to go on the boat, suck a guy or two, and get the info."

These guys used women to kill the drug dealers and had no good opinion of women. The women were useful idiots for them.

I asked him, "Are the girls here?"

He said, "They are all over for us, in every area, and the ones here are very cute."

I said, "The moto girls?"

He told me, "Yes, that's what I said."

The next morning, Maria was at the hotel bright and early, and it was the same crazy sex even before I could eat or get into the shower. So after we took our shower together, I touched her body as if I was kissing her goodbye. I looked at her beautiful color and admired it so. It was perfect, as were her legs and her hair. She then washed my body in a way that her long nails would not scrape me, and she went under my balls and into the crack of my ass. She was so gentle, so nice.

I looked at her and said, "Why haven't you ever let me into the shower with you before?" She looked at me. "This is a special day."

I quickly said, "What day?"

She said, "We've been together for six months."

I said, "Really? Are you sure?"

She just looked at me with those eyes and that face. I had to fight back the tears of joy I felt of her remembering that. To think she was nineteen and so beautiful and the perfect girl, and with every second that went by, I had to fight from being in love with her. I made every excuse in my mind to block that out, but this shower experience was difficult.

We then got dressed and went downstairs to eat. I told her I would get her a special gift later. She just laughed. She was so cute when she laughed. We then walked to the center. It was a big area in the middle of the historic district. There were many tables, so we sat there for a while. And we walked to a church. We walked into the back of the church and sat in almost the same pew as Juan Jose and I sat. I told her I had some things to say. I guessed she thought I was going to tell her how I loved her and all that. But it was not going to be. I told her I worked for these guys and that they were serious hombres and that they knew something about the Italian guys that wanted to take her and her friends out on their boat. She was calm, not in a panic, and seemed not to be surprised.

She looked into my face and said, "You are looking to see if they have drugs?"

I was shocked. "Yes," I replied.

"And you want me to find out?"

I said, "Yes."

"What are you going to do if I say no?"

I took a deep breath and said, "They will kill your grandmother. I know that for sure."

Maria was calm. She said, "Then I have to go on the boat."

I looked at the floor. "I was hoping not, but that is up to you."

She said, "Well, if I don't go, my abuela dies. If I do go, I will have to have sex with those guys."

I informed her that the guys meant business and that they were no joke. "But know that if you go on the boat, it will be an orgy."

At that minute, a hombre walked over to the pew and said to Maria, "Hola carino, I am a friend of Mr. Jerry, and I want you to know I have many friends here. You can see some of them by that door."

And over there standing were three more of Juan Jose's men. He then left, and the look on Maria's face changed. She looked a bit worried. We then got up, and we kissed. She told me she would see me tomorrow with the plan.

Wow, I thought, *tomorrow would come real fast.*

"Are you meeting me at the hotel?"

She then smiled. "Yes, amor, same as usual."

It was the first time she called me amor. Tomorrow could not come fast enough.

"Maria the most beautiful sound I've ever heard"—yes, those were words from such a beautiful song, and they rang through my head all night. But that was not what I woke up to and not the alarm. It was a call from Os. He had several questions.

"You dive, correct?"

I said, "Yes, but I am not an expert diver. I can maybe go up to fifty feet, depends on the pressure and the pain I feel in my ears."

He said, "If they go out on the boat tonight, I want you to blow it up!"

I said, "What?" He told me he could get me a timer and plastic explosive he called C4. I said, "Are you okay? And kill all the people there—the women and all? I thought you needed proof of the drugs?" He then told me he was certain. "Then what do you need me for then? Wait, I have a plan." I also told him, "I am not going to blow up the boat. Plus, I am not that good of a diver." I told him I would get back to him.

That night, I spoke to Maria and asked her to give me her opinion. She told me, "The Italian hombres will demand sex. I can say to them that I am a virgin and maybe get away with it because I am only nineteen. I could get away with giving a couple of them oral or use my hand on them, but the other girls are going to have full sex for a lot of money."

I told her, "They will make an orgy and pay you guys nothing. You will only get raped. Do you know the time? It has to be the exact time they are arriving on the boat. You know, they will sleep on the boat."

She said, "Okay."

"Can you get the women to get them to have breakfast in the restaurant? That way, you can get them off the boat and have to walk back to the boat."

"I see where you are going with this." She then told me she would tell the ladies to demand breakfast before they go and for the men to meet them at the restaurant. She then looked at me. "There are nine ladies and me."

"Once you put the plan together, let me know ASAP."

She then went to try to put the plan together. Then I received a call from Maria. It was lunch. After a late lunch, she told me the time.

She said, "One of the ladies is already having sex with one of the guys, and she said to me that they have a lot of drugs and want to sell more cocaine. But they are moving it out of Colombia to Europe."

"How in the world did she find that out?"

"Well, she was also doing coke with him, and that guy talks a lot."

I asked her to wait a minute, that I would call her right back. I called Os and gave him the info. The plan was going to change because I gave him my plan and the info I had.

When I called Maria back, I told her, "When you and the ladies walk out of the restaurant, make sure you guys walk ahead of the Italians, at least ten feet. You have to tell that to the ladies. Make it like a sexy thing, a tease thing."

Maria picked up on it right away.

I asked her then, "Does this bother you at all?"

She said, "Well, if it was a Colombian hombre maybe, yes, but I don't like Europeans, anyway. And they are selling drugs, so I don't care. Don't worry. Just give me a time."

I said, "It's 4:00 p.m."

She said, "We will walk them out toward the dock area."

"Okay, off the highway, near the big wall, the side way." I then informed Os, and he loved it. He said he would send six girls on motos. I warned Maria to get out of the area as soon as they see the motos.

So nine guys came out at just about 4:00 p.m. behind the ladies. It worked so perfectly. They ran across the highway as the guys trailed them. Then it was the end. The girls didn't miss, and all their shots were to the head areas. It took less than twenty seconds, and all nine were dead. People ran from all over, and the girls on motos took off in different directions. In a blink, they were gone as always, almost like phantoms, and it cost Os about one hundred fifty dollars. I stayed away for days as the police were all over the place, but they didn't care about me. It would go away in a week or two. Maria knew it was time for me to leave and go back home. We said adios on the phone a week later. I said I would be back in a year or two in her area.

She giggled a bit and said, "Mucho besos." Divine.

"I will look for you."

I traveled to Medellin as usual, and the first person I went to see was Os. We had a long talk about the areas I would be traveling to in the future, and he also informed me that a hombre in the Colombian government would be watching and helping. I thought to myself how many people he had in on this, and these were very important people. The way they spoke about the so-called drug lords and the other lowlife dealers, he saw them as objects, not people. And he had a way of using it as revenge. I was yet to know the real reasons why he was doing this.

Now it was time to look at the table and see what women he had planned for me. This time, he chose one for me—a very pretty blonde. She was local in this area. Then he gave me the total info. She was a martial arts expert and was in exceptional condition. She also has a trainer personal, and he was the guy we knew was moving stuff. But we wanted his jefe, the main guy. I looked hard at her photo again and again. I felt that I knew her, but I could not place her. I was sure I had seen her before. I was straining my brain to remember, but I could not remember.

I knew I had to be in shape to be with this woman, so I had to hit the gym and work hard. Again, it was Yuliana who would tell her about me and give her all the details like the fact that I was a gringo, had blue eyes, and was tall—all the things the Colombianas loved. So the meeting was set up for a Friday afternoon. I was dieting the rest of the week and running, doing anything to get in the best shape I could get in a short period of time. One of the things I liked was her name—Sara. It was easy to remember, and I loved it. Friday came quickly, and I was a bit ready. We met at a restaurant that specialized in arepas with anything you wanted on them.

Cool, I thought.

When I arrived, she was already there. I could see she was in super shape, had implants, and had hard-looking culo. Another wow. I could imagine how she was going to kill me in bed, but for now, I had to romance this woman and start the process. It was not difficult. We hit it off right away. Why? Because I could see she was a prepago, a woman looking for things and money. She had a big-face watch that was worth maybe close to a thousand dollars, and her clothes were designers. We spoke about her love for the gym and martial arts and showed me a few videos of her working out and participating in some matches. I could see she was super strong and fast, but I was looking at her face all the time to the point that she wondered if there was something wrong with her.

I said, "You are so pretty."

She smiled, but I still could not place her. Sara then asked me to go with her to a big health show with her tomorrow, which was Saturday. It was at the large arena in Medellin.

I said, "Sure, I would love to go."

The next day, we met at about 11:00 a.m. and took a taxi to the arena. A lot of people were entering, and she had the tickets. There were so many booths with the normal healthy foods and workout videos. Then we passed one booth, and there was her trainer. He ran over and kissed her, and then what was so annoying was that he joined us. It was a good thing in a way. He wasn't a big guy but was in good shape, and every chance he got, he showed the things he could do, like jumping onto two box stands and leaping over things. He was like a little kid showing off. The one thing I could see in his face was jealousy, and when he looked at Sara, he looked like he was dying to fuck her. Hey, who wouldn't? But he was very obvious about it. I thought they might have something, but now I could see they didn't. The shows they had there were cool, and we spent about four hours there. It was cool. It was not my thing, but it was okay. As we were leaving, this guy walked us to the door. I thought he was going to invite himself, but I just gave him the look—the look to get lost. He gave me a smile, like, "Fuck you." I laughed, and then Sara and I got into a taxi. We went to a restaurant in Parque Llaras. We were really hitting it off.

But her phone was busy. Most of the calls she didn't answer. She informed me she had a couple of kids but they were in their teens. "Oh, nice," I said. I asked her about her trainer, but I had to be careful not to seem jealous or suspicious. It was a fine line I had to walk.

I just started with "How long have you had a personal trainer, and what are your goals?"

She said, "Well, I have some matches that I enjoy, but mostly, it's to keep myself in good condition because the gym alone is so boring." She informed me that she'd been training for three years and had the trainer for about a year. When she introduced him to me, she hardly said his name. I could not make out what she said.

So I said, "I didn't quite get what his name is."

She said, "It's Estaban."

"Ohh," I said. "Okay. Cool. A very popular name in Colombia."

She smiled and said, "Si!"

I could see she liked me and that we might be sharing my hotel room very soon, but that night, I wasn't feeling well. I thought I was coming down with something, maybe the flu or a cold. The next day, Sara showed up at the hotel. I had to meet her in the lobby to check her in because there they had to give their identification to join a person in a room. As we went on to the elevator, we kissed, so I knew sex was next. But I wasn't feeling so cool. As we entered the room, she removed her clothes. She had on beautiful red underwear. Her body was looked so strong. And what great tits! Even in my condition, I could not turn that down. But it was a mistake. As we entered the bed, she got on top of me. My god, was this woman strong! She pinned me, and as we started and I penetrated her, she held my arms and pounded me like Louisa—but ten times the power. As she had me pinned, she screamed at me to move more. I was not feeling good and tried to push her off and did. Then I started on her from behind.

She was even pounding me that way. I could see I had to stop. I was going to pass out.

Finally, I had to tell her I was sick, that I had the *gripe* (flu), and then she got mad, thinking she was going to get it now. But it was her who had it and gave it to me. She told me she'd been feeling ill the past few days. I was so pissed off. I remembered her coughing and sneezing a few times when we were first eating. We got up and went to the drugstore and bought all types of medicine. There you could buy amoxicillin over the counter and so many other things. Believe it or not, the next day, I was feeling better, but she was worse. And she was in bed with me, taking all the medicine. I couldn't wait to have my second chance with her when I felt better. For now, I had to give her what she needed and take my time getting the info. I knew something was coming, and what she needed didn't take long, She wanted money and another watch, a special one.

Then after that, I asked her if she knew many gringos. She then told me a story I would never forget. She said she was engaged to a gringo and was ready to marry him, but at the last minute, he backed out.

I said, "Wow, so sorry. What was his reason?"

"He went back to his old girlfriend."

"That was so bad of him," I responded.

She said, "Yes, it was terrible."

I wanted to know more. She went on to tell me what state he was from and some details about him. Then she showed me some photos of them together, and OMG!

I said to myself, *That's him, the guy who was with Louisa!*

I had to put two and two together. And I knew I should be careful in handling this. I went into deep thought. She had black hair and looked different, and now there I was, having sex with both of his ex-girlfriends. I was in shock. But it was also amusing.

Now I was thinking, *Does Os know of this? Did he set me up?* There were many things to figure out.

As I sat in the hotel, pondering all this, it was kind of a turn-on. I also was wondering why he turned down this girl and went back with Louisa. Later, I found out that he was going to marry Louisa and she used him again—this time, to get her papers. Then it soon turned into divorce very quickly. Well, be that as it may, I didn't really care. He was a pure idiot and had been forewarned.

I really was enjoying my time with Sara. She was hot and a sort of interesting. I liked the martial art stuff, and seeing her work out was a turn-on. But her jealous drug-dealing trainer was a problem because I really didn't like him and wanted to end him in a hurry. But first, I had to find out the person who was providing him with the product. After a while, I was able to keep up with Sara in bed. It wasn't easy, but it became more enjoyable when I was able to have some control. I started to see where this relationship was going.

After a while, Sara really wanted to get married, and this was what she wanted. I found out she had a couple of brothers and a sister living in the United States. I guessed she had a plan in her head to get married to be able to be close to them. Sara wanted a big-face watch. She also liked so many, so I asked her which one and said that I was there to buy the one she wanted. So we went back to her apartment and went to her bedroom, where she had a large closet, which was unusual for an apartment in Colombia. When she opened it, I saw that she must have had one pair of jeans, so many blouses, jackets, and a large box with compartments for watches. These were hers and was a typical collection for a woman who was a prepago.

I just laughed and said, "Wow, so many nice things."

Sara sort of knew I was aware of the things some women did for things and money. The thing I really liked about her was that she had no tattoos. I never was into that. But a thing I noticed was that the trainer kept in touch with her all the time, and it was to the point that I had to say something about it.

"Do you know this guy is hot for you?" I said.

She told me, "Many guys are, but I don't want any of them. They can do nothing for me."

I kept quiet and left it at that. After all, she was right, and I didn't want her to think that I was jealous and leave me.

A few days passed, and I had many questions I wanted to ask Sara. I could see we were getting very close, and she was thinking we would take this relationship to the next level. But I always had a trump card. I could throw the relationship she had with John into her face. I could twist that around to make it look like it was her fault, and then I could get out of this. But it was soon time for me to get the information. Os was always pressuring me, but his reason was a good one. He had so many to get to and wanted me to try to get the info as fast as I could. Inside I knew his intentions were sincere, but I knew that if I rushed this, I could blow it. One thing, though, was that I could not handle pressure. I had to do it at my speed. Plus, I knew the lowlife Juan Jose was going to show up any minute to survey the situation and take a closer look at Sara. I used to think he would jerk off in the car with his cohorts while watching some of the girls I was with. And I got the wish I didn't want.

The next day, he showed up, and of course, he made a comment: "Did you come in her face? She has a nice culo."

It was a typical comment from him, but I did respond, "I did those things weeks ago. She loves it all over her, like body cream." Anything to bother him.

Again, I could only go so far because I always needed his protection in case anything went wrong. He and his guys were needed. He wished to have a meeting, so I had to meet him in a church, and of course, we did. I told him what I knew so far and what my plan was.

Then he blessed himself and said to me, "Hey! Don't let that pussy make you crazy, brother."

I always laughed when he said those stupid things, but maybe he had a point. Maybe someday it would really happen. But I thought again if I didn't fall in love with Maria, why would I fall into that trap with any woman? And I sure was not in love with Sara. As with many, it was lust but not love.

I finally had some time for myself away from Os and Sara and others. I wanted to go out to eat alone to think of so many things on my mind. I usually didn't sit at an outside table, but it was a nice afternoon, and I felt like having a burger. Two tables away from me were a few young ladies, so I guessed being alone for a few minutes didn't last. I started to talk with them, and my attention was drawn to a rather good-looking one with a super large chest and a slim waist and a pretty face. I had that feeling that I would be able to get to know her, so I made a move. I started to talk with her. Her name was Laura, she said, and they were having a long lunch to celebrate her coworker's birthday.

"So nice," I said. "Super!"

As the conversation went on, she started to speak with me in English. I thought, *Wow!* But then she said it was because my Spanish was fatal. Oh! But I asked her many questions, such as her type of work. She was a chemist and was super educated and still going to school. I could tell she was bright.

Then the questions came my way, and of course, the first one was "What are you doing here? On a vacation?"

"Well," I said, "something like that."

I assumed she was thinking I was here to pick up women or that I had a girlfriend here in Medellin. I mixed the truth with some untruths. I was interested in her, and I wanted to be able to see her again. A few minutes after that, they were leaving, so I went over and asked for her phone number. She had a cell but gave me her home number. She said her mother would answer but that I should ask for her.

"Make sure you say Laura clearly."

I said, "Of course. I will call you very soon."

She laughed and left.

I called two days later, and we went out. It was super nice. One thing was that she was nineteen, so I asked her how she was a chemist at nineteen? She told me the whole story. She said she was super bright, and they picked her out of the university. Now they are paying for her schooling while she worked for them but had to sign a long contract so they could keep her after she left school. So now I knew her whole story. Not much time after that, I met her family. They were nice people, and her father was gone a long time ago. He left home as the men did very often in Colombia. Then we would go onto the hotel tour. She did everything in bed like she'd been doing this for ten years already, and she did all really super. We were good together and seeing she was bright and very pretty, I was thinking of our future! But in Colombia, you had to be very careful of that, and I was right. She had been with men since she was fifteen and had learned a lot. Most of all, she knew how to lie and use. We were like counter punchers in a ring. Everything we had in common was perfect, and the sex was great, but at home, she used a vibrator and could only get an organism with that. She enjoyed sex but got used to a machine.

But that was not all. She also thought of us as a couple only when it was convenient for her, such as asking for money and things. Otherwise, she was having sex with half of Medellin, and to think this was a brilliant woman. I would confront her about her behavior, but we were addicted to each other. We loved to travel together. She even obtained a visa and was in the United States with me for vacations. But it became a habit for her to cheat, and I was no angel either. I had many women during our time together. We started together when Laura was nineteen, and it ended when she became thirty. It seemed to be in the end—just two people in need of each other in their times of want. Everything was good—the sex, the company, the things in common. But respect was missing.

And during those years, I had so many things on my plate with Os and all the other women, sometimes three a day in three different hotels, including Laura. In the end, I couldn't blame her or myself. Sara was a job for me, and I knew she wanted more or just to try to use me for a visa, but I had a job to do. Soon I would have to complete this one, and not liking her trainer, I was going to really like this one. I was happy to see Sara again. She just came from a workout and showed me the video. She was super. I mean she was so tough and quick. She wanted to talk with me and told me she wanted to get a visa and stay with me in my home.

I was stunned and caught by surprise, and I thought immediately of John and what happened and then thought of her relatives living in the USA. I was sure she just wanted to be with them, and it didn't matter which guy was helping her. She had an agenda, but so did I. And it was to get the lead from her on her friend and the guys who were dealing. I laughed off what she was telling me.

I said, "Well, maybe you can try to get a visa."

But what she really wanted was to get married and have her meal ticket. Would she be the ideal woman to marry? Nah, I didn't think so. Plus, I liked her but again wasn't in love with her. I enjoyed the sex with her, and she was pretty and was good company. But I had to remember that this was a job, and I had to watch what I was doing. I sort of flirted with her, seeming to agree with her, only because I had to start the conversation to get the info I needed. I also knew this would cost me big in material things and cash. Her watch box and clothes were going to get much larger. It started as we sat in the hotel room. I wanted a place where I could keep her contained so she couldn't get up and take off if she didn't like what I had to say. I started with her idiot trainer. I was very blunt.

"You know he is dealing drugs," I said.

Sara just looked at me with a stare and not a happy one. "How do you know this?"

I said, "Do you know this?" She knew I could feel it. So I said, "This is not the time to play games. This is serious." I went on to tell her about the guy I worked for and what he wanted and that if she didn't come up with certain info, things would be bad.

She didn't seem to be scared or worried. She replied, "What do I do? This is really going to cost you."

I guessed right. She was perfect—a perfect prepago. Now I was going to have her remember her list. But before I could get that, I told her to get the info from the trainer about who his supplier was.

She then told me something I never thought she would say, "Do I have to fuck him to get the info? Or suck his cock?"

Wow! I was completely caught by surprise. My mouth was wide open, and my eyes became big.

I said, "I hope not!"

"How do you know I am not fucking him now?" She raised her voice.

I said, "You have too much class for that, and I know you better."

She calmed down when I said that. Then she shouted, "What is the plan! Tell me because this is going to cost you and I have a list!"

I thought to myself, *She thought of that fast.*

Then she surprised me again. She said, "If we are going to have sex, let's do it now. It's going to be our last time, so enjoy it."

She was so permissive. She let me do it anyway. I wanted to do it with her, and she gave in and didn't dominate at all! I thought she was testing me, showing me what I would be missing. A couple of hours passed, and she left.

She told me, "We will meet tomorrow and talk more."

I went to see Os and told him she was agreeing and that she was very pissed off and was going to have a list of demands.

He looked at me and said, "Okay. Did you fuck her for the last time?"

I was caught off guard. That was something Juan Jose would say, not him. But he did, and I didn't question him. He was the card dealer, and I didn't think the cost would matter to him. He told me after this that I would be headed to a farm, a finca, to see someone and that I would have to take a bus.

I looked at him and said, "Okay, we can talk later. I have to get the list from Sara."

Os actually laughed, and that was nice to see and hear from him no matter what the situation.

The next day came quick, and Sara and I met not in the hotel—this time, at the park, like old times for me. Of course, Juan Jose and his crew were watching from his car. Sara had a sheet of paper with her demands. The first one was that her rent should be paid for a year. The second was pay for her travels and for money, visa, and a third credit card with one thousand dollars on it.

I said, "That's a lot to ask, Sara, and I am telling you, those guys in the car aren't going to go for all this." I pointed toward the car, and with that, Juan Jose smiled and puckered his lips to blow her a kiss, a real low-life thing to do. She didn't flinch, not a bit. Then Juan Jose left the car, which bothered me, but he always had to get a word in. He sat next to her and took the list.

He said, "This is a bunch of shit."

Then he went to put his arm on her, and that was a mistake. She took it and almost broke it off in a blink of an eye. He was super pissed. I had to step between them, and I thought she would have kicked his ass. But then he would have shot her on the spot. After twenty minutes, I calmed things down, and we negotiated. She got her visa money and some cash and a watch, which she didn't ask for. But no more. The funny thing about all this was that I thought she had and knew all the info anyway but didn't really want her trainer harmed.

Juan Jose said, "That is part of the deal. You will find a new one no matter where you are, sexy." He always had to throw a comment in like sexy. Then he left.

I told her, "These guys would kill you in a second. They act like they have nothing to live for, so be careful. Don't play with them."

She told me she would get the info, all of it, along with addresses.

I said, "Don't sleep with him."

She turned and looked at me and said, "Don't tell me anything. We have nothing anymore."

I was just ready to go back and complete the mission with Sara when I received a message from Os. He wanted to see me ASAP. When I arrived at his house, he had a few photos he wanted me to see. This was unusual. He always wanted to complete the mission before moving on to another. He then showed me a couple of photos of her black eyes. I mean black pupils. They were so beautiful and so different, but the rest of her was special. I could see she was a bit short but had on high shoes and had the most beautiful smile, and her body was better than perfect. In the photo, she was in a bikini, and she had shoulder-length jet-black hair. It was as if she was molded to be perfect. She was my type for sure.

"Where is she?" I asked. I was thinking that she might be in Colombia.

He told me, "Miraflores Peru."

I just looked at Os with "What! Where!" going around in my head.

He told me he would explain later. "I want to finish with your friend Sara and her friends. Then we will talk more, okay?|

I said, "Sure, I am heading back there now, and I will have all the info, I am sure." Then I turned to Os. "Did you give her what she wants?"

"Most of it."

As I said before, I knew he knew everything. Then he said he would have liked to see her kick Juan Jose's *culo*. I laughed. He told me all would be completed tomorrow.

Tomorrow came, and I hadn't heard a thing—nothing from Sara, nothing from Os. I tried to contact Sara, but no answer. I didn't leave a message, but the next day was different. The girls on the motos received the business they wanted. I heard six of them were on the move and one of them told me that they got the trainer. His life ended, and the maid, the so-called drug lord, was removed and also part of his family also.

I said, "Part of his family?"

"Yes," she said. "They got in the way."

Now these girls never really said anything to me, but this one did. She was wearing a black *Mortal Kombat* mask. When she did, I could see she was very cute but very tough and a no-games girl.

I said, "Great." Then I walked away. I did turn back to see her take off. I loved the super-tight jeans with the black jacket.

Now I knew where I was going next, and this time, it was going to be very weird because I didn't know Peru and didn't know anyone there.

But I said to myself, *Let me hear the whole story.*

I gave Sara a lot of thought that night, and again I knew I might never see her again. But then I reflected on her and Louisa, thinking of sleeping with two women who had a relationship with John.

How odd is that? I thought. And how weird it was that for him and for the two women who hated each other. After all the women I was with, nothing surprised me anymore.

I was in my favorite hotel that night. The next morning, I was going out for a while when I saw in front of the hotel five guys—I mean big boys. Three of them were very large dudes, one was a medium-sized guy, and one was a smaller guy but also in good shape. All of them were well tattooed and looked like they were in the world's strongest men competition.

As I was leaving, I turned to them and asked them, "What are you doing here?"

I could see they were Russian, Eastern European, or something, and I knew they were not here for the food.

The look that I received from the main guy was like, "Who are you?"

Then I asked again, "What are you guys doing in Medellin?"

Juan, the bellman, was in shock and looked very worried. Then I finally got a reply.

"You're American?" the main guy said to me while the others stared at me.

I said, "Good guess!" Then I changed the question. I said, "Where are you guys from?"

The main guys turned to the others and then looked at me and said, "We are Eastern European. You look like Russians to me or something like that." The guy then smiled, and two of the guys went toward the elevator, which was five feet away from them.

Then I hit them with a curve. "Are you here for the girls?"

He looked at me with a stupid grin. "No, we have business here."

I knew they were up to no good, very likely moving products and making deals with drug lords. I then said, "Do you want a good place to get food?"

He looked at me and said, "Yes. Where?"

I told him, "The best place is Parque Lleras in Poblado. It's about ten minutes by taxi. The best time is about 10:00 p.m. The restaurants are mainly outside, and the food is good no matter when you go there."

He repeated the name to me, and his buddy wrote it down. Then Juan told him the same. I went up to my room and called. Os told him everything about these guys. He then told me they were Albanians, really bad guys who come here and make a lot of deals. So I informed Os the time and where I told them to go.

He said, "Well, they may not go there." But he told me he would send four girls, and he wanted me to meet them there and wanted them in front to point them out.

I told Os, "You have to be kidding. Those guys are easy to spot, and that place is crazy busy."

But he wanted to be sure and told me to lead the girls that night. The plan was for me to walk straight in with one girl behind me and the others coming down the side streets. This area had only a couple of streets crossing into the main areas, where the outside restaurant was, and there were plenty to choose from. I knew the spot I would start from, and these girts knew the plan well and were packed to the gills.

I started to walk with a purpose down the first main street toward the small park in the middle and had my head on a swivel. There was no sign of those guys. I went down other streets. No one. Then the final street, and I still saw no sign of them. I went back to the hotel with the girls not far behind. I saw Pedro, another bellman, and I asked him if he'd seen them. He told me they left in a private car, checked out, and left.

Wow, I thought, *Who knows where they went?*

But if they showed up where we went to, all of them would have met their maker. I called Os, and he already knew they left. He told me another time for them. For now, I was to get ready to go to Peru. Os then told me he had guys that would handle those Albanians.

Now on to Peru.

I had another meeting with Os, and we made more plans. Now I was really starting to feel like James Bond. The plan was Peru and Evelyn. Then when I came back Manizales, the next trip was to Valledupar, then onto another along the coast. I hadn't yet seen the other women, but now he turned more attention to my trip to Peru, where Os told me I would be in Miraflores and Cusco and Machu Picchu. I was excited about Machu Picchu and the history of the Incas, and before I went, I read four books on the Incas. Again, I had to remember this was not only a pleasure trip but a business trip.

The girl I was going to be with was super cute and perfect for me and also had black eyes, which I had never seen. I didn't ask much about going to the other places, but in the middle of my questions, Os told me the coast trip in Colombia was going to be the most difficult. I didn't ask why, and I figured that, in many ways, that would be my last job. Os soon gave me the ticket for Peru and told me that Evelyn would have a friend with her. Her name was Rosa.

"You don't want anything to do with her. She is ugly," he told me.

I just looked at him 'cause that was the first time I had ever heard him say something like that. Then he showed me a photo of Rosa, and I guessed he was right.

He told me, "Many beautiful women, as you know, have girl friends who are ugly.

I just laughed and said, "You're right."

He told me Juan Jose would be going down to Peru also but not traveling with me. I didn't like him, but I guessed I needed him.

Os also told me, "This is not only about drugs. When you get there, you will find out the info. Evelyn is the key. You will have to play the game with her. Peruvian women are different than Colombians. And you are super lucky 'cause this is a beautiful Peruvian woman. There aren't many of those."

A week later, I arrived at the Peru airport. My god, I couldn't believe it. There were thousands of people in a big hall, funneling into a couple of rows. What a mess! Evelyn and Rosa were to meet me at the airport, but I couldn't move. It was so tight. There were all sorts of people who came in at the same time from all over.

What a joke! I thought.

It took almost two hours to get through, and I couldn't contact Evelyn. There was no signal. It was terrible. As I pushed my way through customs, I saw them. Wow. I yelled out several times before they turned around and saw the gringo. They were waving at me to come over to them. I could see that Evelyn was beautiful and super cute, and her body was, let's say, wow. Rosa was okay. She was not really ugly. Then we met, and we kissed each other on the cheeks and laughed as I spoke in my terrible Spanish. They spoke very fast, and it wasn't the Spanish I was familiar with, so it was tough putting together what they were saying.

I was also warned about the kids at the airports. On the roads leaving the airport, they would throw garbage cans and other things in front of cars to make them stop them. Then they would rob the passengers. They even had a name. They were called piranhas. They were just little kids but were super dangerous. They fought in groups. I had many things to do. I had to change my money and get to know Evelyn so we can have a relationship and hopefully good sex and get the info I needed.

But I thought to myself, *This is going to take time.*

We sat together in the back seat of the taxi on my way to the hotel in Miraflores, which was in the capital, Lima. We joked, but most of the time, we didn't understand each other. When I spoke about the kids being piranhas, they laughed and said they were piranhas, which was funny. But I knew both of them worked in okay jobs, like secretaries, and weren't prepagos. My approach was going to be important, and I knew nothing of the area.

The next day, both girls were together again. We went to the casinos in the area and played the slots. I could see Evelyn was very aggressive with the one-armed bandits. Rosa left early and said she had to get up early, so that left us alone. We left about an hour later and walked back toward the hotel, and that meant cutting through the church square area, where a beautiful church. A large area in front of the church had many benches and many walkways. It was very pretty during the day, but at night, I was soon to be surprised. As I walked back down some very dark and long blocks, we approached the park area. Now this was about 1:30 a.m.

I turned to my side where Evelyn was and said, "We did okay. We won some change, and I have two pockets full of it."

She laughed and said, "But it's really nothing."

What a beautiful smile! She had everything just lit up. Her eyes just danced when she smiled. So we entered the park church area, and to my disbelief there, had to be a hundred small kids in the park, some with adults. I looked over at Evelyn's face, and she looked worried.

She told me, "Walk fast. Do not look at anyone."

We started to move fast. And then it happened. The kids started to follow us and ask us for money. I mean there were twenty-five or more.

Not good, I thought.

I told Evelyn to walk in front of me and move fast. As we were about to get surrounded, I took all the change out of my pockets and threw them up in the air about ten or more feet away. My god, the kids ran after it like pigeons to bread crumbs. It was so crazy. Then we took off, and just around the block was the hotel.

We got back. Evelyn had work the next day, so I called a taxi for her. We kissed once, and she left. I knew she might be more difficult to get into bed than the others, but I needed to get to that so I could start the process of what I was there for. But for the moment, I had to be smart and not push her.

I also wanted to keep in touch with Rosa. I knew she was very close with Evelyn and they shared most things. One thing I found interesting was that they followed a band in Lima. It was a popular band, and I'd seen a couple of photos of one of the members with Evelyn. I had to remember not to play that hand because the Latinas would think I was jealous, so I had to be careful not to start that nonsense. I had to plan a trip to Machu Picchu with Evelyn. I knew she wanted to go and live in Peru all her life, and not going there is not too good. But many could not afford it, so that was the main reason. It was an expensive trip, even from her area.

One reason I wanted to take her was for sex. I was crazy about her looks and sexy body and beautiful face. Her voice was high pitch, and she had a sort of fast way of speaking. It was a problem, but I knew I could get past that. One thing I had to get by was the guy from the band and her connection to him. I had the feeling that that was one of the guys that were moving products and getting it from. I didn't have any idea yet.

In a few weeks. I asked Evelyn about a trip to go there, and she smiled and said she wanted to go. So I jumped and said I would make the arrangements. She turned and looked at me and said she wanted separate rooms. My face went blank. I was so disappointed, and two things crossed my mind. She was using me to travel, and the guy from the band had something with her. But I also knew she was smart and maybe was just stringing me along.

I made a mistake of showing a friend a photo of her, which I hadn't done of any other woman, and when he saw her photos, he said, "She is really pretty. It's going to take several trips to get in her pants." I just laughed. He knew nothing of what I had been doing for years.

I informed Evelyn I would take her but preferred to have one room. She became quiet and went into deep thought. Then she said, "Well, okay, but two beds." And she wasn't smiling. This was not like any woman I had met in South America. Andrea had a problem with sex, but she gave it up right away. Now I could see a potential problem. I knew she would have many conversations with Rosa about this, and I hoped she would not ask me about Rosa coming.

Soon, all my answers came quick. I happened to be walking toward the center town in Miraflores, and I knew Evelyn was coming to the hotel very soon. I wanted to buy her flowers, and two blocks away, I just happened to be crossing the street and saw her in a car with the band member. So I stopped, went to the nearest doorway, and watched. As she left the car, she kissed him goodbye, but the kiss was on the mouth—not a long one, but still. So now things became more complicated. It would be more difficult to get info from her if I couldn't have something with her. I ran into a local store, grabbed some flowers, and was about two blocks behind her, walking toward the hotel. Even though she walked fast, I caught up with her in no time. I surprised her with the flowers. What a smile she gave me. She looked very happy. As we walked together, she told me she was excited about our trip. Then we entered the hotel and went to the room. Soon after that, we spoke about sex and a relationship. She felt it would be very fast to start something serious together, but as time went on, she might want that.

Wow, I thought. She was an expert. She knew how to play the game and maybe use me, but she didn't know the reason why I was there, and I didn't think she had any suspicions of that. One thing I had to put into my head was that she was very pretty and hot, and in Peru, many women weren't that. It was not Colombia. Soon, we were in Machu Picchu. It was incredible. We had a tour package included, which was cool 'cause going alone exposed you to some bad situations with bandits and so on. We had a three-day tour, and each day, it was something else. But on the second day, I gave her a super nice gift—a beautiful large-face silver watch. I mean it was nice, and she really loved it.

That night, we went to dinner in a nice restaurant for that area, and man, did she drink I was shocked how much vino she consumed! She was not drunk, but she was feeling it. When we went back to the room, we kissed passionately, and I removed her clothes. I had seen her in a two-piece bathing suit, but now I was seeing her naked. She was incredible for a tiny woman. She had a super beautiful body and a solid tan all the way down. She also had beautiful breasts and large, but her real face was so pretty. Her body was fit, and we really had a super night. She gave me oral but not so much, but she was good in bed. And when she was on top, she didn't only look at the ceiling. She looked into my eyes. How many men would fall in love with this woman at this moment? I would have if I wanted to ruin everything, but being with so many beautiful women almost made me indifferent to being in love with them. I almost felt like a performer, like a movie actor. I almost liked the feeling of men looking at them with crazy desire as it was what happened when it was like a job. Now I had to keep this going. Soon I would have to ask questions.

Evelyn and I were getting close. Even though I had a feeling she was with another guy—the guy from the group band I saw her in the car with—I kept my mouth shut. And it was good that I did because she invited me to where she worked, and maybe I could see the flowers I sent her right to her office. Now when I showed up, everyone there would see the gringo. Ha ha ha! Yes, me. I went, and it was about one in the afternoon, just before lunch for the people in the office. I had to pass security, but Evelyn came out to bring me in. I was in shock. She was really taking me seriously to show me her work and to meet her coworkers. But all this time, I didn't know Rosa also worked there. I just missed that. That was stupid. I should have known, but all the people in the office were super.

I received a tour from Evelyn and her *jefe* (boss), a guy about fifty, maybe younger. He was in good shape, had slicked-back hair. They were a distribution center for textiles and showed me how the plant worked, how they shipped, and the many places they shipped to. It was very nice of him to take the time. I was super surprised. He then told me Evelyn was a good person and a very good worker. Then he asked me about where I was from in the States and how I liked Peru. I lied and told him Peru was super. I really didn't think, but the history was really special. I told him that the food was good and so on. As I walked with him, a light bulb went off in my head. What if he was the bad guy who was smuggling products? He then invited me to lunch. It was like he didn't trust me and wanted to know me better. I got that feeling. He was suspicious.

The three of us went to a local restaurant. I remember I ate some spicy meat and some fish there. Her boss was called Diego. Diego started to dig deep, asking about my work and how long I was staying and what other countries had I been to. What normally sounded like okay questions weren't so okay to me. They sounded like a guy wanting info instead of simple polite conversation.

"What hotel are you staying in?" he asked.

"Not far from here," I said.

Evelyn looked up at me as if I was being rude, but then I told him, "Wow, I almost forgot the name."

They laughed. Now I started to feel worried. I felt he was on to me for a minute because I really was thinking that this guy had more than textiles. We started back, about a three-block walk, and like clockwork, as we were entering the office, out of the other door, a side door, about twenty feet from the main entrance, came the guy from the singing group—the guy that was in the car with Evelyn. What a perfect storm! Now all the pieces fell into place. This was the jackpot. All this went through my head. Now I had to call Os and fill him in on what I was thinking. I said goodbye to everyone in the office and her boss. Then I kissed Evelyn on the cheek and took a taxi back to the hotel. As I was leaving the taxi and walking into the hotel, I saw none other than Juan Jose. I knew he was here. It was just a matter of time before he showed up.

I told him I had interesting info to tell Os, so I shared it with him first. His eyes opened wide, and he was surprised I was able to get the info so quickly. But as I was waiting for some insight from him, he then became the same Juan Jose I had always known.

"How does she fuck?" he asked. Always the same stupid shit! "She is super lindo, beautiful face, good body. I love her color."

I turned and said, "She is great."

"Does she suck your cock?"

I knew that if I answered him, he would turn to that. I then informed Juan Jose about her boss and the guy who worked with her and what I saw in the car.

He told me, "She is also fucking that guy."

I said, "How do you know that?"

He just smiled and laughed. He said to me, "Why? Do you think these putas are angels?"

I said, "I don't, but if I think that way, I will screw myself up."

"You are always too sensitive," he said to me. Then he added, "You have a couple of big jobs coming up, and if you still are sensitive, you will fuck it up. So stop that bullshit."

I then called Os and told him what I had and told him Juan Jose was next to me.

He told me, "Work the girl and get the info."

I said, "What can I hold over her?"

Os then said, "It will play out. Her friend Rosa or the guy she likes, we will use them. Once she sees Juan Jose, she will know we mean business." I knew the family or the friends would be used. "You are in Peru because we know this is a big one. We cannot screw this up."

I told him I suspected Diego 'cause of his questioning and how he asked them.

He replied, "Of course. You are a gringo. They suspect a lot. That's what brings the *cucarachas* out. Now they will show their hand. We eventually will get one of the biggest dealers—not here, but the main guy back in Colombia—through this guy Diego."

Time was passing by very quickly, and I was pushing myself not to fall for this girl. The visions of her kissing a guy in the car that day had been in my mind, but I was going to block it out. It wasn't like we were having sex every time I saw her. It was on her terms. She had to be constantly romanced, and that was a real pain to me. I was used to getting it anytime I wanted to from many of the other women. Then a thought popped into my head. Who was going to do away with those guys if it was Evelyn's friend and her boss? I had to bring back many things into my head to block out bad thoughts, but where were the girls on motos when and if they made the trip to Peru? And who was going to wipe out these guys? This was another country, and Os surely knew that, but his power was limited, I would think. Or did he have a lot of connections besides Juan Jose, his goons, and me?

I had a funny feeling Rosa was going to be more involved, and I would start to question her. I didn't know her enough to hold something over her head, so I didn't know. I had to talk to Os more to know who was going to do the end game. I did the next day. I spoke for quite a while with Os. He did have connections and told me that when he got the proof confirmed from me, he would act. I was relieved. I wanted to have more sex with Evelyn and set up a romantic weekend in Cusco, and I was happy to get out of Miraflores for a while. It was a short flight and a super nice hotel. I wasn't happy that I had to go through all this to get laid again. But she was a bit difficult with giving it up for nothing. When we got to the hotel, she was super curious about my life. She asked so many questions about my work and how I could stay in Peru for so long and come back so many times and so long.

I came back with "I do it for you, baby. I think of you all the time, and I want you so badly."

Evelyn smiled, and her big black eyes opened and danced. She looked happy, and maybe I hit the right notes. I wanted her really bad but really only in bed for a few more nights until the deadline came. I had to ask the deadly questions—who, what, and where or else. Else was still the keyword; it wasn't clear yet what I could hold over her head. I knew her mother and her sisters, but that was always pushing it. She could go to the police and point me out as the bad guy, and I would get in big trouble. We had no connections with the police or lawyers in Peru as far as I knew, something else I forgot to ask Os about. After we made love that night—and it was enjoyable—I asked her a question.

"Do you remember when we went out with your boss to lunch?" She said, "Yes."

"When we came back, there was a guy who went into a side door next to us. When we went back, he really checked you out and had a weird look on his face when he looked at me. Who was that?"

She replied, "That guy? I forgot to tell you. I had seen you in a car one day when I was coming back to the hotel. You were about two blocks from the hotel, and he was parked. You were next to him in the car."

She had a blank stare on her face. Then she opened up. "Yes, that is Jose."

"Oh," I said, "he works with you?"

"Yes," she said, "in the back."

Now this was the guy who kissed her on the lips in the car. She was a bit worried. I saw it on her face.

"He looks so familiar," I said. I just said that I didn't mean that. Then she said, "Yes, he also is in a group, a band."

"Really? Have you seen him play?"

She said, "Yes, Rosa and I go often to see them sing. They are good."

I knew the guy was good-looking, and he had a following. I said. "So you are close to this guy?"

She looked at me like, "Are you jealous?" But she said, "Yes, we are friends."

Then I wondered whom I could see who had seen them together besides Rosa. If I asked Rosa any question, I knew she would go right back to Evelyn and tell her. I had a feeling Evelyn was sleeping with this guy, and now I was suspicious more than ever that he was moving stuff, products. Now it was time to get a spy. I had an idea whom I would get. The guy who was asking me for money all the time. He was still around, so I would ask him to help and be my spy.

I walked across the street to see the idiot I threw into a window of a restaurant, the one who was always asking me for money. Standing behind him was a familiar face, the pretty moto girl, the only one I'd seen so far. She looked nice. She was in a blouse and a skirt. She looked like she worked in an office. That was the first thing I said to her.

And she had an answer: "How do you know I don't?"

I just laughed. She told me she had many things to show me. She was worried I was falling for Evelyn and wanted to show me things that would change my mind.

As if I could read her thoughts I told her, "I am not in love with Evelyn."

She looked at me and said, "Good because I have many photos to show you."

I asked her, "How many days have you been here?"

She laughed but not jokingly. "I came down right behind you," she said. This was a serious girl.

No juegos from her, I thought.

We went to a restaurant, and she showed me the photos of Evelyn with the guy Jose from the band. There were many photos of them making out while hanging out at the beach with friends. Rosa was in a few of the photos. She had direct attention to my face as I looked at the photos to see if I had emotions toward Evelyn, such as pain.

But I surprised her and said, "Okay, I have a plan to get it out of Evelyn." I finally asked her for her name.

She looked at me and said, "Call me Lulu."

I said, "What? Lulu? What is that?"

She repeated, "Just call me that." She had more photos, and they were of Jose dealing but using his band members to do so. He was a small guy, but he was leading the way. She then told me to get more info from Evelyn as soon as possible, like now. She would be dealt with also. She wanted confirmation and a lead to someone bigger. I ate a salad. She ate something else—spicy stuff, I think. This Lulu was a very serious person but kind of sexy and also pretty. I asked Lulu if her friends were here with her.

She just looked and smiled and said, "When you get more, call Os, and give it to him."

In my head, I was starting to put in order whom I feared the most—her, Os, Juan Jose, or the police in Peru. Inside I knew that the police could be paid off. They didn't make any money and would turn their heads when something went down. It was the same as the police in Colombia. To me, it was a smart move 'cause the bad guys would go after your family and you, and the risk was not worth about five thousand American dollars a year.

The next day was big the day I would confront Evelyn. I felt very bad. I didn't know why it was always the same to me. But I did feel bad, so I gave her the typical talking to. I needed some info, and I told her whom I was working with. I said that if she didn't provide information, they would kill her friend Jose and Rosa and some more. She was in shock. I told the same as many others, but her voice became real squeaky and high. She started to cry. She almost had me crying. I felt so bad for her. But she was the one who got involved with that guy. As she broke more and more, she told me she did think he was dealing drugs along with his friends in the band, but she was more concerned about whether telling me would save him.

I said, "Maybe, I think so." But I lied. Nothing was going to save him. I asked her several times who his connection was.

About the tenth time, she said, "I saw him meeting with Diego many times, and they seemed close—too close."

Jackpot! I had that feeling after he had so many curious questions when we were in the restaurant. I said, "I hope you can forgive me, and we can see one another again."

She looked at me with tears coming down her cheeks. "Don't hurt Jose, pleaseeeee. Do me that favor."

I shook my head, and my eyes went down. Then she openly wept, and I said, "Do you love him?"

She cried more and left. That day was the last time I saw Evelyn. She was such a beautiful girl. The call went to Os. That night, I was invited to a super bad area where I met Juan Jose, his guys, and Lulu. They had Diego tied to a chair and were giving him a beating so badly that I thought his eye would fall out. I walked out. I'd had enough. They threw the head of Jose at Diego. I became sick and started to throw up. I left quickly. I didn't want them to see me do that. It was worse than any horror movie I'd ever seen. I was so nervous.

Lulu was outside, and she said, "See you in Medellin."

I just turned and said, "Yep, you will."

During my travels in Peru, I met two other women. Both were pretty—not outstanding, but pretty. One was a speech pathologist in a major hospital in Peru, and the other one was a pretty girl. And the best thing was that they both had visas to travel. A few months later, they visited me at different times and stayed with me for a couple of weeks. The most amusing thing was that the speech pathologist told me she could not give me oral sex 'cause it might damage her throat. It would affect her career. I almost passed out laughing. Ten minutes later, she gave me oral like an expert. That was not the most interesting thing. Eight months after, I left Evelyn and saw her for the last time. She had a baby, and it wasn't mine. She was pregnant by Jose. She seemed happy. I saw the photos but never contacted her or spoke to her.

Now after a trip home, I was back again in Medellin. I was back in my favorite hotel, and I was waiting for Laura to come by. I hadn't seen her in a while, and we were going to take a trip to Guatape after we spent a day or two here. I had always liked Laura. We had a long relationship that lasted on and off for twelve years. She was good in bed, was very intelligent and very pretty, and we liked similar things. Knowing she was going to be late, as all Latinas usually are, I went to sit outside by the hotel pool. I sat for a few minutes, got up, and went to the front desk to talk to one of my buddies for a minute. Then I went back toward the pool area, hoping to get the same table. No one was really there, so I thought I would. I then saw a middle-aged man cross from where I was sitting and go to another table that was to my right. Facing the pool as I was when I went to sit down, I noticed that he and I were the only ones outside in that area. What I noticed next almost changed my entire life. Next to my chair was a shopping bag from a popular store; it was a supermarket shopping bag, so I relaxed and sat the bag a bit under the table to the left of my chair.

First, I was worried and said, "No one left this there by accident." Now I was thinking it might be a bomb. Nah, who would want to kill me, the gringo?

The guy was still sitting to my right. Louis, the waiter, one of my favorite people in the world, came out with a beer for this guy, and Louis gave me the look, the "be warned" look. Finally, I grew big balls at that moment. I looked in the bag and pulled it over so I could see in it. It had bills tied together, like they just came from the bank, and they were not small bills. They were one-hundred-dollar bills. I only saw what was on top. I dared not pick anything up. I could see it was Ben Franklins in all their glory, and a whole shopping bag full of them. Only God knew how much money was there. I took a quick look to my right, and the guy was drinking his beer, just waiting to see what I was going to do. Again, Louis was standing by the doorway to the pool area and gave me a second look, this one very even more concerning.

I gave Louis a look and shook my head side to side slowly as if I was telling him, "Don't worry, I got this."

My next move changed my life. I sort of figured this out quickly. If I took it, I would die. If I didn't, I would confuse them. But it was either one of two things—a severe warning to stop being involved or a trick by Os. So in fear, I picked up the bag, walked it over to the guy, and said, "I don't want it, and you can stick it in."

I left it next to him and walked out. I was really happy Laura didn't show at that moment, or it would have been very hard to explain. And he would have seen her face, which could have been far worse. As Laura let me know, she was in the taxi and on her way.

Louis said to me, "You did the right thing."

I thought I did. I wondered how much was in the bag. I was told when I shared the story with Os just to see his reaction that it was anywhere from one hundred and fifty thousand to half a million.

Os smiled, one of the few times he ever did, and said, "Mr. Jerry, you're an interesting guy."

I just laughed. Os asked me to go to another area on a bus. It was close to Santa Barbara. I was to meet a guy who was going to set me up for my next trip to Manizales. I had some fear of these things traveling on buses, but I would just see what would happen.

He told me, "After you meet this guy, you will meet his women in Manizales. The photos were wow! She is a *triguena*."

I said, "What?"

All I saw was beauty. She was a little dark-skinned, and that was what we call them—triguena. Okay, I was looking forward to that trip. The next day, I was off to Santa Barbara. This was in the mountain area, but the bus was taking me to an area a few hours away. I figured the bus was a mess. It was very dirty and full of old ladies who didn't smell like spring rain. I sat alone, making sure I took up two seats. After about two hours from the heat and the smell, I was spent. The bus was starting to slow down, then start and stop. I looked out the window. OMG!

There were about ten guys with automatic weapons stopping the bus. Shit! I thought I was almost crying in a panic as they approached the bus. I knew then that I was dead, but two old ladies saw the condition I was in and that I was a gringo. They pulled me toward the back of the bus and lifted the back seat, which was a long seat along the back of the bus. It took all of us to lift it up. This was happening in seconds. I jumped into the space underneath the seat, which also contains a spare tire and engine parts. the ladies all sat along those seats. I was wondering if they saw me. Did they notice anything? I couldn't breathe. It was so tight, and I was sweating so much and knew I was done. It seemed like I was under that seat for hours, but it was only about twenty minutes. I heard the voices of the men as they asked questions toward the women. Finally, the bus started to move.

I was under the seat for about twenty more minutes before the old women lifted the seat and helped me out. I looked like a grease monkey. I was full of dirt, but I was happy and finally safe. I could not thank the women enough. I gave each of them some pesos. We came to the destination. Finally, it felt like twenty-four hours had passed. I got off the bus, and everyone applauded. I bowed and thanked everyone. I was thinking that those were Colombian guerillas at that time. They were taking people's coffee farms in the area, I was told. I went to the area where I was to meet Juan. He was sort of a strange guy, a real farmer. He looked strong but never shut up. He was strange for an old Colombian guy.

I was still wondering what the hell I was doing there. Then Juan took me to his barn and moved all the crap he had on the floor of the barn. He opened a door on the floor and showed me what he had. It must have been every automatic weapon I had ever seen, and I knew nothing about guns. Even when Os showed me his stash, I couldn't care less, but what the hell! I looked at all of them. They looked new, and he had cases of rounds, enough to start a war. After about an hour, Juan took me to his house to eat. I was just eager to wash up, even though the bathroom was outside and had a hose. We ate the very typical *piasa* food, which was especially good. Several women were preparing it. The women would not sit with us. They would eat in another room. Juan said nothing at the table, and neither did I. But soon a call from Os came in. I was to return his call ASAP. I did. He asked me about the weapons.

I said, "Os, I know nothing about those guns. Only what you showed me!"

He said, "Tell me how they looked."

I said, "They look new, brand new! How many—it looked like a hundred or more and many rounds of clips. He said, "Okay, I will contact Juan."

He said, "I heard what happened to you on the bus. I am glad you are okay."

"How the hell did you know?" I said.

He said, "I will talk to Juan later about the weapons."

To me, I thought the whole thing was stupid. Why did I have to make that trip?

He told Juan to take me out of the area by horseback and that a car will be waiting for him. After two hours on a horse, my ass fell asleep, and my balls were blue. I hated it, but it was good to leave there in a car, not a stupid bus. And I wondered why I did not go there by car in the first place. I was really pissed off. I wanted to be in two places now—home or back at the hotel. I didn't even think of the triguena or the Manizales trip.

Now I was off to Manizales, which was a long trip and, as I would find out, a lot longer than even I expected. As I was leaving Bogota, they told me the volcano in Manizales was active, so they were going to fly to Pereira, which was a mountainous and coffee country. When I arrived in Pereira, I would have to take a bus to Manizales. Now I was not too happy. I was thinking of the experience I had not too long ago on a bus and that I was going to be the only gringo on the bus and so on. Soon as we landed, they took us to the bus, and I was on my way. Luckily enough, the bus was going to take us to the airport in Manizales. It was a little over an hour, but the ride was okay—no drama this time.

So then I was on my way to meet this triguena named Sofia. Soon, I made it to the hotel via taxi, and soon, Sofia was to arrive. The one trip we were to make was to the volcano, and I couldn't wait. Also, the hot springs came from the sulfur water around the volcano, and to be extra cool, the volcano was active. After two hours, Sofia arrived, I met her in the lobby, and she was nice, real nice, and super pretty. She had a great color and a nice body. She also had a very pretty smile, one you always get when you first meet.

Her first question was strange. She asked me, "How do you know Yuliana?"

I said in English, "Boy, does she get around."

Sofia looked at me and said, "Que?"

Good. No English was good for me sometimes. So I just told her, "An old friend."

She seemed to be okay with that. Then we went to my room, and I told her that I had a few gifts for her, which I did. She loved them. They were simple things, but it was a nice watch. I always knew what they loved. Then she told me she had to use the bathroom. After a minute, the mirror was on the outside wall, facing into the bathroom. The first thing she did was take a pill from the typical birth control box. Then I knew we were off to the races. I moved to another part of the room because I didn't want to see anything else she was doing. That would be a turn-off.

Then she said she was ready, and we went out to eat at a Chinese restaurant. It was cool. The food was good, but the several paintings of Mao around were unsettling.

I looked at them and said, "It is what it is."

After that, we went back to the hotel. Then we planned our trip to the volcano and to the sulfur pool, and then soon after that, we went to our room. When she removed her clothes, I could see she had super body, almost perfect. Her color was beautiful. Then we kissed, and it started. What I noticed first was that she was always wet.

Incredible, I thought. *Superhot. Now am I going to see what the pervert Juan Jose told me about these triguena women? Well, maybe. We will see.*

And she stayed the night. I was very happy with this. She informed me she would have to go home the next day to get all her stuff to travel because it was going to be very cold at the top of the volcano. I didn't bring a coat, only a hoodie, and that wasn't going to be enough. So we also had to buy more clothes, wool hats, etc.

Now on our way to the volcano, we had two other couples in our jitney. There were several stops to see the beautiful landscape. The mountains were magnificent. The views were spectacular. One couple were from Germany, but the others were locals from Colombia, so I started a conversation. We started with the usual—names, where you were from, what you did for a living. That was the part that made up part of my trip. The Colombian guy told me he was a cardiologist, and I looked at him. He looked like he was in his late thirties or early forties.

Then I said, "What do you mean *used to be?*"

"Well," he said, "they were only paying me about two thousand a month for saving people's lives and would not pay me more."

I said, "Wow, that is terrible."

He said, "That is why I am not doing it anymore."

So I asked, "What are you doing now?" His reply was so surprising and funny I almost died.

He said, "I am doing plastic surgery."

I said, "What?"

He then told me he was making about fifteen thousand a week and only had three people working for him. It was a piece of cake considering open heart surgery. I was between laughter and amazement. He really seemed to be a good guy, and I thought that was cool.

I said, "Making that money here is incredible."

He said, "Yes, it is, but that's what all the girls want now, and they will find the money to pay for it. They get bank loans, all kinds of stuff."

All I thought was that he made fifteen grand a week. Then he asked me what I did for a living. That was easy for me. I told him, "I'm an engineer." Then the follow-up was what type of engineer I was. I said, "Stationary." I did not follow up with anything I was doing here.

One thing I knew was that Sofia was way hotter than the girls they were with, and he was eyeballing her several times. We finally arrived all the way to the volcano. Many were breathing into paper bags; they were so out of shape. I was one of the few that were up there that didn't have to do that. We went above the volcano and took many great photos and videos. I needed this trip to be sure there would be no pressure, and it was nice to be with a superhot woman, Sofia, and enjoy that also. We got back to the hotel. The next day, we went to the sulfur pool. It was even better. Water ran directly down the volcano and into a larger pool. I felt like I was fifteen years old when I came out of the pool, but the big mistake was getting the water in my eyes. That was not a good idea; it burned forever! But I really enjoyed it and could only wish I had one like that at home.

I also found that Sofia's niece was moving products, which I hated, but most of the time, you could tell when they had super nice things and no job and were not really pretty enough to be a prepago. That was always a big hint to find. Her trail was easy. The guys were delivering it from a corner *tienda* (store)—not the owner, but a kid working there. I didn't think Os wanted me involved in that one. He said he had two really big catches coming soon and that this was more of a relaxing trip, a beautiful trip with a very beautiful woman and good sex.

Sofia and I continued our relationship for several years till she got knocked up by another guy. This is something they do when you are not with them twenty-four seven. It was the same with Evelyn. When I found that out it was adios, I had much more things to do.

All was perfect for me to be with beautiful women and have long relationships with them and know that I always had an out and a serious one. This was a reflection of my life not wanting a commitment and to have it all—the perfect storm, I feel that I was doing good for many but taking advantage of the situation. But it wasn't easy. It was super dangerous. I had great fear of my life and my family, and at any time, everyone was at risk. No one in Os's world played games. They might play with you, but there was always something behind it. Things with him had a purpose. I often wondered if he needed me. Maybe I was a distraction or something else, but this was a close-minded guy and didn't let many in. Not even Yuliana knew all of him, but she was completely dedicated to him. And how she knew all these women I met was incredible.

Maybe me being a gringo was the reason these women wanted to be with me. When I had time to think, those insecurities from my childhood came back to me—the fears, the loneliness. For me, this was a way to cover those things up, and it was easy to block out many of the things I saw here in Colombia. I think Os knew me. Despite all of my faults, I was noble, and I always had a sort of the white-knight syndrome going on in my head. To do all he had done, you could not be stupid. He knew there were people looking for him. To me, he was part of the government, the police, and the mob, but I had a feeling the thing that went on in his life turned him into this vigilante type of guy. Then I heard the story from his own mouth, and I believed it.

It was table time again. There were fewer photos on the table, and there were two I wanted to meet. I picked one.

Then Os told me, "Not that one. You should wait for that one."

I laughed, and I didn't even bother to ask why. I knew he wouldn't answer. So I picked the other from an area near Venezuela, a superhot area where I had heard that the women were superhot. I could see she was pretty, and there were four more photos of her always under the top one. But unless I picked the main photo, I could not see the rest. I had to play that game. Some of these photos had sexy photos, and some were very average, typical photos.

Her name was Eliana, and I was leaving soon to meet her. But it was not in the area where she lived; it was going to be in Bogota, the capital. I thought that was a bit strange, but this is what she wanted. I already thought she was hiding something. Bogota had a lot of history and great old churches and was a hot bed of corruption. Many of the killings went on there. I asked Os if the moto girls would be there.

He said, "No, not there, but when you travel to where she lives, they will be around, maybe a bit later."

It was a super short flight, and it was so funny because the airport was so crowded it took a while to find each other. Out in the parking lot, with such a crowd, we saw each other, and yes, she was pretty. She had such a pretty face, nice large breasts, nice butt, but skinny legs. She was sweet and spoke good English. I could see she was super educated and still very young but naturally bright. And a conversationalist. It seemed that she could not wait to talk. She wanted to know my whole life right away, and I didn't like that at all. I knew I had to lie. I found my real life very boring. We took the taxi right to the hotel.

"Very beautiful hotel and very nice suit," I joked with the front desk woman. Both were laughing.

The girl said to Eliana, "Where did you get him? He is so funny. The guys here are so boring."

Eliana laughed and said, "He's the gringo from Pennsylvania."

The girl smiled and said, "Get me one of those now!"

We all laughed, and Eliana and I went to our room. Bogota was not Medellin. It was colder, and the people there dressed like it was winter here. But to me, it wasn't that cold, maybe in the low sixties. So the heat was on in the room, but wow, before I could give Eliana the gifts I brought for her, she started to remove her clothes. I didn't even open the bags. She was in bed naked. I could see this was going to be a crazy experience. I took off my clothes and jumped right into bed with her. She was super aggressive, totally in heat like an animal, bringing me to flashbacks of Louisa but even more aggressive.

But there was a problem. Her vagina smelled, and I mean it smelled really bad—so bad it was a turnoff. It stunk up the whole room. I did my best to avoid the smell, and we had sex for what seemed like forever. As soon as we finished, we both jumped into the shower. I was trying to remove the odor from my penis, and I was trying to clean her with soap.

Then I told her, "What is that smell?" She said she had a small problem. I looked at her and said, "Don't worry. We can go to the pharmacy and get something."

After the shower, we went directly to the pharmacy. I bought a few douches, and we went to eat and headed back to the hotel. When we got back, she used one of the douches. Then she jumped back into bed, being in heat as she always seemed to be. But the odor didn't go away. She said to me that she had things to tell me. I was super worried now that she had something I could catch. She told me she started having sex when she was thirteen years old and had so many lovers it caused her to get many cysts. She had to go for an operation soon after she left. My head was going around and around. Then more stories came out. She told me when customs was going through her things, she had, like, ten or more different vibrators in her luggage, and they saw them. She said she was so embarrassed. I just listened. I thought my teeth were grinding, and I didn't blink.

I was thinking, *Who is this woman? And she's studying to be a doctor? OMG! She should be in porn. This girl is insatiable. What am I going to do with her? What did Os get me into!*

But all that aside, she was super fun to be with. She was always smiling, was super funny, and had such a sense of humor, but despite all that, something was missing in her. The next day, we were going to tour Bogota, and I knew that was going to be a trip—and I mean a trip.

The more I got to know her, the more I could see how intelligent she was and that she always tried to cover it up. She laughed a lot, flirted quite a bit, seemed to be carefree, and was very promiscuous. When we went to the museums, she knew everything—super sharp, very quick. She knew her history. She would act like the girl everyone wanted to be with for the rest of their lives—sweet, honest, affectionate, and at many times, brilliant. Now I could see her showing some of herself. I thought of where I was going to find a weakness in her so I could find out the info I needed to know. As all that was going through my head, she told me she was fluent in several languages and that there were many good Italian restaurants in Bogota. She spoke fluent Italian. She said she had spent a lot of time in Europe and studied there and that much of that time was in Italy.

Now I wondered, *Does she have connections there? Is that something I am going to have to find out?*

We then went to eat. Then we were going to check out several churches. Italian, of course, was on the menu, and she did speak very good Italian.

She asked, "How many languages do you speak?" She did say it in a nice way.

I joked, "Of course. I barely speak English."

She laughed. As we sat and ordered from the very large menu, she ordered a bottle of wine, the one that she liked. I just wanted water but ended up having one glass while she finished the bottle. She was feeling good after dinner, and as we walked, she put her arm inside of mine as we walked along. It was not something you saw often in Colombia. Many didn't even hold hands. She was being so sweet. We then jumped into a taxi and went to a very old church built in the fifteen hundreds by the Franciscans. It was amazing. There was so much gold in the altar. I really loved it. There were also guards with automatic weapons, walking around in the church, and as I was taking pictures, they asked me to stop. I asked very politely if I could take one more. They said okay, so I did and then stopped. But as we were walking out, I could see that Eliana was a bit upset. Her eyes were tearing up a bit. I just put my arm around her and kissed her on the cheek.

Then we got into another taxi and headed to the Monserrate Sanctuary, which was up on a mountain. We had to take a train up the mountain and cable cars down. When we got there, a long line was ahead of us, but it moved quickly. It was super cool. The top was terrific. There were the stations of the cross and the gardens. We took so many photos together. Then we walked toward the church. This time, Eliana was a bit hesitant, but I waved her on. A mass was going on, so we went and sat in the pew. I kneeled to pray, and so did Eliana. It amazed me 'cause I knew she was not a religious person. Then she started to weep—and I mean crying big tears—while holding her face with her hands. I almost started just to see her doing this. A minute later, after such emotion, she got up and walked out with me like nothing happened. I could see her emotion was real, but she shut it off like turning off a faucet. That stunned me a bit, but now I could see a little crack in her armor, just a bit.

We then headed down. I always looked around and checked out the people around us. This was what I did and was used to doing.

Much of the time, it was to see if the girl I was with was being checked out, and Eliana was sure being checked out by many hombres. Now we were back to the hotel to enjoy the pool, and I also had to remember to take my vitamins because I knew the sex I was in for. With Eliana, it was not thirty minutes to an hour; it was a several-hour affair, and it was no joke. I had to keep up. In a couple of more days, she was headed back home, and so was I for a few weeks. Then I would return to her area and hope to meet her family members, who were located in a city close to Venezuela. The next two nights, she would tell me what her family did for a living. I could not be more impressed, but seeing how intelligent Eliana was, I knew they had some things going on. I also knew Eliana had come from money.

I was home for a while and kept in communication with Eliana all the time, even though the first couple of days home she sort of shocked me. She told me she was having sex with another guy, a friend she called him, but I shouldn't have been shocked at all. I knew she couldn't keep her pants on for long. I acted surprised and disappointed with her. I had to do it in a bit of a salty manner. If I didn't, she would think I was a weak man. In Spanish, they called it a *pendejo* (asshole). I told her I would be heading to her area very soon, and we would talk then. Eliana didn't seem to mind and seemed happy that I was coming. One thing at least was that she was honest about her sexcapades.

I didn't tell her I was in Medellin at the time. I had a meeting with Os.

He told me, "This is a very big deal, and we want you to find out which of the family is the key."

I told Os, "I am headed up there soon, and I will start to get more serious with her and get to know her family." Then I told him about Eliana. I said, "Os, seriously, she acts goofy sometimes, but she is super intelligent and street smart and can snap at you. I thought I found a couple of weaknesses. I will see. But she is not going to be easy. She has big money, and as you see from the photos, she's very pretty and cannot be trusted. She will sleep with anyone at a moment's notice. She is a very strange bird, very unpredictable."

Os didn't say too much. Not much went over or under his head, so I just went on my way and got ready to travel. It wasn't a long trip. I had to stop in Bogota to change planes. then she would meet me in the airport near her home. The next day, I left Medellin and met Eliana. She looked beautiful as usual and had that special smile showing all her teeth with that nice mouth.

When I saw it, I thought, *How many guys' cocks have been in that mouth other than mine?*

But I didn't really care. I had things to get done. She wanted to take me to eat before going to the hotel, but I wanted to get to the hotel first.

She said, "You know, once we are in the room, we're not going to leave."

I laughed and said, "You're right! Let's eat!"

It was super hot outside. It felt about one hundred degrees. The minute walk to the taxi, I got sunburned. Soon we arrived at the hotel. It was very average. The photos looked good but barely above a dump. It was a small town with little to do. I saw that no one spoke English. After some pretty good food, we went to our room. The air conditioning unit was so noisy I told them they had to change the room. I always hated to complain in front of the girls because they took it personally about their country, so I had to be careful when complaining in front of them. Eliana was super cool in letting things go by. She told me she could stay in her mother's guest house tomorrow.

I looked at her and thought, *That's good, but I need to be alone sometime to put info together and get rest so I can think clearly.*

I knew sex with Eliana was number one on the menu, and it was going to be long and hard like being at the gym. To give you an example, the first night in her hometown, we were at it for three straight hours, and breaks were rare. I dared not ejaculate. I had to just stop, wait an hour or two, and then start again. I never permitted her to take all those vibrators out. I never wanted to get into that. She wanted to do that a couple of times.

I laughed one time and said, "You act like they are your trophies."

She smiled, but she looked like she took that personally. I had to be very careful with her. I was not a psychologist, but I could see she was not all there all the time. I really wanted to get into her family. She started to tell me about their work, and I had an idea. But wow, her mother owned one liquor distributorship, her brother was doing his internship to being a doctor, and her father owned another liquor distributorship. I could see they could buy this town; maybe they already did. As soon as she told me about the distributorships, I knew where I had to look, but this was going to take time—a lot of time. If Eliana was as smart as I thought she was, I knew her parents and brother were twice of her. Now I had to play the dumb gringo and think as a smart gringo and ask the right questions. Getting to know not only her family but, more importantly, her friends.

The next day, I was going with Eliana to go to the guest house and stay there for a while. Then I was thinking that I wished to meet her friends as quickly as possible. She had plenty of friends, some girls and some guys and some gays. Out of all of them, I had the feeling that the gay guys would do a lot of talking. All the parties would start on Friday and end on Sunday afternoon. And it was Wednesday, so I had to get my shit in order to meet the parents and brother and then the friends, or I would be found out. Remember, I was the gringo, the oddity for them, so I will be the main attention.

Now it was party time. We went to Eliana and her brother's house. It was a rather large house several miles from the guest house I was staying in now, and her parents' house was an amazing place. There was a big pool; it was a modern house and relatively new. There were a couple of maids, and as you can imagine, many people for the party. I could see this was super good for me to get some info before I met Eliana's parents. Her brother was an intern and was very close to becoming a doctor. He was a thin guy, somewhat tall, and good-looking. I could see all the hot women that were around, but also there were several gay men around him. They were very open about their sexuality. There were two gay men especially close to her brother, so I became interested in the conversation they were having. I had to get involved.

Then the bongs and the marijuana came out. I would never and had never done those things. I was squeaky clean on those things. I walked around with a beer, and many said, "Typical gringo." I just laughed. I could see a couple of the main guys who controlled the sharing of the pot. That was easy, but I had a feeling Eliana's brother was involved, especially when they had a main room where many were joining in, doing the cocaine. And this was not just doing the lines of cocaine. They had, let me say, bags full. They were small bags, but there were several of them and wide out in the open. Eliana walked into the room I was wandering around in, and she put her arm into and around mine, a sweet move, and kissed me on the cheek.

I asked her, "Do you do this stuff?"

She replied, "I have but not in a long time and not anymore." She told me she was stuck on vino, and she laughed.

"Good," I said. I had to be careful not to judge, especially her brother or his friends. I had to play along but ask questions, so I asked her if her brother was gay.

She laughed. "Why? 'Cause he has a lot of gay friends?"

Again I had to be careful. "Yes," I said."

Her smile left her face as she said, "No, he is not gay, but if he were, is that a problem?"

I knew had I stepped into a trap. Eliana was super smart, and she was also very liberal. Now I had to change the subject for a few minutes. I said, "He has so many friends and a lot of people that really like him."

Her smile was back. Now I had to find another approach. Maybe I could talk to a few of her brother's friends, but now it was difficult because of her on my arm. Then another thing. I thought of how many hombres she'd had sex with in this house. Many of the guys were really eyeballing her, not just because she was pretty and sexy. But did I really care? No. I had bigger issues—how to talk with these guys and ask them where they got so much cocaine. Given the way these guys were handling one another, I was sure they would be open about it.

Eliana stepped away for a few minutes. This was my chance, so I engaged in conversation with a couple of guys in the, let's say, the cocaine room. They thought I was very interested in buying some. I was surprised by how talkative they were. These two guys and one woman pointed to the other room. I didn't really understand.

Then they said, "Ask Pedro."

I said, "Eliana's brother?"

They nodded yes, and I thought he had something to do with it. But he was not the big money man, so now I was suspicious of her family. This was an opening. As I was going to ask a couple of more questions, Eliana came back and asked me if I was having fun and if I wanted to go into the pool.

I said, "I am going to go downstairs and get some food."

She said, "Let's go!"

We went downstairs. As we walked, I said, "What a house! Very nice people."

Eliana laughed and said, "You really think so?"

I said, "I like many of them."

I could see she thought I was just being polite, and she knew I was not a drug user and didn't like it. The food we had was super. I loved it.

I had to stick around, so I said, "Let's use the pool."

She laughed and said, "Super!"

More information was going to come, and I hadn't even met her parents yet. Thinking to myself, I felt this could be an opening. But it would take a lot of time, and when I got back to the guest house and while Eliana was busy, I called Os to give him an update.

Then it was time to meet the parents. Well, one at a time, because they were separated. The trickle conversation started, and Eliana was in a talkative mood. These things were good, I thought. She told me how to act around her mother, who also owned a liquor distributorship, as did her father.

We were going to meet her mother at a restaurant just outside of town, so now Eliana took a car. They had cars, motos, homes, and money, but there was a big tie-up in something illegal from what

I could see. I thought it was up to me to get the info to Os, but I wanted to find out who was moving the product. I wasn't that bright to ask many of the pertinent questions, but I could be tricky and joke around to get some answers. The restaurant was a bit dark. There was little light. There was a singer piano player, and it was very classy.

As Eliana and I walked in, her mom had already had a couple of glasses of vino. As we approached her mom, I introduced myself.

"Encantado," I said.

She smiled and said to me in English, "I am Iza."

I smiled, kissed her on the cheek, and held Eliana's seat for her. We sat, and as I looked around, I could see that the food was special, so I couldn't wait to eat. I was starving. We ordered, and her mom started the conversation.

"What work do you do?"

I told her I was an engineer back home.

"What kind?" she said.

I said, "Stationary."

She looked at me strangely then said, "How did you meet my Eliana?"

I looked at Eliana and said, "We met through a friend."

"Which friend? I know most of Eliana's friends."

"It was someone back in Medellin. Yuliana," I said.

"Okay, nice," she said.

I started my questioning. "Eliana tells me you own a liquor company."

She told me the name. "Yes, it's true, and I am hoping Eliana follows in my footsteps, but she took a better road, studying to be a doctor."

I could almost see that she was measuring me up. I had to be slick, so I changed the subject and said, "I met your son. He is also studying to be a doctor, right?"

She smiled and said, "He is my pride and joy."

Wow, to say that in front of Eliana was really something, but I guessed the number one son was considered to be number one, and that was from a successful woman, his mother. I didn't want to get so much into the party her son was at, but I was starting to see, with her mother's ways and the weird looks she was giving Eliana, that they didn't really get along. I mean, the first time she met me, her mom threw a big insult—backhanded, I would say. Then Iza told me that she and Eliana's father were separated. This was after she finished the bottle of vino. Every time I saw a woman drink like that, I would get flashbacks of my mom, who would be loud and sad after two drinks. It was something that was stuck in my mind. To this day, I had to prevent her from drinking. Then I blocked it out as I did through her entire life.

Eliana never ate a lot but loved to pick through all the different foods, so she liked to pick from everyone's plate. Her mother wasn't buying the story of us meeting through a friend she had never heard of. She was asking Eliana how she knew this girl from Medellin. Eliana blocked it out. She didn't really care. Her mom didn't know what a sexual freak her daughter was either, I thought. I didn't really care what her mother thought. This wasn't serious to me, and Eliana couldn't keep her pants on for five minutes, no matter what guy was with her. I remember asking her if she would do two guys or a guy and a woman. She looked pissed and said loudly, "No! I am not into that!" But who knew? Maybe she just didn't want to admit she did it or that it was a possibility. In a couple of days, I would meet Eliana's father. Now that was going to be interesting. He was also in the liquor business.

Time passed quickly when I was with Eliana. It was sex rump after sex rump, and the smell didn't go away. Soon she was going back to the hospital to get an operation to remove some things in her vagina, and hopefully, that would be the end of the odor. It was getting embarrassing to have the maid come into the guest house, and it smelled like the most terrible odor you could imagine. Every time she did come, I asked her to clean the sheets. It was not me who was putting out that odor!

The funny thing was that she would say "Altra vez" over and over.

I laughed and said, "I know. I am not the only hombre that has been in your bed." LOL.

The maid just looked at the ceiling and rolled her eyes. I laughed again. I knew the meeting with her dad was coming soon, so I was again going to call Os and give him an update. I was thinking that this stuff was getting old. I loved sleeping with all these beautiful women but not finding out stuff and having the risk getting bigger and bigger since I was away from Medellin more and more. It was such a weird feeling. When you imagine the things you would like to have in your life, one of the things is to have sex with beautiful women. And now I had slept with literally so many, hundreds, and I'd found that I could have one anytime I wanted to. So now I started to size them up, like how were their asses, breasts, faces, waists, and so on. But I really never found love with them, only good sex.

I would get flashbacks to my mother calling my father a gal-livanter. I really didn't know what the definition of that word was, but I thought it had to do with not being home and having fun and maybe cheating. Many expression and things stuck in my head all throughout my life no matter where I was or whom I was with, and I would also think maybe many of those things affected me in keeping a solid relationship with a woman. The closer we became, the more I wanted to leave no matter how beautiful the woman was. I always looked for a reason to leave, always measuring them up, like, maybe their ass was too small or they had a pimple. They were stupid things, but they counted for me.

At one time, I was dating the runner-up to Miss Colombia. She was only twenty-two years of age and won so many beauty contests. I mean she had everything. She had personality, talent, and so many positives, and she wanted something serious with me. But even when we had sex, I would look for faults, and believe me, she really had none. Eliana walked in with a lot of food for breakfast—healthy fruit and special breads and all that, even some waffles. They were all from a health food store. I really liked all the food. It was great.

She told me a bit about her dad. "He is a strong man, a no-non-sense type of man. He always wants straight answers."

I said, "He sounds like your madre."

She laughed. "They are the same but bang heads a lot, and Dad likes his mujeres women and some younger than myself."

"Okay," I said, "let's see when we go for dinner later."

I asked Eliana about her brother and his friends out of the blue. I said, "Where did they get all those drugs? I mean, there were piles of cocaine and pot, everything!" It was a shot in the dark. Maybe she would say something, and I was thinking she was too smart to fall for that. Well, I got lucky. A confession was coming.

Elaina replied, "You know, Colombia has a lot of drugs." I stayed quiet. She continued, "They control everything you have, and though my madre and dad own the companies, they have to take on much of that."

I was still quiet until I had an opening. Then I said, "Why are your brother, who is close to being a doctor, and you, who is studying to be one, involved in that?"

She said, "Well, not me. It's my brother's friends that help move the drugs."

I said, "The guys at the party with him?"

She said, "Yes, remember the gay guy Santi? He and his friend and one other there are the main guys. They make a lot of money. My brother knows what they are doing, but he does not agree with them."

I just shook my head and said, "I am sorry. I am sure your family had to build their business to have it controlled by the drug lords."

I wanted to know so much more, and now I had a big opening, but I feared this was really big. Holding something over these guys' heads was far above my pay grade, so I had to find out as much as I could and then give the info to Os and Juan Jose and then get the hell out. But now I had names, and after the conversation tonight with her dad, I could only hope that Eliana would bring it up. She told me about it, but maybe it was not a good idea. I was getting scared, far more than before.

Before I met her dad, I called Os again to tell him more. He was super happy, but he wanted photos of the guys and names.

He told me, "Her brother is not safe."

I responded, "Safe from what or whom?"

He said, "From meeting his maker."

Shit, I was worried big time. Let me pick through this and get more info and get the hell out of this area. Now I didn't even feel hungry.

I was getting ready to meet the dad, and Eliana was putting on a very nice dress. I didn't quite have those types of clothes with me, but to my surprise, Eliana had a nice shirt for me and a jacket. It was nice to do that for me. She was such a weird person to figure out. I never really tried. I knew I would never have a serious relationship leading to a union. She had too many issues for me, and I didn't know if she would survive this. I never did know what happened to the women afterward. I gave the info to Os and Juan Jose, and they did what they had to do. Eliana, as many others, was the person who would lead me to the right people. Each of these women was so different in so many ways and how to deal with them was my biggest issue. Now I knew how goofy sometimes Eliana was. I knew now that she was super intelligent and knew how to play the game.

We left to meet her dad. This time, we had a driver, and in fifteen minutes, we were at the restaurant. Her father was already there, and the place was the restaurant her mom had been at when she met us. This was special. I didn't know why I had to meet them, but this was a great opportunity to get more info. As we spoke, I could see that this was a super smart guy, just like her mother, and his questions were very typical. But this time, as Diego from Peru, he really wanted to know what I was doing here and what type of work I did and what was my full name. I had nothing to hide. LOL. So I told him all with not a problem, and the one question was very easy.

I said, "I'm here to be with Eliana."

He thought this was going to lead to marriage, and to my amusement, Eliana laughed a bit when that came up. She covered for me to get out of that question. Her father looked into my eyes during our conversation and while asking every question. I was aware of that, so I did the same. I grinned at the end of my answers. He would say several things to Eliana during our dinner and even asked her how my Spanish was. She said it was passable but far from good. He understood more than he spoke.

During this, I was becoming more and more curious. Who called for these dinners? And why? And what was the reason for meeting the parents and now putting me in the guest house? Sometimes I was a little slow figuring things out. After a couple of hours, we left again. Her father looked right into my face, and as soon as we left, he got right on his phone—maybe normal, maybe not.

It took me a couple of days, but I asked Eliana, "Was it you that wanted me to meet your parents?"

She said, "Not really. It was them they were curious of the gringo I was with."

So be it. Now I knew something was up for sure. I had to get moving, and I knew Juan Jose was near for sure. I could smell him. It was his time to snoop. The weekend was coming, and there were more parties on the agenda. This was a second good chance to find out more. Again, soon Eliana was going to get those cysts removed, and that would mean no sex for a month. I wanted to get into her friends more and her brother. I knew her parents had something to do with all this, and the drug lords had them wrapped up, but I could never get the info from them. That was way too crazy on my part to think that, and they are way too smart.

The weekend came fast, and it was party time. It was the same house, the same cast of characters. Plus, there were several very hot women, friends of Eliana. None of them had men with them; they came alone. This time, I came with a purpose to get names and areas, and since they had seen me before with Eliana, they would feel good talking with me. But I had to be alone with a few I thought would be able to give me info, and of course, her brother—I knew he knew everything. The first guys I saw were Pedro, Santi, her brother, and her gay friend. They were super friendly toward me, but I wanted to talk to them separately to get some names and areas. I tried her brother first. I knew how to open the conversation, using the meeting of their parents as an opening.

It was party time all the time. I often thought when they studied or worked. I knew Eliana was super smart, as was her brother, but this was crazy to me. At one point, I was thinking when the orgies would start, but I was waiting for Juan Jose to show and make some dumb comments. Now my attention was toward Santi and her brother Pedro. These gay guys who were at the party were not closet types. They were very flamboyant and super talkative, so those were the guys I hung around with. Eliana was always walking around and flirting or God knows what, but it was the info I was interested in. These guys would love to gossip, and no matter how many times I was there, they were so curious about me as far as being a gringo and being in this area and my apparent super interest in Eliana.

They knew how much she screwed around; they called her a free spirit, and some called her a puta. They would make comments like "Does the gringo have a *grande pene* [big cock]."

This was the amusing part of being there with these guys. They were funny. I was sitting with Santi and a couple of his friends above the pool, and the cocaine was flowing. The air was full of the smoke from the pot smoke. I almost felt myself getting high from that. As much as they offered these things to me, I never had and never would accept. They took all that in stride. I never had anything forced on me, and I liked that.

Again, I would ask, "Where do get all this stuff from? Isn't it illegal?"

Playing the game, they would say, "It's passed down from mami and papi."

Pedro's head spun around and just looked. I didn't think he heard, but apparently, he did. To my surprise, he just laughed. I found it so interesting how normal they found this, and it was such a part of life for them that they couldn't care less about anything around them. If Juan Jose walked into this, I couldn't imagine what would happen. A body count maybe.

I then spoke to Santi and said, "How do you get all this stuff? My god, it looks like you would need a big truck for every party."

He again laughed and said, "We take turns picking it up. Two trips to get ready for the weekend."

I played super dumb and said, "Who pays for it? You?"

He said, "No, silly. It's from the family. Didn't Eliana tell you? She must have. You are here all the time, so I am sure she wants to be with you. And I heard you were with her mother and father."

I turned and saw a couple of hard-looking hombres who did the security moving toward us. They apparently didn't hear what was said but were told to be close to me. Now I remembered how her father questioned me, so now I was being watched. This wasn't very good for me, but I knew now where it was coming from, and I could see I had to be very careful. Eliana was coming over toward me. As always, she had a big smile. She gave me a super kiss and got very close to me. Then the security people backed off and went to another area. Then her brother came over and had a long conversation with her about certain people being with her and how control was being lost.

Then Eliana wanted to go to the front of the house and walk, so we did. She told me she was thinking of going to the United States and that she would visit me there. I was happy. I thought that was cool. I enjoyed her and the sex. She then told me that her mother was very ill and might die.

I thought, *Wow, this is terrible.*

She told me, "It's cancer."

I told her, "I am so sorry." But I really didn't care. I knew her mother was a drug dealer through others, but she still was. And so were her father and her family. Maybe the lords were using them, but it still was a crime against humanity. They never thought of how many poor people they were killing and the damage they were doing to their country.

We then sat and spoke. I was very blunt and said, "What's going on with all the drugs all over the place?"

I got a bit emotional, and to Eliana, what I said was judgmental. She got upset. She knew how to twist things around, and I always had to remember she was super intelligent and could get very emotional.

I then grabbed her and kissed her and said, "Let's not argue over that. Let's pray for your mom."

She paused and thought and said, "Let's go to the house."

We went and had our psychology session called hard sex. She told me she needed me, and I was surprised she was very independent but also a bit crazy. Even after hours of sex, on and off, she would break out the vibrators. She told me she was going again for the operation to remove the cysts. I needed time. That was good. Now I would call Os and tell him the latest news.

As I spoke to Os, I told him more info and my opinion.

He said, "Juan Jose is theirs. Point out the characteristics that you've seen and tell him as you told me."

I said, "Eliana is very intelligent, and it's not easy to get into her head 'cause as smart as she is, she is also loca."

He said, "You have some time, but still, be careful because this is leading to the big one soon."

"Huh?" I said. "What big one?"

He replied, "Soon after this. I have the girl already picked out."

My head was starting to spin. I was already getting worried and tired of this. It had been going on for years now, on and off. I would never share this with Os, but I feared people were starting to recognize me and I was becoming known. There are so many that were killed by them, and I was Os's prostitute. It was cool in the beginning, but now I wanted something serious in my life, not this serious game of catch-the-drug-lord. I feared Os just as I feared the drug dealers. When I looked in the mirror, I tried to understand what I was doing and justify all. But now it was time to sit with Eliana and talk seriously about all the drugs I'd seen.

When I finally spoke with her, it was like talking to a mentally ill two-year-old. She knew about all the drugs, but she was all over the place.

"Why do I care?" she said. "Who am I to ask these questions." And so on.

I told her, "You are so special, and I want you so bad. I worry about these things."

She almost barked like a dog, like a growl. I was thinking that she was possessed. Then she said, "Look! Many do drugs and a lot of drugs. I told them many times to stop. I don't like it, but they do what they want to!"

I was getting nothing, and I didn't want to blow it all up. Then she got up, went to the bathroom, and came back.

She looked at me and said, "These are stupid guys."

I said, "Who?" Now I was playing really stupid, and in the past, when I pulled something like that, she never played along. She just got real angry. Now she was getting close to that point. I knew she was protecting her parents and all, and I tried to make this a normal conversation, but it was difficult to ever have a normal conversation with her. She always went off the deep end. Her temper was as hot as her sex, and when she got like this, I could not touch her. So I just talked normally.

Then I asked again, "Where do you think the drugs are coming from? I think your brother may be using them. Do you think so?"

Like Dr. Jekyll and Mr. Hyde, she became calm and said, "Well, he does use cocaine, and I hate it, but he says he needs it to study. It was Santi's fault and his friends."

I stopped the conversation. Now I had something. "Let's go eat," I said. "I'm starving."

She smiled, and we left.

Now I was going to meet with Juan Jose and give him the names and a few photos, but I was going to ask him to leave Eliana's brother Pedro for last, meaning if he didn't need him, he needn't go after him. The next day, I was super tired. I didn't get much sleep, maybe only four hours. It was always a long night with Eliana. I was able to get away for a couple of hours. Eliana had a meeting with the doctor about her medical issue, when to go for an operation. I told Juan Jose where and when. Again, his first questions were about the puta.

As he said, this time, I told him, "You couldn't handle her."

He replied, "I see your eyes. You can't either."

We both laughed. Now I gave him the photos and the names of all I knew.

He said, "These guys are gays?"

I said, "Yes, they are."

He said, "It will be easy. They squeal like women. There are parties every weekend."

He said, "I know how to find them."

The one thing about Juan Jose was that he was super sharp and a professional in what he did. He always had a purpose and never played games, such as a shark going in for a kill. Though I didn't really like him, I feared and respected him for that. He seemed to be jealous of me, though, or maybe envious. It's probably because of the women. He could see how hot they were, and I was treated like a king. But this was a business, and I never loved these women. It was a job. I always hoped he knew this. I wanted to find someone I could be in love with but not yet. I knew this part of my life was coming to an end and wondering whom Os picked for me instead of me picking. Now Juan Jose was on the move, and he was going to get what he needed.

I met Juan Jose, and we spoke at length. It was good 'cause Eliana was recovering from her operation, so she was out of the way. She really didn't give me anything in words, but by taking me to meet her family and friends, I digested a lot of info and knew now whom we could use to get the info to help lead us to the top. Os was really involved in this more than normal, about the same as he was in Peru, I felt. He had whispered before that this was leading to big things in the girl I was to meet soon. I saw that Lulu was here now and a few other girls that wore bandanas over most of their faces. Even with the bandanas, I could see they were cute and had great bodies, especially in jeans and boots. But like Lulu, I would bet they seldom smiled. I knew one thing—they were good killers. I would not ever want to cross those girls, so sleeping with them was literally putting your life in danger.

I had a feeling Juan Jose would go after what he considered the weak link, and that would be the gay guys. I assumed Pedro would be right behind them if he didn't get the info right away. He always seemed to always start with the weak and then go up the ladder. I knew it was going to be a bad few weeks, and many were going to be killed. I counted the days till I was going to inform Eliana. It was much stress for me. I had the feeling her father was going to be one of the casualties. I never knew how far they would go. It was their because they had a brother who died of an overdose of drugs. I thought it was fine, what they did. They were wiping out some of the real bad guys. Maybe they would be called vigilantes or whatever, but if there was a good cause for Colombia, this was one of them.

The day finally came, and now all the action would start. I made sure I kept out of the way. The girls were ready and on standby. Juan Jose and his guys—and there were plenty of guys I hadn't seen before—were also ready. These guys also had bandanas on. From what I could understand, the Colombian government was in on this too. This won't be the only time. They would even at a time approach me a few times to ask me to do more work. Santi and his friend would be the first. Juan Jose at times made it look like he was a government agent, and the guys he, let's say, dragged in for questioning were legal. But far from that, if they didn't lead him to the leaders, forget it. They, let's say, woke up dead or had been beaten that you would wish you were dead. He had about ten guys waiting by. The guys he wanted he had followed and took in. When he brought in Santi, he never came out. A couple of his friends also would never be seen again.

In these farm areas, no one would ever look for them or care to find them or their bodies. They were disposable. Lulu would keep me informed. She said they were bringing Pedro in soon, and it was now because he was there, taken in with a hood on his head. I thought if he came out, it would be a miracle. I had no feeling either way with all these guys. You almost had to look at them as objects, not human, and I always had to worry about me. I never knew if they would turn on me. In my mind, I always thought Os had an affection for me. Maybe it's because of my relationship with his daughter and what I did for him, but still I hadn't really spoken to him about the reasons for all of this. I had already spent twenty-two years traveling back and forth to Colombia and doing these things and hadn't had a serious relationship for a long time. Maybe he thought of all that. I was feeling sorry for myself, even if it was a really weak reason. I was having sex with some of the most beautiful women in the world. So that was another checkmark in the positive.

After a few hours, I still hadn't seen Pedro and Lulu, so I didn't know what was happening. I really wanted to leave, but I needed a ride and would not enter the area. Now I heard a noise, and it was another car coming with more, let's say, prisoners or hostages or whatever. This was bigger than I expected. Now it was going to be an all-nighter. I was hoping Lulu would come out, but she didn't, so I had to wait.

I was hoping deep inside that they weren't going to kill Pedro, but I still haven't seen him of yet, and I wanted to leave. Lulu came out, and she finally gave me a ride and two on a moto. It was a challenge, but we made it back to the guest house. I asked her if she wanted to come in. I was just being polite, and I knew Eliana was staying at her mother's because of the operation she had. Lulu shook her head left and right in the negative manner. I was really being polite. I would never pull something on Lulu, not at all. I knew they were going for Eliana's father. This would happen very soon, and I expected they would hold on to his son until they got to him and then possibly get more info and kill them both. In such a weird way, I wished this would get over faster. I want to get home and then come back when we were going to start what I hoped would be the last one.

I was so tired and depressed. It was so difficult not being able to share any of this to even my close friends. The only thing I shared was the hot women I was with and some photos of the girls. Even in this book, I am going to tell everything, not all. Lulu was my best informant, and I did put that trust in her. I even had her phone number but never left a message and used other phones to contact her. That was the way she wanted. And believe it or not, she did have a real job. She worked in the police office. Seriously, I had to laugh when I found out. But few knew what Os was doing and just closed their eyes and ears because one way or another, if they said anything to either side, they and their families would be gone. Period.

About a week later, Pedro was still nowhere to be found, and Eliana was not only worried but super pissed off. She still had to wait a month for sex. She told me he wasn't answering his phone. I would say nothing as of yet. I was being very coy. The only thing I said was, in the next party, maybe he would show up. Then she said that many of his friends weren't answering either.

I looked at Eliana and said, "I don't know. I am sure he will show up."

A couple of days later, I got in contact with Lulu. She told me he was still alive but that the father won't be for long. They either weren't getting the info they wanted or did get it. Another couple of days passed, and I was feeling a lot of pressure from Eliana.

At one point, she said to me, "You know where he is, don't you?"

I was in shock! I turned and laughed at her. "Are you kidding?" I said. "Would I know that?"

She was so smart. I had to be very careful, but if I told her now when I didn't need to, two things might happen. She would go to the police, or I would have to tell Os and she would be killed. We went out to eat that night, and I told her I had to leave to go back home. The next day, I left. By the time I walked in my door at home, I was informed that Eliana's father was killed. The one good thing was that they let her brother live, which was strange. I couldn't figure that out. To me, that was a loose end, but something happened. From that point on, Eliana hated me. She would not say why, but the hate was real. Years later, she obtained a visa to travel to United States, and I happened to speak to her when she was here. But she was just angry and said she was with someone now. That was no surprise. I knew that would happen. It happened when we were together, so it was no big deal. She always felt I had something to do with it. Things started to go wrong when I came into her life. It was a true statement and was very familiar comments that I heard in the past. Sometimes I felt like the grim reaper.

Now I had a meeting with Os, and hopefully, this would be my last journey, which he and I would have a long conversation about.

Os spoke about this, which was difficult to figure out sometimes, saying that the Peru experience and the one with Eliana were leading up to this next one but that he needed certain proof and certain characters. As I arrived at Os's home, I saw the photos of what I thought to be the girl of my dreams, the one girl who really stopped traffic!

We always speak of soul mates, love at first sight. What is one man's desert is another man's ocean. There're so many sayings. I've had so many relationships in my life, whether it was for a purpose or for a relationship, and I never really found myself in more than lust or simply wanting to have company. Sometimes when I was with someone, I was as lonely as if I were alone. In many of the experiences I've had, they were for a purpose, but I still had an opportunity to fall in love. Even though Os told me to leave that behind, it was still a feeling and a want and something I could control.

Now I was going on my next mission. Hopefully, it would be the last one. The way Os spoke to me and the look he gave me said that this was the big one—the one he wanted. So he was counting on me to get the info he needed to wipe out this new bunch. This was not going to be easy for me. This was to be a super heartbreak for me and would put me in a position to hurt the love of my life. It was a journey that would last five years. To this day, I still never got an answer to how Yuliana knew all these people and who her contacts were. All I knew was that she was right on all the time and was always able to build a relationship with me and the girls before I was seen or heard. They all knew one thing—that I was a gringo. Where I was headed now was not very far from where Eliana was living, more northeast.

When I first saw the photos of Carla—yes, that was her name—I said, "Super body, cute face, and breast implants." I could always tell. It was not hard to tell, but even with the photos, I could not see how really pretty she was and how sexy her body was without even trying. The area I was going to was superhot. I had a short haircut, plenty of sunscreen, and when I was ready to travel, I received a phone call from Carla. I was super surprised. We spoke a little, but she told me she and her brother-in-law were going to pick me up at the airport.

I said, "Great. That's super nice."

As I arrived, I started to walk out of the airport. My god, it was like a desert. The breeze was hot, and the heat took your breath away. It had to be the hottest place I have been to. I had a million taxi guys ask me if I needed a ride as I looked back and forth, looking for the car. I knew she told me it was a white one, but which way? Then I saw her coming. It was an incredible view. This will be not the first time I will say this, but she stopped traffic. She had on jeans and a tight golf shirt and platform shoes. I had to remember to keep an eye on my luggage because I knew what could happen, but I lost vision of everything but her. As Carla came closer, I took my bags and went toward her. She was a sight to behold. She was perfect in every way. Tomorrow she could star in any novella. Everything she had on was a perfect fit.

I walked toward her and almost couldn't speak. I finally got out, "Encantado de conocerte [nice to meet you]."

She looked at me, and I had sunglasses on right in my face. She smiled and said, "Lo mismo [the same]."

I still almost could not speak. I finally got a word out, and as soon as I did, her brother-in-law came and not in a cheap car; it was a very expensive new Honda. I kissed Carla on the cheek, and we left. We both sat in the back seat as her brother-in-law drove us to the hotel. I almost didn't know what to say.

Then I finally got to know his name. It was Marco. He was married, well, maybe to Carla's sister, whom I guessed I would meet later or whenever. Finally, we made it to the hotel after driving through some of the worst areas I have ever seen. Carla told Marco she would see him later. We checked in, and she checked in with me. Remember, in Colombia, both parties had to check in, and their identification was needed. It was mostly because there were so many *prepagos* in the country. As we entered the room, I had several gifts for her, mostly sexy lingerie and panties, perfume, and candy. Wow, did she love them all of them! She sat at the desk and started to open the candy and was doing a job on it.

I asked her if she was hungry, and she said to me, "So rico."

All I saw was her no matter where I looked. Then I took my bags off the bed, and she went and posed on the bed on her side with her arm holding her head up. She was perfect—the perfect smile, perfect everything. I knew then that my feelings were very different, and I was only with her for an hour or so. Soon I went over to her and kissed her, really kissed her. She stepped back and removed her blouse. Normally, by now, I was super erect, but for some reason, I had nothing. This feeling I had was different. I wanted her, but then I didn't. It was like I found some respect. But then she removed her perfectly fitted jeans, and I almost had drool coming out of my mouth. She had a perfect tan all the way. I never forgot the beating of my heart. It was pounding so fast, and my thought was that it was far more than lust. It was like being in the greatest art museum in the world and seeing the perfect painting by Rembrandt. I finally stripped down, and everything was coming normal with myself. Now she removed everything, and the kissing was perfect. She performed oral, and I did the same with her. Then she got on top of me as I was on my back. She put her knees deep into my thighs and pushed with great passion. Nothing on her body moved. It was a hard body yet soft enough to enjoy. We had a couple of hours of passion, and there were even times when Carla looked into my face. So much so soon, I thought she told me she would meet me tomorrow at her grandmother's house.

I asked her quickly, "Do you want something to eat?"

She turned around, waved her finger in the negative manner, and said, "See you tomorrow."

That night, I didn't sleep much, and I was tired. I had Carla on my mind, and then I knew this was going to be difficult this time, for sure.

This must have been a trend now—going to meet a family again. It was usually something very serious. It should have been between two people, meeting the girl's family, and this was only after a couple of days. Os and Yuliana told me before that being a gringo opened doors here in Colombia. There was a lot of trust. Colombianas went for the blue-eyed tall gringos. That part I knew already, but meeting the family was what I was here for. But there was a big problem. Every time I saw Carla, my heart jumped. It was as if I had no control. But staring at her with such wanting, such a feeling was almost embarrassing. And I had a hard time controlling it.

Carla came to the hotel and picked out the clothes for me to wear. I had never had that done before. But it was okay. She even wore the jean shorts I liked with a super tight top. My god, I wanted to be with her every second. I had to get my head on a bit better and go now with her and meet the family. When we went downstairs, her brother-in-law Marco was there along with his wife, Carla's sister. As we walked toward them, I was introduced.

"This is my sister Inez."

Right away, Inez spoke in English—and very good English. I could see right away that she was very educated. She was not pretty, was a little heavy, but was not ugly either. I was told she was a lawyer and had a big practice in another area, about a two-hour drive from there.

As we conversed in the car, Carla didn't say a word. Her sister did all the talking. Marco said nothing; he only smiled once in a while. I could see now that Carla, though aggressive in sex with me, was very private. It seemed that her sister talking so much bothered her. We finally got to their grandmother's house. It was nice but nothing special, but when I was observing, Carla barked a bit at Inez. I could not make it out, but it sounded like "Don't talk about me." When I walked in, their grandmother was sitting. Their tia was there, along with many kids, and the other sister also came in. I quickly learned that they all worked. One was a manager of a telephone company. One was a teacher. A few were attending what they said were the best universities. Some of the nieces looked very hot, with great bodies. An old uncle was there. Another younger uncle was also there. There were so many people, and their attention was on me.

Carla didn't smile when people were complimenting me on my blue eyes and height and so on. Her other sister was sort of plain, and but this time, I was wondering if Carla got all the looks and the others the brains. Soon the other sister introduced herself.

She said, "Hi, I am Millie."

I smiled. She also spoke very good English—again, well educated. Now all the food came out. There was a lot of food, and there were many places to sit. The house was not very large but was very clean. Many sat on the steps outside and ate, but I was at the main table. Then the questions flew at me.

One of them said, "Carla never says anything about her life. She is very private. We were very surprised we even got to meet you."

I almost looked at Carla's facial expressions as the questions came to see how she felt about them. She hardly picked her head up from looking at the dinner plate, but I knew she was waiting for my answers. I had to answer them in a way that would not offend her privacy and blow this whole thing up. I had to make sure my feelings didn't get in the way either. I didn't really know if Carla was super into me. Sex is one thing; real feelings are very different.

One thing I noticed was that many calls were being made into the tia's phone, and every time she answered, she had a pad and pencil with her. Several times, she left the table. Every time she would come back with a shy smile on her face and pan her eyes downward. And at the table, everyone would become quiet. Then when she sat down, all would go back to normal. I wondered what that meant. That pad was put away very quickly. Why hide the pad?

After dinner, Carla and I were not allowed to help. We all sat across from one another and spoke. Carla didn't say a lot, but she did smile once in a while. She seemed happy when we took photos together, but I had to be very careful with her. I saw that she had a very short fuse with her sister. Later, I received a call for Os. I didn't answer and would talk with him much later.

Sitting in the grandmother's house, I noticed a couple of people missing—the parents. I thought these would be people I would meet sometime in the future. I didn't want to bring it up to Carla because she was the type that if she wanted to tell you something, she would. She surely seemed to be secretive. Now the other sisters were a bit more open, especially Inez. But I was seeing that Millie and Carla were closer. They would share much more intimate things, and they also were closer in age. I had to be careful in getting any info, and when I spoke to Inez, I had to make it clear that this conversation was between her and me. I never really came out with those words, but she was super bright and got that I was worried about upsetting Carla.

I asked Inez about her parents, and she would not shut up. She told me her father had a business and her mother helped him. They were very busy, and her mother was in the United States. Her father was traveling in South America, but they would be back very soon. She also told me they didn't get along and were really separated, but both live near. I didn't want to be pushy by asking what they did for a living. Not yet. But I did bring up the brother, who was not at the grandmother's house either. Inez said he was busy. He was an engineer, and his work was all over the place.

Besides she said, "I don't think Aria shares any details of who she is dating with him." It was not that she didn't love him; it was that he asked too many questions and she was very private, so it bothered her. She then got into her father. "As much as we love him, he plays around a lot, so my mother has had enough of him. They still run the business together, but that's it."

I was thinking, *Now I've found my fountain of info.* Sooner or later, she would give me a lot more info.

Carla always had one eye on me. I could see she liked me, but she was very worried her sister was talking about her. Millie was her opinion person. She would give her info as if she would give her information, as if me, her new partner, was worth the effort, and if I would fit in.

One of the uncles approached me and asked me if I liked guns. I said, "Sure, but I don't use them. I don't care if another does."

Then he got up and brought more.

My god, I thought, *why would he do this?*

He asked me if I would like to shoot a few. I said no. I was spending time with Carla and had to go back to the hotel in a few. He had a weird smile on his face then and moved his arm in a way to say, "Yes, you want to go to the hotel and fuck her, right?"

Now this was her uncle. How crude was he? *Wow!* I thought. Carla was super pretty. Anyone could see this, and her body was beyond perfect. But her uncle? Doing those things, he reminded me of Juan Jose. Carla and Millie then asked me to go around the corner to get the kids ice cream. That was cool. I could get away from the strange uncle. We bought a lot of ice cream pops, and of course, I paid. But this area was so hot. We had to hurry to get back. It was funny almost running back. After we gave them out, we left and went back to the hotel. I told Carla her family was nice and that I looked forward to seeing them again. She just smiled. There were times I thought there was something wrong mentally with Carla. She never spoke a lot to me, but apparently, she told her sisters, especially Millie, her inner thoughts of me. We took a taxi back to the hotel.

She told me she could not spend the night because she lived with her brother and he got mad if she didn't get home the same night. So she would stay until 3:00 a.m. and then leave, which was strange, but who cared? I would share a bed with this special girl whom I was falling for. Her brother called a couple of times, but we were making love. One of the things with Carla was that she did everything great in bed. And another thing was that I was making love with her, not just having sex. I really wanted her, and I thought it was becoming obvious to her, but I also thought about how many guys felt that way about her. When I was alone, I missed her, and now I knew I had a big problem. Now was this something I would share with Os. I didn't know I had to wait and see and think this through. I could not him not having faith in me. I had to wait this out for a while and see what happened, but I hated this uneasy feeling I had from being in love.

It had been months, and though I had made many trips, I hadn't met the mother or father. I was thinking that Carla wasn't serious with me. I hadn't even met her brother yet. Then a surprise came. Her father must have said something to Carla about me and wanted to meet me. Now I was curious because he wanted to meet me, and now I was wondering if Carla had a good reason for me not to meet certain members of her family. It seemed the day before the meeting, Carla was angry with me as if it was my fault. After knowing her more and more, I knew she was super private and that sharing anything about her was not going to happen. I always depended on Inez to give me info, but I didn't want to push it. As for Millie, I knew that if I asked any questions, she would tell Carla right away, so I was tightlipped with Millie. I was figuring out why, but I really knew the answer.

One thing that worried me was the father; this could be a problem. I remember previous meetings with parents that were drug lords. When I went to the grandmother's house, I seemed to see hombres in the distance, and the same guys always about a block and a half away—one always, sometimes two. It was amazing how professional the family was. Some were schoolteachers, doctors, lawyers, owners of companies, and engineers. In the house, there were always pads and pencils ready by the phones, and many had long lists of names on them with checkmarks all over the pages. I first saw them by the counter in the kitchen, then also by the phone in the bedroom. I took a chance one day. I wrote down the names. There had to be hundreds, and the tia would write more all the time. From what I could see, she had very little fear of the police or anyone. I remember Lulu telling me about the numbers of police officers who would turn their heads for fear that their families would be killed.

As the months and days passed, I only knew a bit more than the first day. But now, with a chance to meet with Carla's father, I thought I would know where I stood. The next day came quick. The taxi took us. Carla was super quiet. As I took her hand in the taxi, she cracked a smile and looked at me. I was so in love with her. At her smile, it was as if she removed her clothes and jumped into my lap. Now we arrived at a really nice house. There was a large gate, two guards, and throughout the area, a couple of dogs. I thought I was visiting a prison. As I got out, Carla gave the guards a look, which I noticed, and I was not frisked. That was the meaning I got out of it. Carla wore a tight short black dress, and she was superhot hot as usual. I wore shoes, which was rare for me. Now when we entered, I saw maids, butlers, and gardeners all over the place. It was so crazy.

Now a man approached. He was not very tall, maybe up to my ear. Then he kissed Carla and asked her how she was. Then he looked toward me and said, "Hey, a tall gringo!" Then he introduced himself. "I am Marco. You must be Gerard." He shook my hand and had a strong handshake.

Then he proceeded to show us around—really, me. As we walked, I got the typical questions.

"Many told me of you," he said, "but as you must know, Carla is very quiet—unless she gets angry. Then she will cut your heart out." He laughed. "So be careful."

He asked Carla if I had met his wife yet. She said no, and he explained they had some issues. He asked me where I had traveled to in Colombia and in South America. I told him only a few places. I had to lie. I didn't want him to try to put things together. I was a bit nervous. This guy had a big aura about him and had a lot of confidence; he was sure of himself.

As he walked with Carla, he joked with her. "So you are very serious with the gringo. Wow, that is different for you."

She was not amused. I could see it in her face, but he was super curious about how we met. I said it was through a friend, and Carla said the same.

He pushed that a bit with "Wow, a mutual friend in Colombia! That's curious."

I didn't follow up with anything. I was very worried he was fishing, and I didn't want him to find out anything. It was very difficult not to get involved in a long conversation because Carla didn't say much and I was left alone in the cross-examination by her father. Every word he said is toward who I was really. I was used to it, so I played the game well. The food was super. There were all different types of seafood, and I had a beer, only one. Then I drank water. I was always polite. I laughed when it was appropriate. He had a big garden, so we sat outside and spoke.

Three times he asked me what I did for a living. I said to him jokingly, "I won't forget no matter how many times you ask that."

Even he laughed, and Carla smiled. I could see now how I would be followed.

He came out with a nice surprise. He said to Carla, "Why don't you take him to the island?"

Carla liked that. She said, "Yes! Good idea, Papa."

We finally left. I felt a bit relieved but only for a moment. I asked Carla about the island, but she really didn't say much about it. She didn't even ask me what I thought of her father. She was always weird that way. But I knew who would tell me about the island and her father's opinion of me—her sister Inez.

The long-awaited meeting was over, and a few days later, Carla wanted to take me to an island. I thought, *Wow, this is cool!* I was wanting to do some deep-sea diving, so I asked Carla about diving equipment I could rent. She knew of a place right away, but she informed me she was more of a sunbather than a diver and enjoyed going up to the water to her waist but no more. I was very excited to do this, so we were making the plans.

Then in the middle of our conversation, she said, "Don't worry. All will be ready."

I responded, "What?"

She told me her father owned a boat and that they would pick us up. The boat had a lot of diving equipment. I said okay. I was starting to pay more attention now. The next day came fast, and we were met by a car in front of the hotel and taken to a port in the area. We didn't even have to take food. The boat was really nice, about forty feet long, and looked new. Soon we went aboard and soon took off. What a beautiful ride. My head was on a swivel, swinging back and forth. Then Carla removed her blouse and shorts, and I had never seen anyone look better in a light-green bikini than her. I told her that my head was only in one direction now, and she actually laughed, which only made me happy. I loved it when she showed emotion in a good way.

Then the boat started to slow down, and it came very close to a beautiful island. Believe it or not, the guys on the boat carried Carla to the beach. I could not stop laughing as I put on my diving suit. While my guide and I got dressed, the guys were talking.

One said to me, "That is her father's island."

I said, "He owns it?"

They told me, "Yes, he does."

My head almost exploded as I put my tanks on. I waved to Carla as she put her towel on the beautiful beach. I asked the guys, "Is there a house there?"

They said, "No, but they will start soon on one."

When I was in the water and seeing all the beautiful fish and the five-foot-long big-mouth groupers that passed me regularly. I enjoyed everything. I was down almost an hour and finally went back into the boat. And then I went on to the island to join Carla, who took me on a little tour of the island. I didn't ask her if it was her father's because I knew she would get upset and ask me who told me, and then that would start an argument. Carla always wanted to be in control, and if you tried to take that away, she would flip. She hated opinions of her. And most of the time, she wanted things on her terms. Despite all that, I loved her. She could be difficult, but I made excuses for that. And I do remember what Os told me—to be careful with her. I didn't tell him I was in love with her, but Os could figure things out very fast.

When we got back to the hotel, I told Carla I had to go back home for a while. She always had this smile that made me crazy for her, and she had it on then. Soon we made love. She went home after that. She wanted me to rest because of my long trip. I didn't tell her I was first stopping in Medellin. I had a meeting with Os. The next day, I flew into Medellin and was met by Juan Jose at the airport. Hearing his usual crude comments, I just laughed them off. After all, this had been going on for years. Juan Jose did tell me that it was a big meeting and was very important. When I arrived, I was very tired, but we met anyway.

As Os and I sat alone, he told me straight why all this was being done. He sounded as if this was a last mission, but he said all this was because of him! "Escobar! I loved her so much more than anything in the world, and he took her from me." I sat in silence. His voice went up and down. He was so loud sometimes that I thought they heard him a mile away. Then he told me that he blew up a hotel she was in in Bogota. "He took her from me, so now that he is gone, I am taking as many evildoers as I can."

I was frozen sitting there very quietly, sometimes nodding my head in agreement. I looked at him with tears in my eyes and said, "I understand." Then I got the big surprise.

He said, "Are you in love with her?" I turned around and just looked at him. He said, "I see it. I knew that sooner or later, you would meet one that you really loved. Be careful, Gerard. You may have to kill her."

I said, "I don't kill anyone. That's what you guys do."

He said, "You may have to before she kills you."

I knew what he meant. Now I was sweating.

After I have been taking this all in, especially the meeting with Os, I had to really think this time. I had a strong feeling this was going to come to a bad end. I really wanted to be with her so much. Carla was all that was on my mind.

When I was alone, I would think, *Of all the super beautiful women I've been with, why this one?*

I would look at this logically, but inside I knew love wasn't logical at all. I didn't want to put out of my mind. What her family is, though, I had little proof. I knew inside what they were, but I was also worried I would accept them as they were. Now I was seeing what love was. It was very confusing, especially here in Colombia, where, in a second, I could be killed just for the fun of it. No one played games when it came to that. Carla and I spent many days together. We went to Panama, where I had a contact, a woman. She was very nice to me in the past, and someday I might use her, so I had to keep the peace with her throughout the years. We also made trips to Costa Rica and San Andres—two places I really loved.

The problem was that Carla never wanted to stay long, so we had to travel back, and it was a pain because I would travel for a weekend here and there. Almost all the time, Os would fund me, and I always had a feeling Juan Jose was not far behind me. In all the places we traveled to, I was asked by many, "Who is she?" Many thought she was a movie star or at least in the novellas. It was difficult when we were on the beach. People would see her and come up to me and ask me. And the saying "She could stop traffic"? I finally saw it with Carla. When she crossed the street, it would happen. I first saw it in Colombia, twice in main towns. One time she wore a Colombia soccer shirt and denim jean short shorts. My god, she looked incredible! I used to just watch as all the cars stopped to let her walk in front of them. What was so strange about it was that she seemed not to even notice.

As many weeks passed, she told me her mother was coming back from the United States and that she wanted to meet me for a whole weekend. Now I started to sweat. Why for a weekend? I assumed she was talking with Carla's father and trying to put two and two together and figure out where this gringo really came from. The next day, I was back at the grandmother's house, and Inez was there, so I was going to try to ask some questions before Carla, who went back to her apartment, would get there.

The info about the island was correct. Before I said a thing, Inez said, "Oh, you guys went to my father's island? Super!"

I said, "That place was so beautiful."

As we had some small talk, Inez told me, "We have such a big family. Did Carla tell you we have many tias and tios in Italy?"

I said, "No, she didn't. You know her. She doesn't say much about anything." But inside my head, I knew I had to find out more about them. Then again, jackpot!

She said, "Here is their email. You can talk to them."

One thing I knew Carla hated was when I spoke to any one of her friends or family members without her knowing first. Inez gave me their names and the part of Italy they lived. This was getting better each minute. I had to remember, so I got a pencil and paper from her tia's drawer in the bedroom and wrote it down. I saw many more names by the telephone when I went into the bedroom. I didn't know, but they were planning a baby shower for Inez. She was a bit overweight, and I had not noticed that she was pregnant. Now this was something else going on, but maybe it was an opening to get more info.

The next week, we were on our way to see the mother. She apparently wanted to spend a few days with us before she went to be with her whole family at her mother's house. I bought a small gym bag and a change of clothes. A driver took us there. It was a bit farther than her father's house, and again, Carla looked stressed. And I knew that with any word I said, Carla would jump down my throat. So I just kept quiet. It was like any bit of stress would set her off, and she had the weight of the world on her shoulders. But to me, it was as if she had a hard time keeping secrets, and she did this to protect all the secrets; in other words, the attitude kept people from asking.

Her mom waited. Inside the gate were guards, dogs—all the usual things. It was the same as the father had. I was greeted by a more-than-average woman. Her makeup was perfect. Her hair perfect. Her clothes were not off-the-rack kind, and my first impression was that she didn't look like anyone in the family, maybe a bit like Millie. She was very stern and looked like no nonsense.

The first thing she said to me even before she introduced herself or I got a chance to introduce myself was "Isn't she the most beautiful girl you've ever seen?"

I looked right into her face and said, "Yes, she is number one." Then I introduced myself. "Hi, I am Gerard."

She stuck out her hand and said, "I am Anna." Then she led us inside. "You know, I just came back from your country."

I said, "I know." She asked me where I lived, and I told her, "Pennsylvania, not far from New York, about an hour and a half drive."

She said, "Too cold for me. I like the warm weather."

I laughed a bit. I could see that here was superhot. Then she had the maid bring in some iced tea and lemonade. The conversation was the same as always: what work I did and so on and on. She then told me she was going to be a grandmother again but did not seem overly happy about it. I almost made a big mistake. I was going to ask her what she was doing in the USA, but I caught myself. The one thing she told me was that she had a sister in New Jersey.

I said, "I grew up there. What part?"

She said she thought it was Bergan County. I didn't want to push anything by asking what town. I was sure Inez would tell me. She then said, "You met Carla's father? Interesting character he is." I nodded slowly. She said, "How many women did he have around him?"

I just looked at Carla as if saying, "Can you get me out of this conversation?" But she just smiled and asked her mother what we were eating. Of course, it was Carla's favorite fish. I was so tired of fish; all they ate was fish. But I played along.

Dinner was, as they say, super Rico! As we sat, more stories came out—about the education of the kids and how smart they were and how all of them finished at the top of the class. Then she wanted to know how serious I was with her daughter. All I said was that I cared for her very much, but I knew that she was seeing my eyes and knew that I was in love with her.

Then another odd question: "Do you know if she loves you?"

"Certainly, I hope so, but that is up to her," I responded. I could see Carla smile. That was all I needed to see—for now!

After a few months, I was learning so much. I had a big list of names for the tia's list and the full names of the relatives living in Italy. One day, we all were sitting in the abuela's house—well, all except the mother and father, who never seemed to be around that house much. I was having a conversation with the abuela and joking around. Mille and Carla were sitting just across from me, and something very strange came out from Millie's mouth.

She looked at me and said, "You know, my sister can get any man she wants."

I pulled my head back, looked at Carla, and saw that she looked pissed, as if I said something wrong. I had no idea where that came from and why. As I said, I never wanted to pursue any potential issues.

But I did say to Millie, "Where did that come from?"

"Carla was thinking you were looking at other women."

I looked at Carla but was speaking to Millie, who to me was a potential troublemaker. I said, "Why get hamburger when I have steak?"

They both laughed at that and repeated it to their abuela and tia, who could not stop laughing.

Whew! I thought. *I got out of that argument!*

But I would never cheat on Carla. I loved her too much.

I had seen the mother and father several times during the years and also provided Os with a lot of info. There were so many names and phone numbers, maybe five hundred or more, the address and locations of the father and mother; and several of their properties. So now I knew something was coming soon.

It was midweek, and I just traveled from home. I was super tired. I checked into the usual hotel, and just inside the doorway was Lulu. I was a bit surprised, but I knew then that something was coming. Maybe the biggest surprise was Lulu in a dress. She looked pretty good, I must admit, but she told me she needed to talk and seriously.

"Well, I said I never knew any other way of speaking with you than seriously." I thought I would get a smile, but I didn't.

She said they had a plan for Friday. "We know his routine and the woman, and we already spoke to the woman he is with usually."

I never really commented on what or how they did things, but this time, I said, "The woman? There is more than one he screws around with, correct?"

She said, "This one is my friend."

I assumed she was a moto girl and that they set her up with him. The family already told me he had several girlfriends and how their mother hated him. I knew the mother was the major person in the family, the main person.

I knew that when Os made plans for these things, he was precise, but not this time. The father took off for the United States the next day, and their plans were ruined. For now.

According to Carla, the mother was returning very soon from the United States. I offered that info to Lulu. I was sure they would plan for another day to end the father. Monday came around, and the mother had returned. It seemed that despite the fact that they didn't like each other, they were working in tandem. They were never together, not even for five minutes. All the words were sent by the kids. I assumed the brother was the one. I had never really seen him all these years. The mother came back Sunday night in a direct flight from New York, I was told. Lulu was still around, and now I was worried that the mother was going to be the first one to go down. What was I to do? I was super scared about this. I was in a panic on what to do with Carla. Where could I take her? How should I deal with this when it happened? I had to call Os! He did confirm this with me, and it was her first now and some others later. The minutes seemed like hours. I didn't know how or what hour, but I knew it was coming.

"A good plan violently executed now is better than a perfect plan executed next week" (General George Patton).

Even though the mother had avoided any routines, she was still human, and she had a couple. One was going to see what new artwork came in. I never knew if this was smuggling or a legit operation, but she went to this area to see what came in. The deliveries were on certain days. And from a person on the inside, we learned that Tuesday was the day. She had two guards with her and a driver. At 1:00 p.m., she arrived at the, let's say, auction. From what I was told, there were six girls. Two bikes had two girls on them, and two other bikes had one girl each, including Lulu. They waited and hid well, and it wasn't easy. This was just off a main street, so they drove around for some time, never together, mixing with other riders.

At 1:45 p.m., the mother and guard walked out. He was carrying a medium-sized wrapped painting. The driver went to open the door. In a matter of minutes, hundreds of bullets seemed to fly. Two of the girls were using automatic weapons. People ran in all directions. The last bike rode on the sidewalk, and I was sure they were all dead, including the mother. She made sure to fire several bullets into the head to the guard, the chauffeur, and the mother. From what I was told, she was unrecognizable. Now I had a lot of consoling to do. I left the hotel because I was going to meet Carla at the abuela's house. I was wondering in the taxi when she was going to find out. God help me.

I can't say how much pain this caused the family. Hundreds were at the funeral, many of whom I didn't know or haven't seen. I didn't really care. I knew what she was doing, and I only comforted Carla. I wondered if they ever thought how many she killed by moving products. I could think how happy Os was. I knew he had more to do in this family and had many names. After a week of this, I had to return home but had a stop back in Medellin. Os met with me and several others, including Juan Jose, his crew, and a few of the girls who again wore bandanas to cover their faces. The new plan was to wipe out a few every week that were on the list, the list I forwarded.

I was hoping he would hit the family in Italy. They acted like they were so holy. I hated the use of the church, knowing what they were up to. The father came up in the conversation a few times, but I always thought the United States government would get him, especially since he spent more time there. Os had connections all over in the police department and in the USA.

He often said to me, "If I have a million dollars, I would give it to you."

Then I would joke and say, "You mean dollars, not pesos?"

When he asked me about my relationship with Carla, again my eyes would look toward the floor. He would say to me, "I knew sooner or later you would fall in love." He knew it. He asked me if I was going to marry her.

I looked at the floor and said, "I don't know."

He knew I wanted to, but he also knew I might be in danger. The family wasn't stupid and may put things together. Weeks after things started to calm down a bit, Lulu and the girls were knocking off many on the list, sometimes two a day. When I went to the abuela's house, I could see the stress on the tia's face. I would just say hello then sit and talk with whoever was there.

That night, Carla and her sisters and I went out for pizza. I tried to face the street side all the time so I could see if Lulu was coming by. You never knew, so I wanted to be able to get out of the way. Inez said something I could not believe as we were eating, and by the way, the pizza was good for Colombia.

Inez said to me, "We are still taken care of, you know."

I was in shock. Why did she tell me that? I had to take a breath. I didn't think anyone else heard it, so I said, "Really? That's good."

I thought Millie heard it, but the music was loud, and she didn't. Thank God. In my mind, she was a troublemaker and put a lot of crap into Carla's head. She was the type whom you'd think was a good person but wasn't. She was jealous of Carla's beauty and of Inez's success in her career, even though she had plenty of money and ran a telephone company. Everywhere we went, people gave their condolences, but it looked like it was from fear more than concern. I always received a long look from people there, like, "Do I know you?" or "Who are you?" It was nothing new to me. For over twenty years, this had been happening. Most of the time, I winked, which was very funny, but not to the recipients.

This last trip, I bought something with me, and it was going to be a big surprise for Carla. We were in the hotel, and she looked a beautiful as ever—so *lindo* (cute), so beautiful. I went to the safe and pulled it out *the ring*! This real beauty cost me a small fortune, so I did the normal thing and asked Carla to marry me. She looked like death. I had never seen her so scared. I was lost for words. I then told her that there was no rush. Then she smiled and put the ring on her right hand, which Latinas did. She also told me she loved it but could not wear it.

She explained, "Here they would cut off your finger to get it."

I nodded in agreement, but I thought I would pity the fool who would try that on her or a family member. That was a night of super passion, as you could imagine. The next day, she told most of her family were expecting her father, who was still in the USA, and her brother, whom they all feared. I wasn't really sure if she ever loved me completely, and I got a reminder from Os. I had been with Carla for almost five years, and I knew I was being watched by both sides. I was in the hotel and received a call to my room to come down to the lobby. There was a person who would meet me there. I asked the name and all but got nothing.

I went down. I never feared meeting people because I knew that if someone was going to kill me, it would not be difficult. I walked toward the front desk, and a guy stopped me.

He said, "Hi, my name is Joseph."

Of course, I said, "Who are you? How can I help you."

He was Colombian but said he lived in Canada. Os contacted him and wanted him to talk with me. We sat in the lobby and spoke for a couple of hours. And the conversation was all about Carla. The things he told me were not unbelievable but disturbing, and he had proof.

The paperwork showed she'd had several abortions, and there were many photos of her in bed with several other men. And as the conversation went on, he said she'd had an abortion from when she got pregnant by him. He explained how they owned several doctors. She was also connected to a guy in Maracaibo Venezuela and still traveled to see him. A few things I said was that she told me she was worried she could never get pregnant, and I knew she had family in Venezuela and many places. I knew this guy really hated her for the things she did, as in playing with good people.

Now I knew Os was sending me a stern message. Did this stop me from loving her? No! But I had a sort of sick feeling. Joseph was a good guy and a sincere guy, and since that day, we became friends. Even today we are still friends.

This was a mess for me. I felt so much love for Carla, but this stuff would be always on my mind. Now did I really believe this stuff that was told to me? I didn't know. I was very mixed up and had to get my head on straight because I knew more things were coming and I didn't know if Os was going after more family members. What I did know was that many people were snooping around Abuela's house and the father's house. I was still in the clear. No one bothered me. But getting back to Carla… I could never ask her anything. She had a bubble around her, and she deflected everything with her attitude. She was the beauty that could not be questioned. I found it so strange. I fell in love with her again; it was almost instantly. The thing that bothered me most was the comments by Millie. She had a very sharp tongue, and I could get her back, but that would cause unnecessary issues. I waited to see what was next.

The first thing I thought of was her brother getting killed. I didn't know him at all, and I'd seen him several times from a distance, but I was sure he knew of me. The only one I wished to talk to was Inez. At least she spoke and enjoyed my sense of humor. It was understood with her that I knew what was going on, so she often told me small stories about when they were small and the places they were taken to and who watched them. As we sat on the steps outside Abuela's, I saw Lulu go by on her moto. After weeks, she was around again, and I was wondering, if I wasn't sitting here next to Inez, would she have been a target? But it wasn't that.

I called Os that night. Lulu just wanted to give me a heads up about something big that was going to happen. I knew the father was in USA, so I figured he was safe. Maybe the brother? I didn't know. Then I heard from Lulu that she told me American agents were watching everything, and in her opinion, something big was going to happen. She brought me a helmet that barely fit, and we went for a ride. She showed me where all the agents were. From what I could tell, there were three.

There was nothing that escaped Os. He didn't want us to be obvious, but it was super cool to see all this. She told me a police captain was a very good informant for them. He was a good guy and was behind Os and what he had done all the way. Remember, Lulu worked in a police office.

I got a little personal with Lulu. I asked her if she had someone.

She replied, "I don't talk much about me." Then she waved her index finger back and forth, saying no in that matter.

Then I asked her, "What do you think of my relationship with Carla?"

She looked at me with that look as if to say, "Are you kidding?" Then she did the same thing. She waved her finger back and forth in the no manner. Lulu was still the only one of the mote girls I knew

313

and saw. And she looked cute, and she ran her life like a dedicated employee. She did what she was told to do. And I would guess she made good money from Os.

I then asked Lulu how Yuliana was doing (Os's daughter). She said she asked me the same thing about you, then was surprised I was in love with Carla. Lulu told me Yuliana wondered how I was going to get myself out of this one. I just looked at Lulu and asked her to say hello to Yuliana for me.

The next day, big fireworks were on their way. Carla's father was doing his business in the United States. We all knew what he was doing, but he never got caught. He always had a fall guy. But not this time. The feds and the SWAT team surrounded his house and several other places where he had small warehouses, storage places. He gave up without a struggle.

How was I going to handle this one with Carla that's the first thing all this happening in the matter of a couple of years. Now I have a headache and a real big one. And the family is going to be in huge turmoil.

While all that was going on, more stuff was just coming. Most of us were sitting in Abuela's house, except Inez. I was told she was coming in a few. To no one's surprise, Inez was pregnant again, the third one. When she arrived, she was dressed to the nines, and her makeup was perfect. There had to be ten of us there. For what I didn't know. But there were no friends except for me; only the first family members were there. It was getting dark when I heard the noise of cars coming. Now, on this street, the only thing you heard was kids playing, but I hadn't noticed any special noise. Now, on most of these homes, the living room was off the front door, and outside was a one- or two-step stoop. The house number was to the right of the front door; front to back was the living room, a small kitchen, an open outside laundry room with no roof, and a large slop sink for washing clothes. The bedrooms were off to the sides. If you went to the laundry area, you could easily climb the wall and go into the back of another home. I always looked when I went into a house for a way to get out besides the front door.

As we were sitting and chatting about the mother, I quickly turned my head. Two men—and they were not small guys—were coming toward the front door. I could see from the way that they wore their jackets. They were armed sipper, only catching the bottom part of jacket; other sides were puffed out. As they knocked on the door, I was headed toward the back of the house until the tia stopped me; she said they were friends. All together, four large black SUVs. Now it was completely dark out. Two other guys came into the house. They scoped the house in a second and told all of us, "No phones, no cameras."

I was still standing between the kitchen and the living room. Then *she* walked into the living. I had to look several times to take this all in. It was one of Colombia's biggest stars right here, and soon I found out why. She was also pregnant, as was Inez, and they happened to be friends.

I said to myself, *You have to be kidding. All these people are connected!*

I could say that Carla was hotter for sure. They also spoke, and this star complimented Carla for being so pretty. Then it was my turn.

"Who is this gringo?" she said.

I was almost speechless. Then I said, "Wow! Your English is perfect."

She laughed and said, "Thank you."

I worked very hard on it. Then I said, "I am with Carla."

"You are a lucky gringo."

I laughed and said, "Yes, I am."

Then she said, "How do you like Colombia?"

"I have come here many times," I said, "and I like it."

She shook my hand and said, "Come see me in my concert."

I said, "Of course. Good luck with your baby."

She smiled, spoke a bit to the others, and then left as she came.

Now that was the talk of the family for a while. This was not the first star I was around. We visited another big star's house nearby, and what I found out was that the sister went to school with her brother and that he was the one buying a lot of products. Needless to say, he was on Os's list. After this, another big day came, and a very bad day for the lieutenant of the deceased Escobar was coming and coming quickly.

I would say that was a nice thing having a face-to-face meeting with a Colombian celebrity. Now what was coming was super big, and the last few weeks were a big warning sign. This week, I went to Medellin. I didn't want to be anywhere near what was going to happen. I knew the father was about to return within the week, and Lulu gave me a hint. Something big was coming soon. What I didn't know was that it was not going to be in Colombia.

It was a Tuesday, and I was just going to see Os when Juan Jose showed up at my hotel. He did not say, "Did you hear what happened?" or "Do you know the news?" He said that he was done. All I said was "Where and how?" I thought he would have been shot, but in the United States, that was very complicated. He told me, "Let's go see Os." We jumped into his car and drove off. It was like New Year's to Juan Jose. I've never seen him smile so much unless he was busting my chops about the woman I was with.

One thing popped into my head. Carla—I wondered how she was. I couldn't call her now because it would look like I knew something, so I had to play it smart. We arrived at Os's house. Here is the difference. Os smiled rarely and never really laughed. Four of us sat in his back house, where he kept his weapons. He then told all of us even though Juan Jose seemed to know what happened.

Then he told us what happened. He said, "The lieutenant is as good as gone, yet you never know." I was a bit confused. Though I've known Os for so long, I still feared him and knew in a second that I could be missing. Then he looked at me and said, "This morning, the United States government caught Lieutenant Marco."

Now he wasn't really a military lieutenant, but he was one to Escobar. It was one of his right-hand men, even though Escobar was killed years ago.

I asked Os, "How did it happen?"

He looked again right at me. His eyes never blinked. Then he went into the story. The government of the United States, with info from certain people from Colombia, had set up an operation for about a year. I didn't interrupt, but when I heard "certain people," I knew whom he meant. Then he went into details. The SWAT team was there also, and what they got him on was smuggling, which carried a life sentence in prison. I mean he was moving tons of cocaine through the years, and on the day he was taken, they had all the evidence the authorities needed. What Os explained was that he used his ex-wife as the fall person. He tried to pin the entire drug trade on her. That was his plan. That was why we had to get rid of her first.

So we knew she was the smart one and that, sooner or later, he would screw up and the US government would get him. The problem was, he would have a trial, and that worried me a bit. But he would never return here either way because if he returned here, he wouldn't last a week. I sat for a couple of hours and listened to what Os had to say. He told me to wait after everyone left and that he wanted to talk with me. After everyone left, it was my turn. He explained to me that he was expecting the family to split up, especially the brother. He was a target.

Then he said that he expected Carla to take off as soon as her father was convicted.

I said, "Take off where?"

He said, "I think Venezuela or Panama. She has a lot of family in Venezuela, and some of them are targets. Her family in Italy is on the menu."

I put my head down. I didn't know what to say. I was so sad for Carla, but everything they had and obtained in the past was because of blood and drug money.

The trail took months and many witnesses. There were many who would not testify, but the evidence was overwhelming, and smuggling deserved a life sentence. The family was a mess. They could only get news from a couple of people that were family that were attending the trial. I spoke to Carla often every few hours, but I had to stop it because she was so upset. It was better for her to be at her abuela's, with her family.

> Sometimes the only way to heal our
> wounds is to make peace with the
> demons who created them.

—Dr. Ishio Serizawa

Even though I was so much in love with her, I knew many in her family were evildoers. We got so many names. So many were terminated. Now there was a severe warning all around Colombia that you would get caught. No matter who you were, where you were, you would get caught! Now the day came. Marco, the lieutenant, was convicted on all counts, and he was to do life in prison. The family was devastated. I knew they would be, and the cost of the trial was in the millions. This was automatic smuggling according to the law. And as the father tried to set up his ex-wife, he also set up the operation, which went flawlessly. And I knew Os had a lot to do with this. He was one of the most honest people I have met, and he was always a man of his word.

And with that, I went to visit Carla. I called first, but she wasn't there. So I asked some of her family, her tia, her sisters—as many people as I could. They said she left with the church.

I said, "What church?"

And it was all the same little info—more bullshit. Some said she was in Central America. Some said she was in Panama. Some said she was in Venezuela. She was all over the place! This was a super joke to me. Out of the blue, she left? Why was that?

I went back to Medellin to talk with Os, and he told me this would happen. "I remember you should have realized she was a bit loca and now is hiding from you and all."

But he said, "You know the one sister—you know, the one called Millie?"

I said, "Yes, you're right. They are close, but she already lied to me, so I am at a dead end." Os told me he was going to send someone to find her. I was super worried. I thought her end would soon come. I asked, "Os, please don't kill her."

He didn't say a word, but I knew most of the family members were on his list and if she was not at home, she was a better target for him. I was very nervous. I spoke to Lulu about this. She said she had nothing to do with it. I finally told her I would pay her to help me find Carla. She looked at me and agreed to it. Money always talked here in Colombia.

A few weeks passed, and the family members were still deliberately misleading me. I was super pissed off, so I traveled to Central America and went to some cities, only the main ones, and put her photo and her info on billboards and poles all over. I was hoping the family would see these. And guess what they did! They weren't happy about it.

Too bad, I thought. Now I was even more angry.

More weeks passed. As I came back, Lulu told me that there was a guy who knew where she was. I was so down and depressed, but this was a pick-me-up. Soon I met up with the guy and with Lulu. He told me she was in a major city in Venezuela named Maracaibo. I knew it; it was where much of her family was. Lulu stayed in Colombia, and the two of us traveled to Venezuela on a bad bus.

What a mess this thing was. I tried starting a conversation with this guy, who was called Paco, but he said little. The bus trip took hours. Finally, we stopped to eat. The guy disappeared for a bit and came back with a large long bag. I asked him what was in the bag. He told me it was a weapon, that we would need it. I almost shit in my pants. We got off the bus before the border and were picked up by a small van. At this time, I didn't worry anymore. I thought my life was going to end. We went into Maracaibo. It was about twelve thirty in the afternoon. He took me to an area where there was a school.

We must have been about a hundred yards away, and I could see Carla. She was sitting there with a guy and talking right outside. I almost was going to yell to her, but now the bag with the rifle was open, and he already put it together. This was not a run-of-the mill gun. It was high powered and had a sight. Now I knew why he took me here; it was so that I could see him kill her. I had tears coming down, and I told the guy to let her live. I said I would give him the money he needed. As the conversation went on, he seemed not to care about anything I said. I pleaded with him, but I had to watch out; he might kill me.

Then his phone rang. He didn't answer it. Three more times a call came. Finally, he answered. He told them he had her right in his sight. They asked him if I was there. Of course, he said yes. I couldn't make out the last part of their conversation, but he started to take the rifle apart. He said one thing to me: "If you go to see her, I will kill her for sure." He told me that she was fucking another guy and that I better put that in my head and be very angry with her. That night, we took the last bus back to Colombia. We didn't speak for the whole trip. I found out later that the brother was shot and killed. That day was the last time I saw Carla. I never heard from her, and I didn't try to contact her. She most likely never knew and surely would never know I was there. I remember the blue dress she was wearing, and I had that vision of her sitting in that chair stuck in my head. I thought of these words often: "Sometimes the only way to heal our wounds is to make peace with the demons who created them."

Years later, I was in the Poblado, in Medellin, and a woman I was with, Pao, went to one of the big supermarket chains. As we were shopping, we checked out, and a young guy with a white shirt stopped me and spoke perfect English to me. Pao had no idea what he was going to say. *Thank God*, I thought. He told me he recognized me. I was completely startled. I took several looks at his face. I looked at his name tag; it had his name and his position: store manager.

I again said, "How?"

He said he was with his uncle who was a politician and that, at that time, I was around. I really didn't remember that incident he was talking about. He then did something very strange. He got on the microphone loudspeaker and called all the store associates to come to the front of the store. Within a minute, the front where the cashiers were along with the customers were packed in the front of the store.

He told me, "Please wait a minute." Then he said in a very loud voice to everyone, "Este es el hombre que ayudo a rescatar a Colombia." It meant "This is the man who helped save Colombia."

I looked at Pao. She had a confused look on her face. I told her we had to get out of there. Then I raced toward the floor, and I could hear the people cheering and applauding in the distance. Of all the things I had been through, this made me real scared.

My connection in Colombia had been disappearing through the years. Os passed away from cancer. I had never seen his daughter, Yuli, again. I never heard a thing about Juan Jose, but I did see Lulu one more time. She hugged me then winked at me, and then I never saw her again.

I spend a lot of time in Colombia now but will never live there. The underbelly is there, though it has improved. But I still cannot resist the most beautiful women in the world!

About the Author

No one—not my closest friends, not my family members, not my coworkers—knew what I was doing in Colombia. Many assumed things but never knew the truth. It was one of the most difficult secrets I kept in my life. After surviving downtown Jersey City, and the teachers and nuns, I was starting to find my own way, playing a lot of sports, which I enjoyed immensely. I always remember how that helped me escape life.

There was a time I was so good in sports that I went to try ice-skating for the first time. The head of the Jersey City Recreation Department, who knew me, saw me putting on ice skates. She knew it was my first time doing so. And then she saw me fly around the ice like I have been doing it my whole life. She said in front of all the bystanders, "Gerard is an athlete." And I was! I never used any sort of drugs. Maybe I learned from my brother's experience.

I was finding myself in the world of education and different jobs. Finally, with the example of two guys I worked with, I took school seriously and went to trade school and engineering school. It took me many years to get degrees, and I pushed myself, still living with Mom in cold water flats. I landed a great job that helped me build three different homes, each one nicer than the next.

At times, I still find myself feeling lucky and a bit insecure that I don't deserve all the success I have had. My many trips to Colombia and all of South America sort of helped me build an interesting life that led me to this book. For many years, I sang solo in church at mass. I am still Catholic. I also play Santa Claus for many poor kids in Allentown, Pennsylvania, buying them food and gifts. And I did the same for Thanksgiving, buying and giving out Turkeys for the church—all that for sixteen years.

Maybe things I learned rubbed off on me. Mostly my mother generosity did the trick for me. Tom again comes into the picture: "Gerard, do you know where you came from and all the great things you have done?" Yes, I do. Some good, and some not so good.

I went on to build three homes (and I lived in them), and I also had my own business. One guy that worked for me went on to be very successful in the field, which I am very proud of!

Please look forward to the next book titled *Colombianas: The Most Beautiful Women in the World*.

CPSIA information can be obtained
at www.ICGtesting.com
Printed in the USA
BVHW041005271121
620613BV00007BA/128/J

9 781662 434358